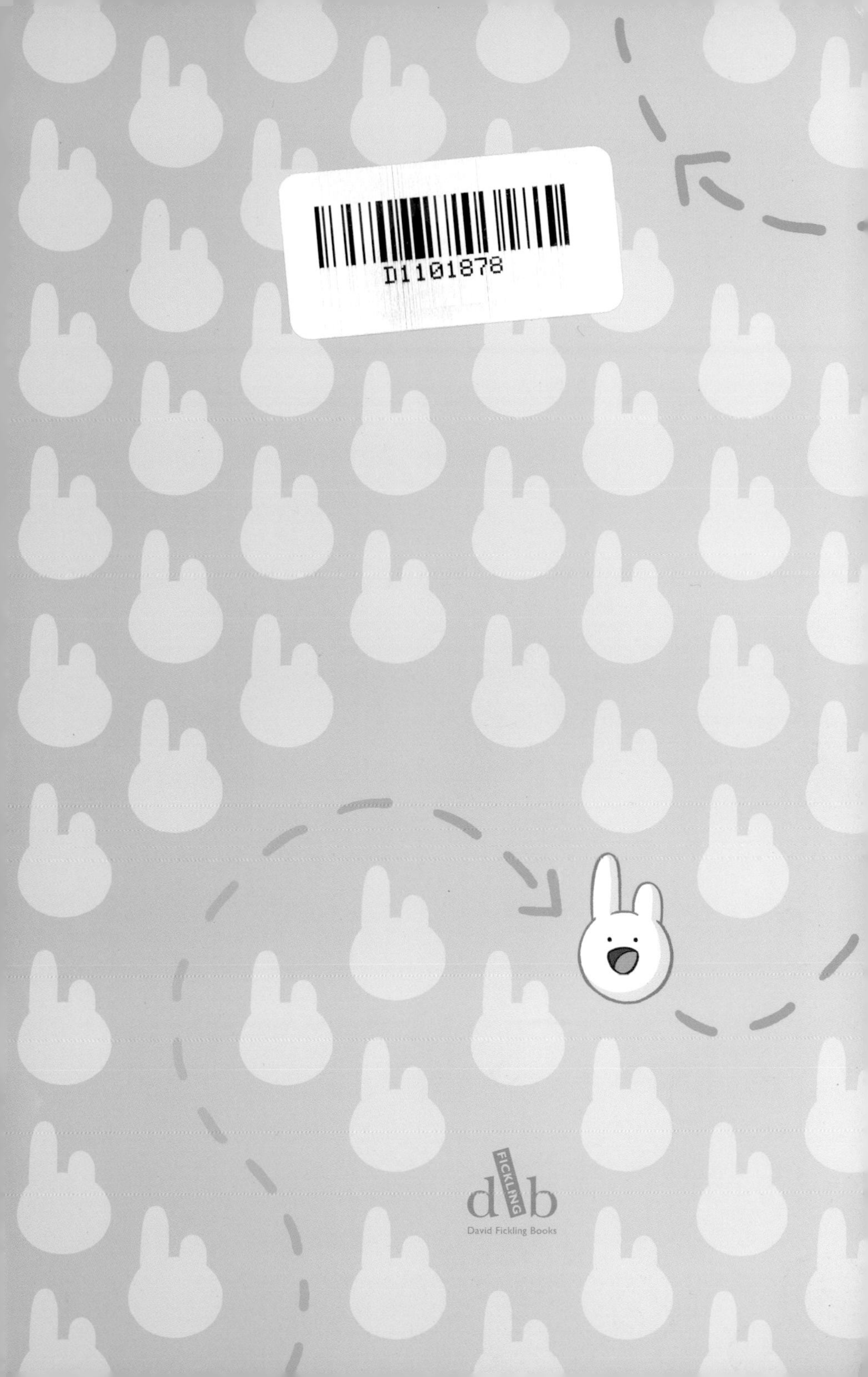

FICKLING
dfb
David Fickling Books

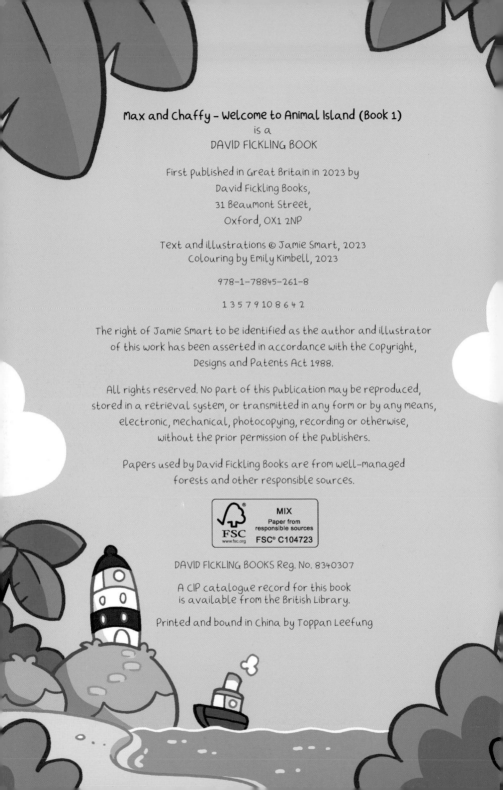

max and Chaffy - Welcome to Animal Island (Book 1)
is a
DAVID FICKLING BOOK

First published in Great Britain in 2023 by
David Fickling Books,
31 Beaumont Street,
Oxford, OX1 2NP

978-1-78845-261-8

1 3 5 7 9 10 8 6 4 2

Papers used by David Fickling Books are from well-managed
forests and other responsible sources.

MIX
Paper from
responsible sources
FSC® C104723
FSC
www.fsc.org

DAVID FICKLING BOOKS Reg. No. 8340307

A CIP catalogue record for this book
is available from the British Library.

Printed and bound in China by Toppan Leefung

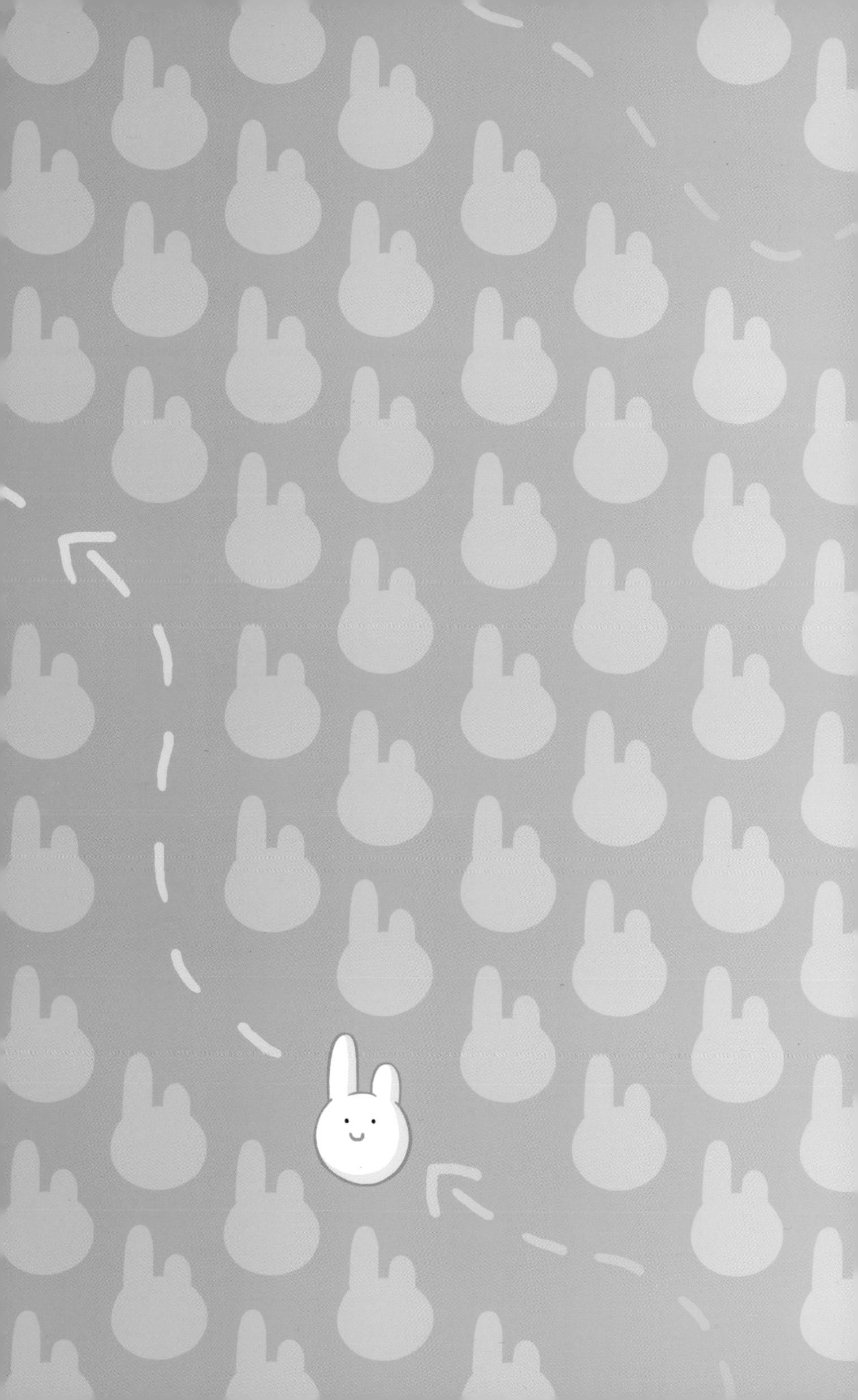

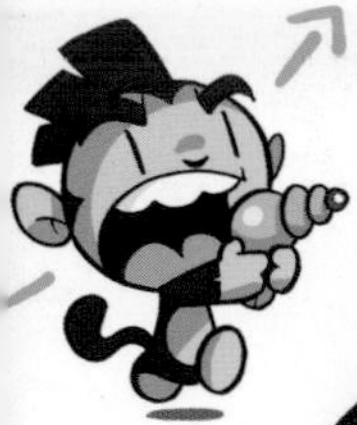

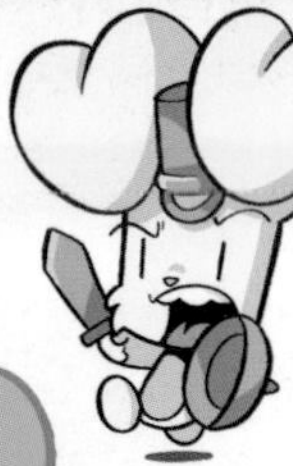

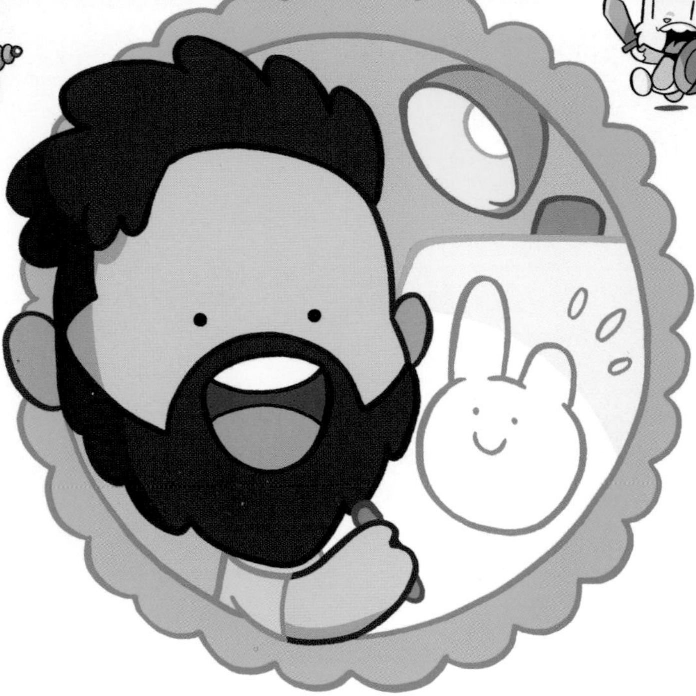

Hi! I'm Jamie Smart.

I hope you loved reading about Max and Chaffy.

I really enjoyed writing and drawing it.

Thank you to my friends Emily, Rosie and Katie

who all helped me make this book too!

I've also created other books, like the best-selling

BUNNY VS MONKEY and LOOSHKIN

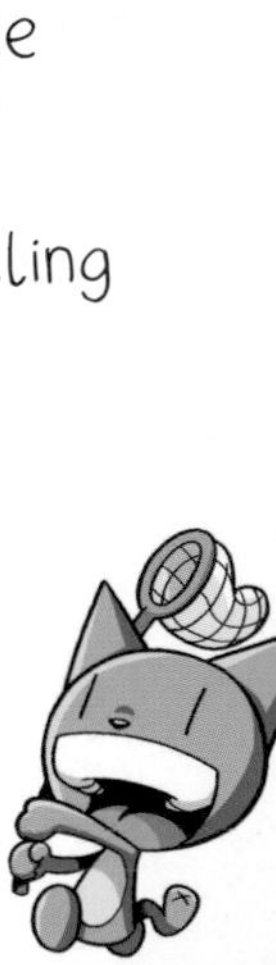

Making up stories and looking for chaffies

are my two favourite things!

FICKLING
db
David Fickling Books
Welcome to
Animal Island,
Max & Chaffy!

Far, far across the ocean . . .

chug!
chug chug!

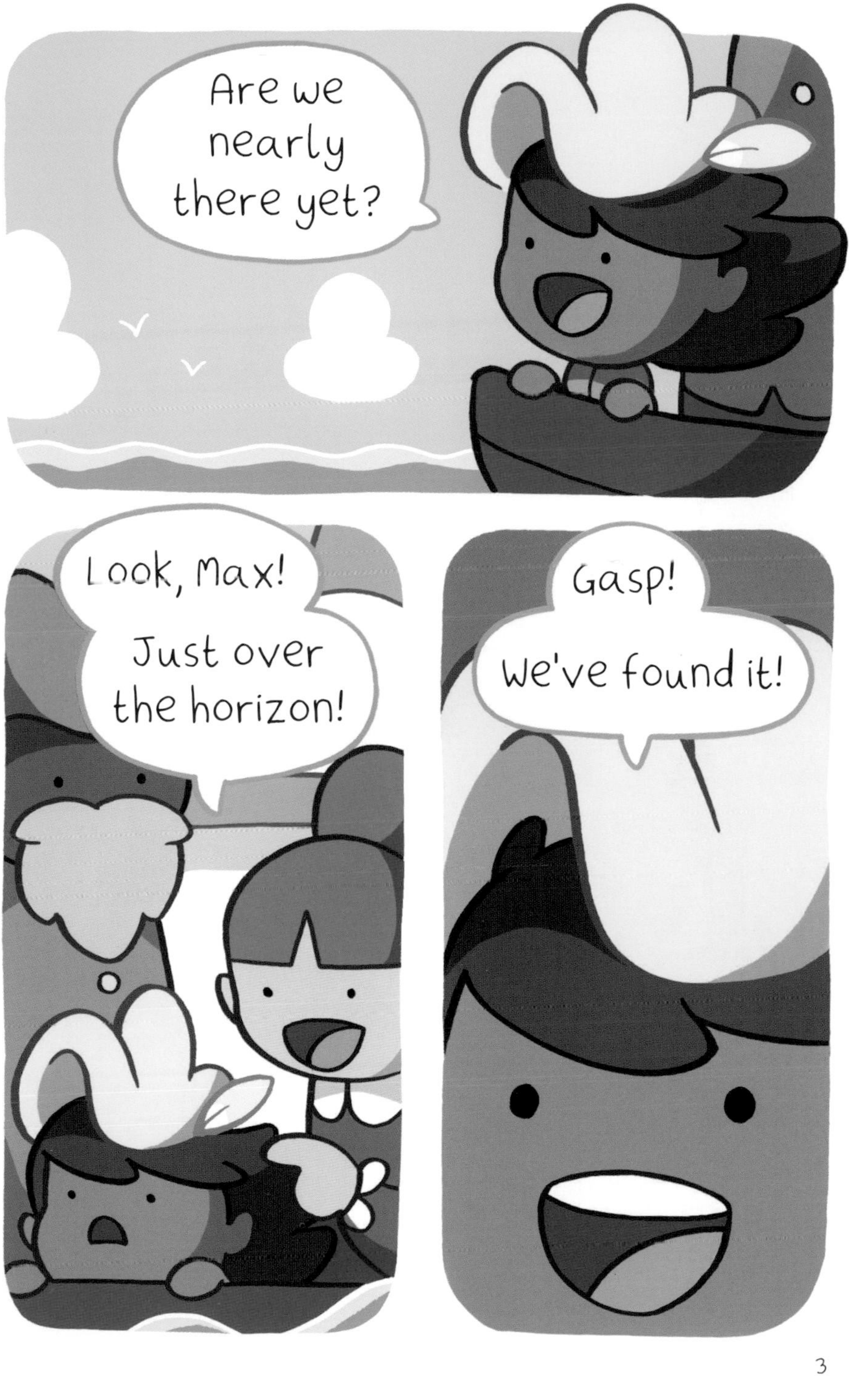
Are we nearly there yet?
Look, Max!
Just over the horizon!
Gasp!
We've found it!

welcome to Animal Island!

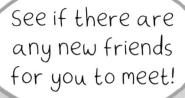

Here you go, Max. Look through my binoculars!

See if there are any new friends for you to meet!

I hope so . . .

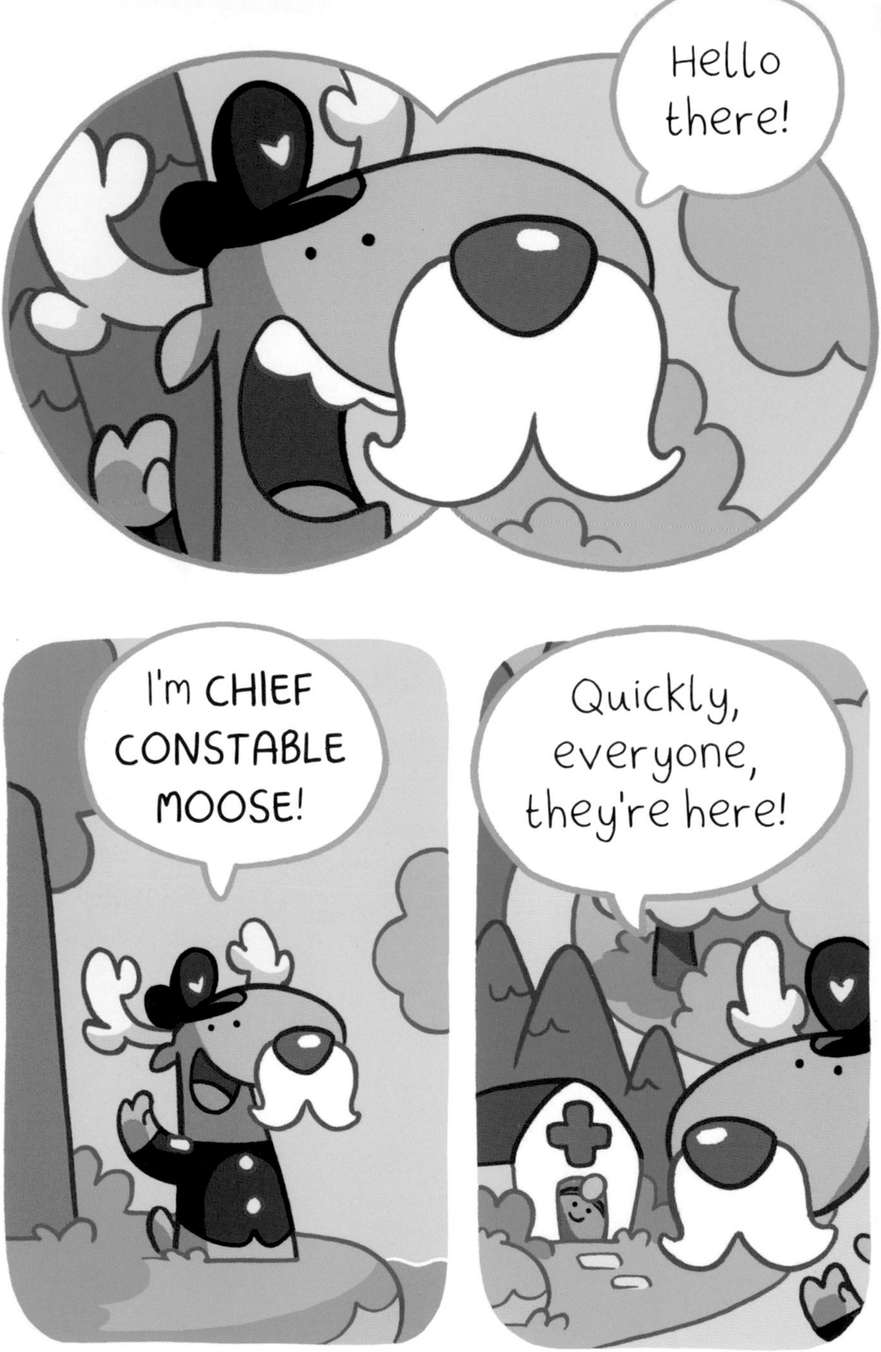
Hello there!
I'm CHIEF CONSTABLE MOOSE!
Quickly, everyone, they're here!

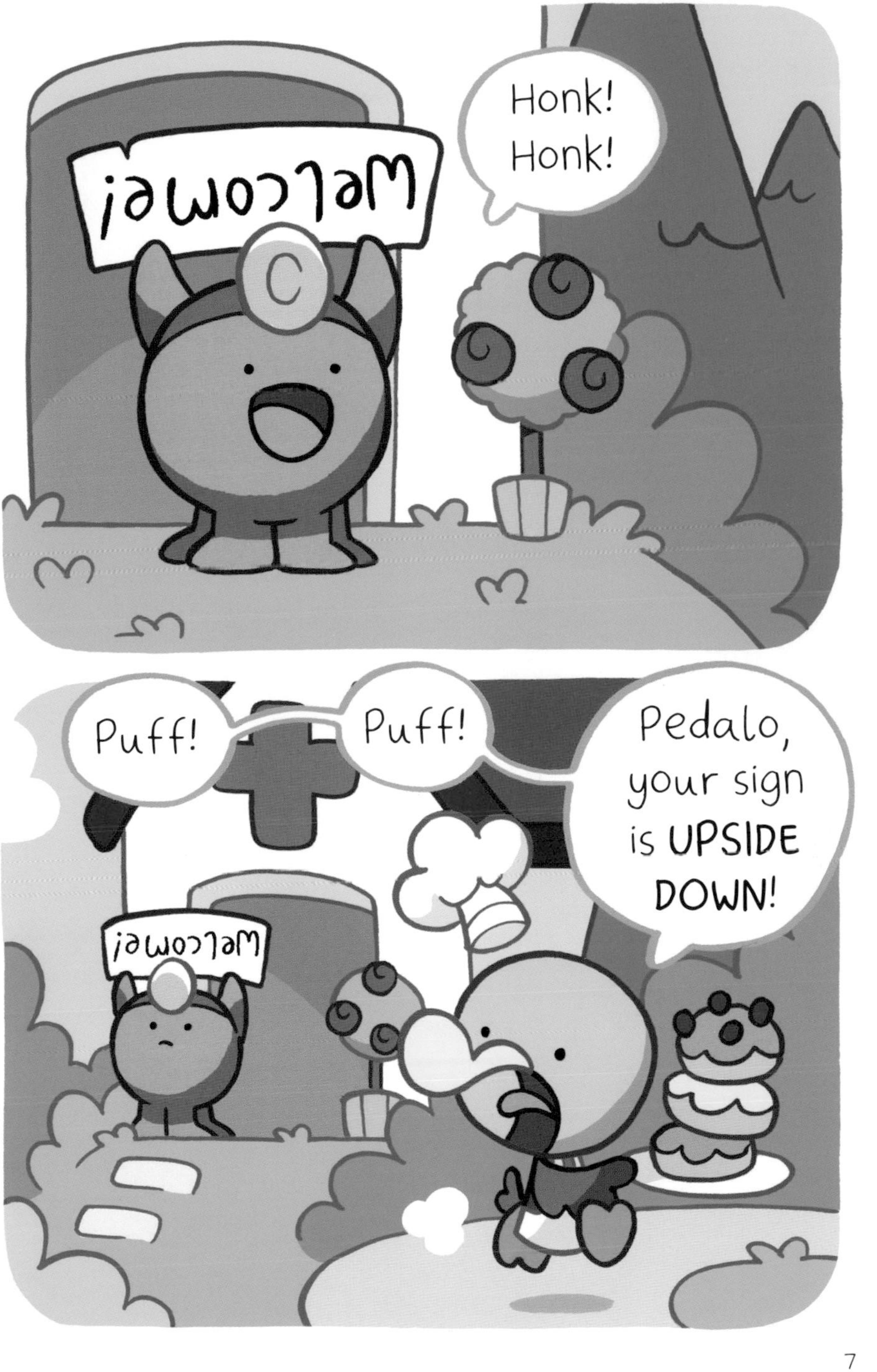
Welcome!
Honk! Honk!
Welcome!
Puff!
Puff!
Pedalo, your sign is UPSIDE DOWN!

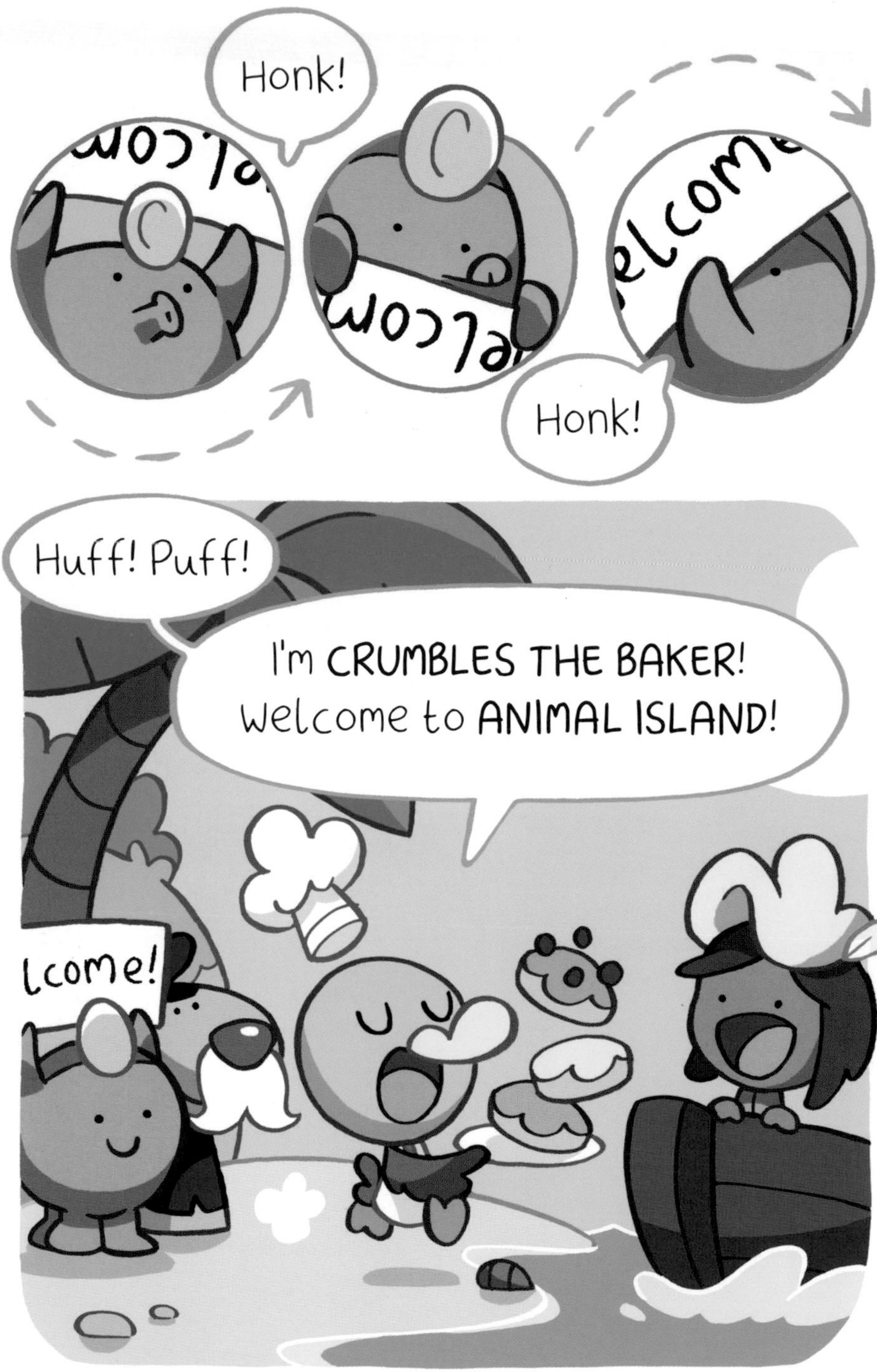
Honk!
Honk!
Huff! Puff!
I'm CRUMBLES THE BAKER!
Welcome to ANIMAL ISLAND!
lcome!

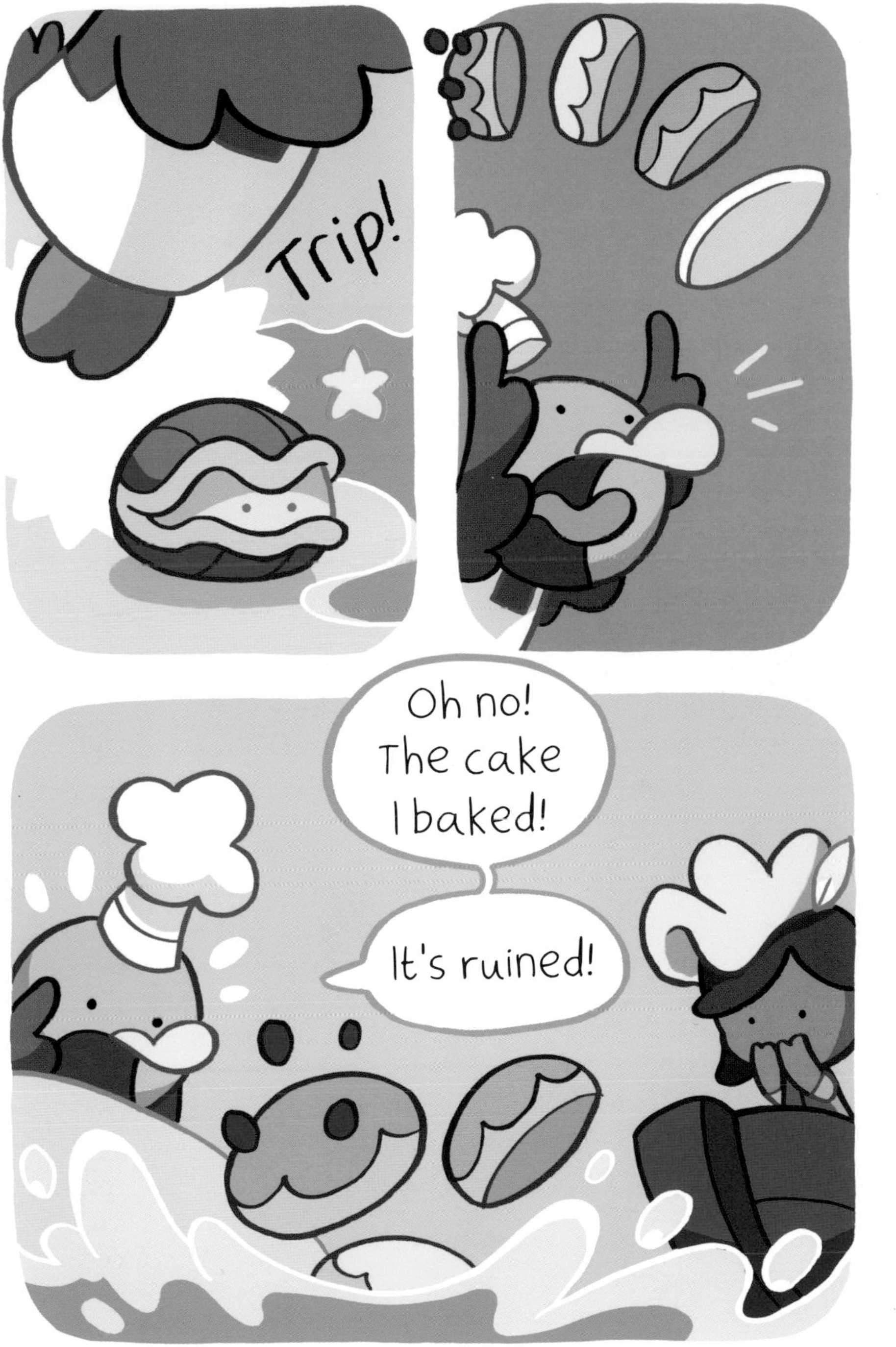
Trip!
Oh no! The cake I baked!
It's ruined!

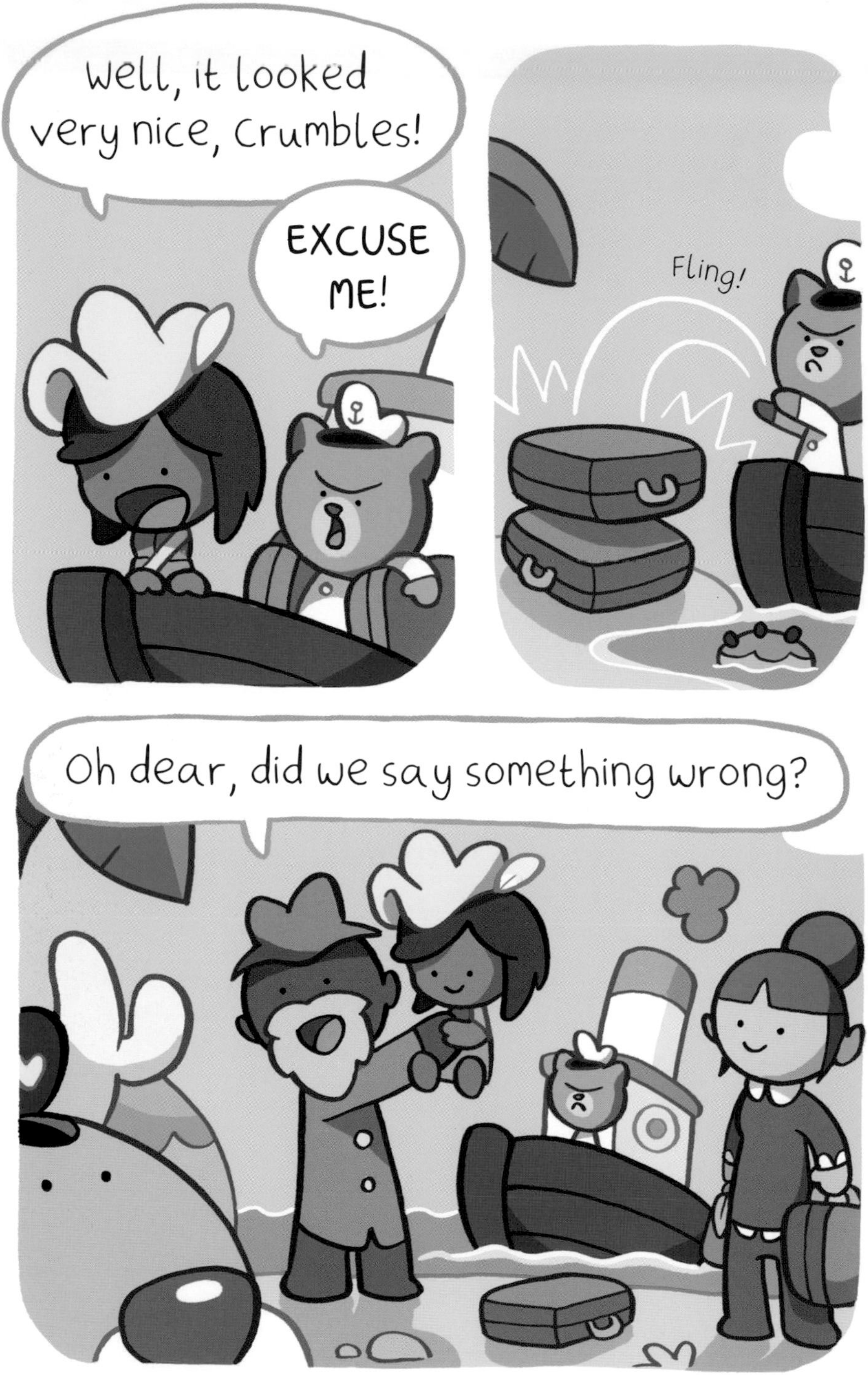
Well, it looked very nice, Crumbles!
EXCUSE ME!
Fling!
Oh dear, did we say something wrong?

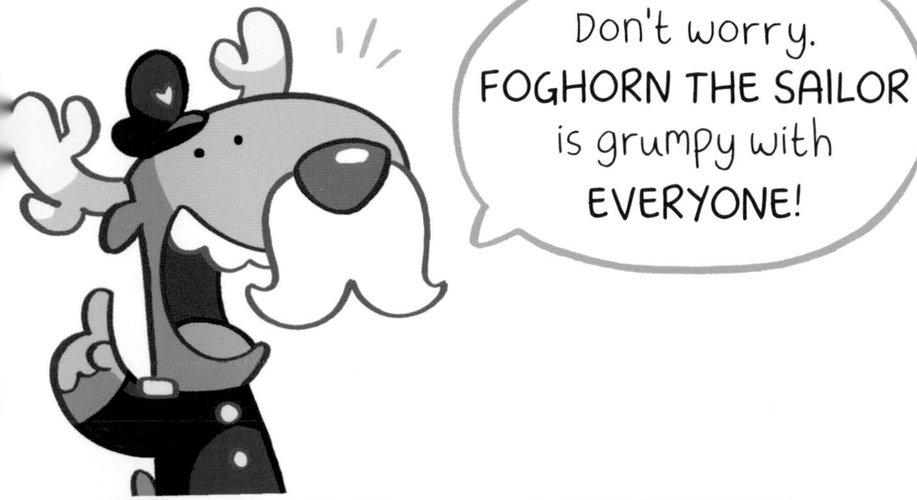
Don't worry.
FOGHORN THE SAILOR
is grumpy with
EVERYONE!

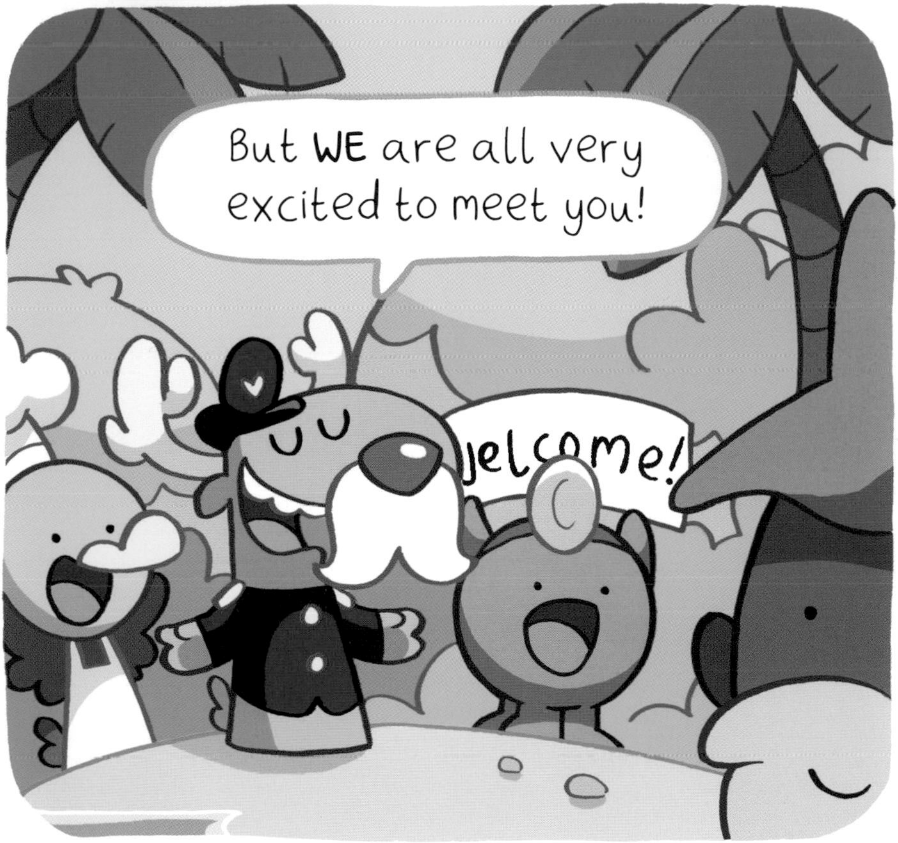
But WE are all very
excited to meet you!
Welcome!

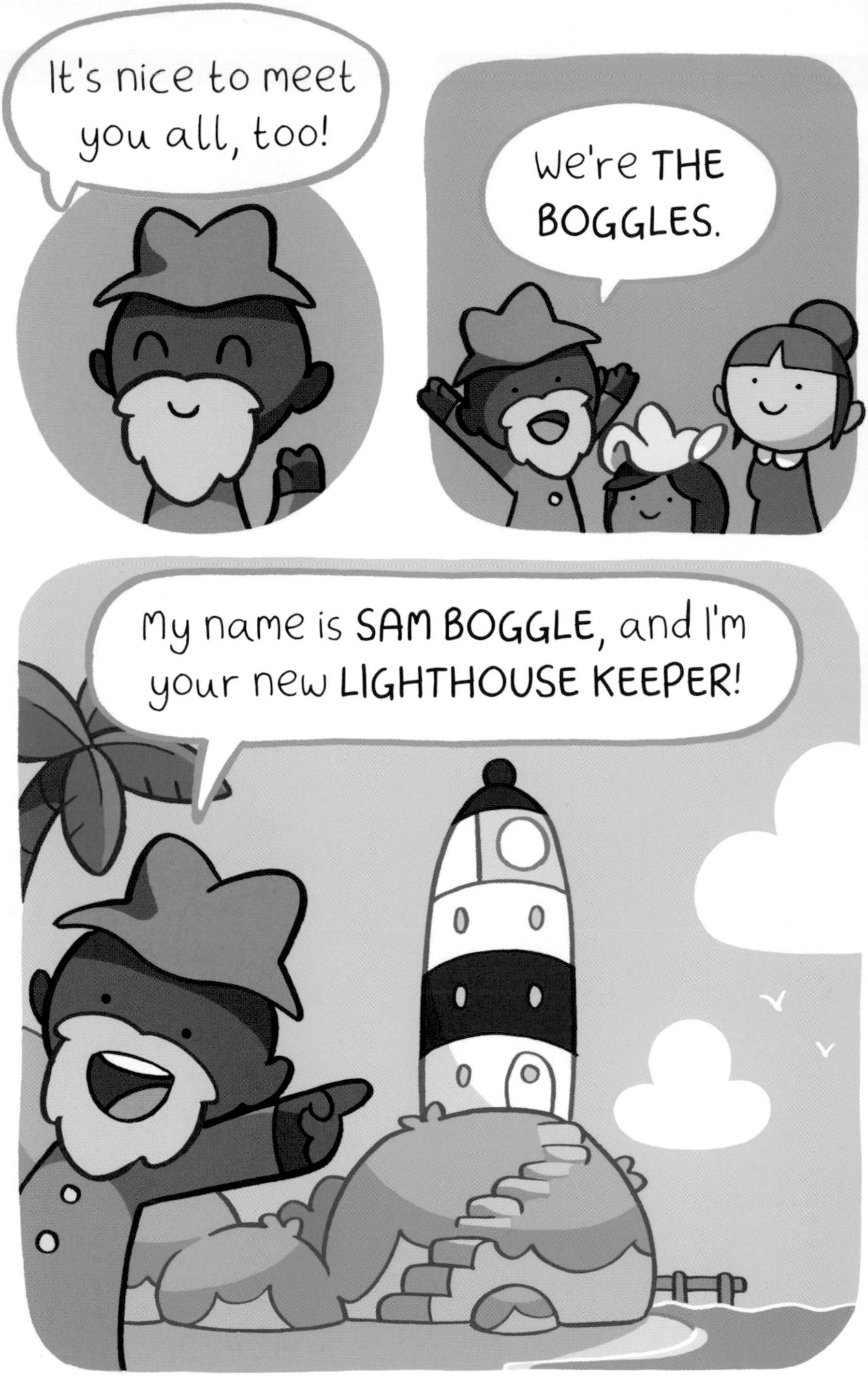
It's nice to meet you all, too!
We're THE BOGGLES.
My name is SAM BOGGLE, and I'm your new LIGHTHOUSE KEEPER!

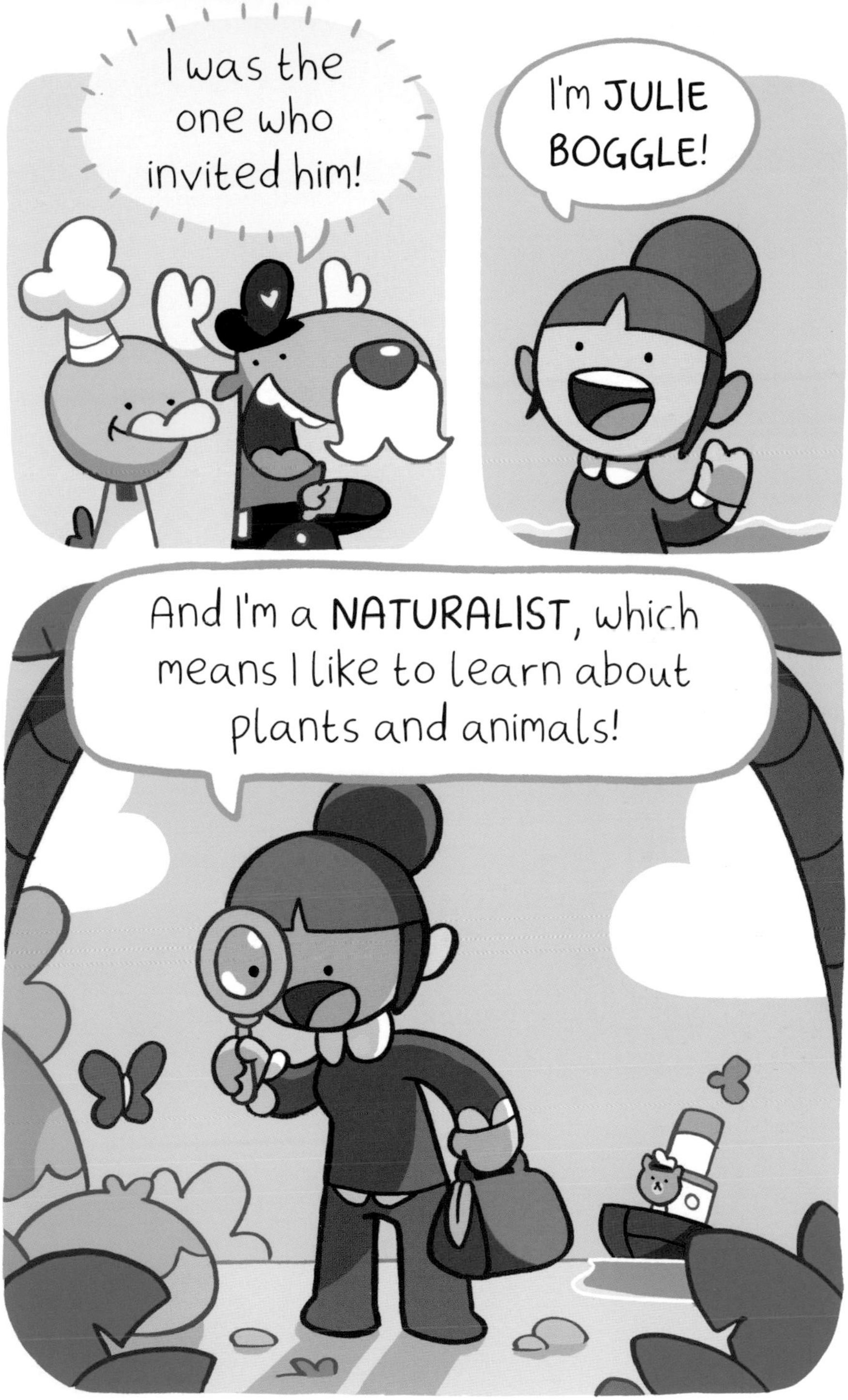
I was the one who invited him!
I'm JULIE BOGGLE!
And I'm a NATURALIST, which means I like to learn about plants and animals!

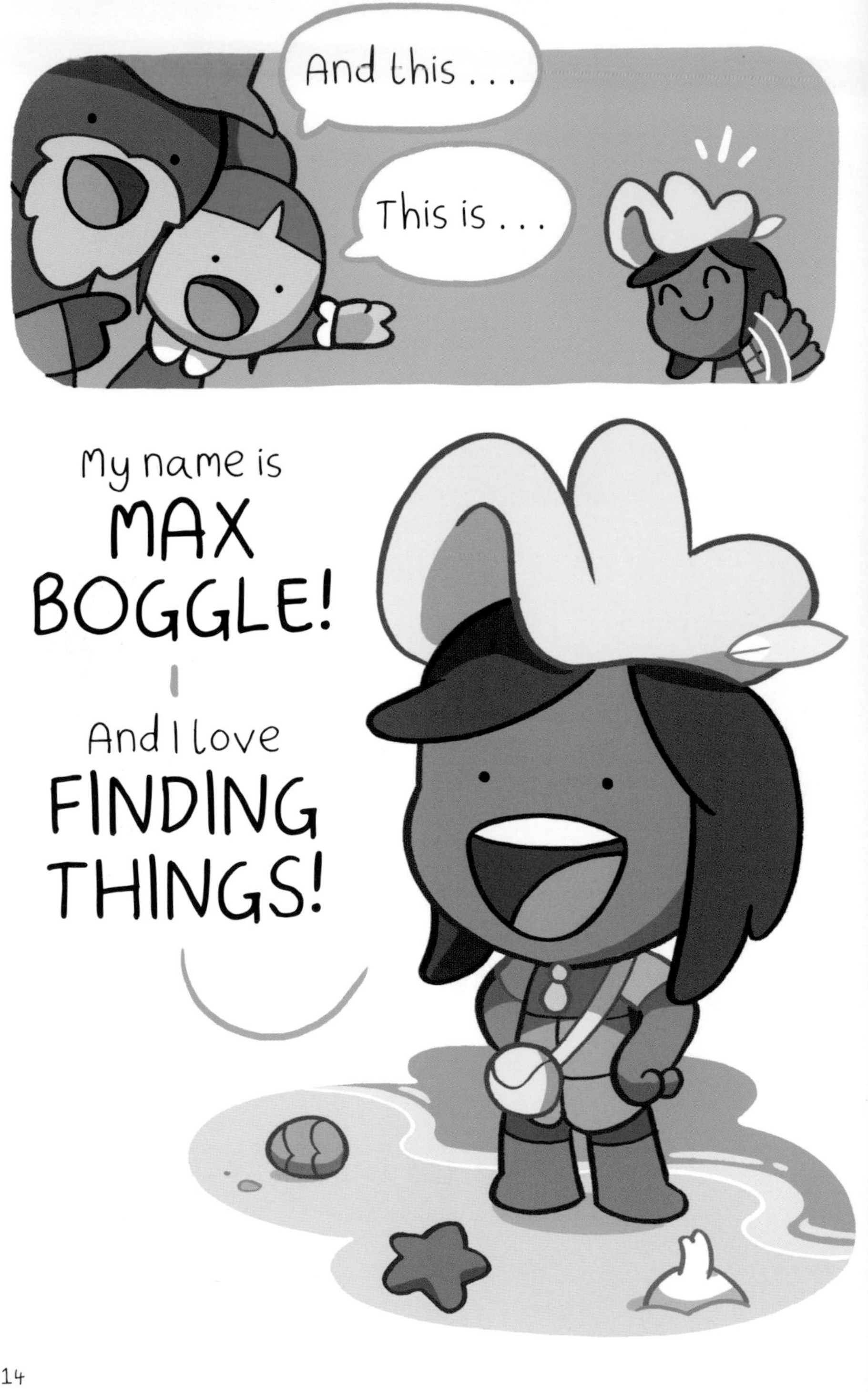

And this . . .
This is . . .
My name is
MAX
BOGGLE!
And I love
FINDING
THINGS!

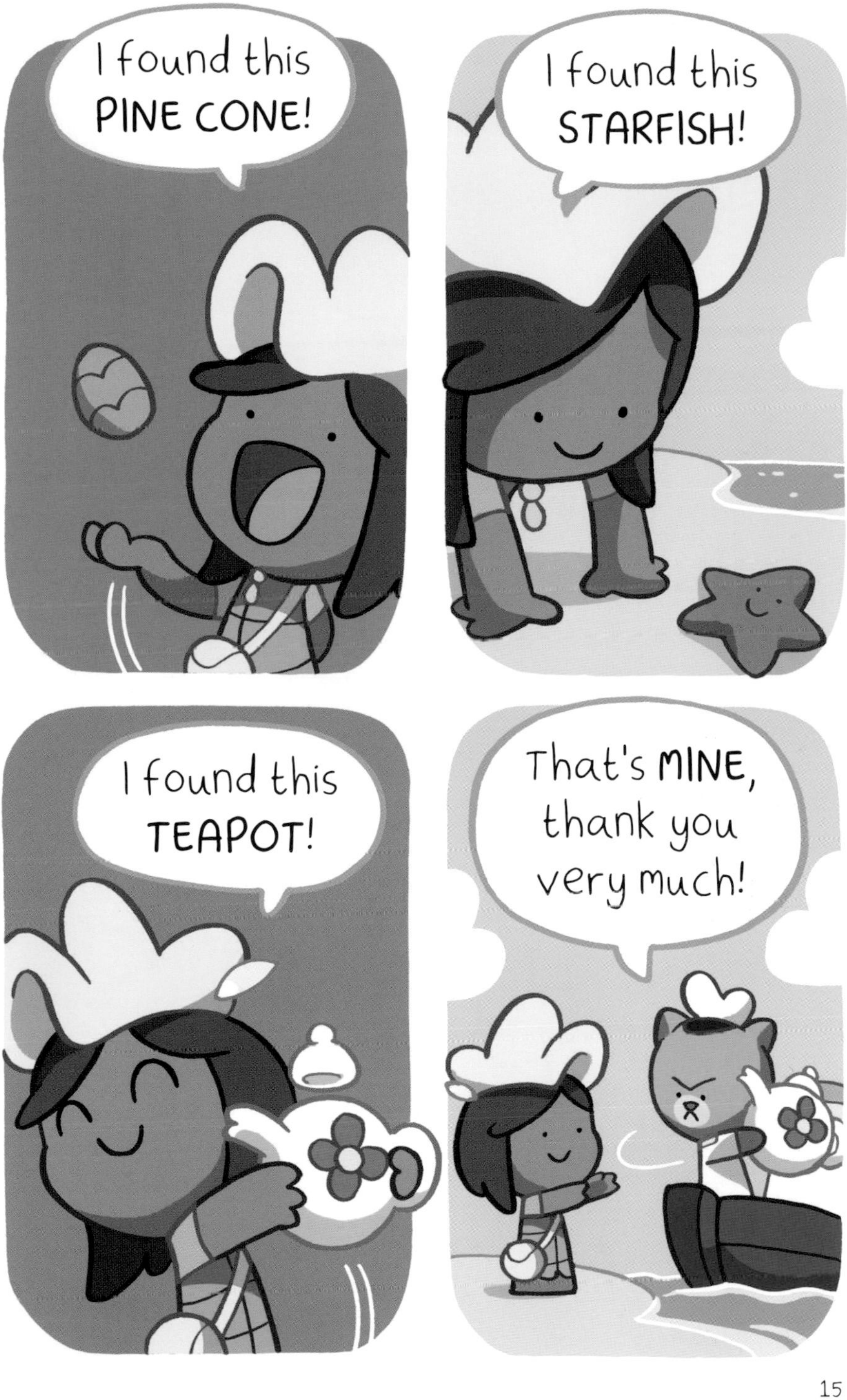
I found this PINE CONE!
I found this STARFISH!
I found this TEAPOT!
That's MINE, thank you very much!

Now, if you don't mind, I have better things to do!

Hee hee! Foghorn's funny!

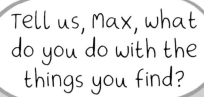

Tell us, Max, what do you do with the things you find?

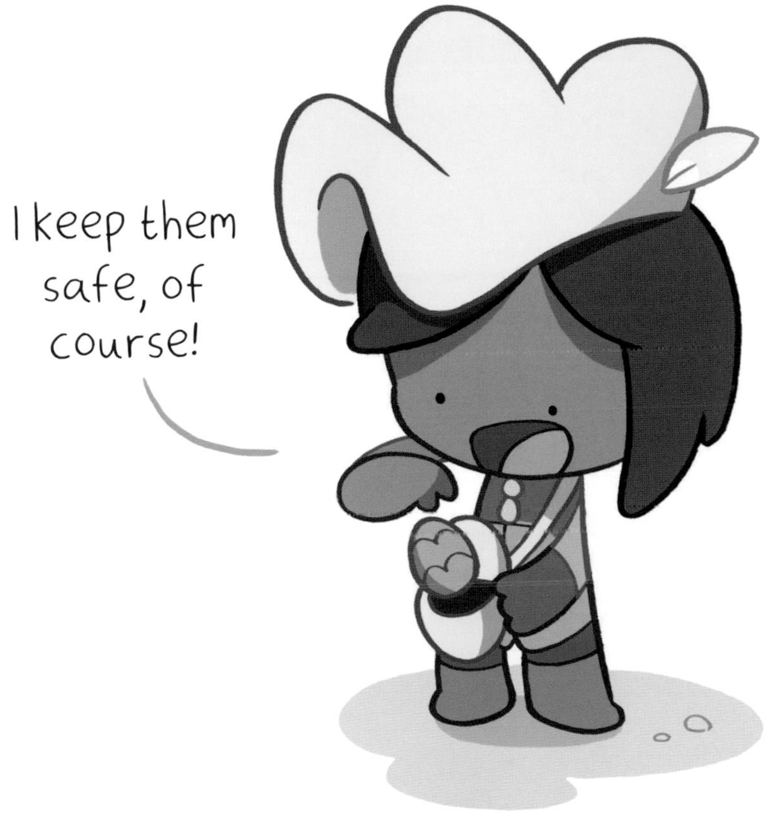
I keep them safe, of course!

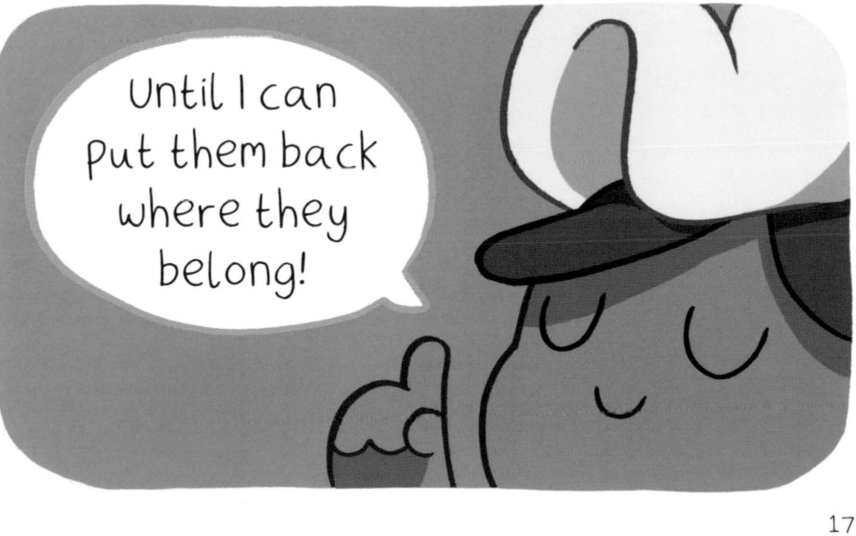
Until I can put them back where they belong!

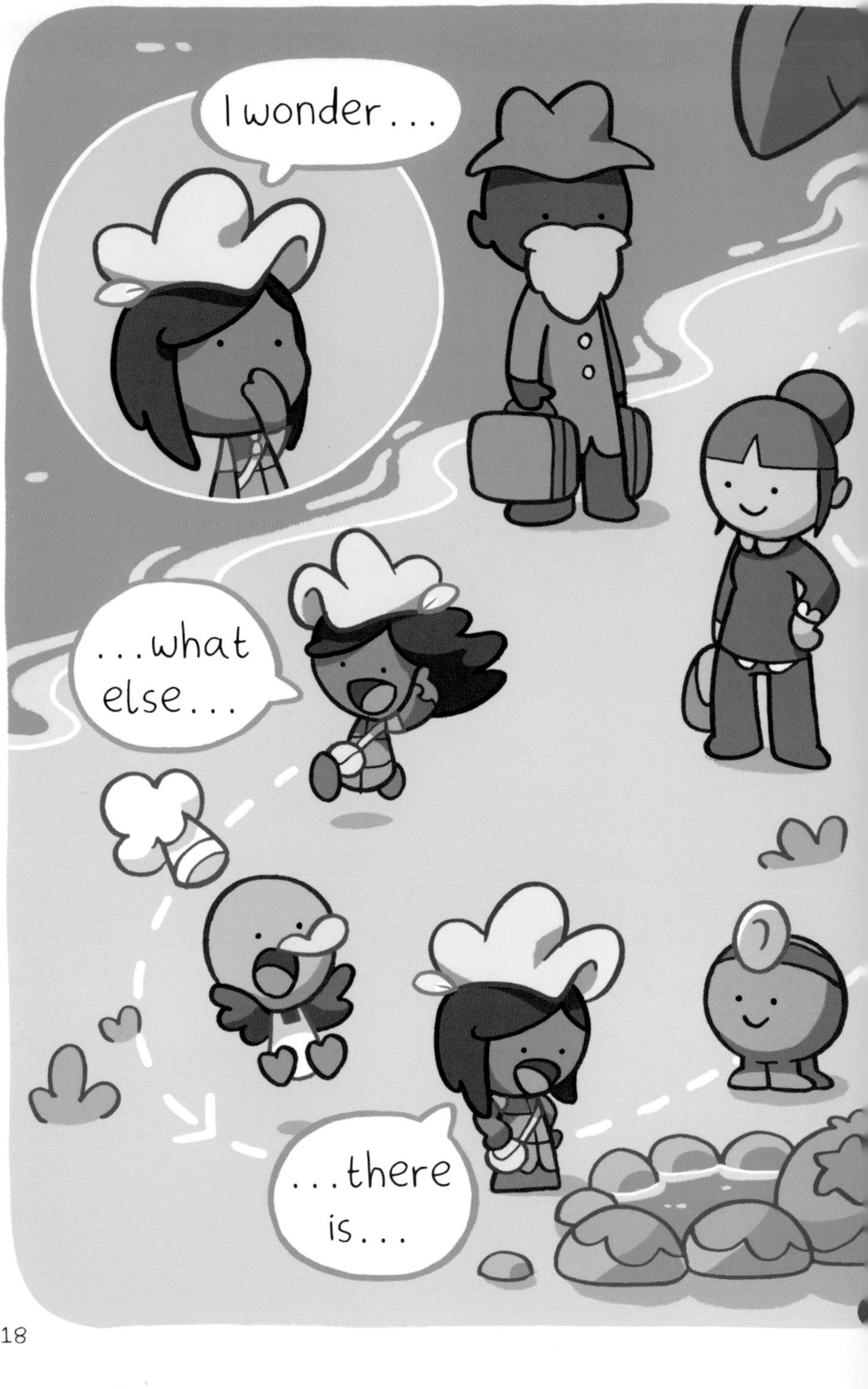
I wonder...
...what else...
...there is...

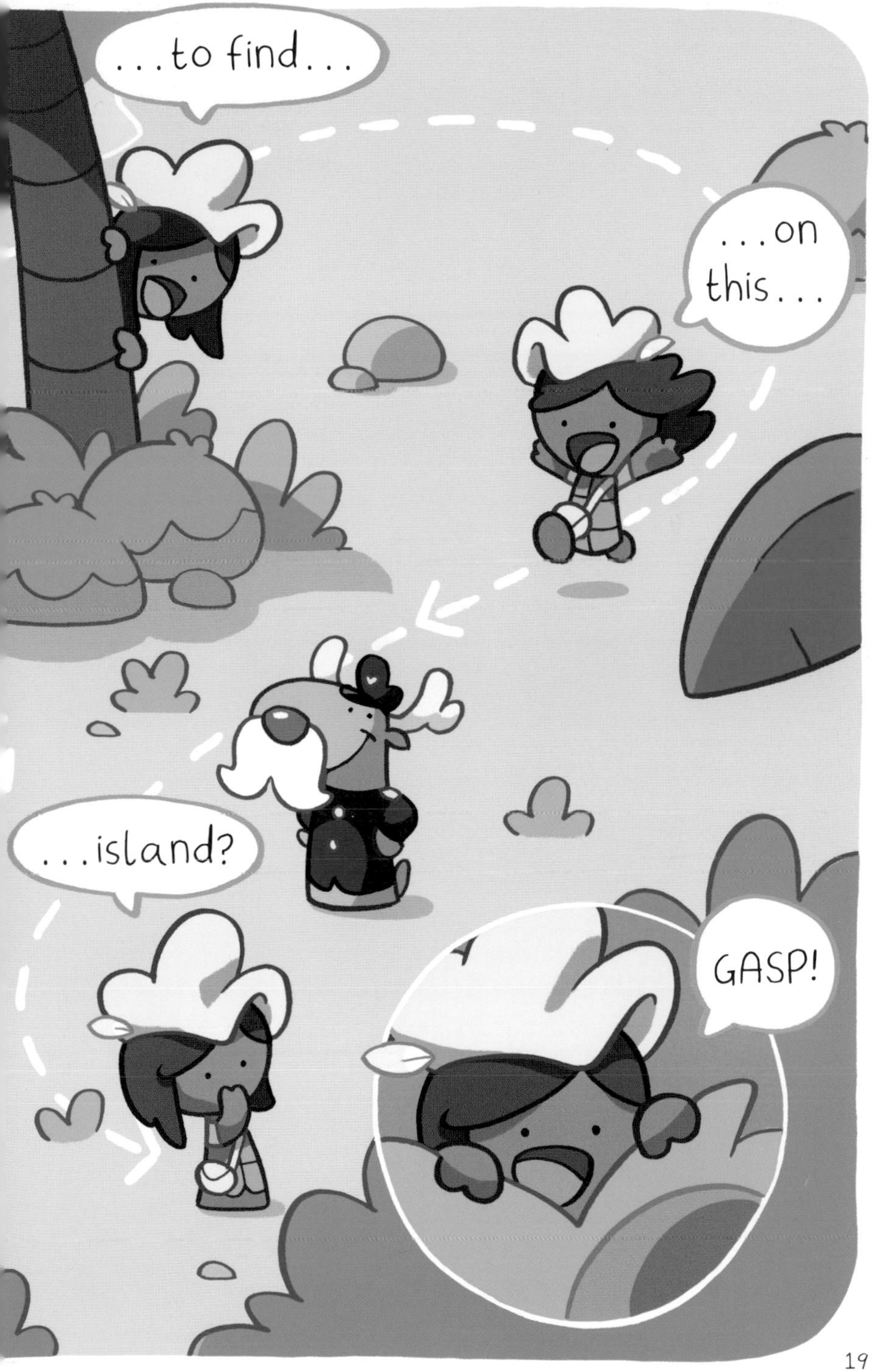
...to find...
...on this...
...island?
GASP!

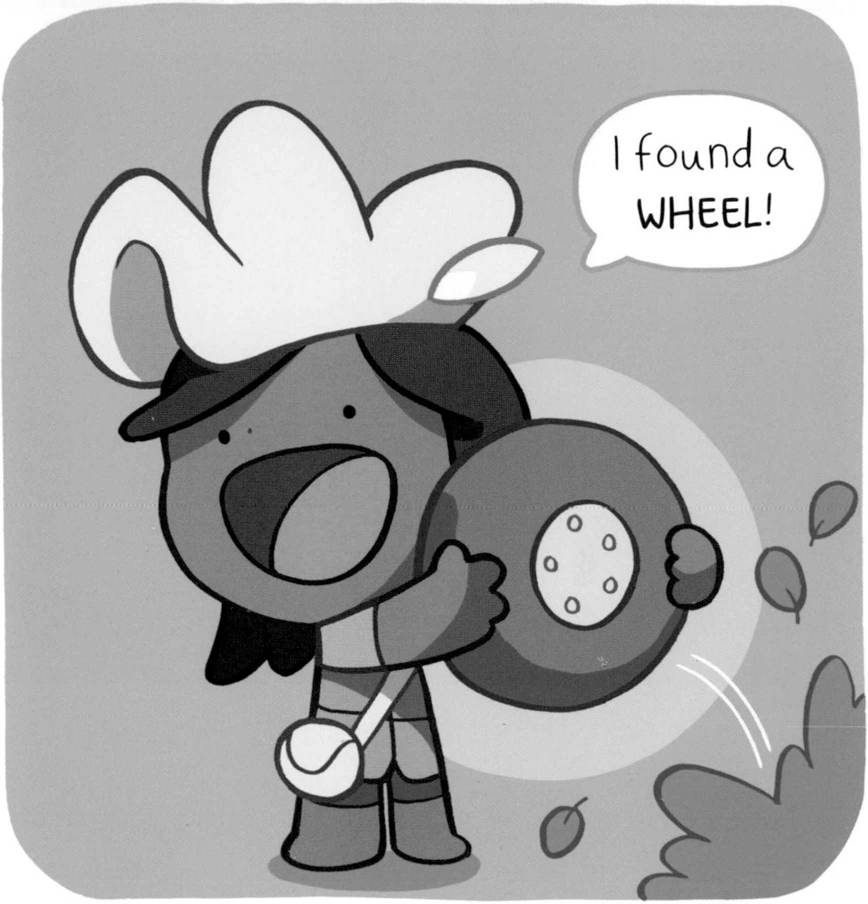
I found a WHEEL!

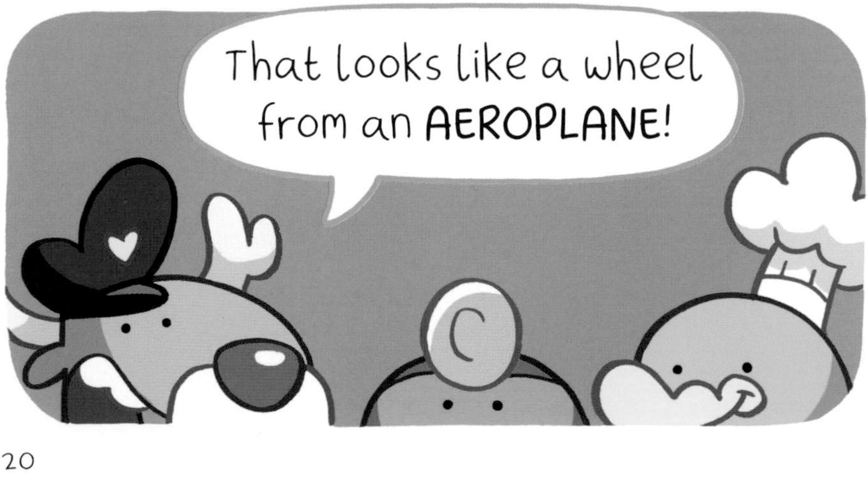
That looks like a wheel from an AEROPLANE!

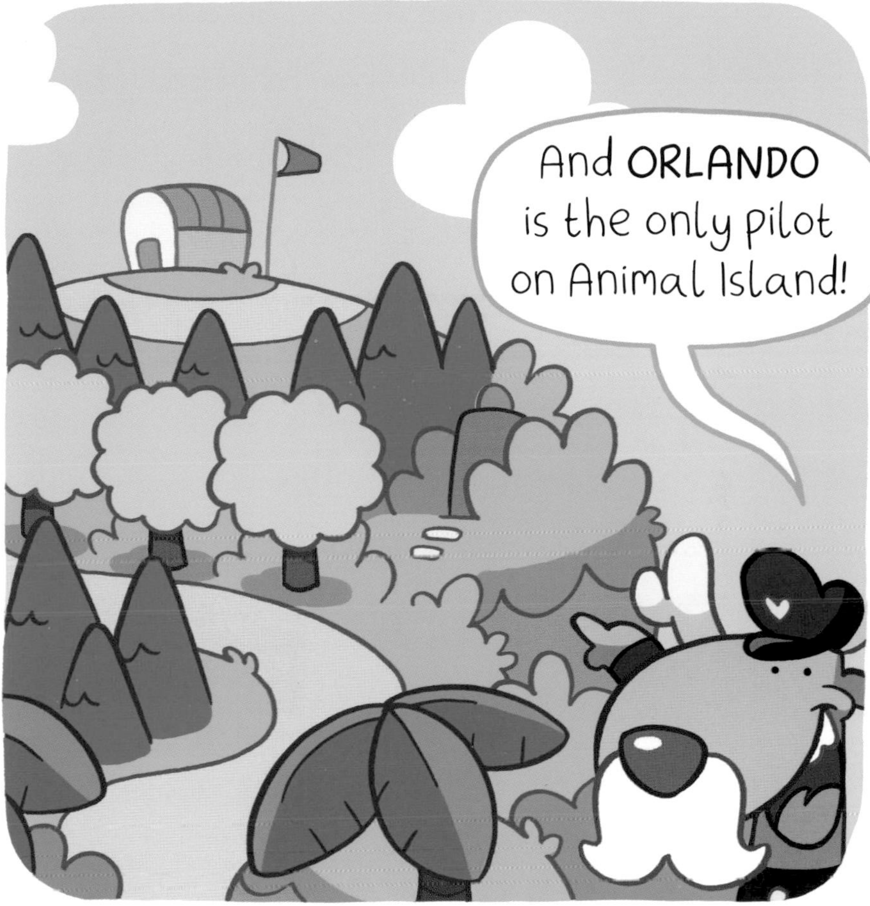
And ORLANDO is the only pilot on Animal Island!

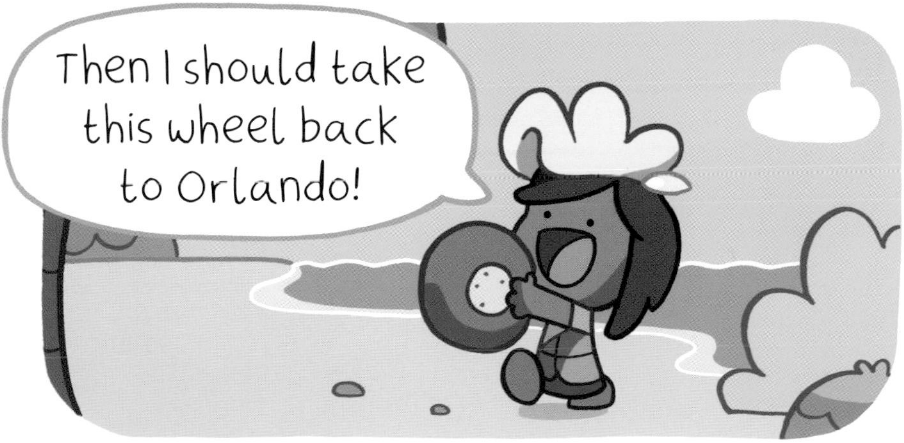
Then I should take this wheel back to Orlando!

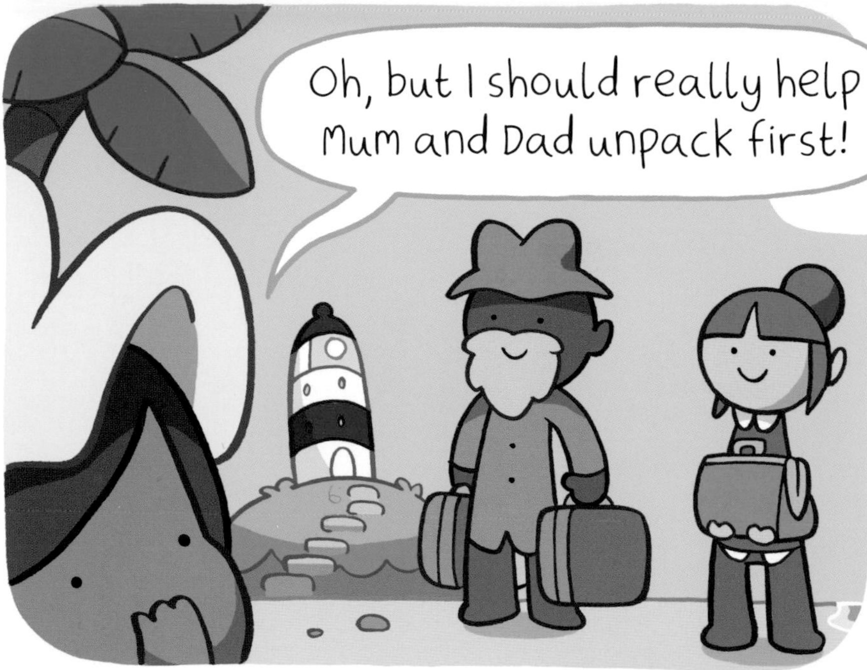
Oh, but I should really help Mum and Dad unpack first!

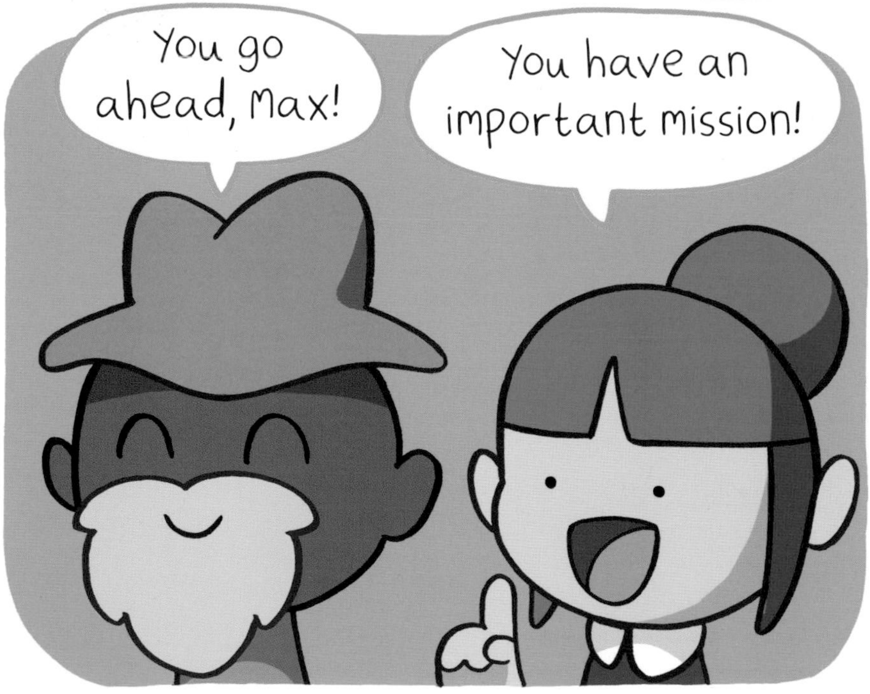
You go ahead, Max!
You have an important mission!

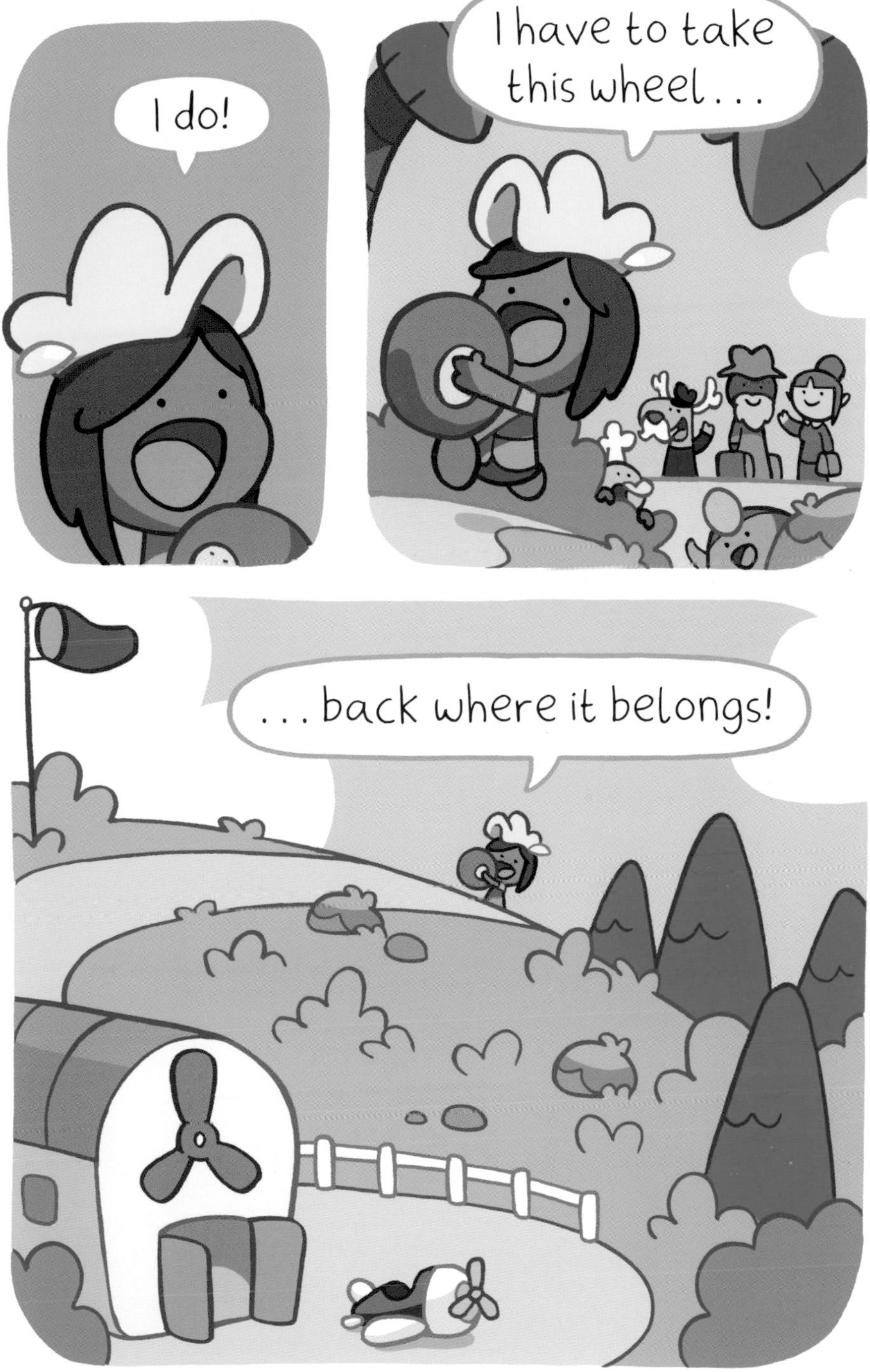
I do!
I have to take this wheel...
...back where it belongs!

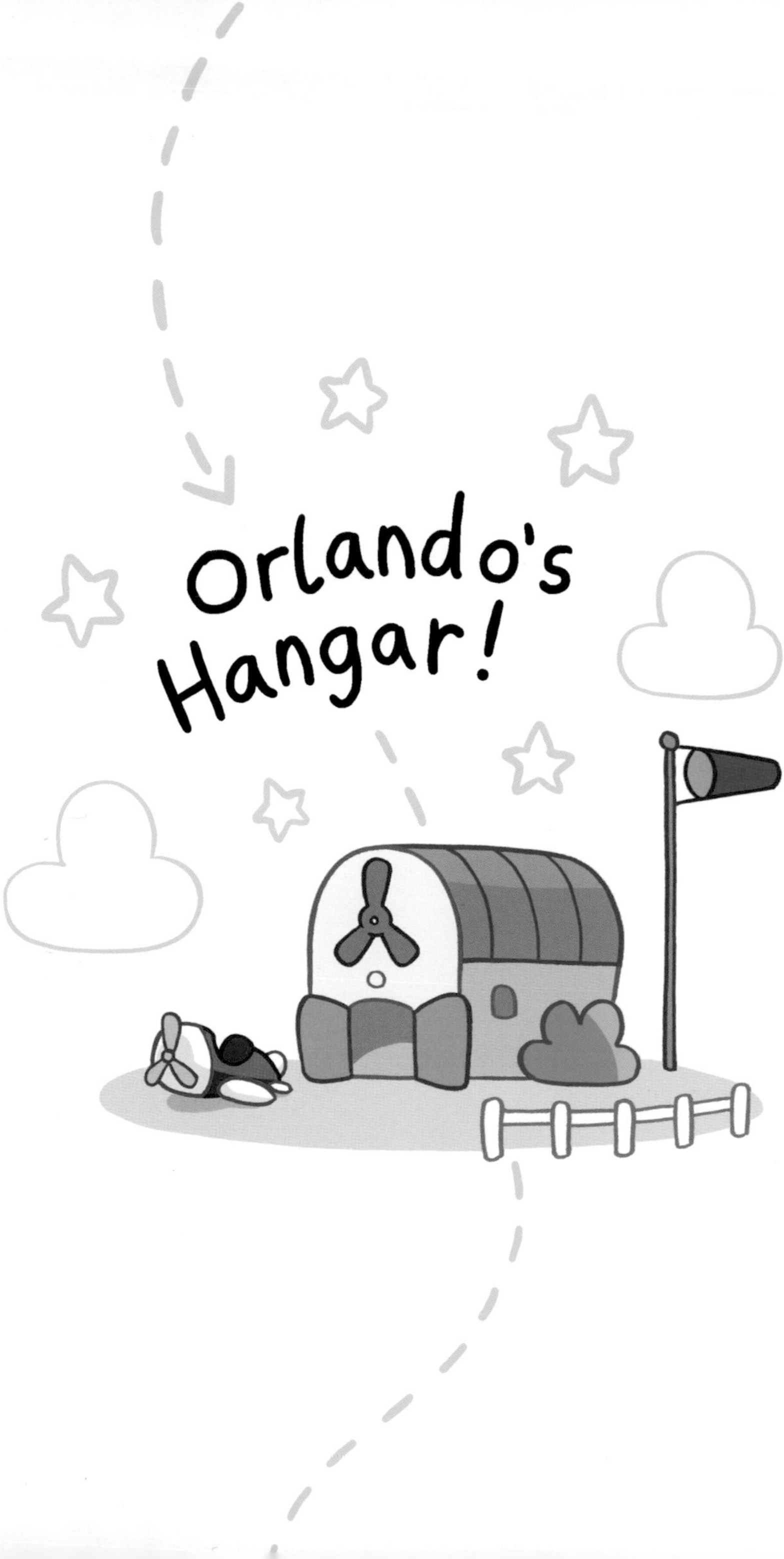
Orlando's Hangar!

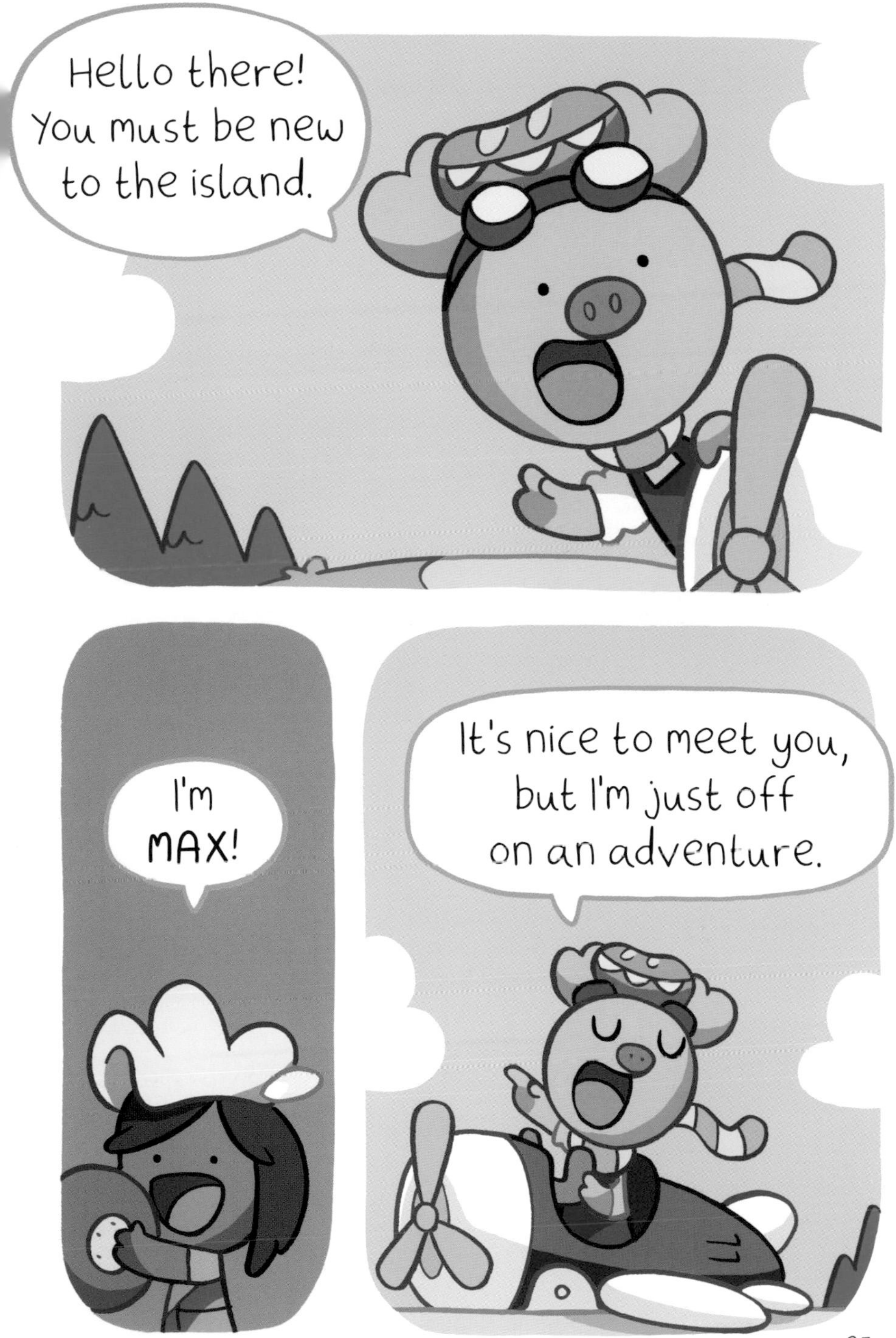
Hello there! You must be new to the island.
I'm MAX!
It's nice to meet you, but I'm just off on an adventure.

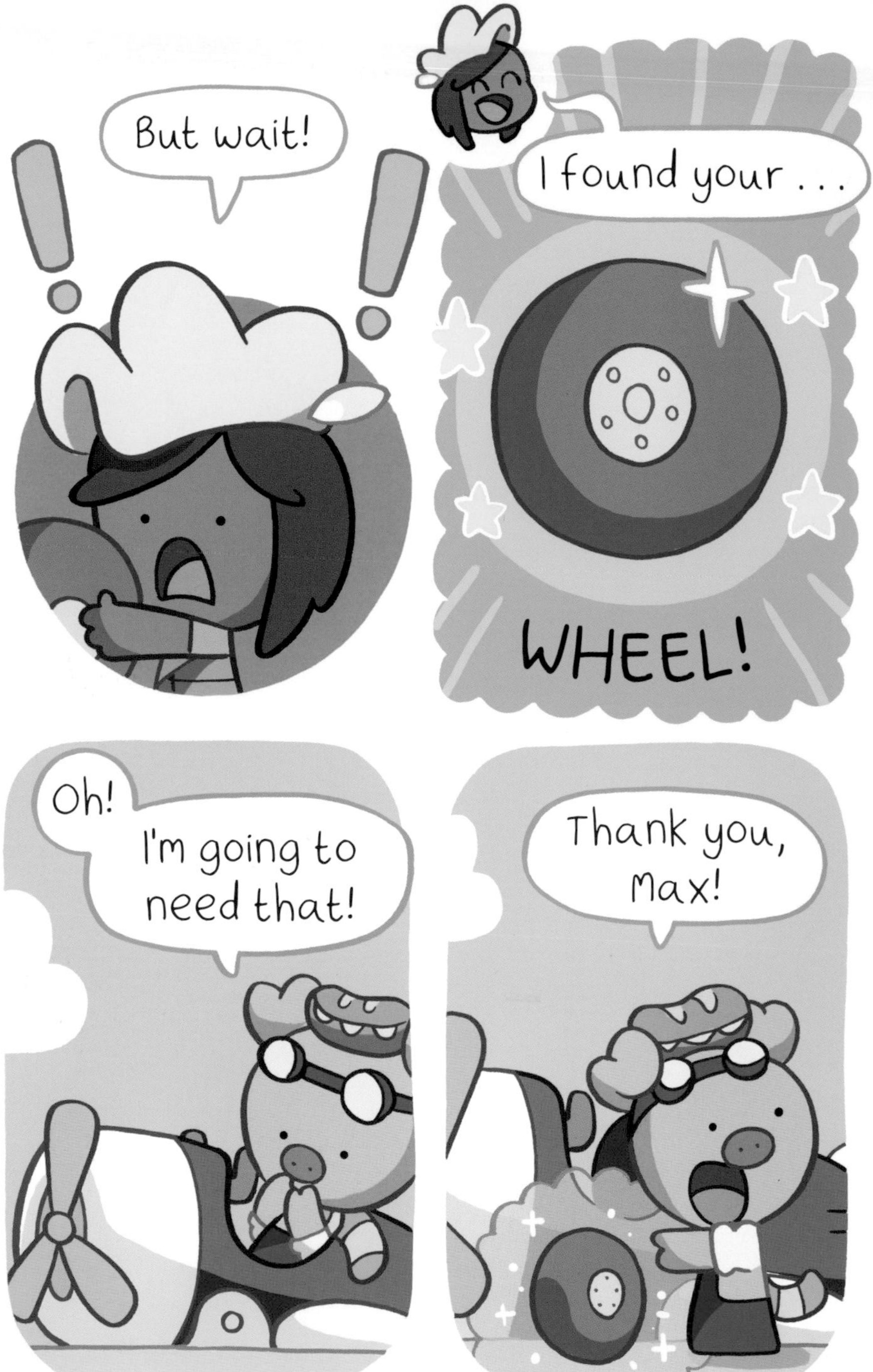
But wait!
I found your . . .
WHEEL!
Oh!
I'm going to need that!
Thank you, Max!

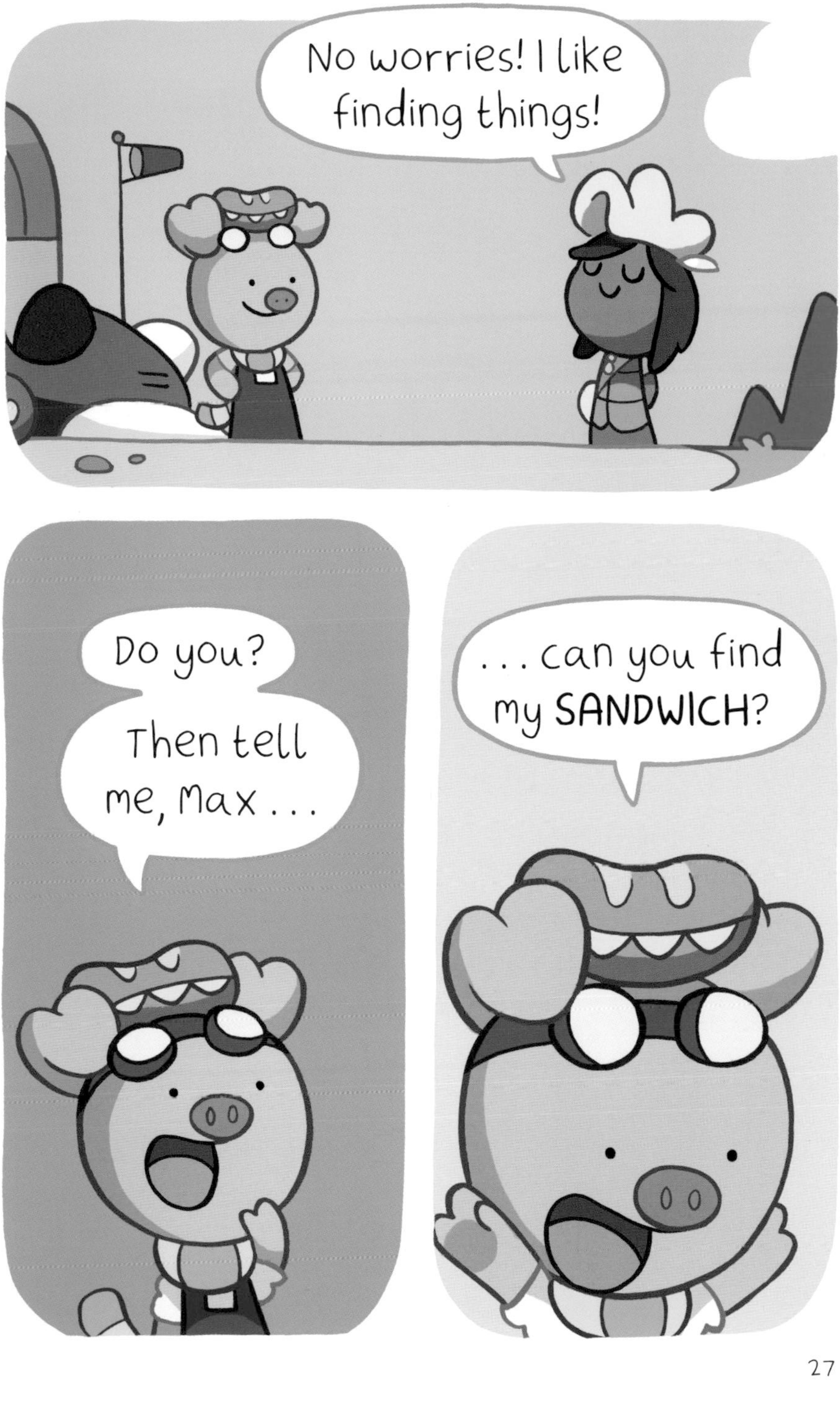
No worries! I like finding things!
Do you?
Then tell me, Max . . .
. . . can you find my SANDWICH?

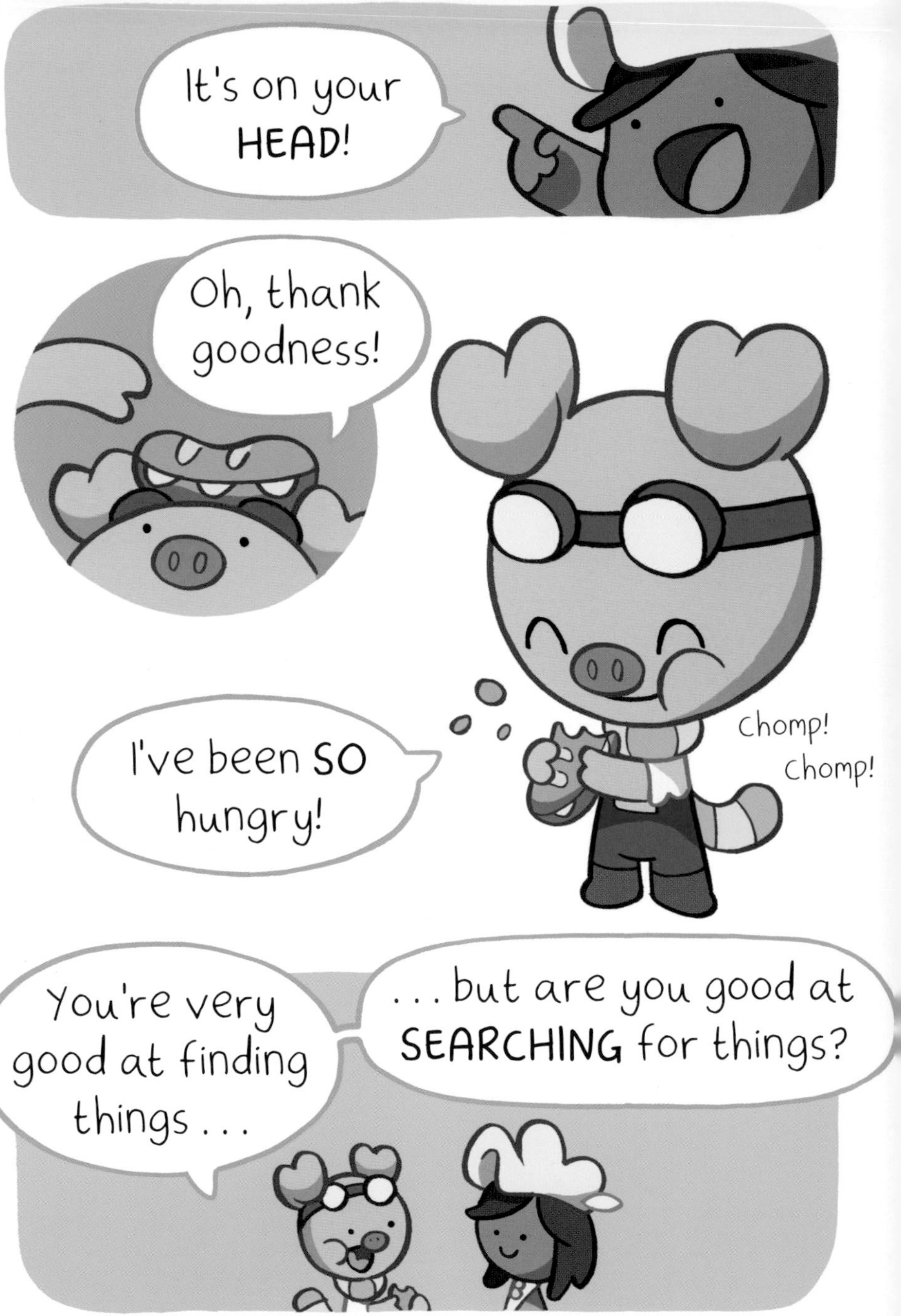
It's on your HEAD!
Oh, thank goodness!
I've been SO hungry!
Chomp!
Chomp!
You're very good at finding things . . .
. . . but are you good at SEARCHING for things?

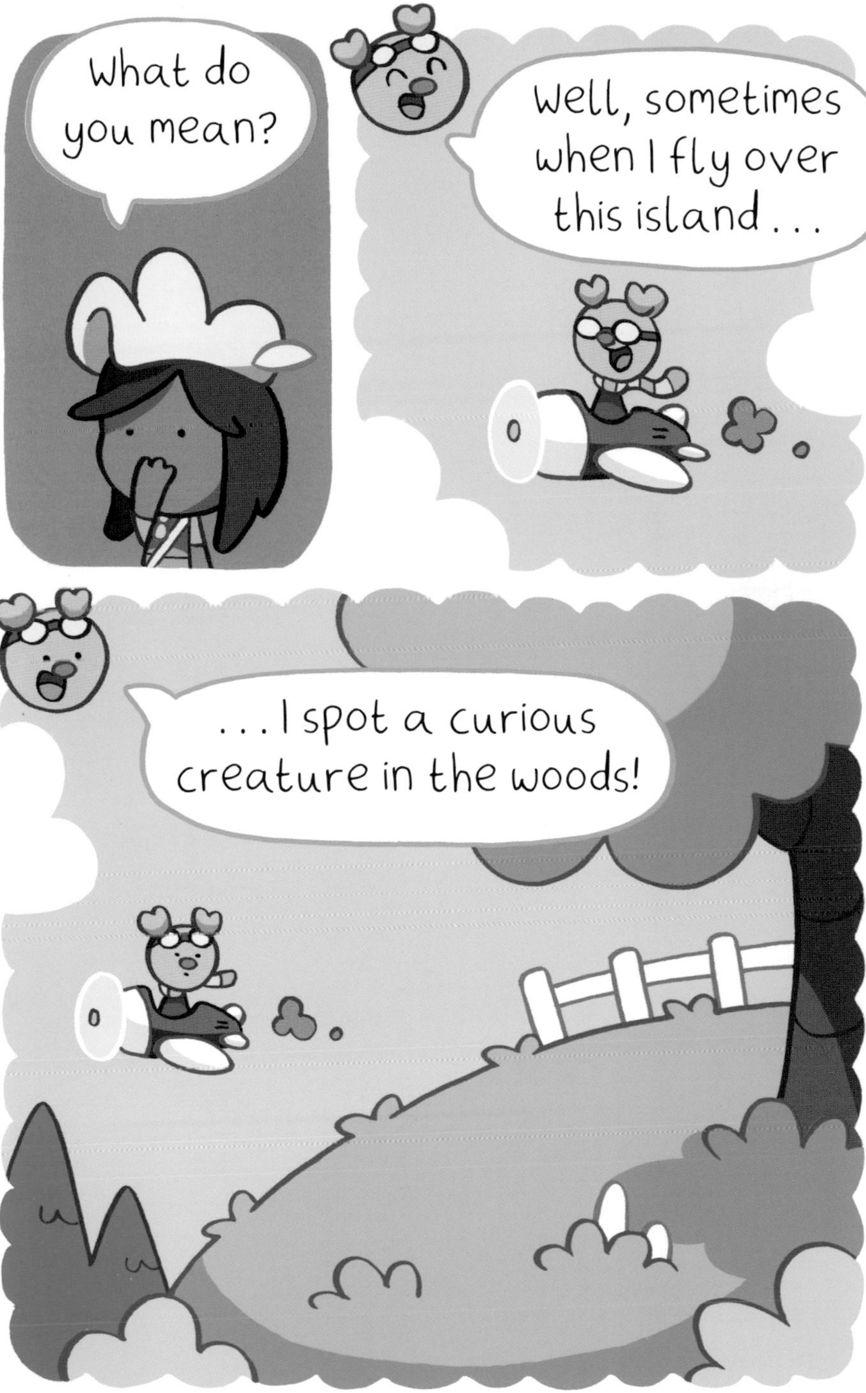
What do you mean?
Well, sometimes when I fly over this island . . .
. . . I spot a curious creature in the woods!

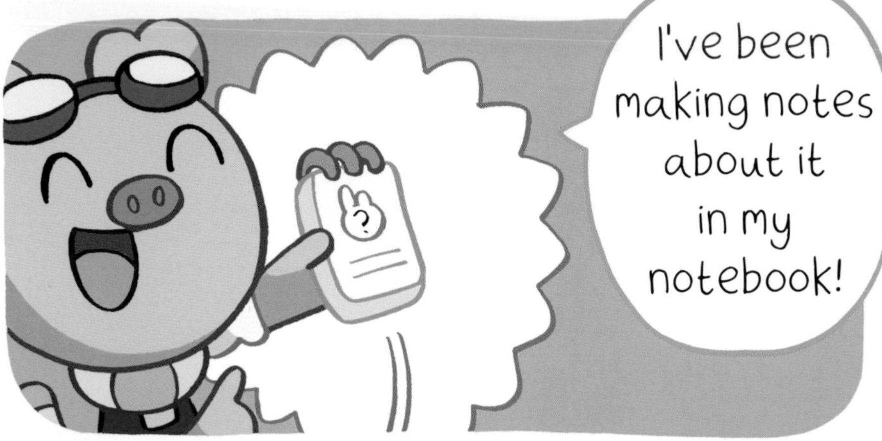
I've been making notes about it in my notebook!

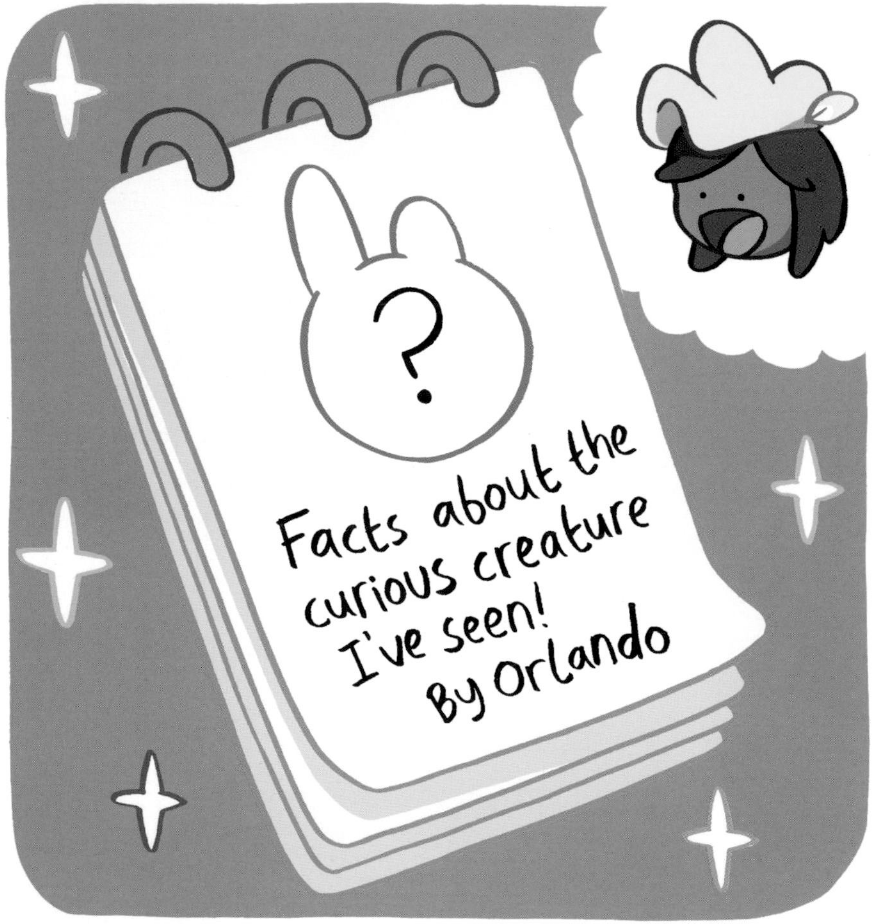
Facts about the curious creature I've seen! By Orlando

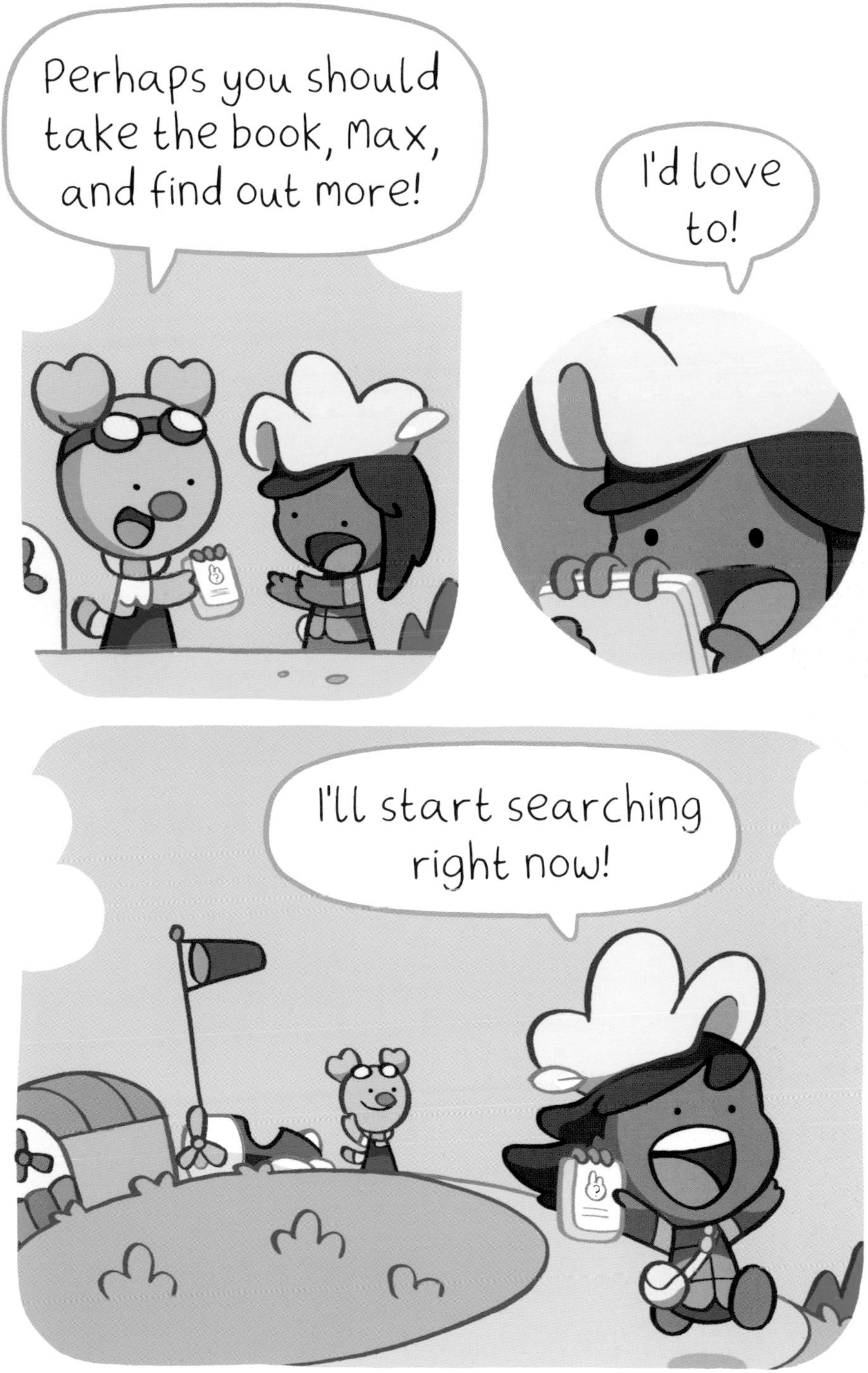
Perhaps you should take the book, Max, and find out more!
I'd love to!
I'll start searching right now!

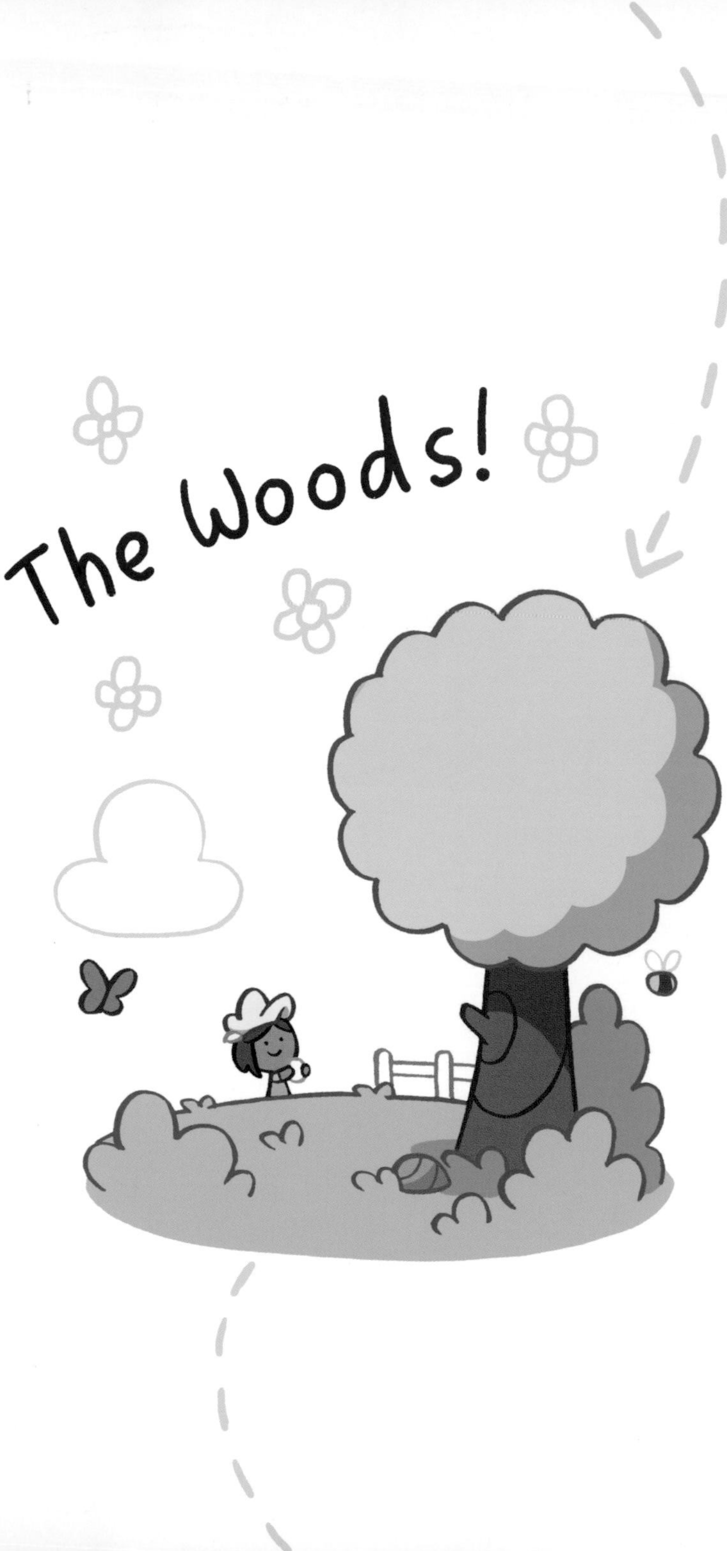
The Woods!

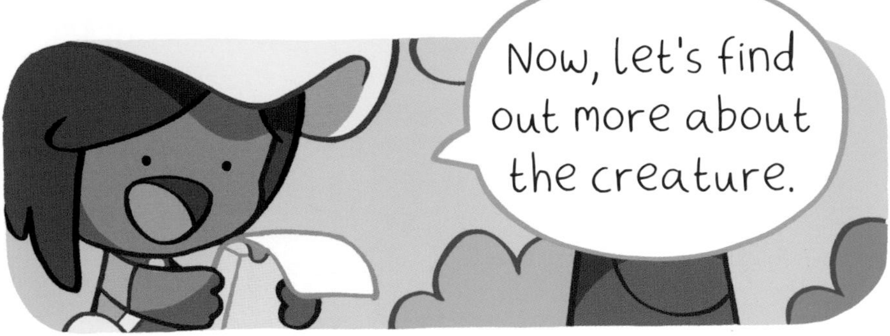
Now, let's find out more about the creature.

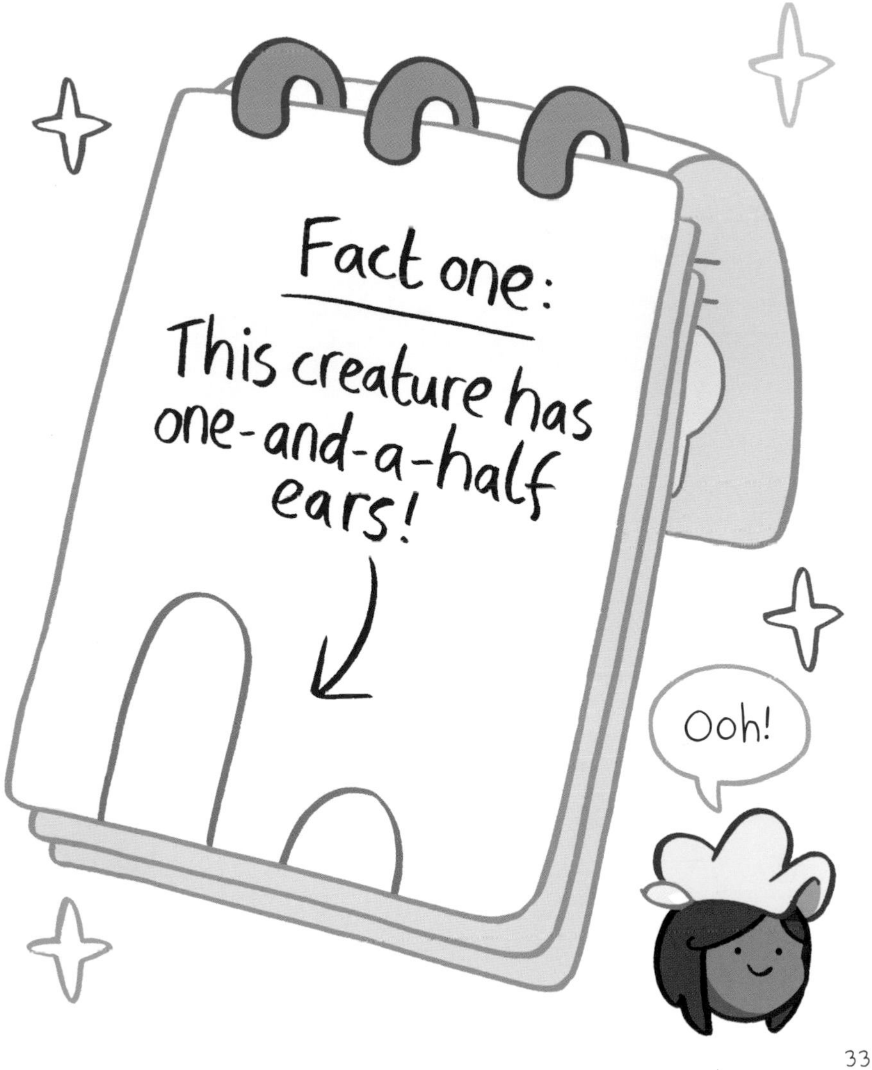
Fact one:
This creature has one-and-a-half ears!
Ooh!

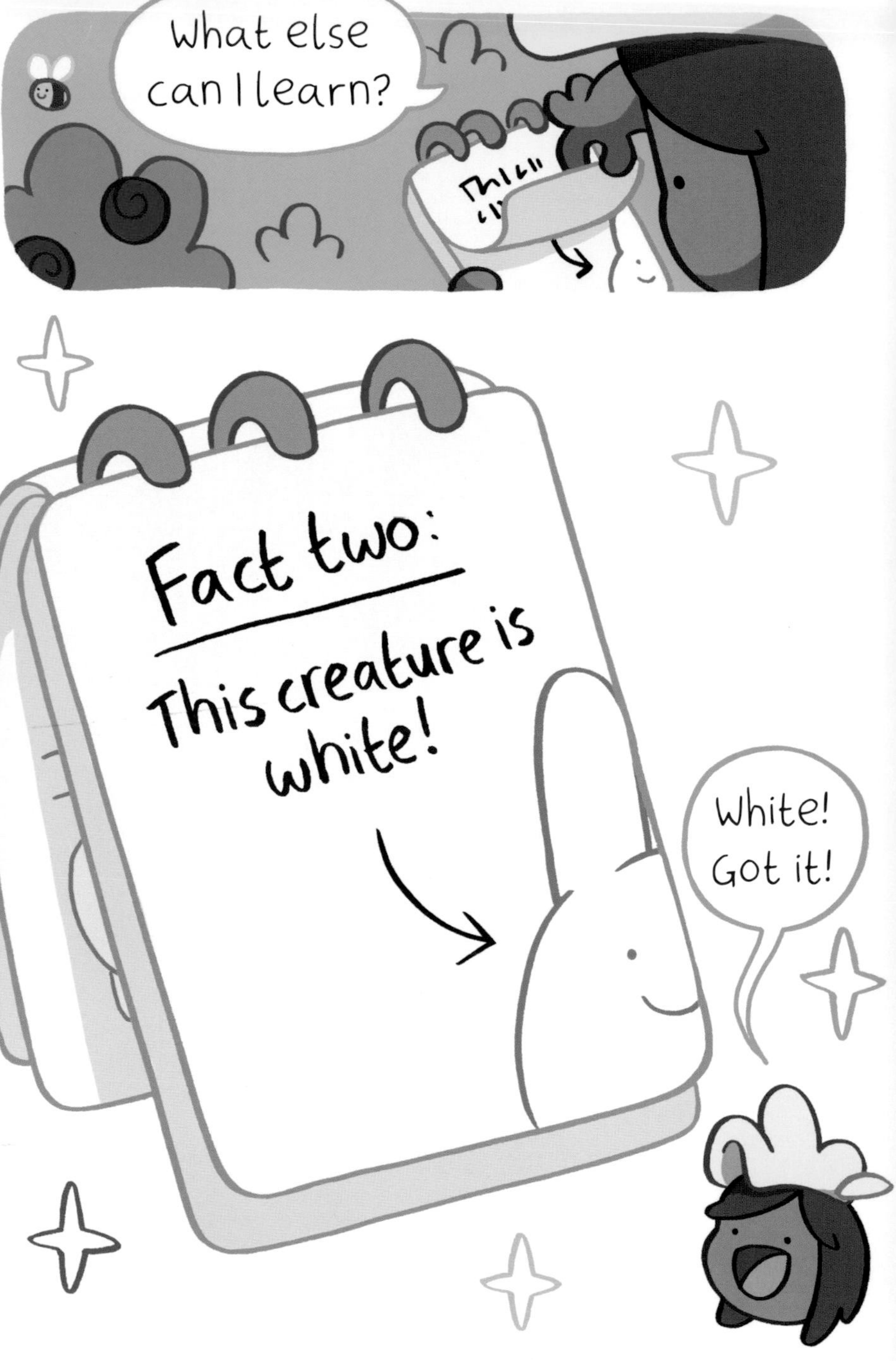
What else can I learn?
Fact two:
This creature is white!
White! Got it!

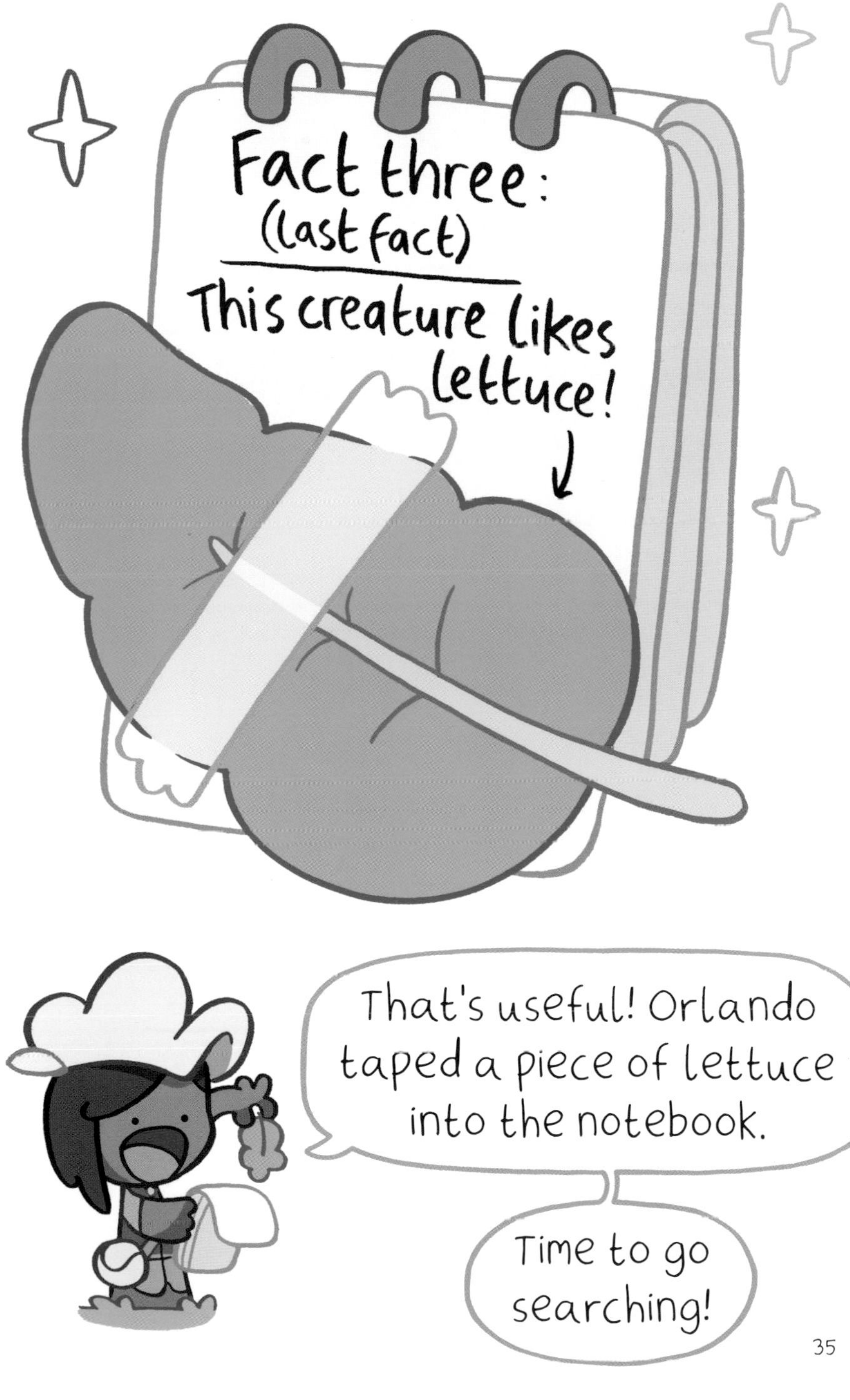

Fact three:
(last fact)
This creature likes lettuce!
That's useful! Orlando taped a piece of lettuce into the notebook.
Time to go searching!

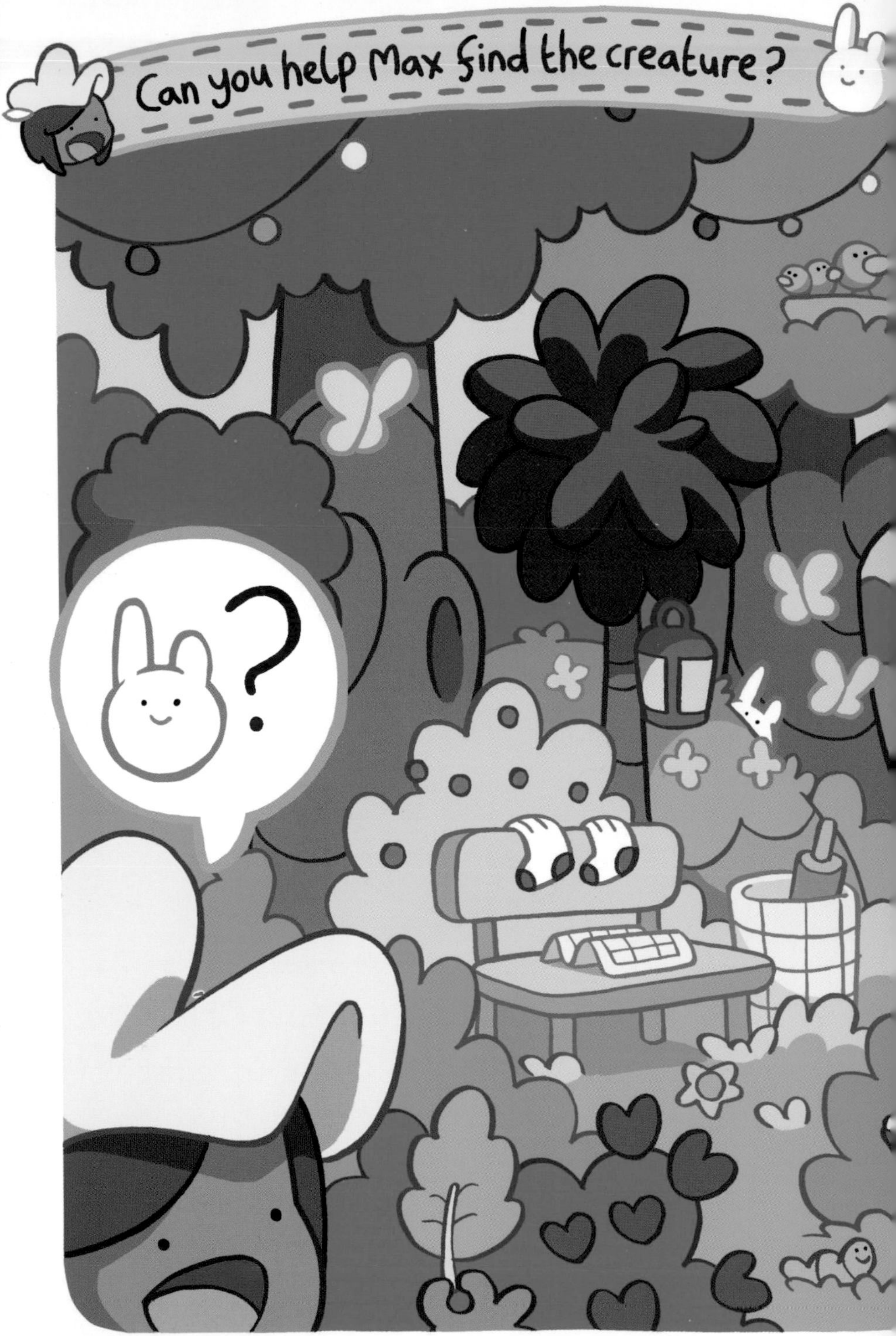
Can you help Max find the creature?
?

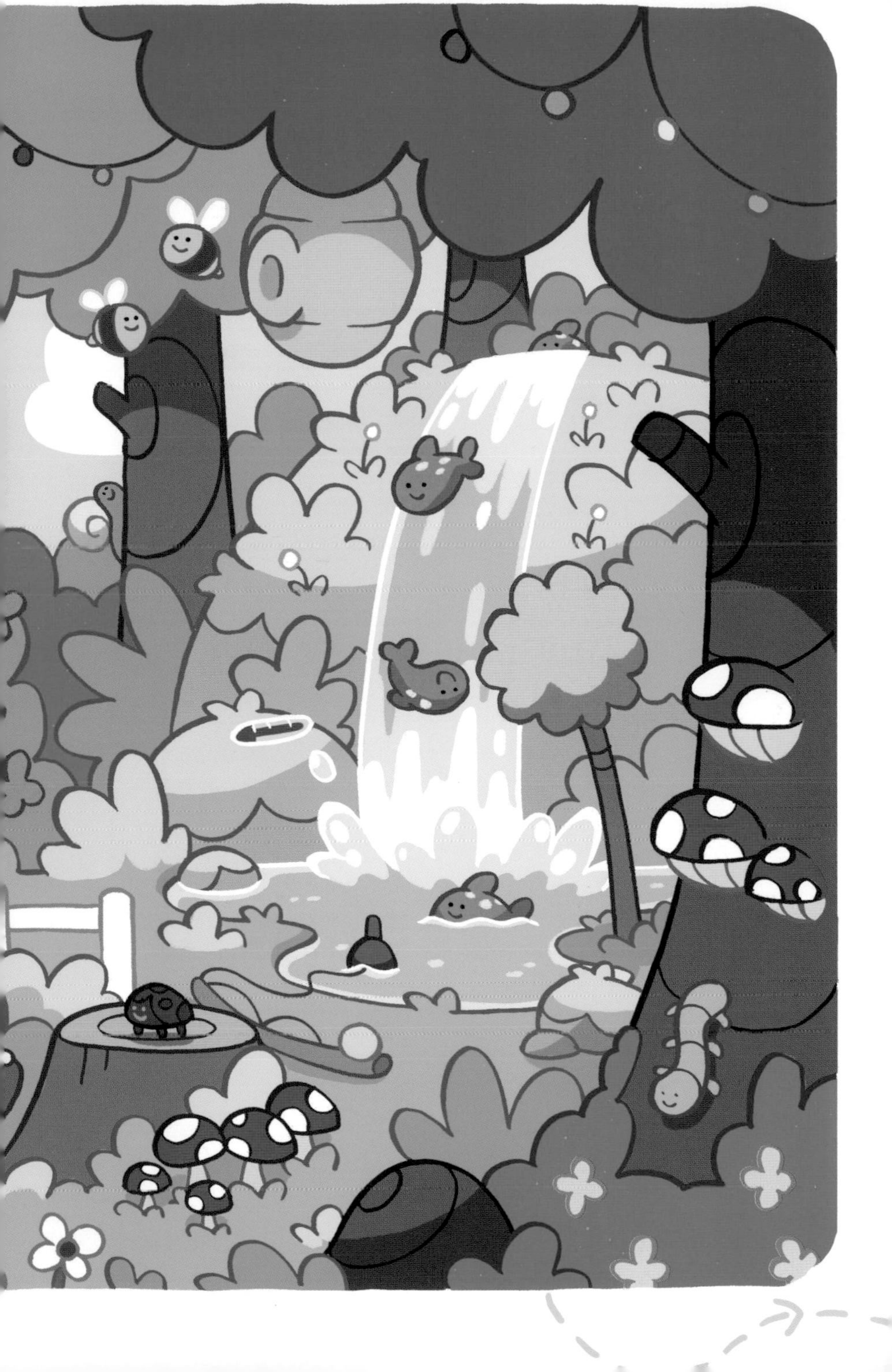

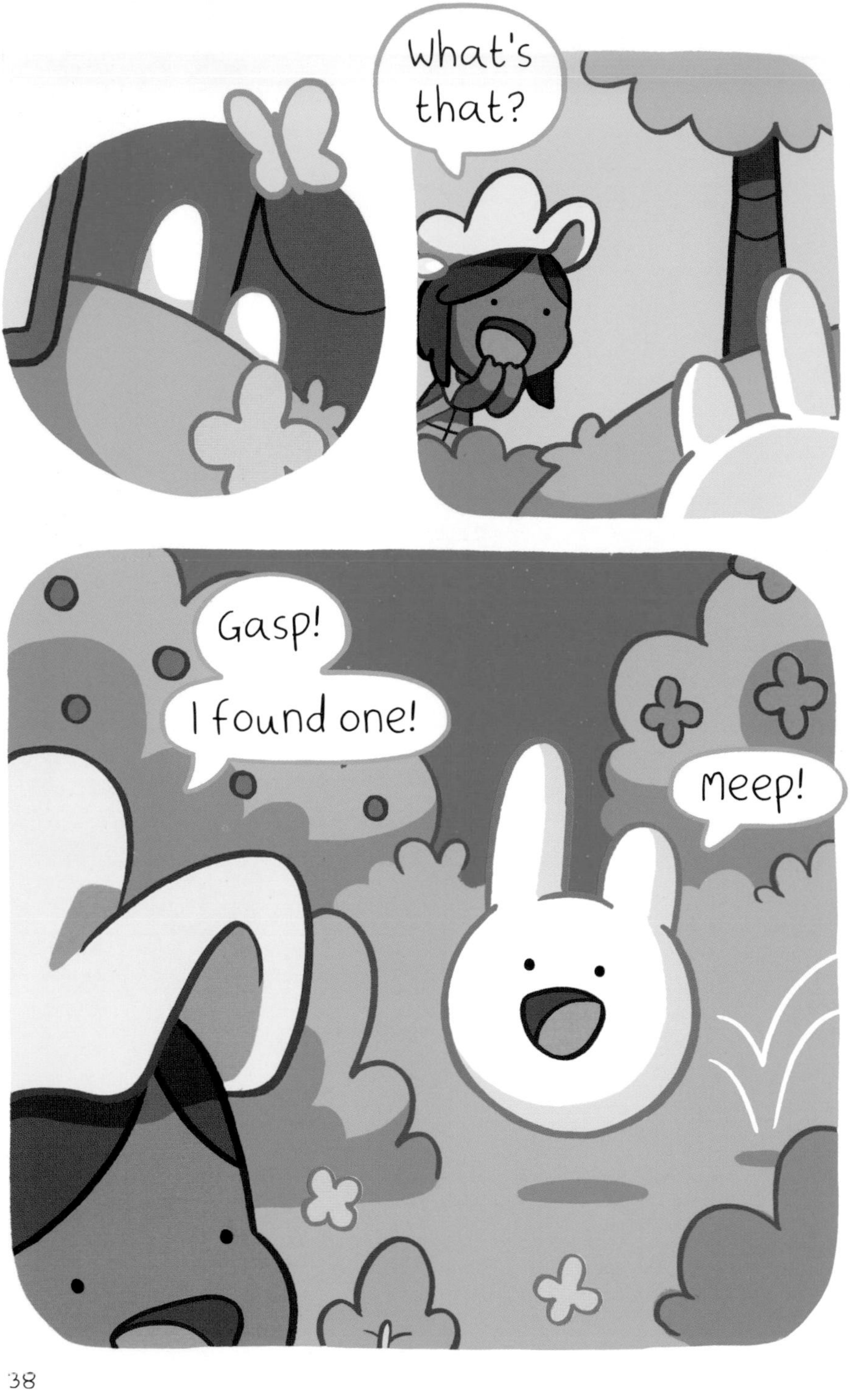
What's that?
Gasp!
I found one!
Meep!

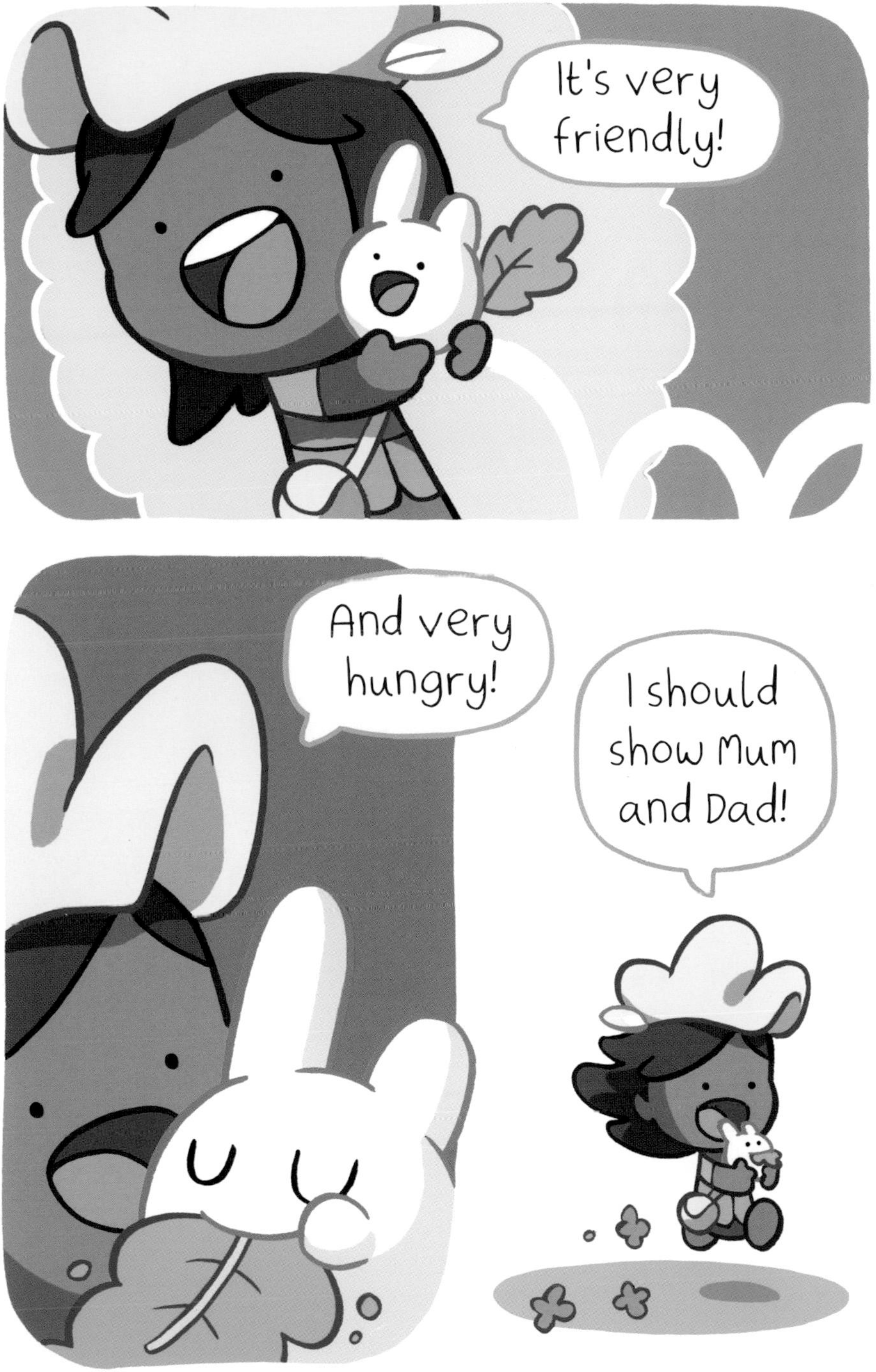
It's very friendly!
And very hungry!
I should show Mum and Dad!

The Lighthouse!

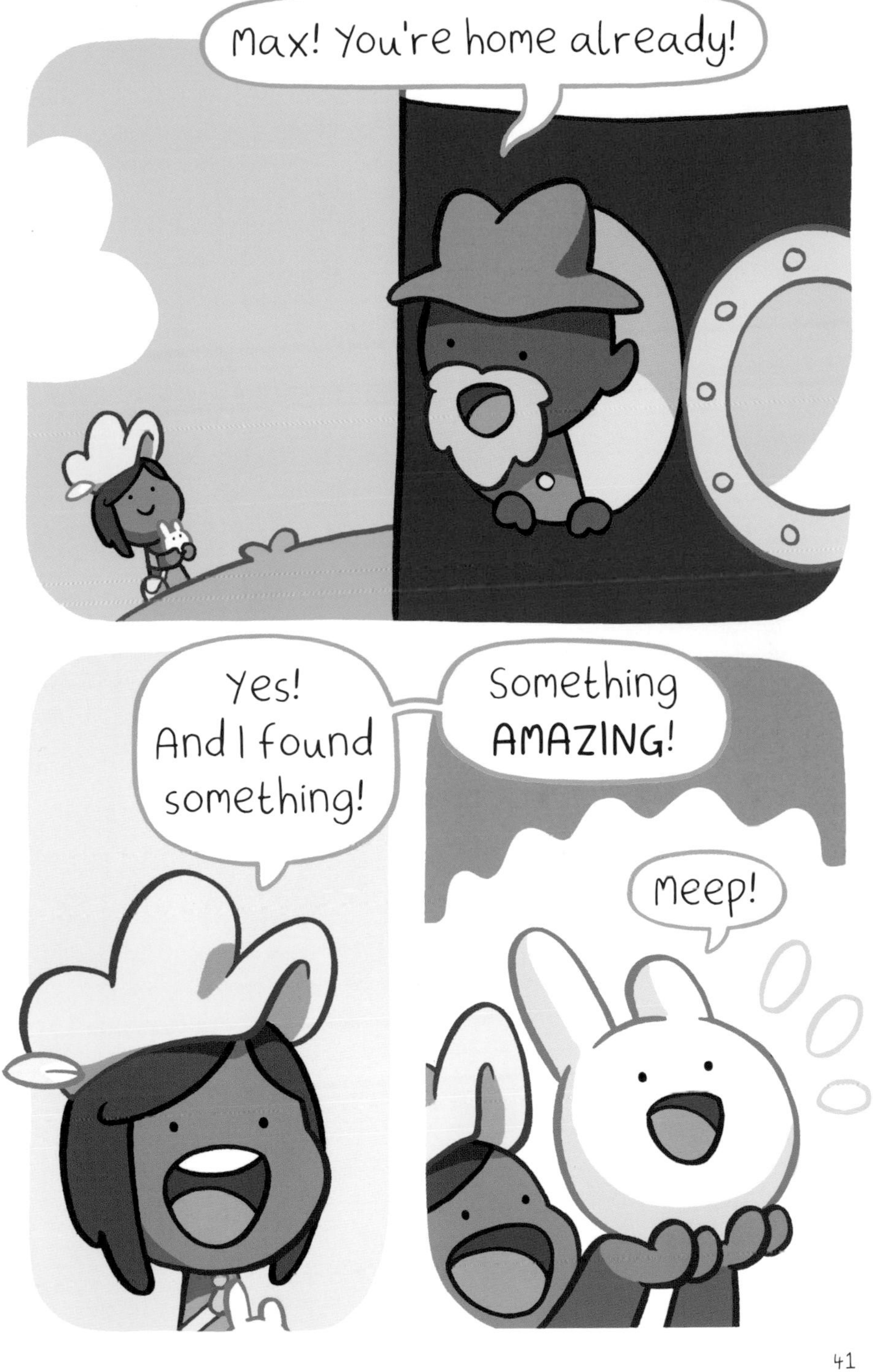
Max! You're home already!
Yes! And I found something!
Something AMAZING!
Meep!

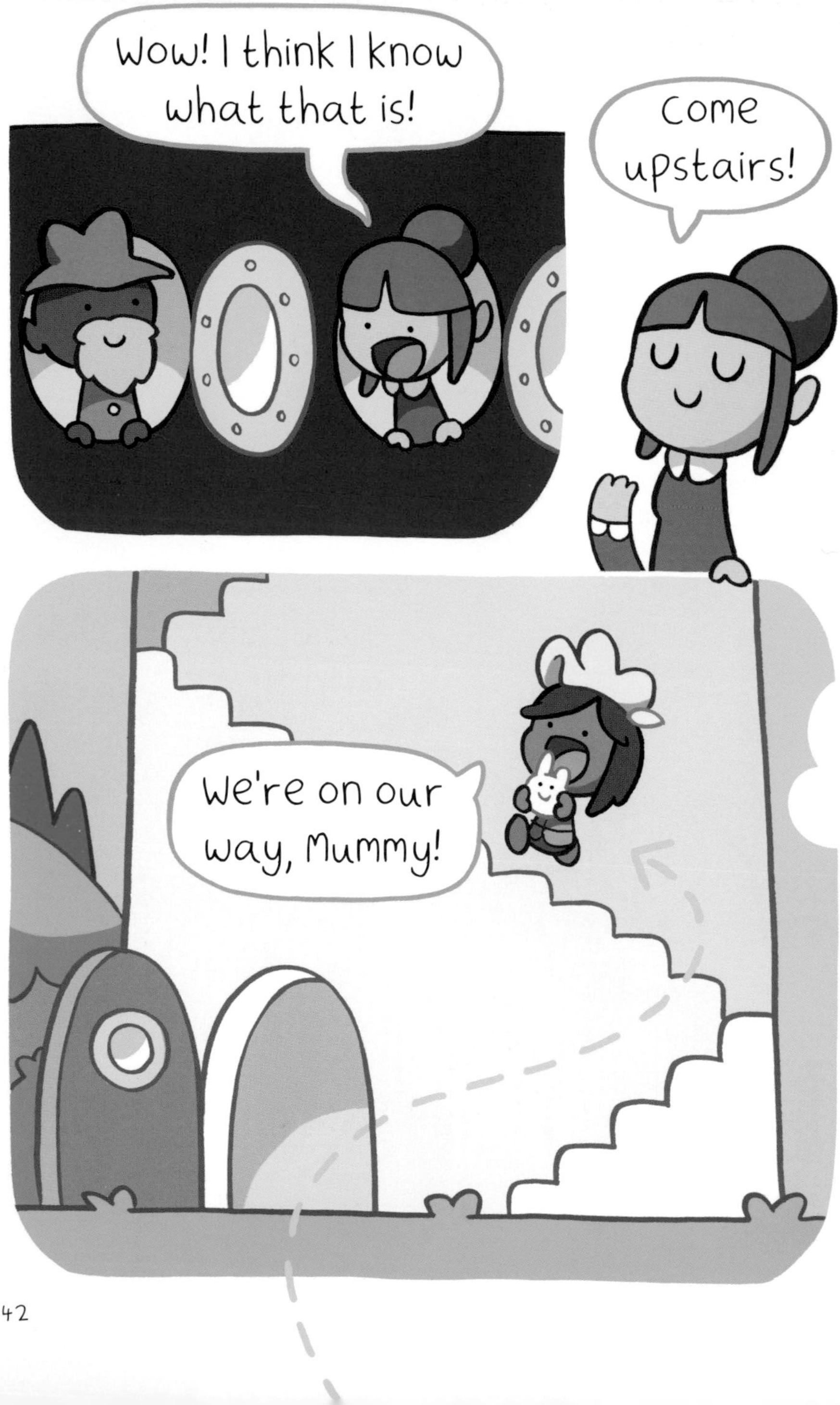
Wow! I think I know what that is!
Come upstairs!
We're on our way, Mummy!

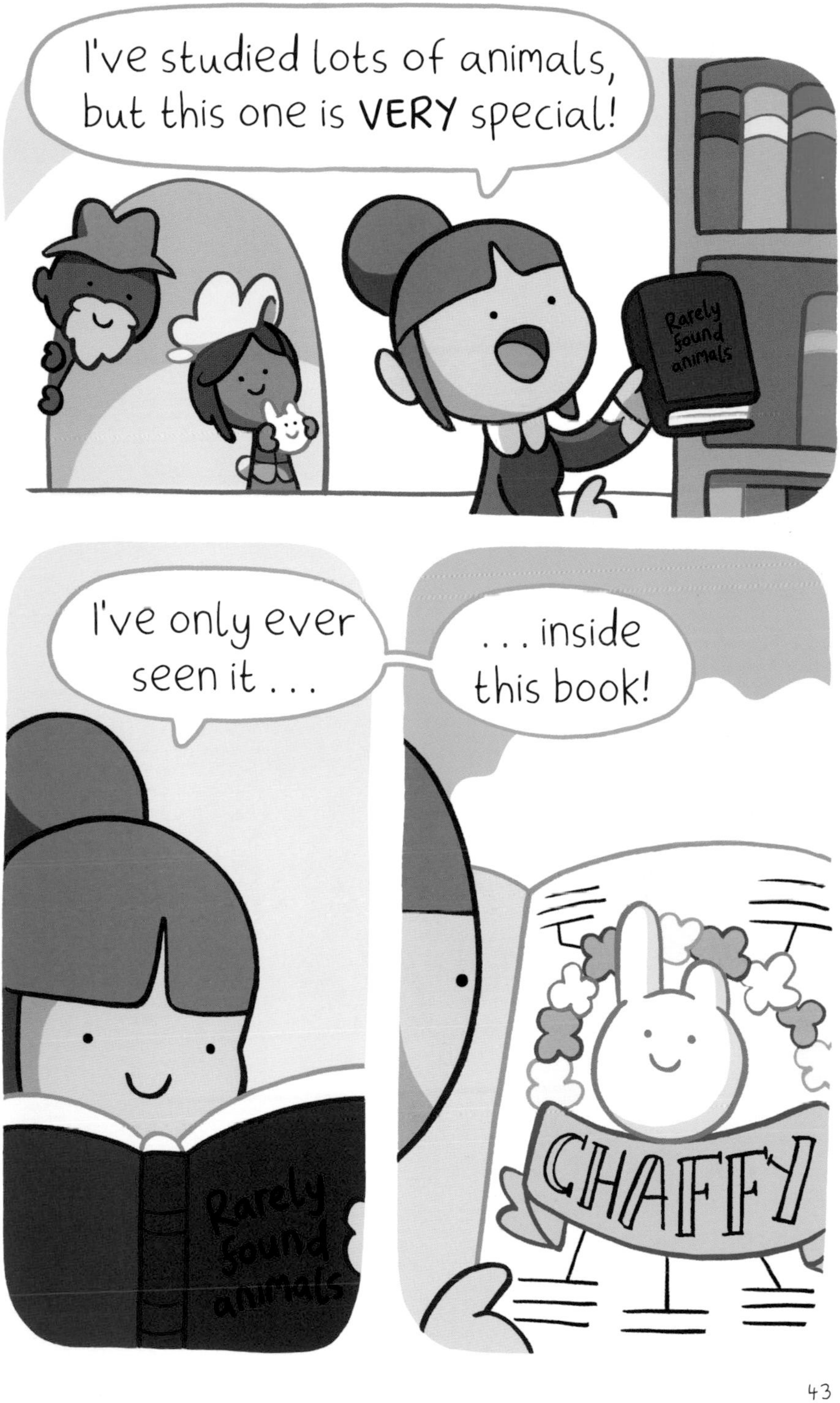
I've studied lots of animals, but this one is **VERY** special!
Rarely found animals
I've only ever seen it . . .
. . . inside this book!
Rarely found animals
CHAFFY

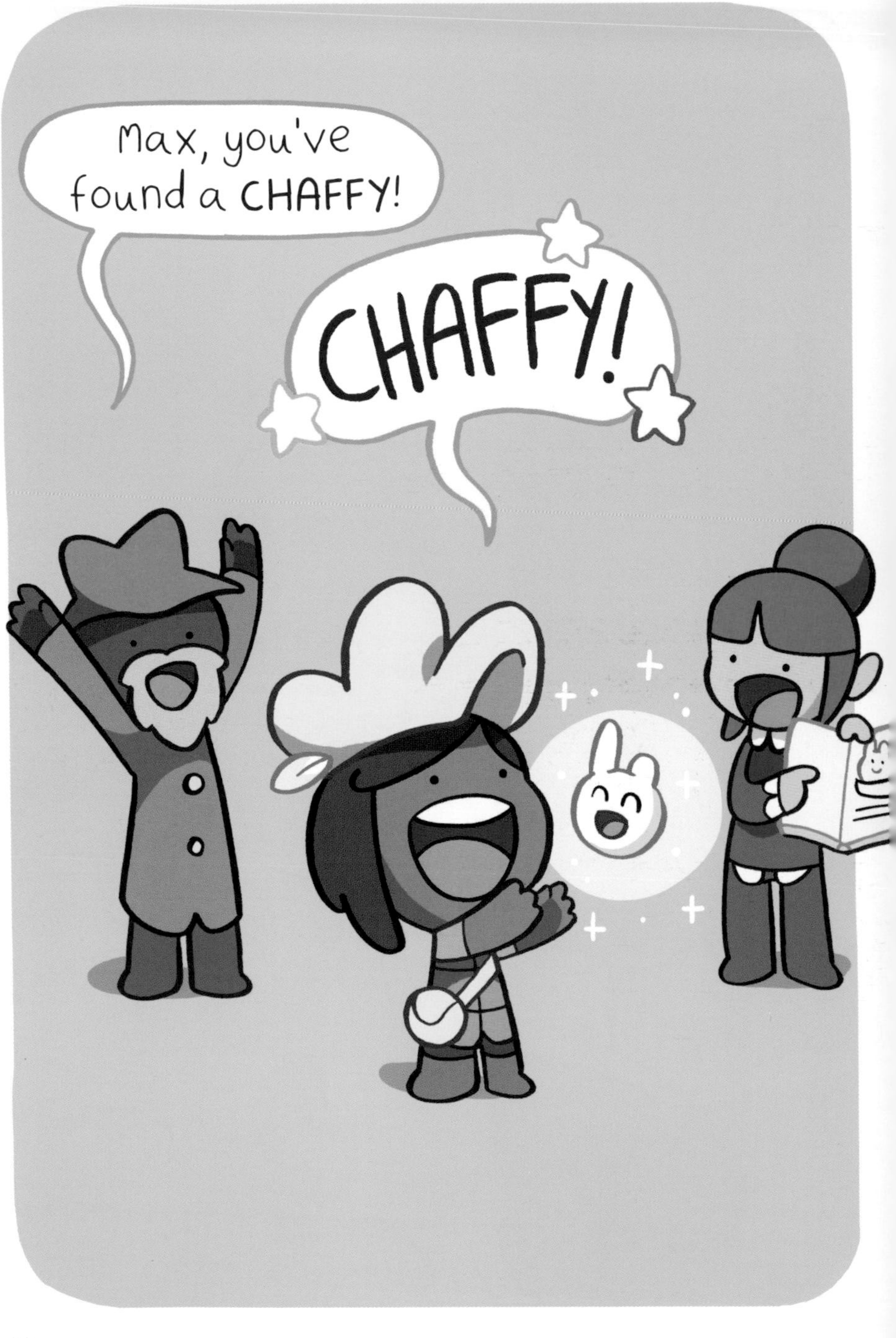
Max, you've found a CHAFFY!
CHAFFY!

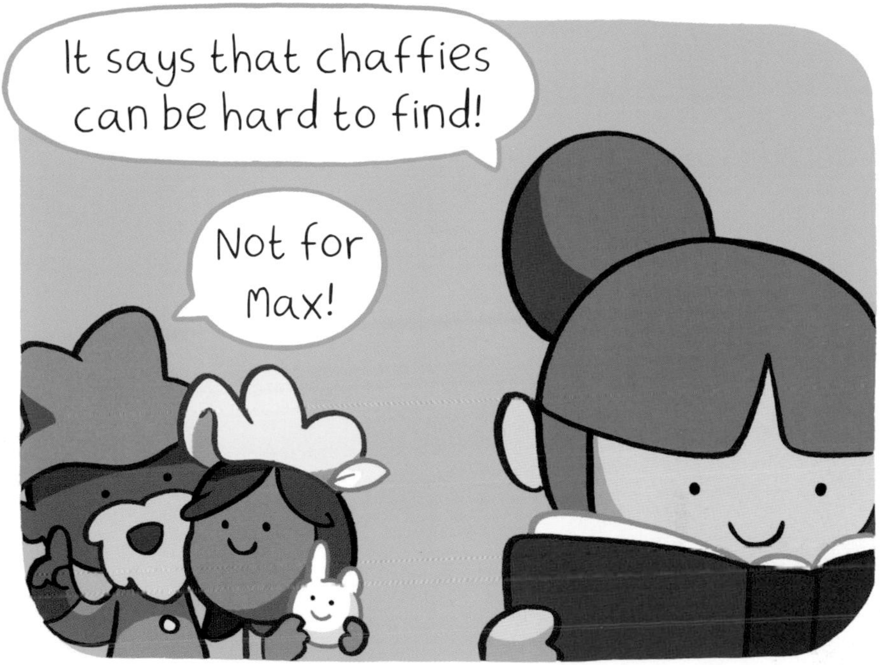
It says that chaffies can be hard to find!
Not for Max!

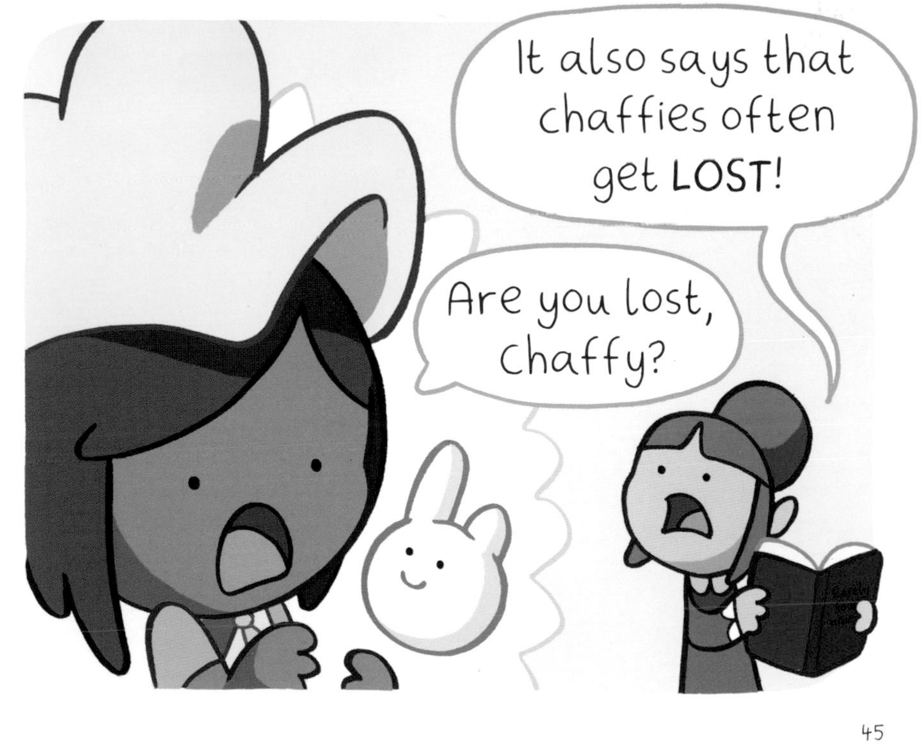
It also says that chaffies often get LOST!
Are you lost, Chaffy?

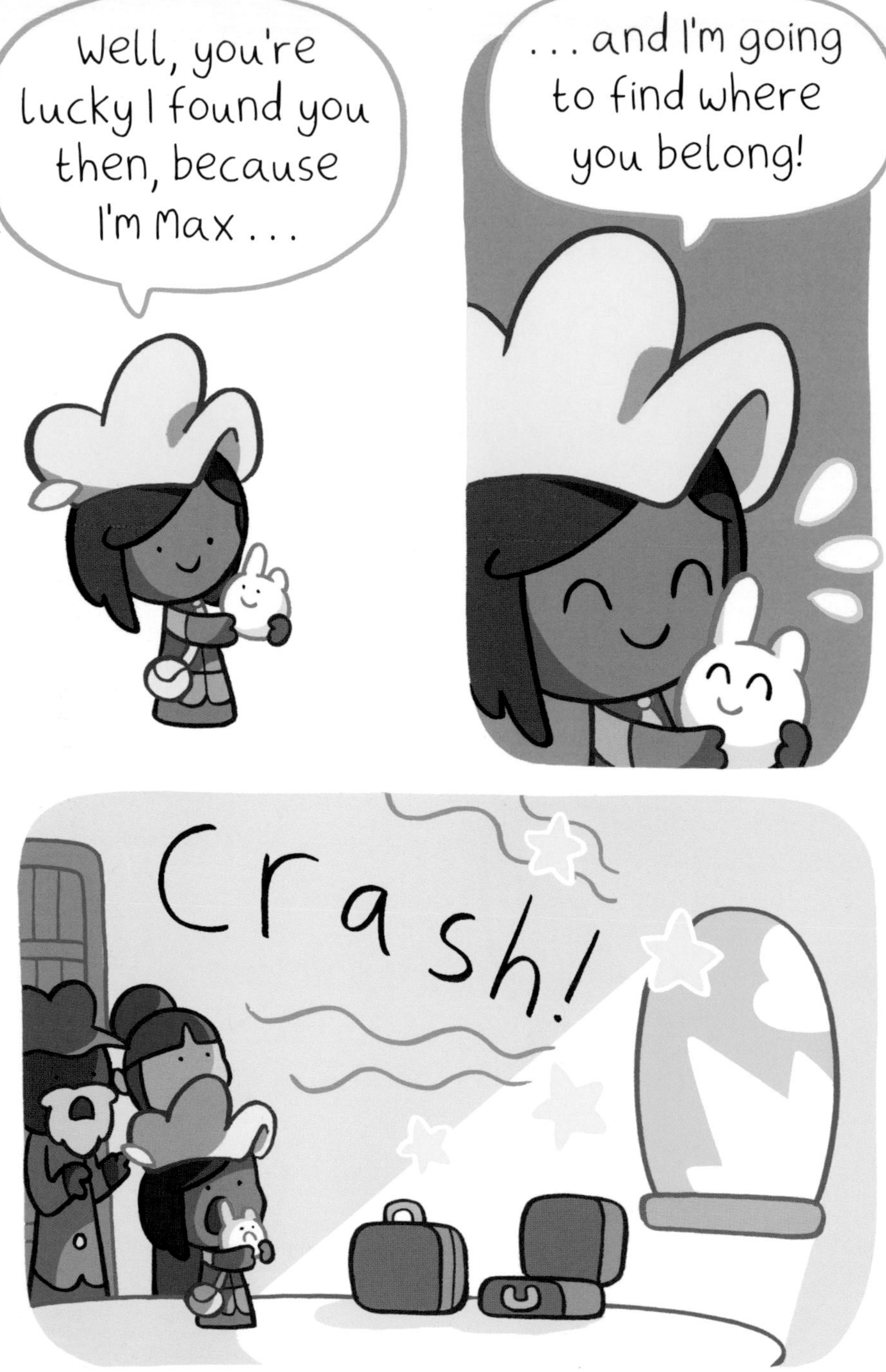
Well, you're lucky I found you then, because I'm Max . . .
. . . and I'm going to find where you belong!
Crash!

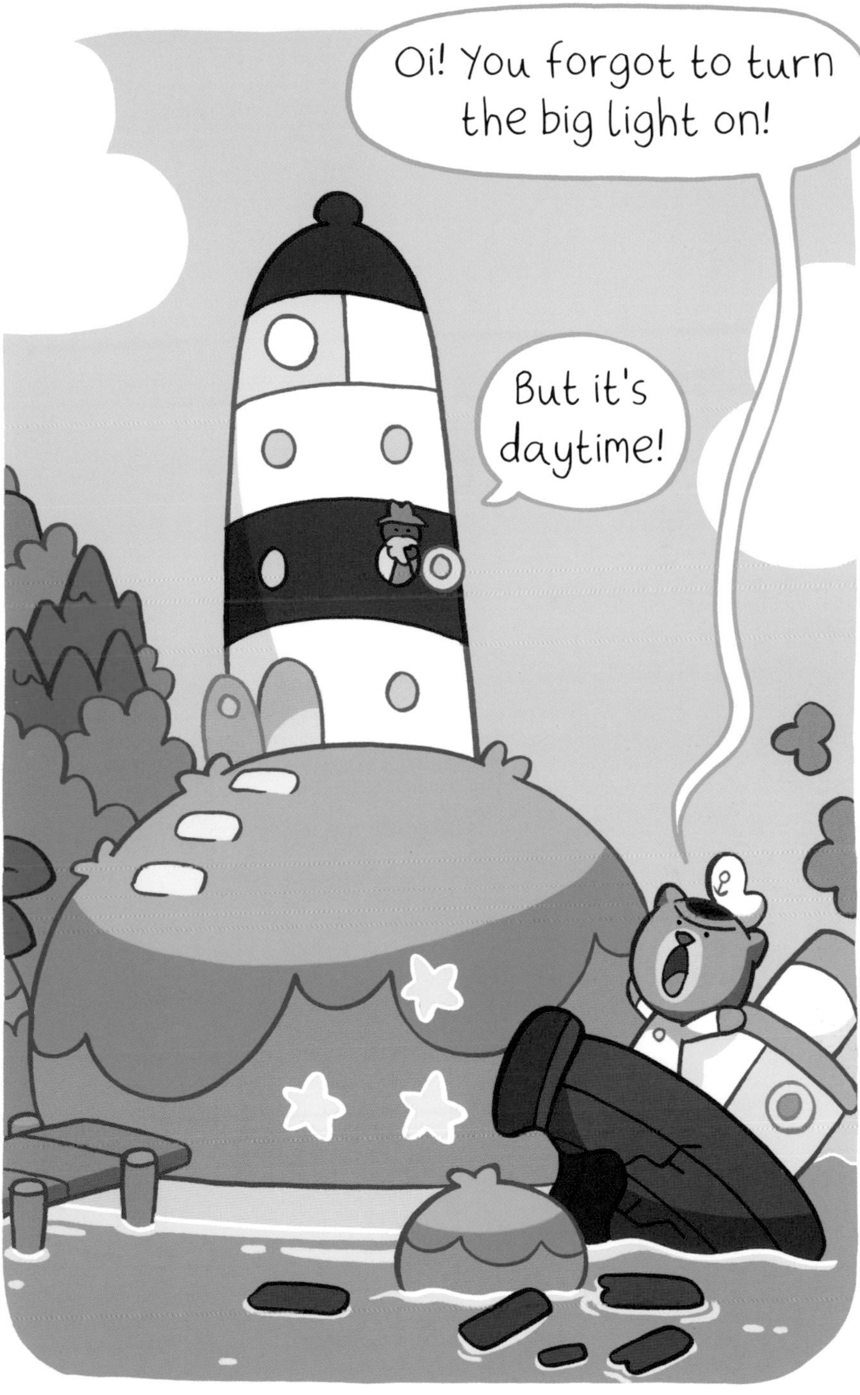

Oi! You forgot to turn the big light on!
But it's daytime!

Foghorn's Boat!

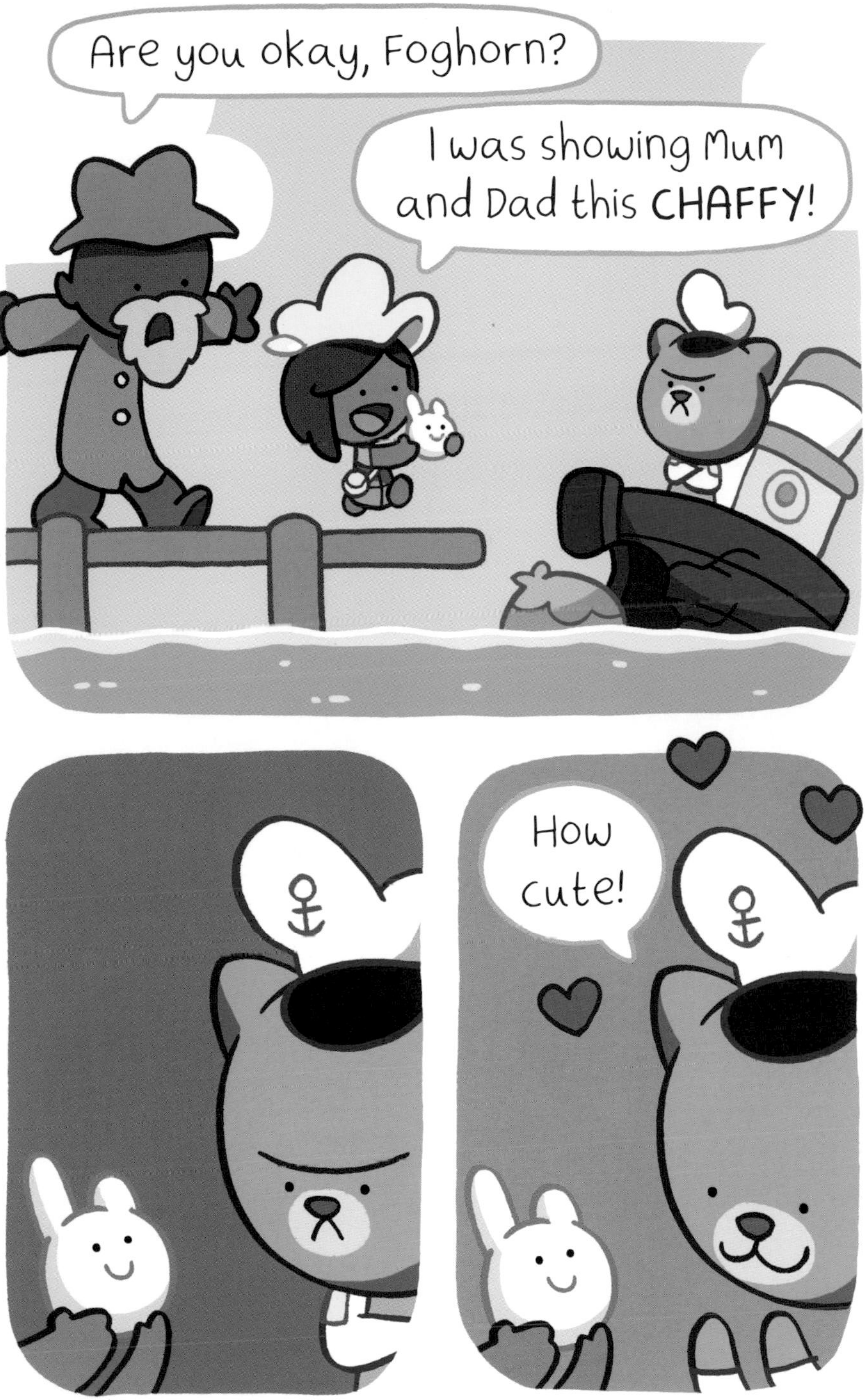
Are you okay, Foghorn?
I was showing Mum and Dad this CHAFFY!
How cute!

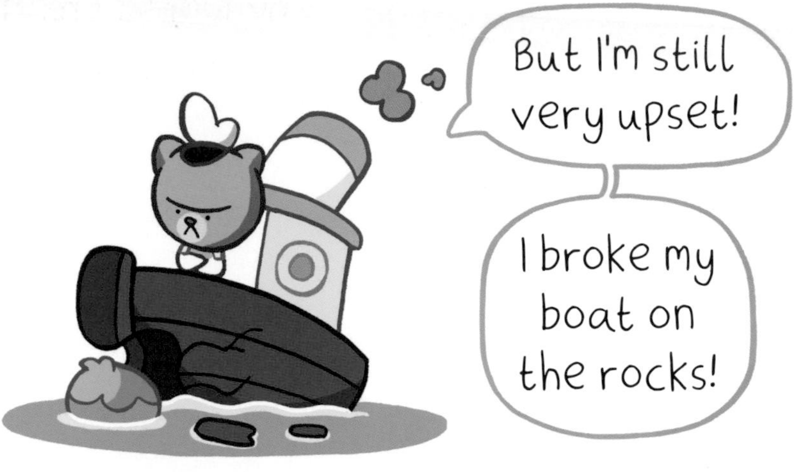
But I'm still very upset!
I broke my boat on the rocks!

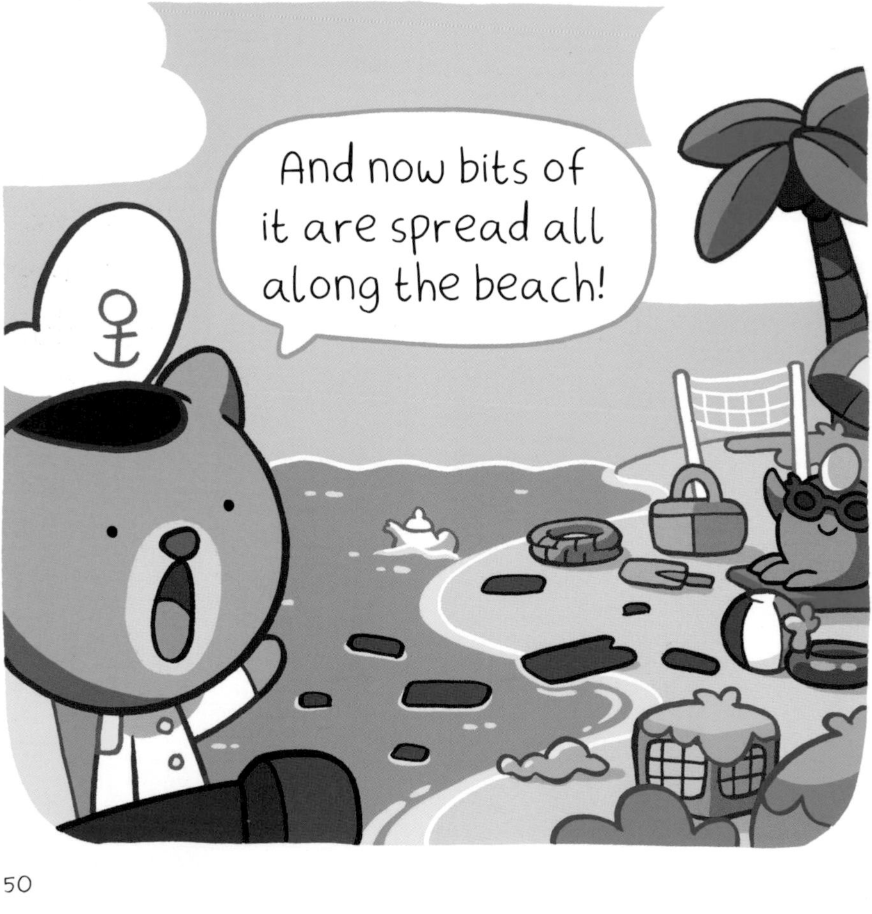
And now bits of it are spread all along the beach!

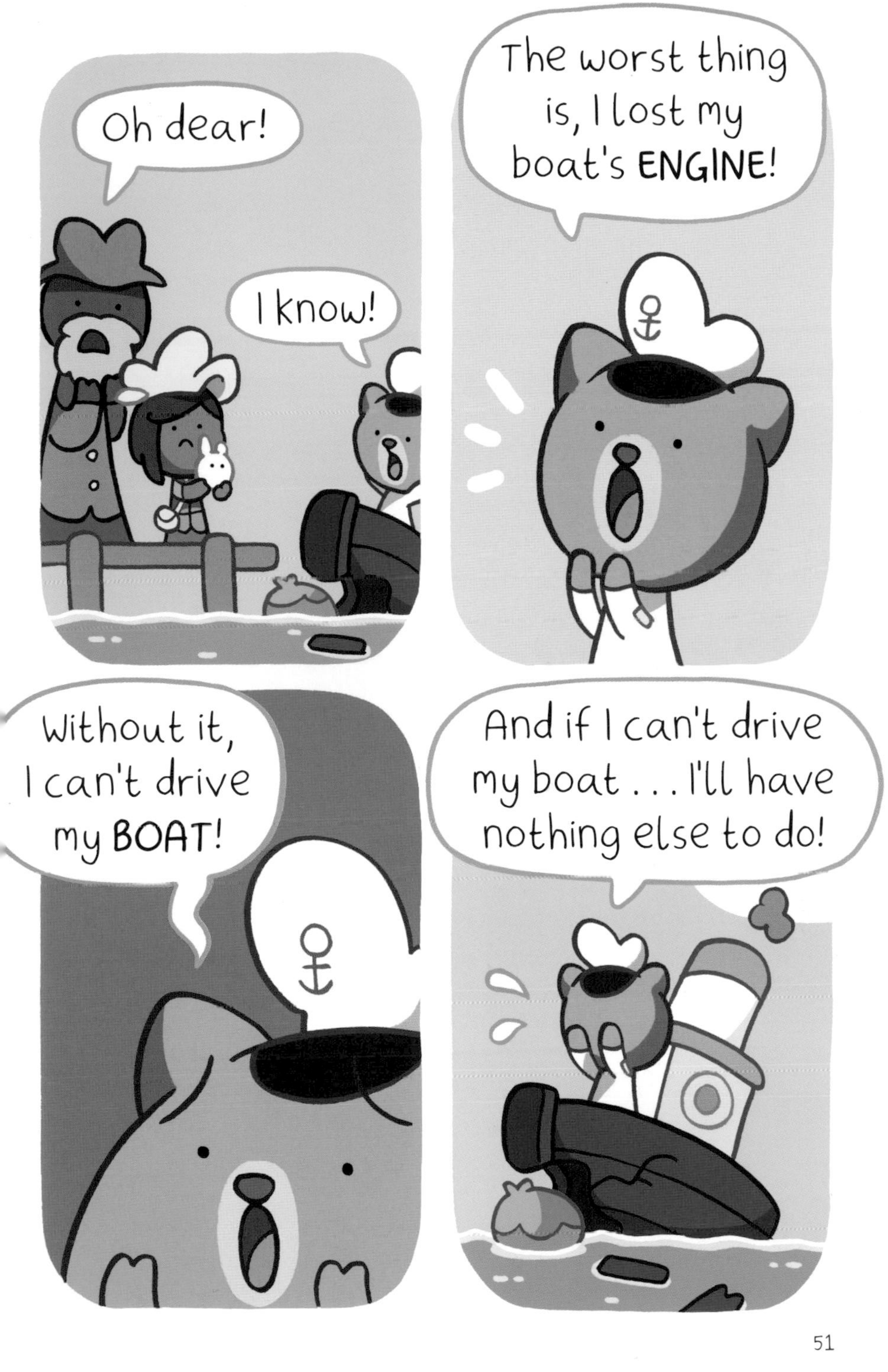
Oh dear!
I know!
The worst thing is, I lost my boat's ENGINE!
Without it, I can't drive my BOAT!
And if I can't drive my boat . . . I'll have nothing else to do!

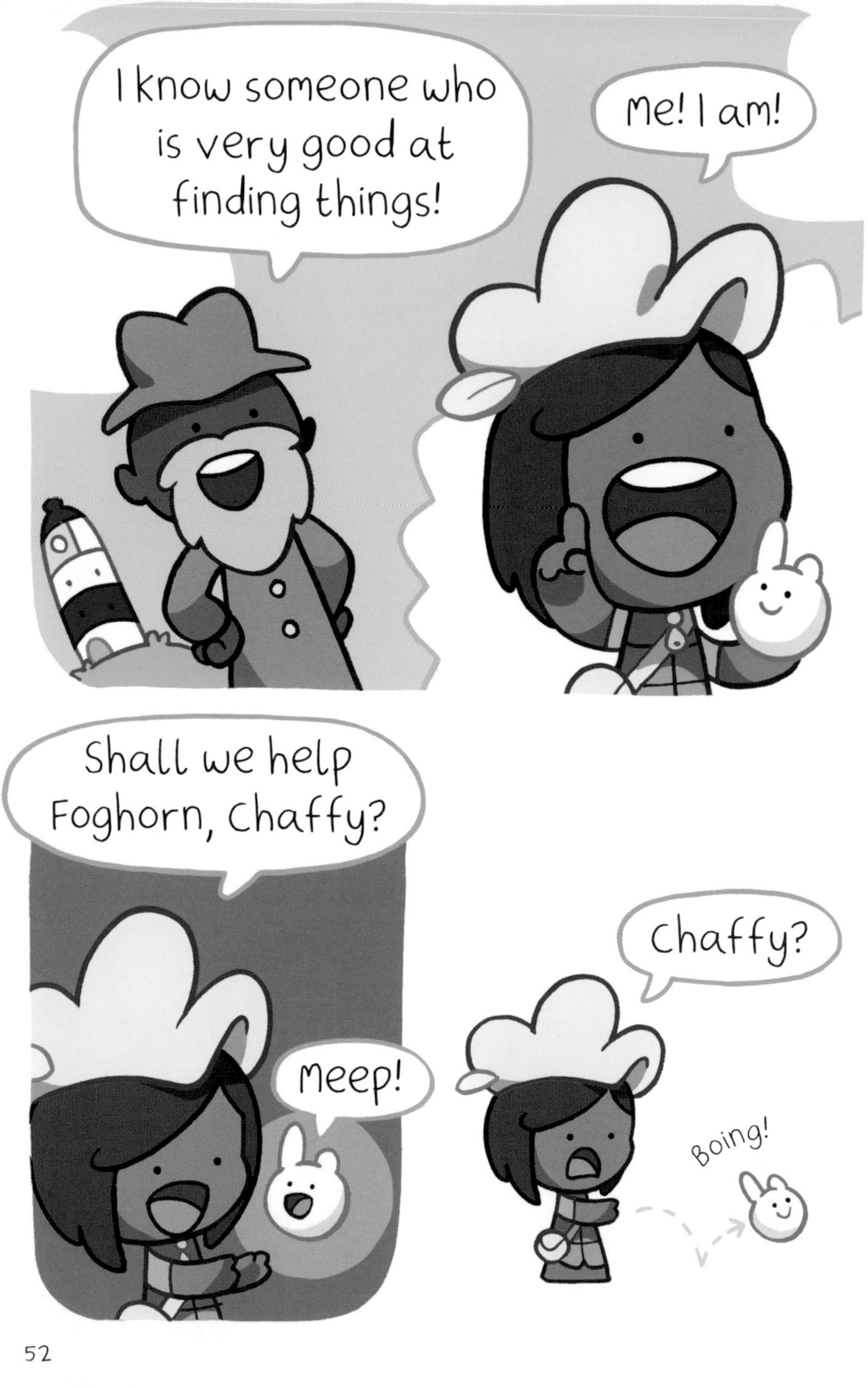
I know someone who is very good at finding things!
Me! I am!
Shall we help Foghorn, Chaffy?
Meep!
Chaffy?
Boing!

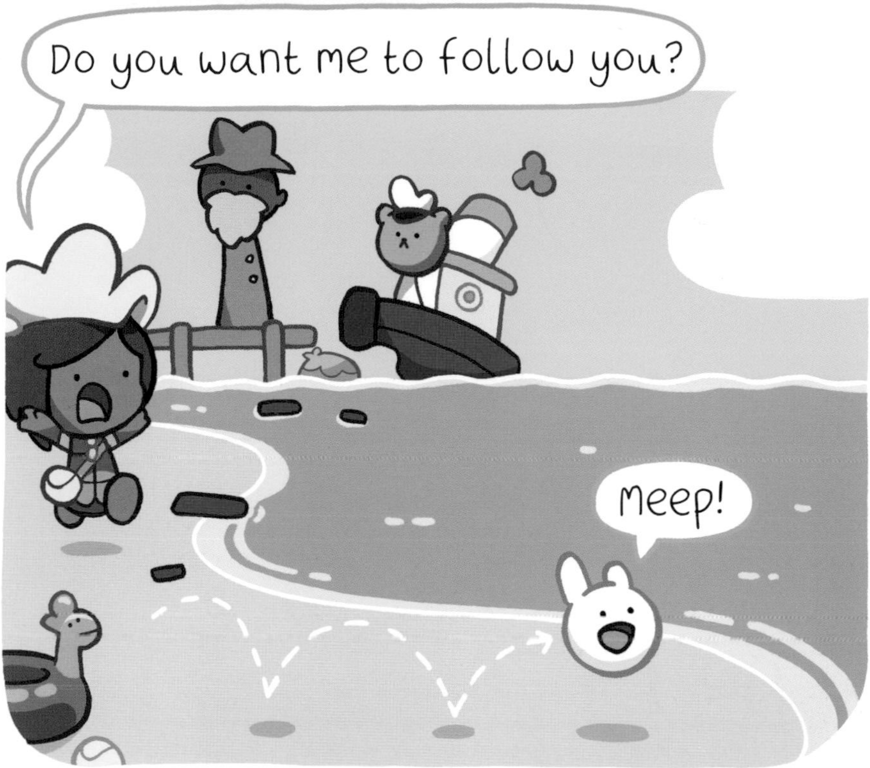
Do you want me to follow you?
Meep!

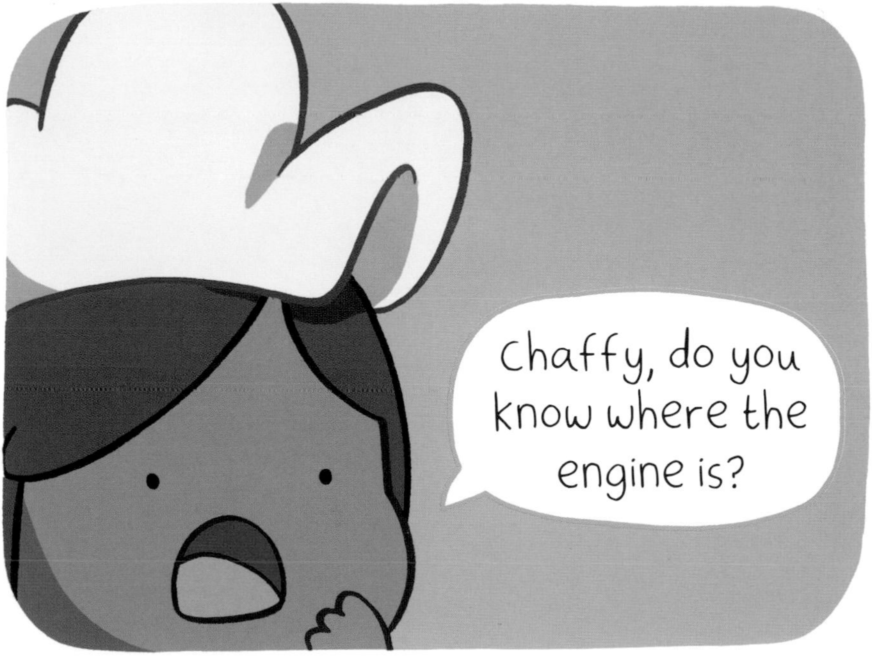
Chaffy, do you know where the engine is?

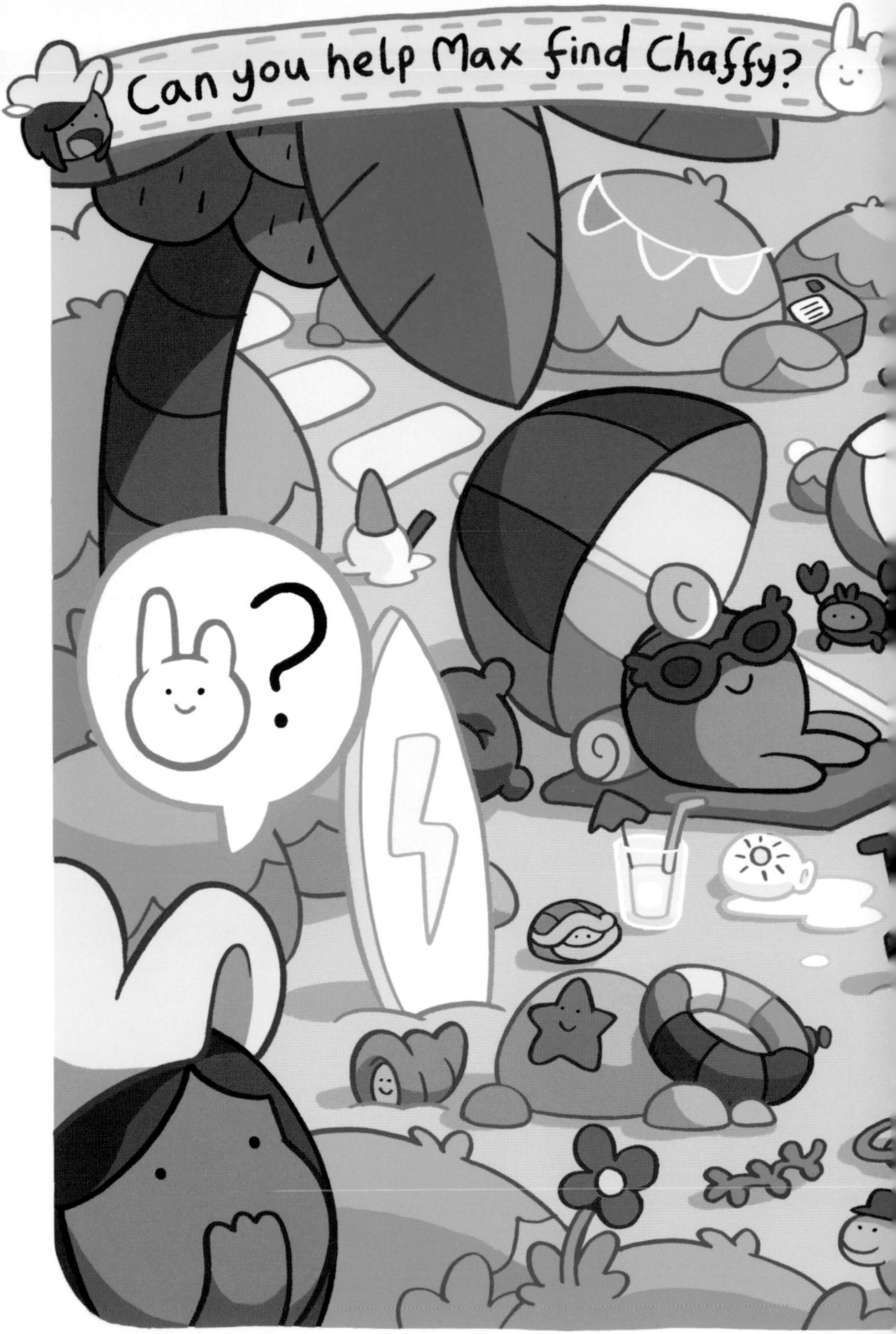
Can you help Max find Chaffy?

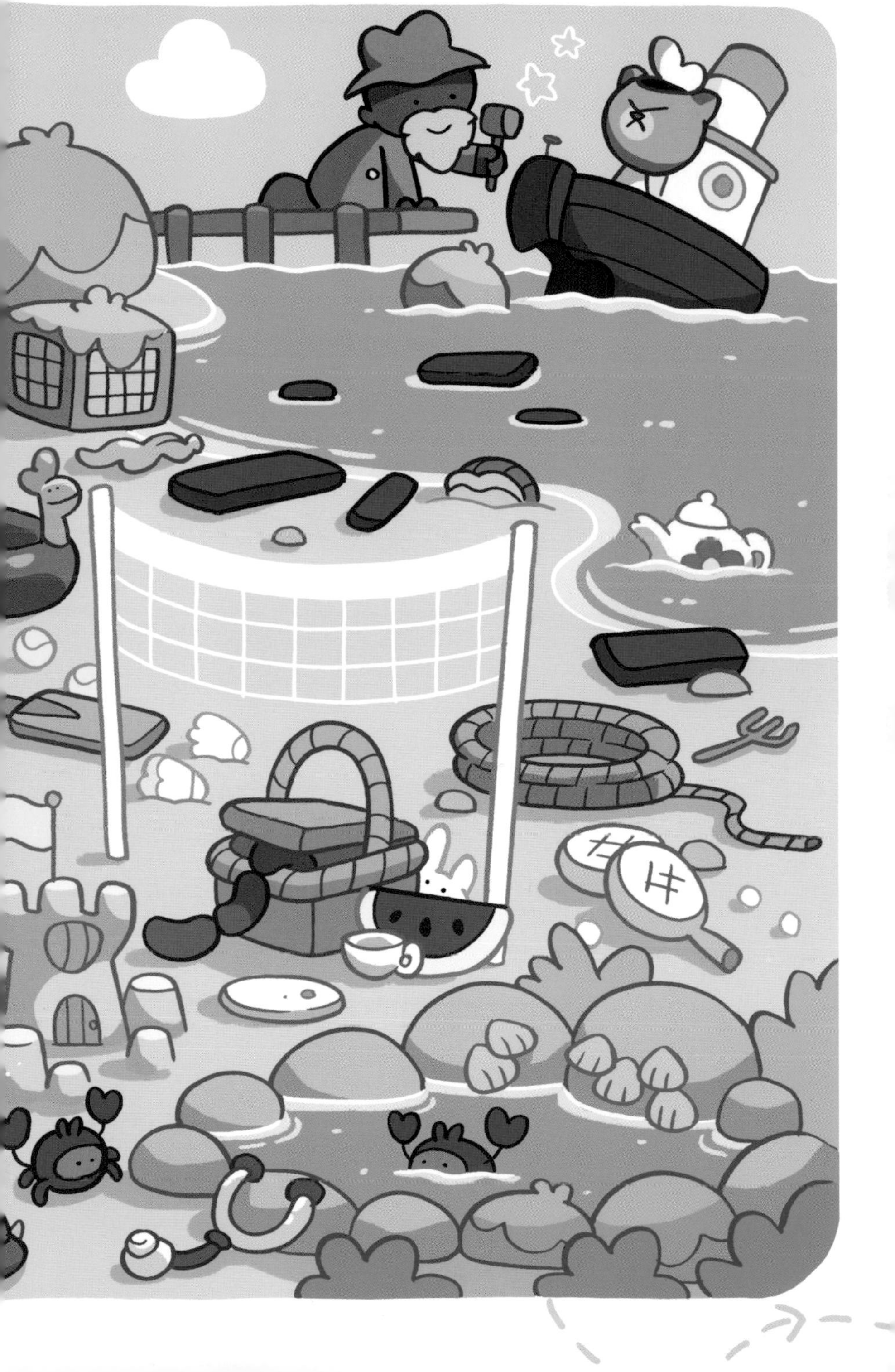

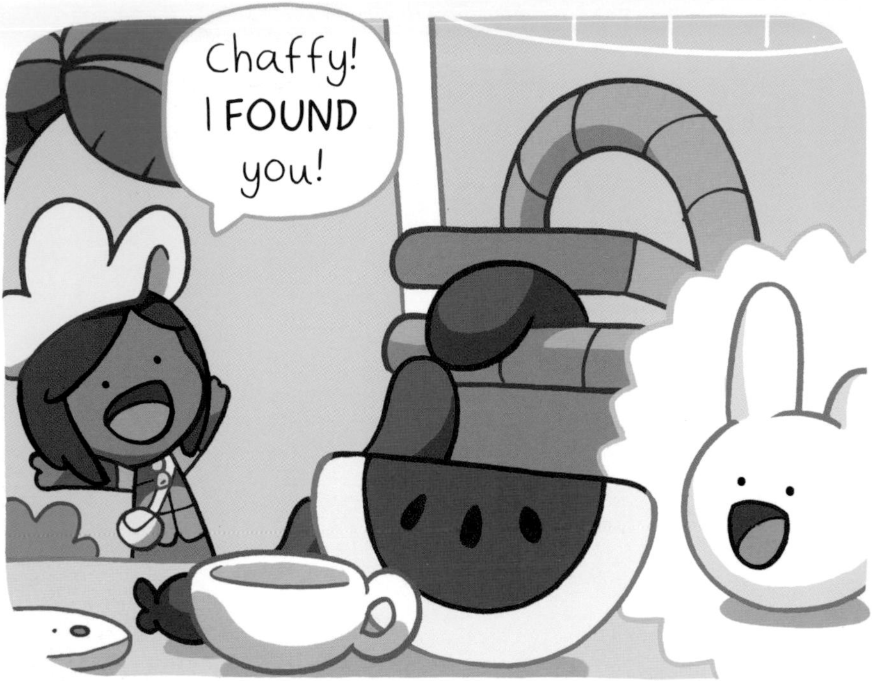
Chaffy! I **FOUND** you!

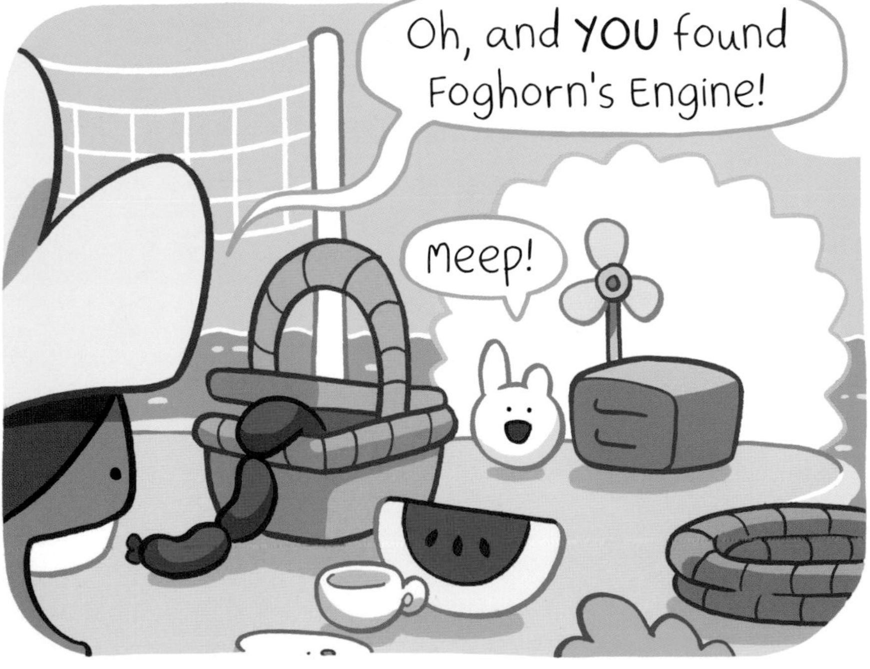
Oh, and **YOU** found Foghorn's Engine!
Meep!

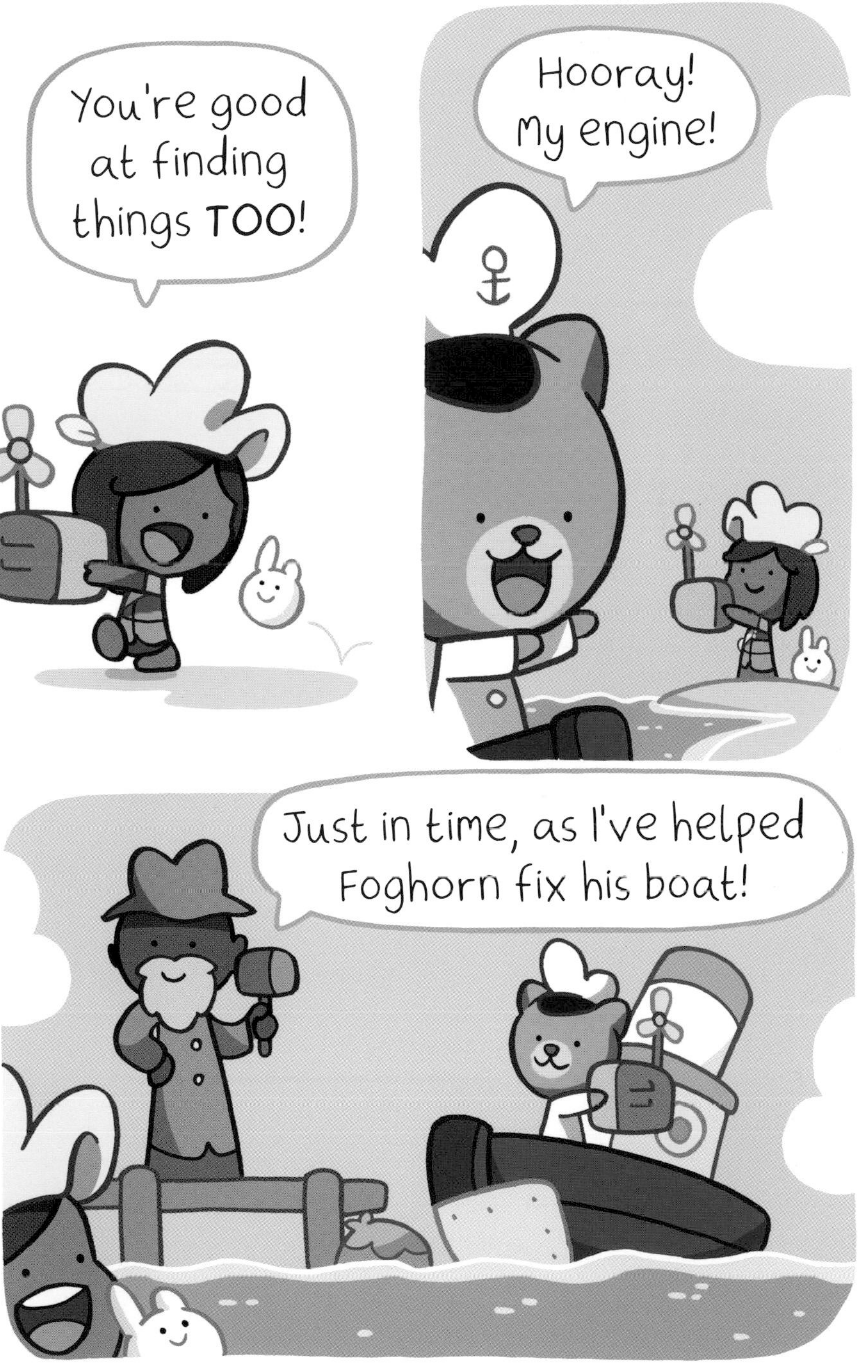
You're good at finding things TOO!
Hooray! My engine!
Just in time, as I've helped Foghorn fix his boat!

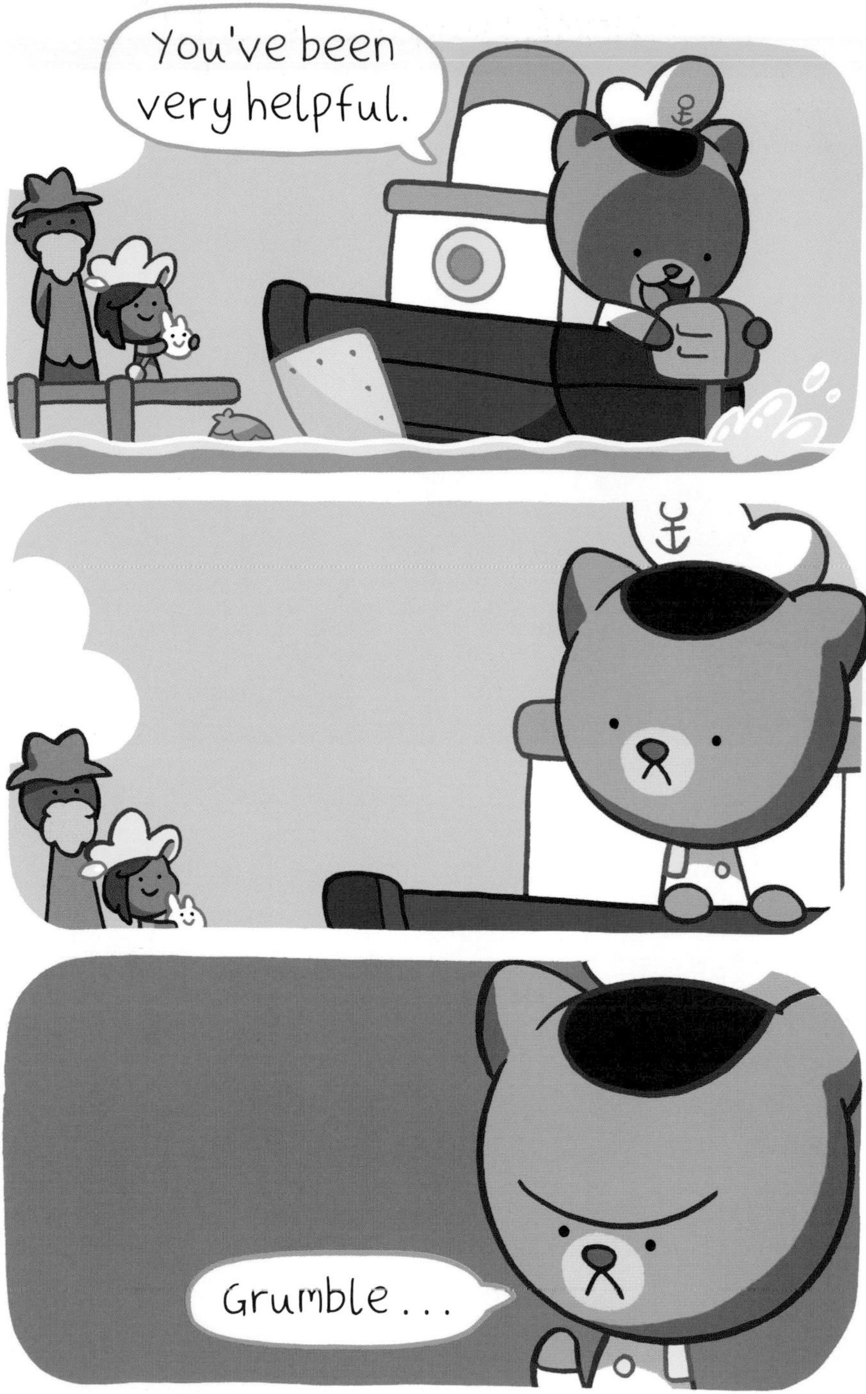
You've been very helpful.
Grumble...

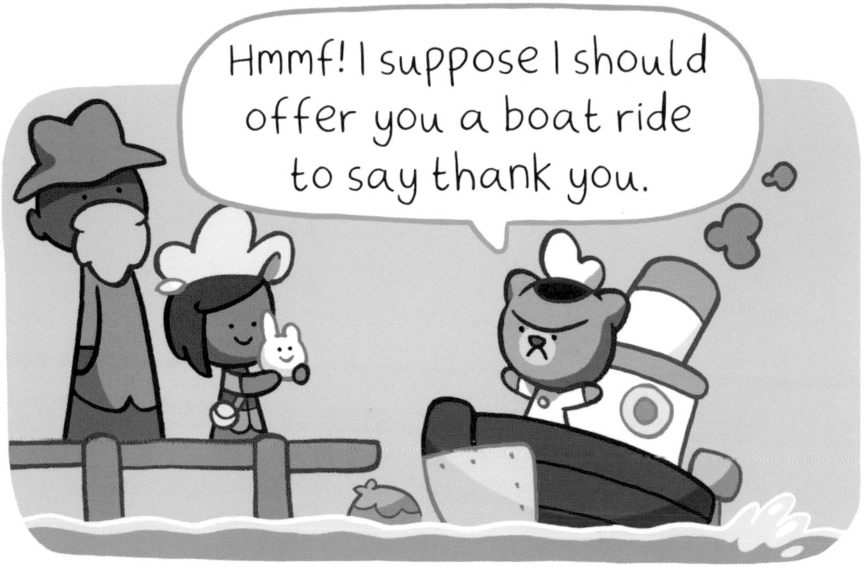
Hmmf! I suppose I should offer you a boat ride to say thank you.

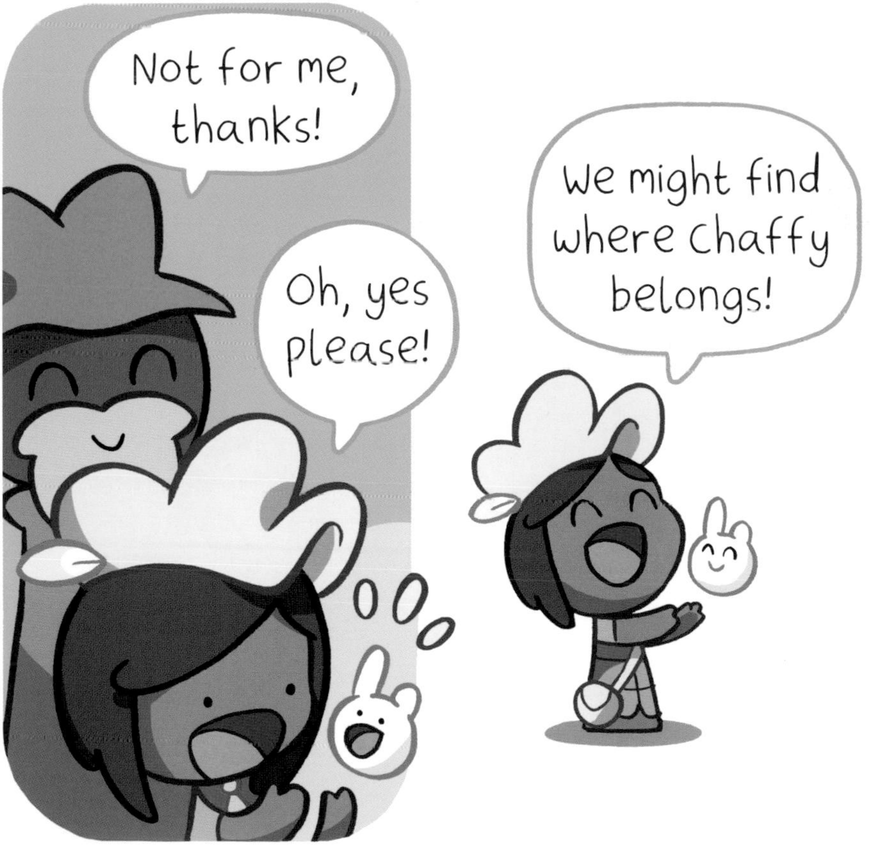
Not for me, thanks!
Oh, yes please!
We might find where Chaffy belongs!

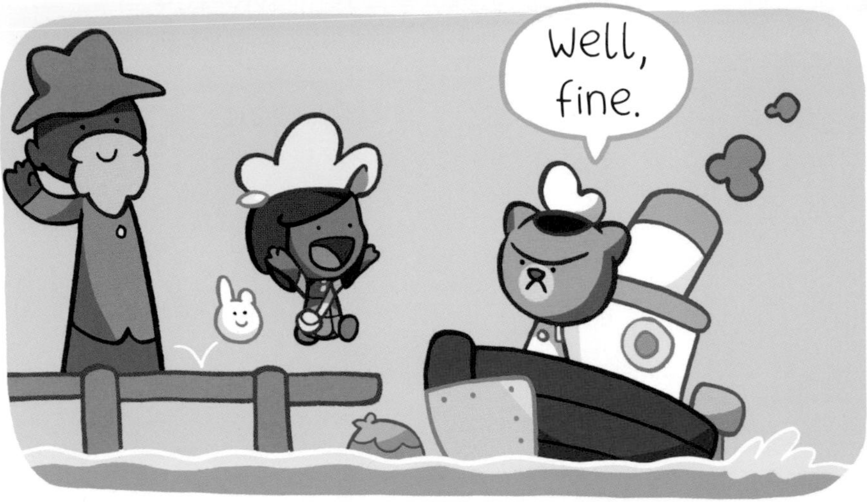
Well, fine.

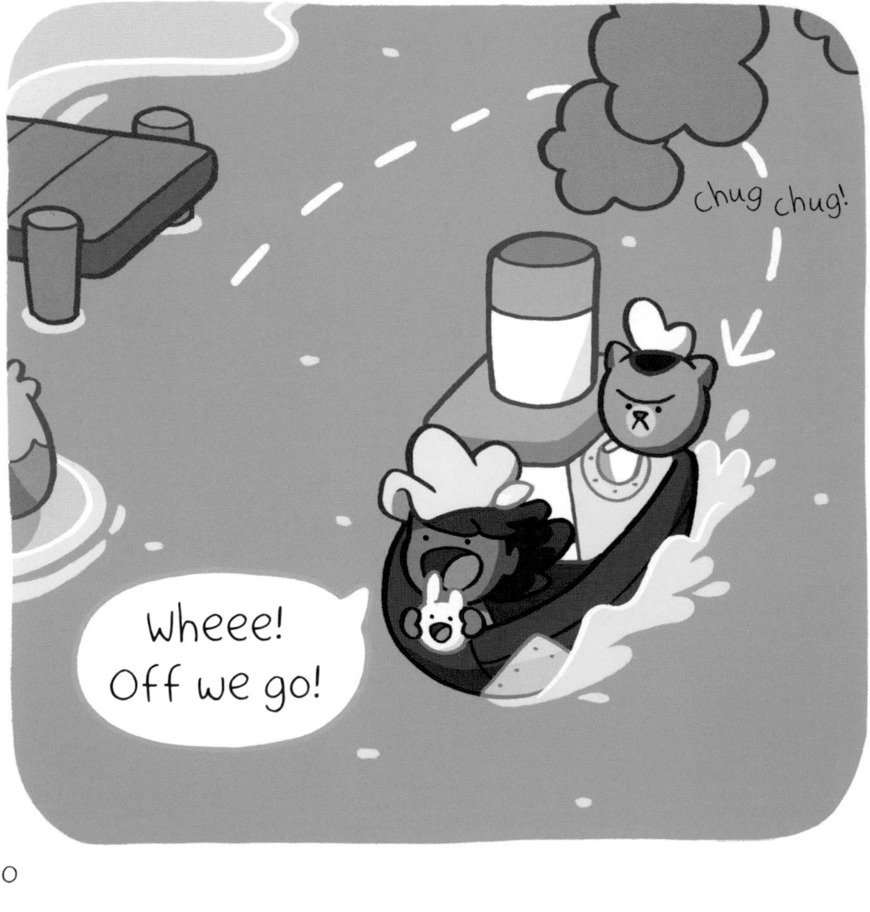
chug chug!
Wheee! Off we go!

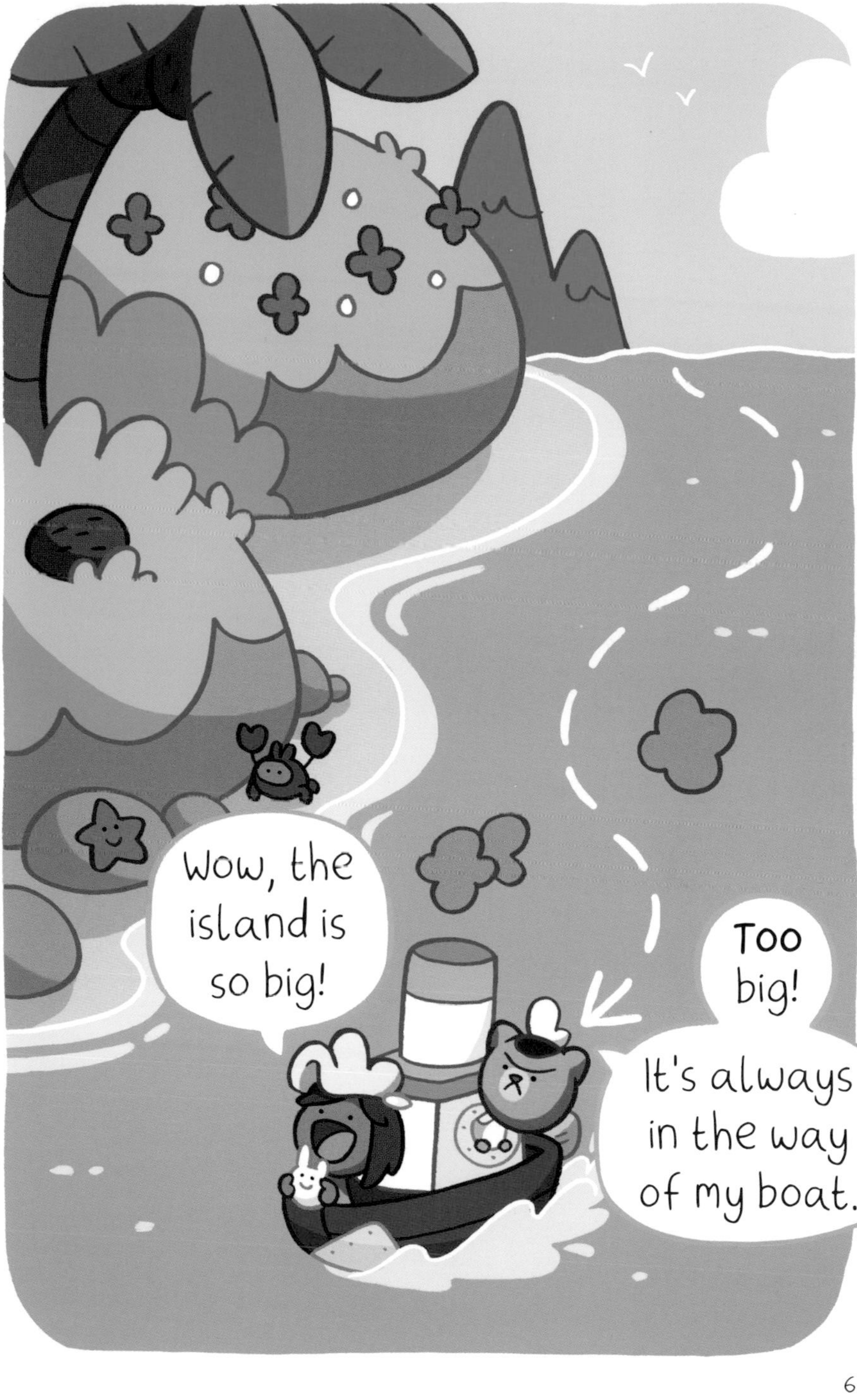
Wow, the island is so big!
TOO big!
It's always in the way of my boat.

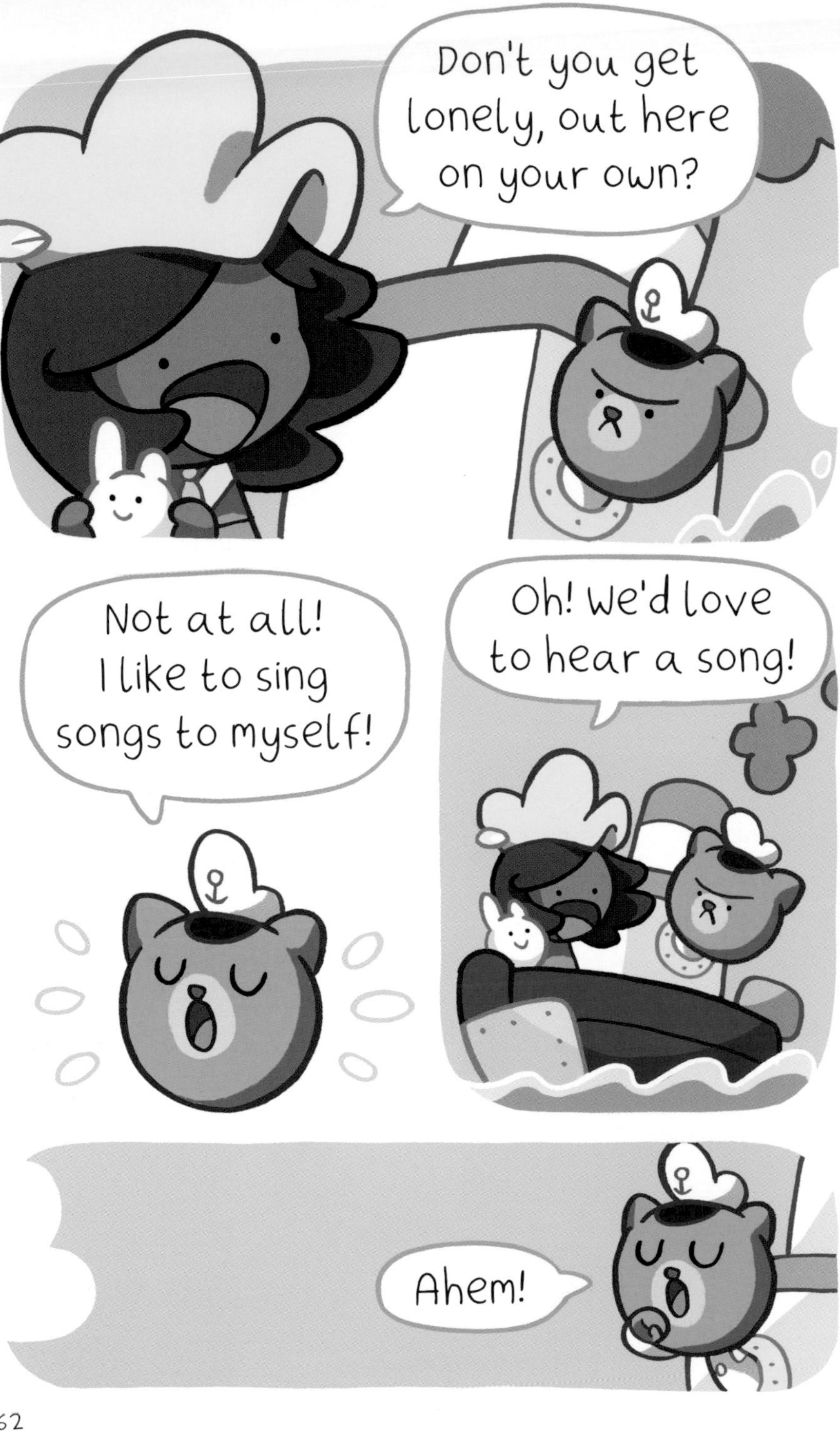
Don't you get lonely, out here on your own?
Not at all! I like to sing songs to myself!
Oh! We'd love to hear a song!
Ahem!

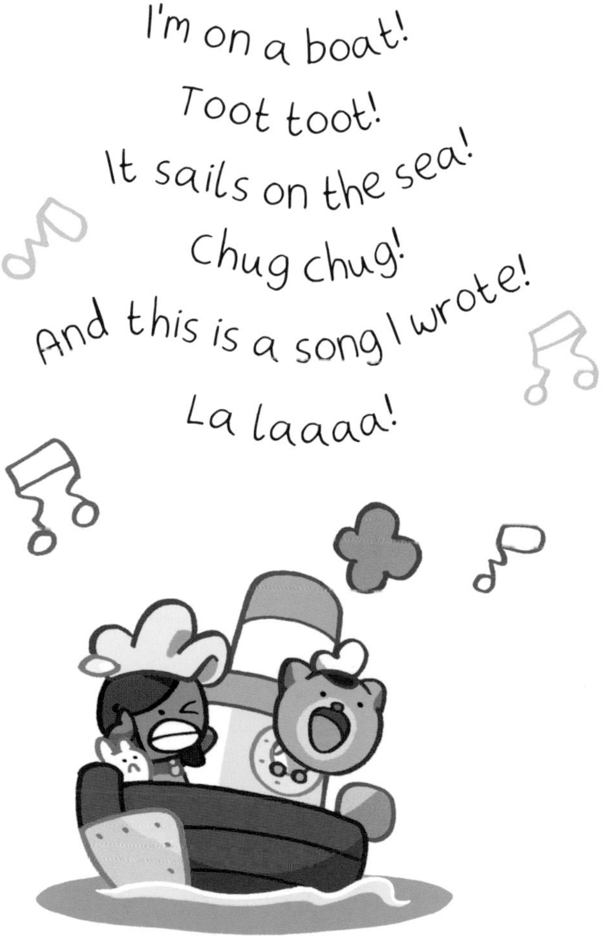
I'm on a boat!
Toot toot!
It sails on the sea!
Chug chug!
And this is a song I wrote!
La laaaa!

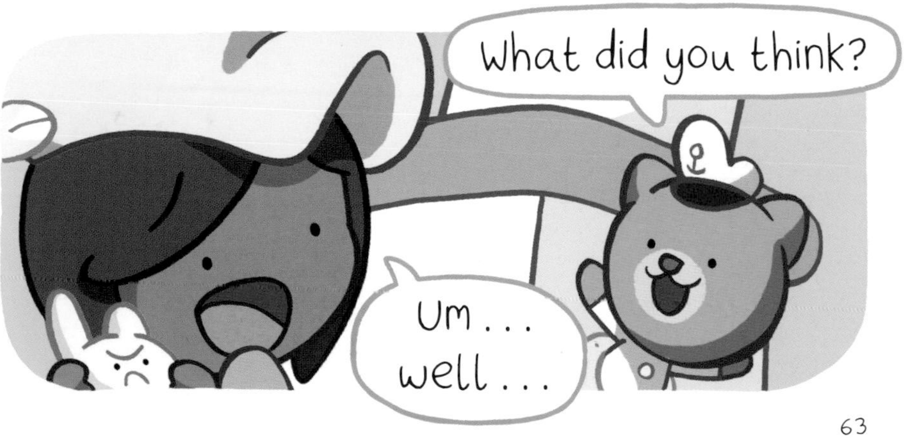
What did you think?
Um . . .
well . . .

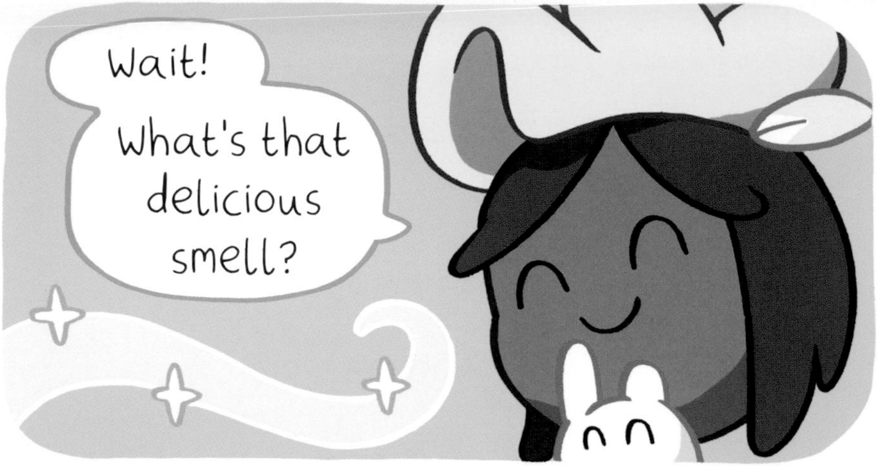
Wait!
What's that delicious smell?

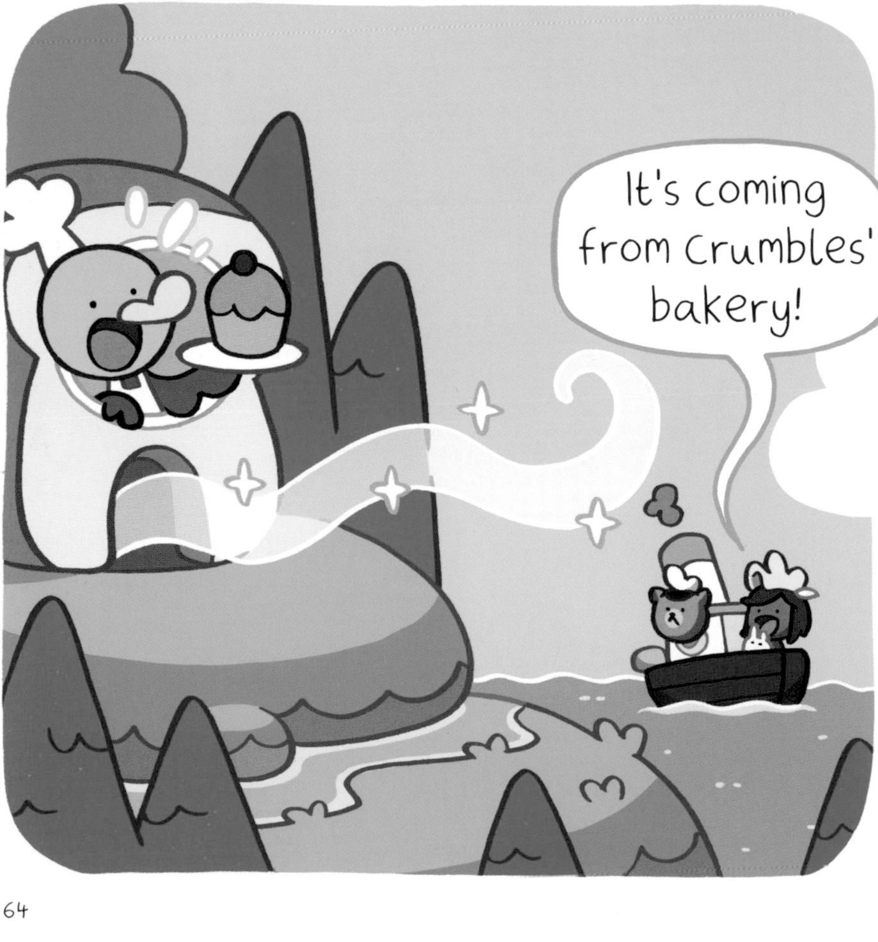
It's coming from Crumbles' bakery!

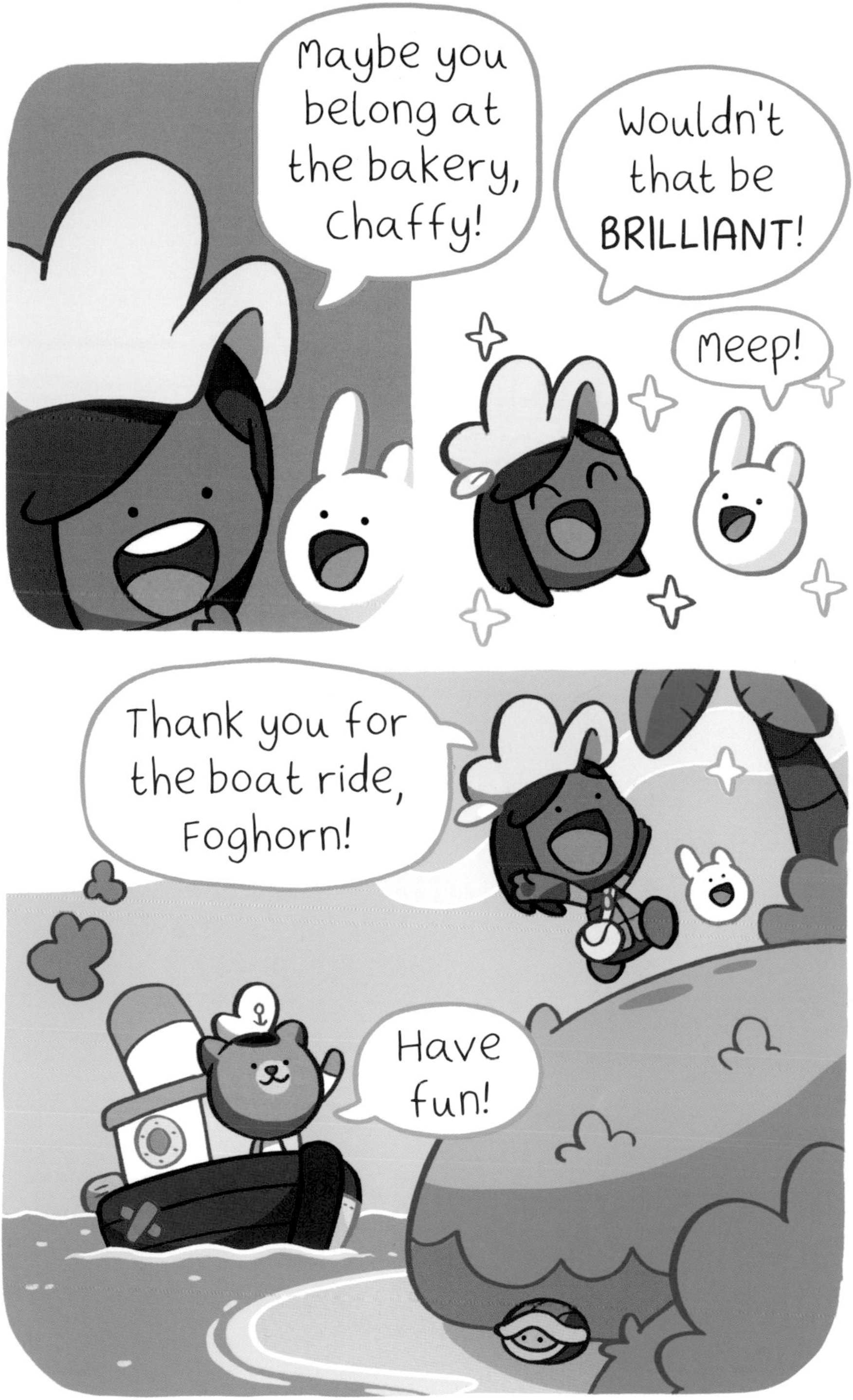
Maybe you belong at the bakery, Chaffy!
Wouldn't that be BRILLIANT!
Meep!
Thank you for the boat ride, Foghorn!
Have fun!

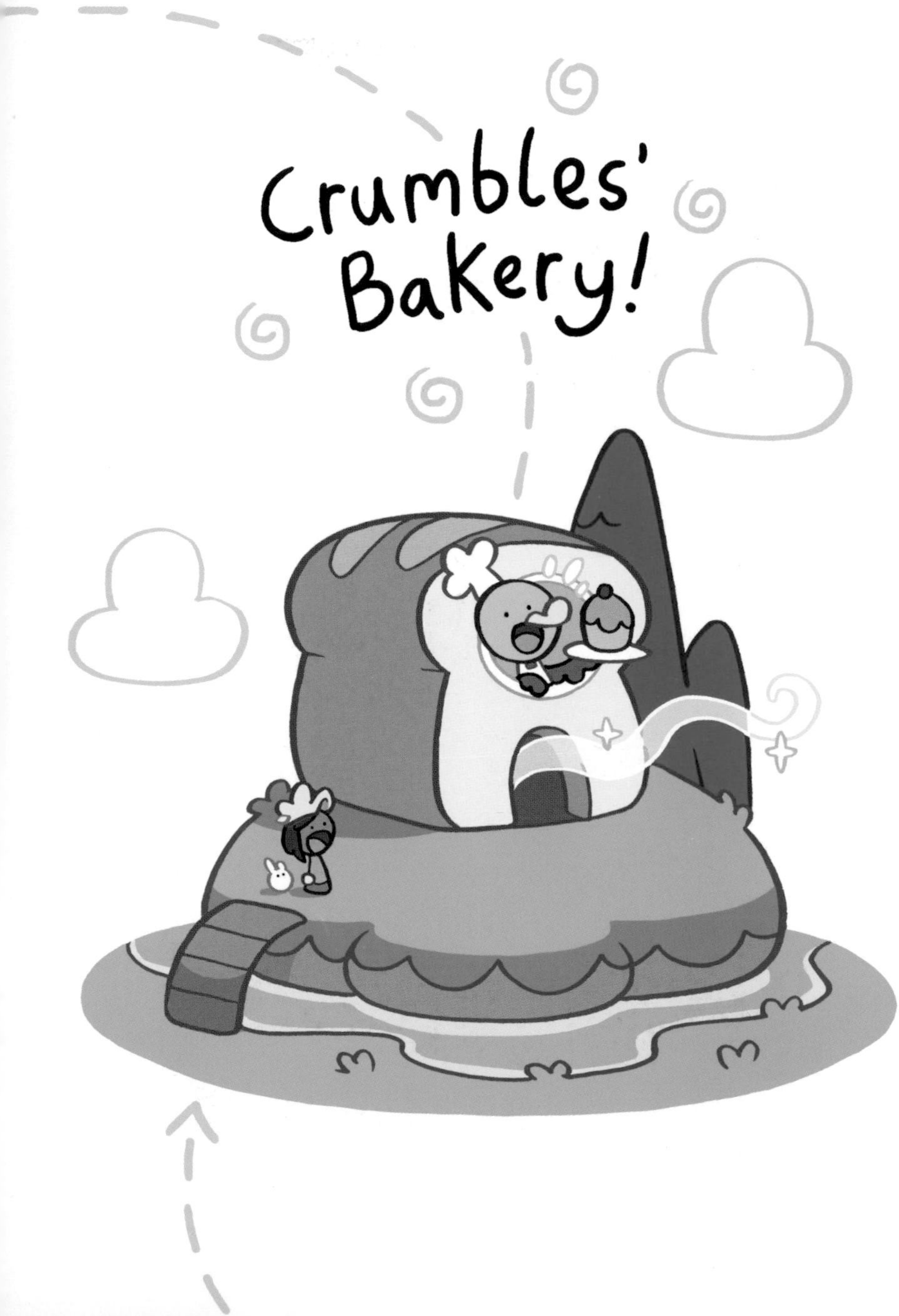
Crumbles' Bakery!

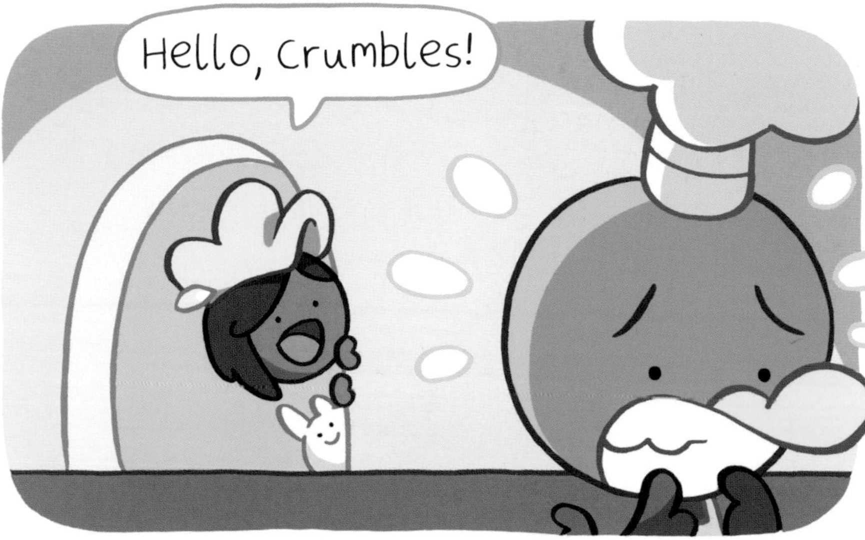
Hello, Crumbles!

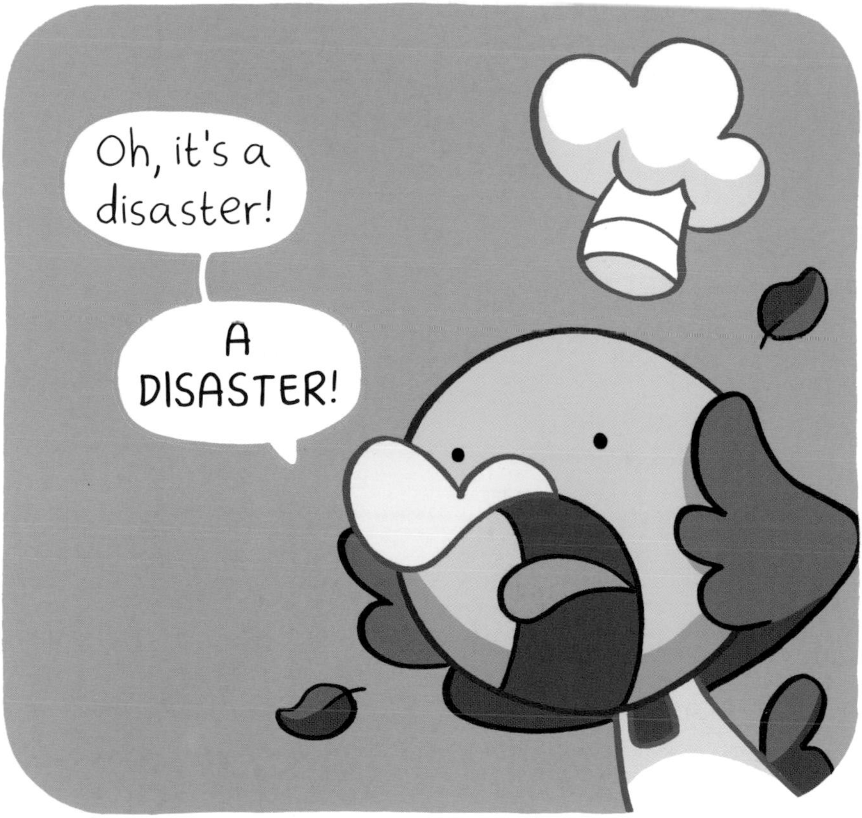
Oh, it's a disaster!
A DISASTER!

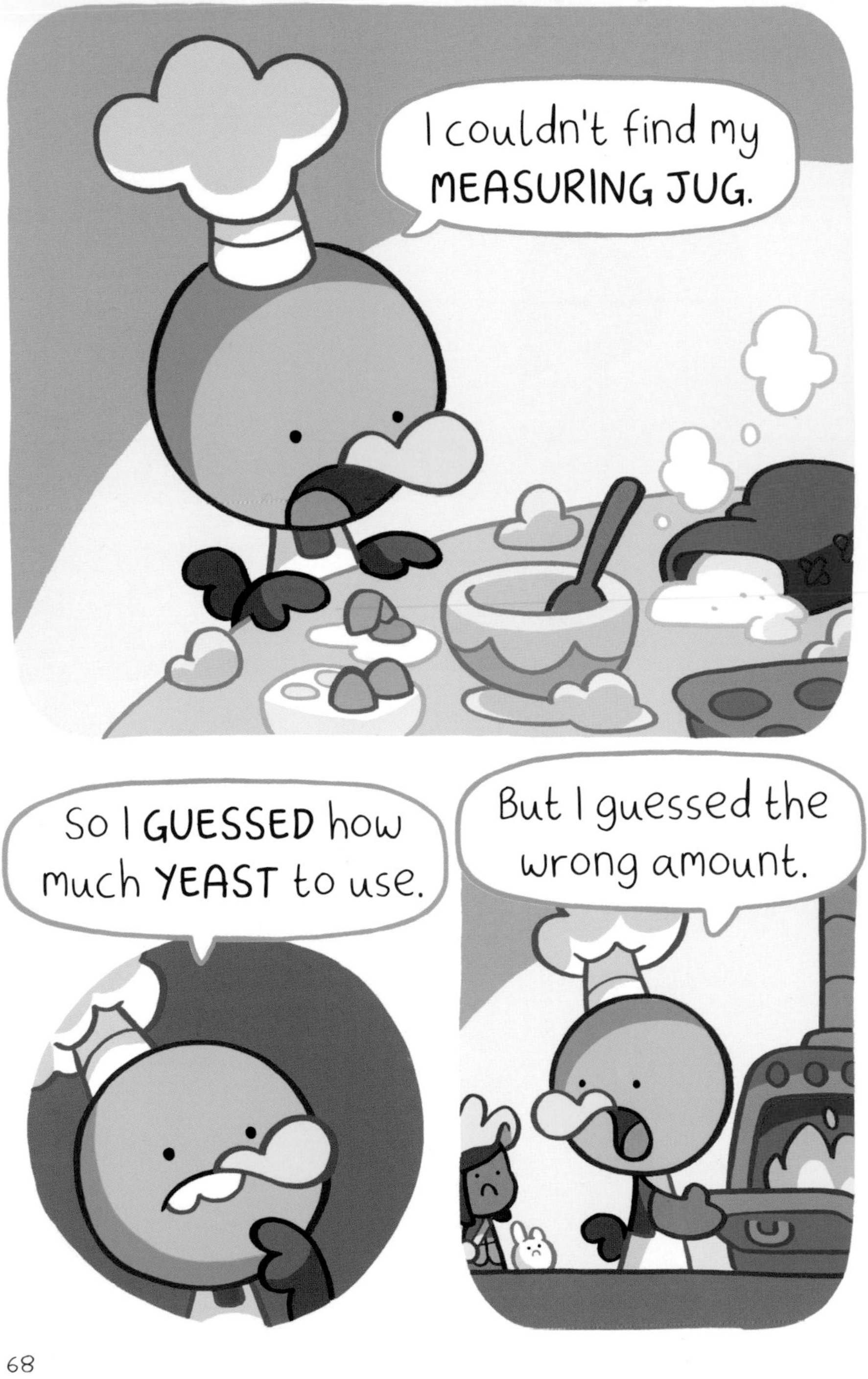
I couldn't find my MEASURING JUG.
So I GUESSED how much YEAST to use.
But I guessed the wrong amount.

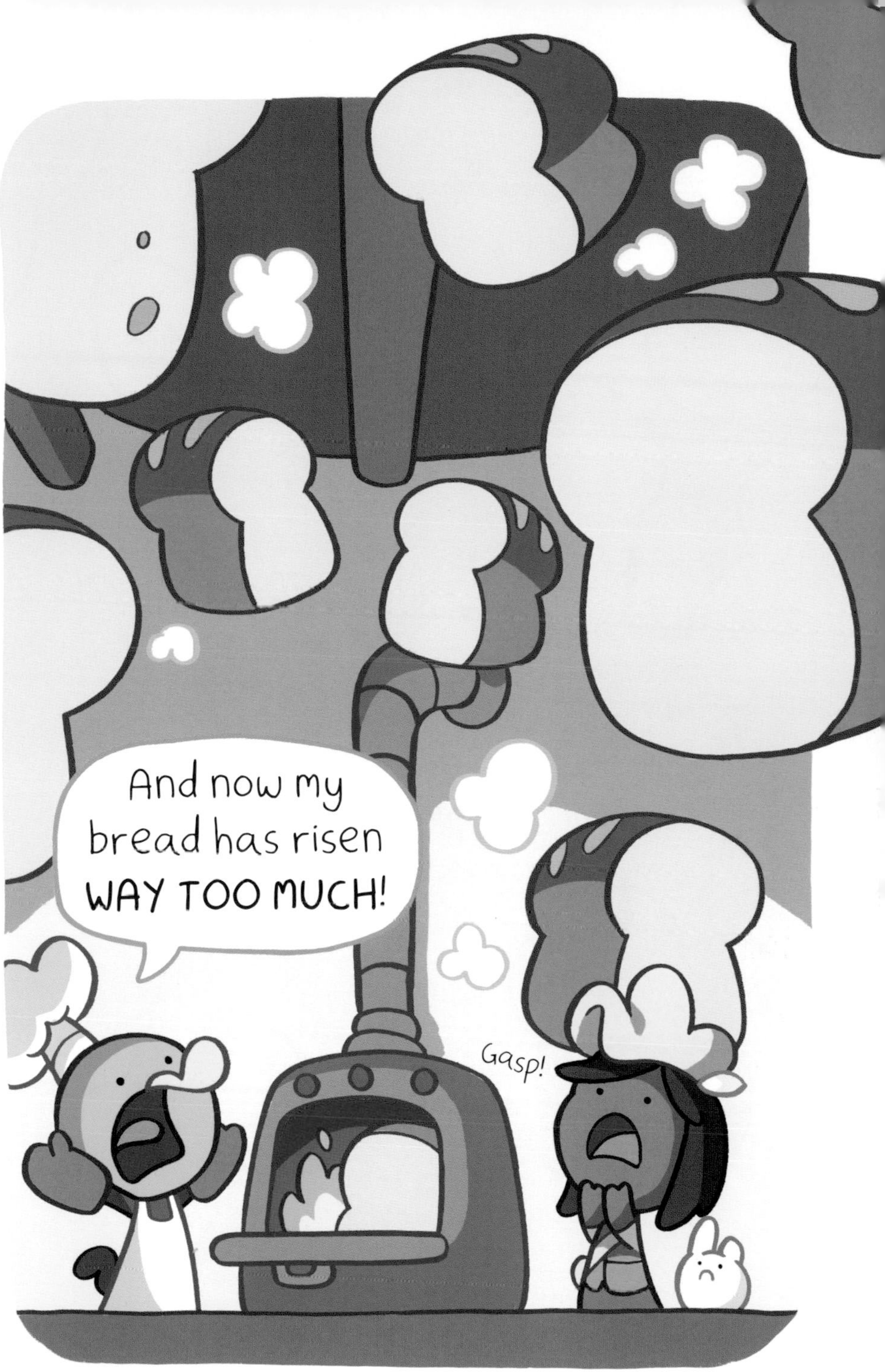
And now my bread has risen WAY TOO MUCH!
Gasp!

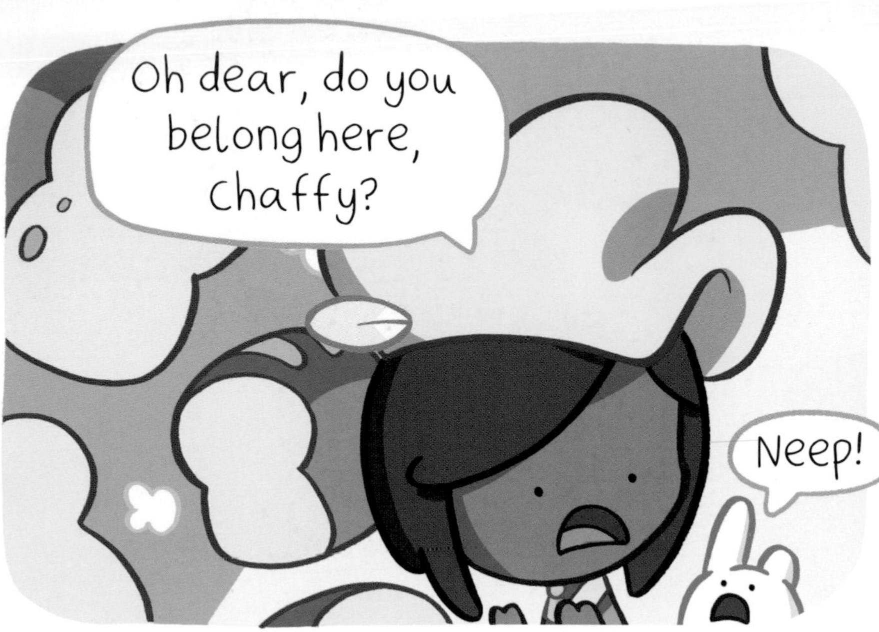
Oh dear, do you belong here, Chaffy?
Neep!

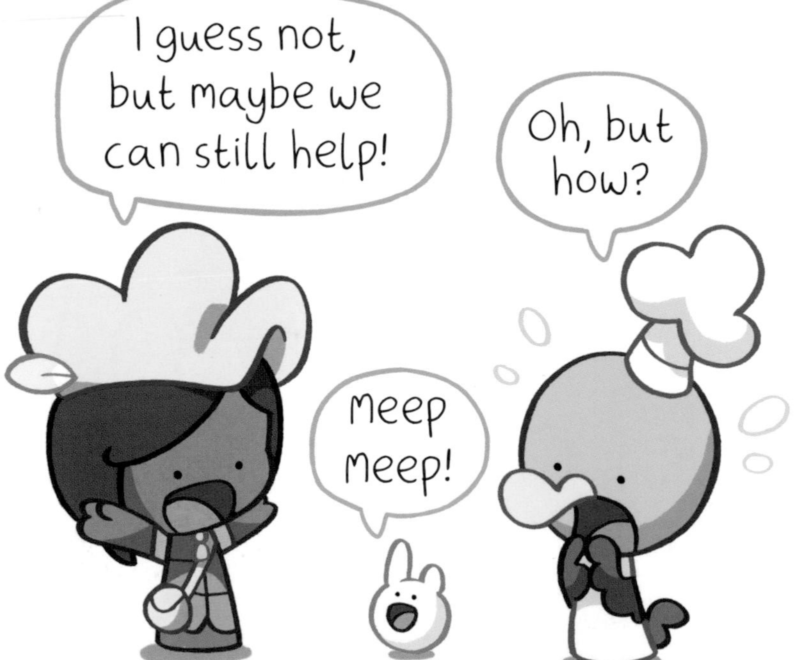
I guess not, but maybe we can still help!
Oh, but how?
Meep Meep!

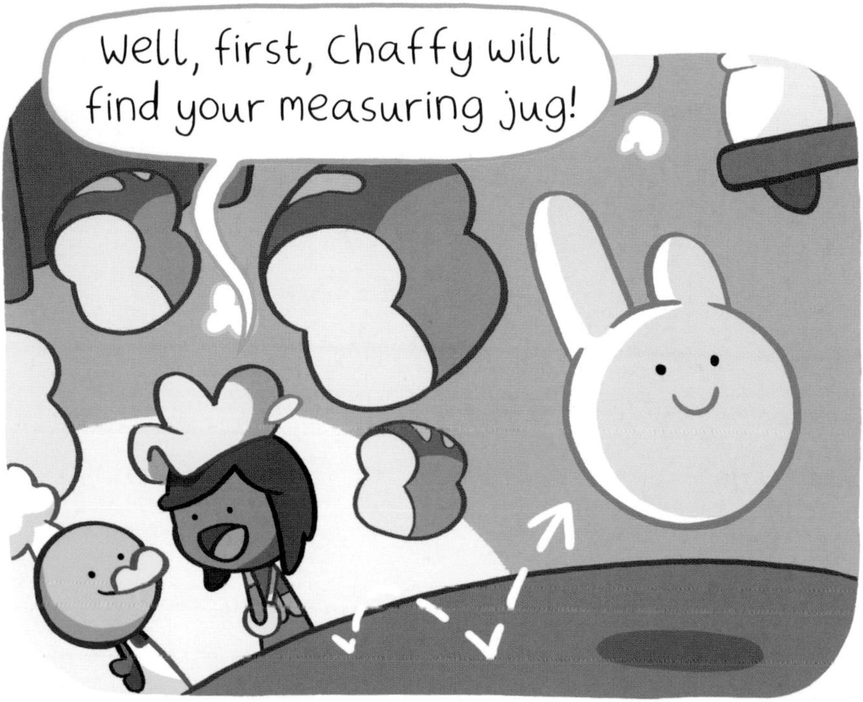
Well, first, Chaffy will find your measuring jug!

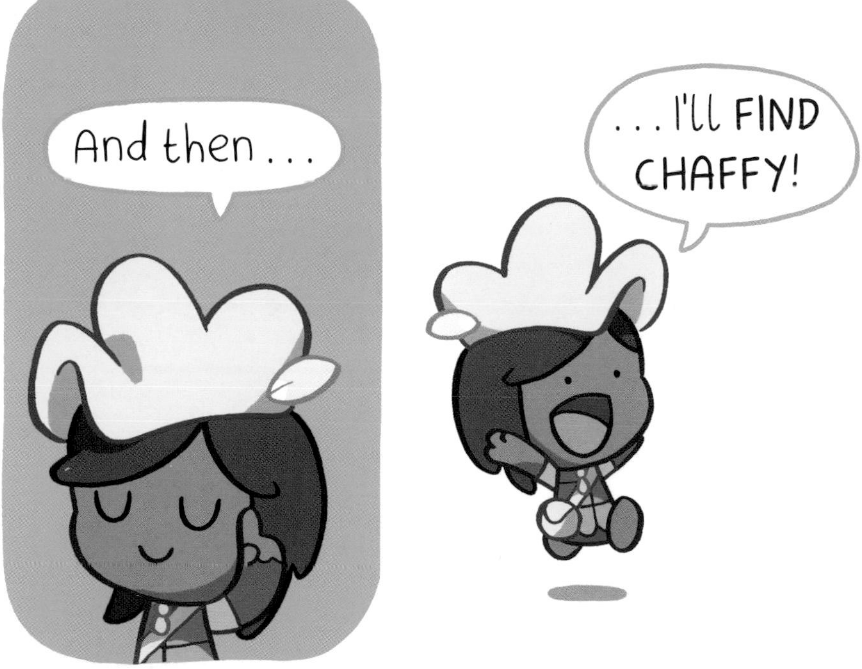
And then . . .
. . . I'll FIND CHAFFY!

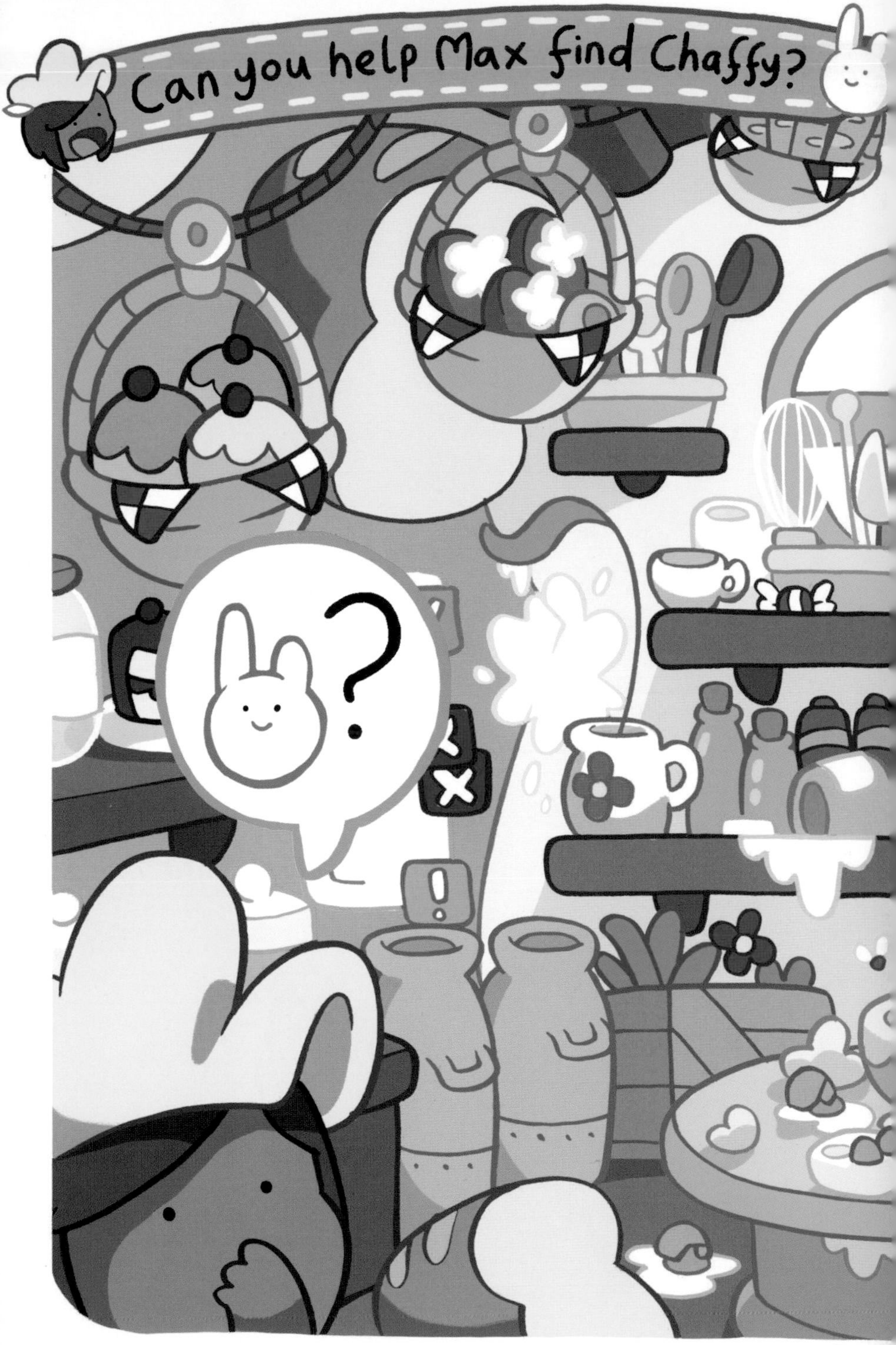
Can you help Max find Chaffy?
?

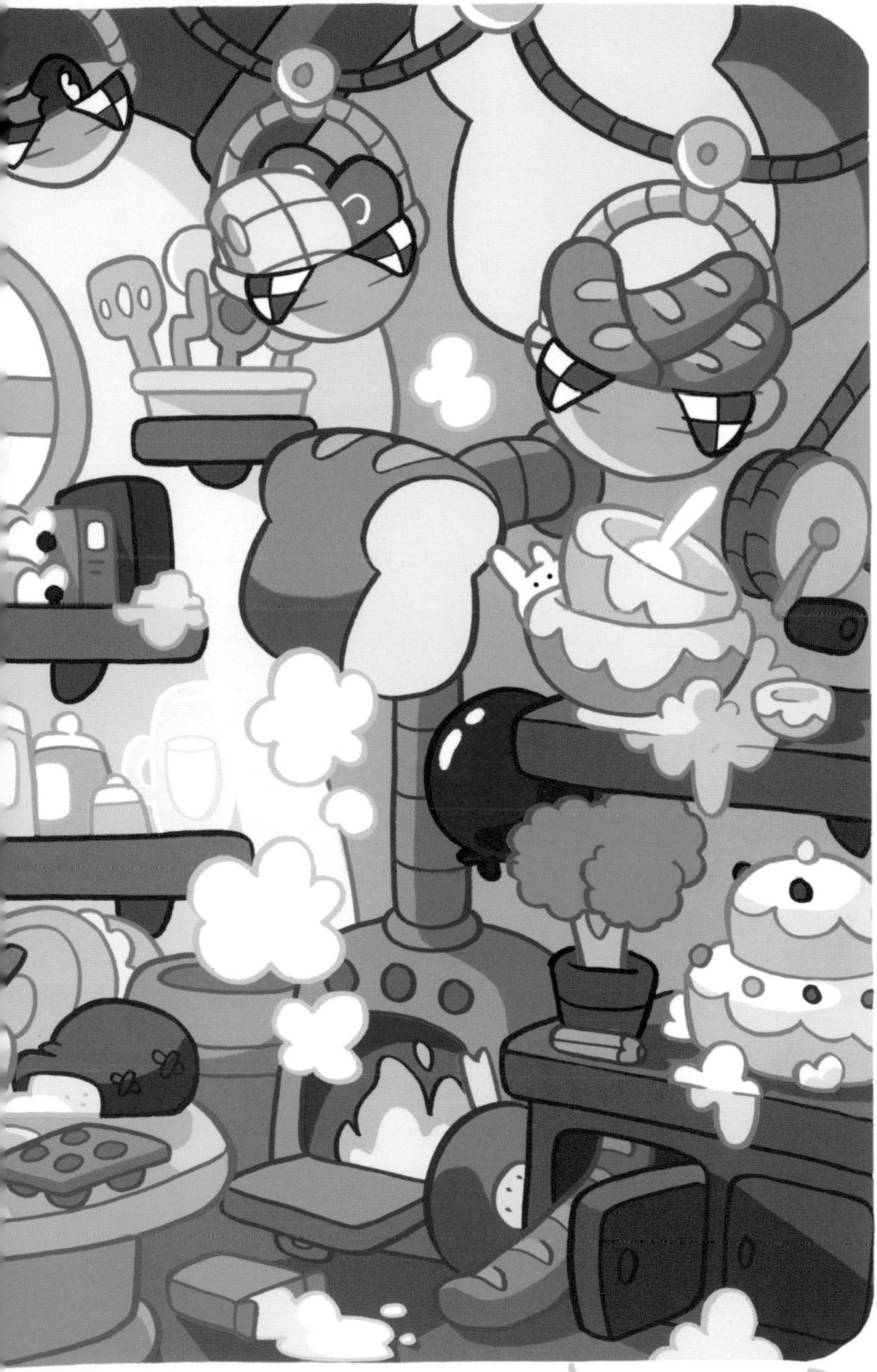

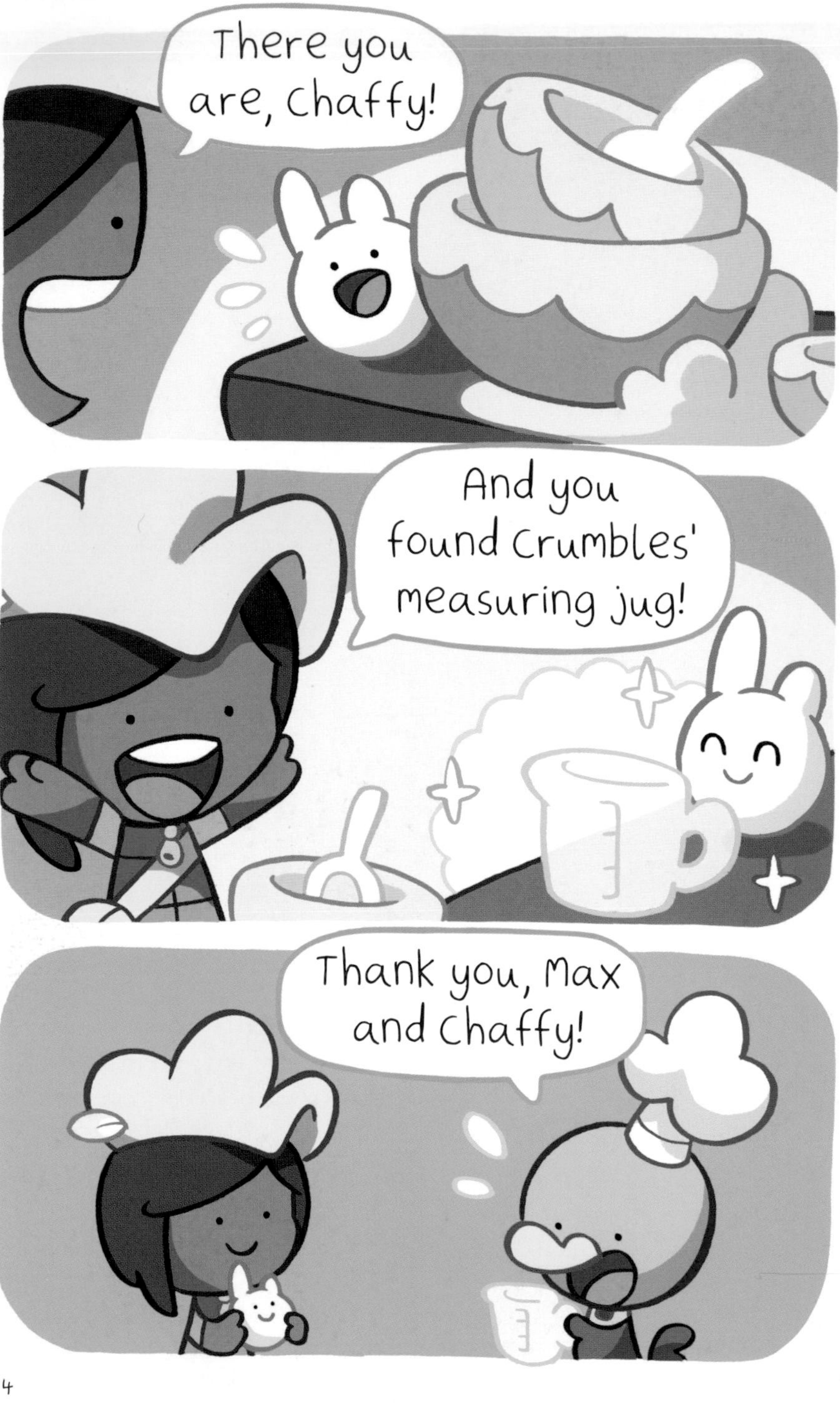
There you are, Chaffy!
And you found Crumbles' measuring jug!
Thank you, Max and Chaffy!

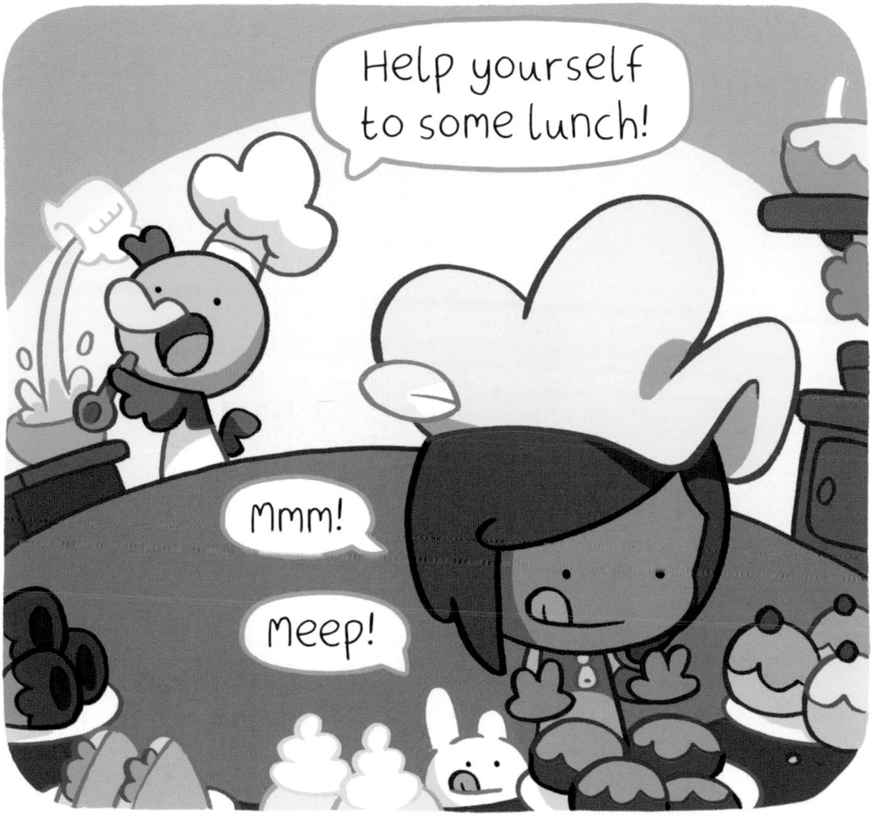
Help yourself to some lunch!
Mmm!
Meep!

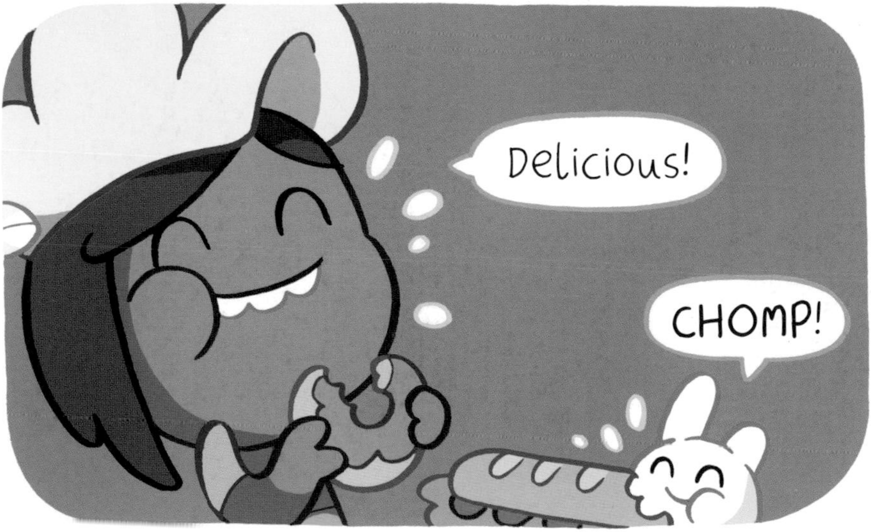
Delicious!
CHOMP!

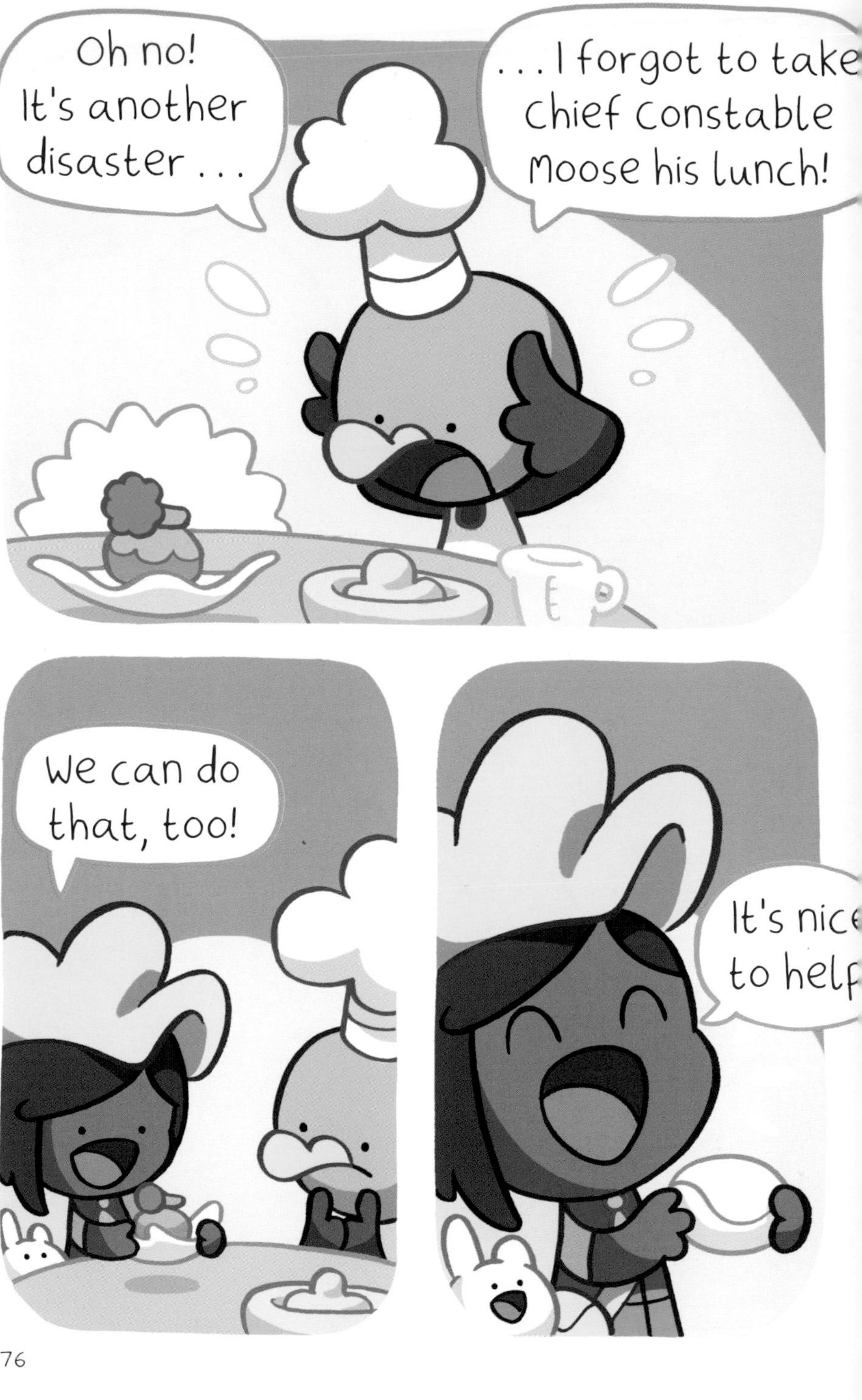
Oh no! It's another disaster . . .
. . . I forgot to take Chief Constable Moose his lunch!
We can do that, too!
It's nic
to hel

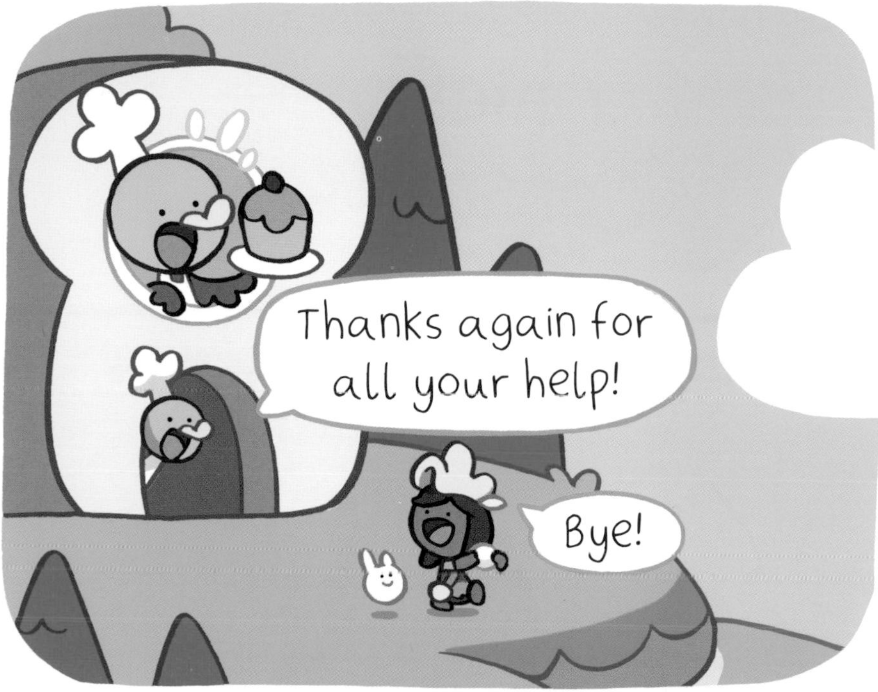
Thanks again for all your help!
Bye!

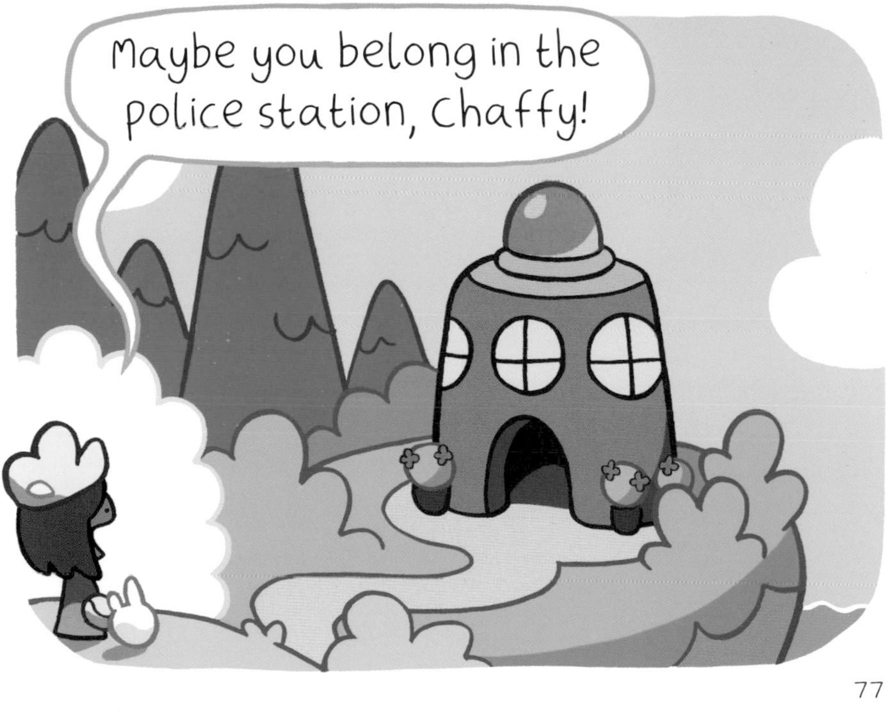
Maybe you belong in the police station, Chaffy!

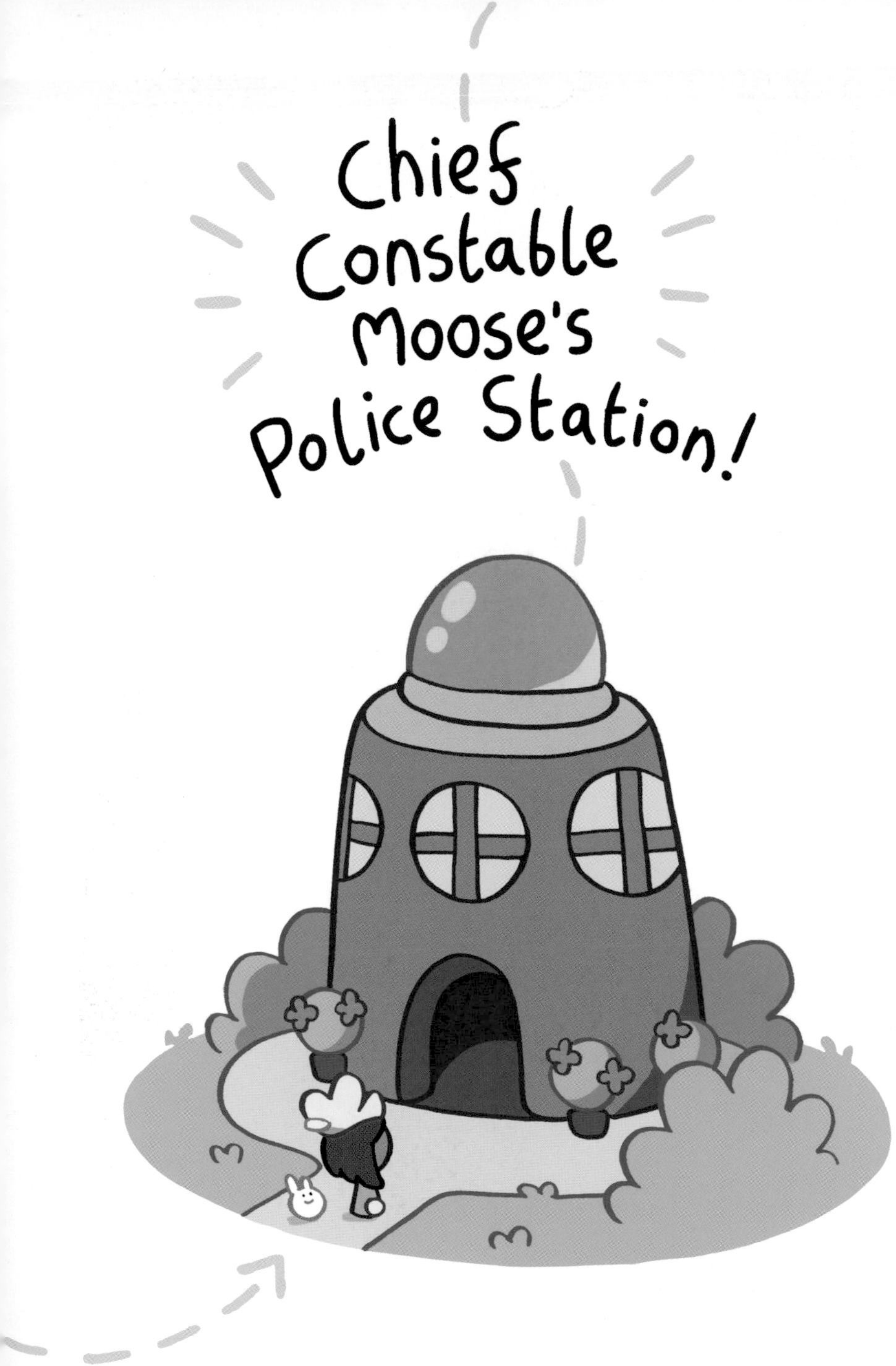
Chief Constable Moose's Police Station!

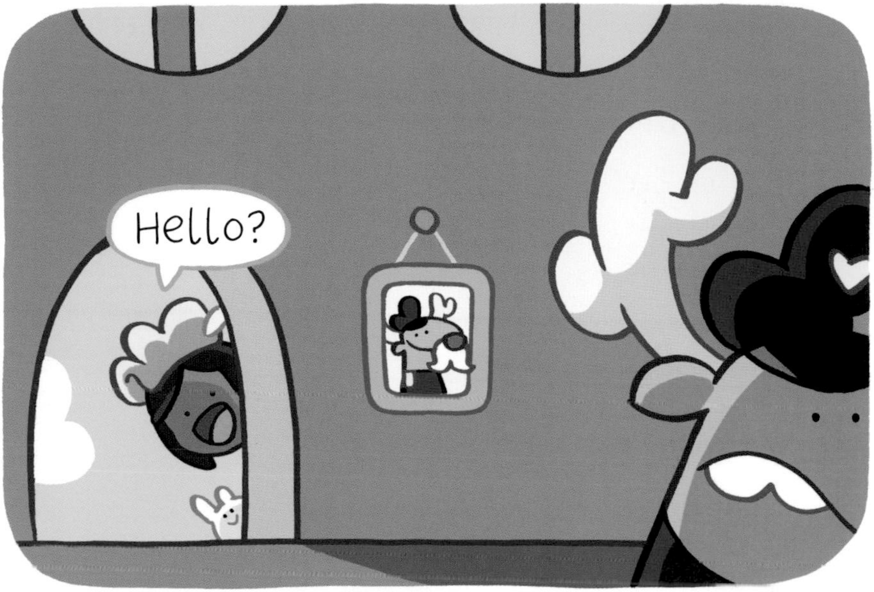
Hello?

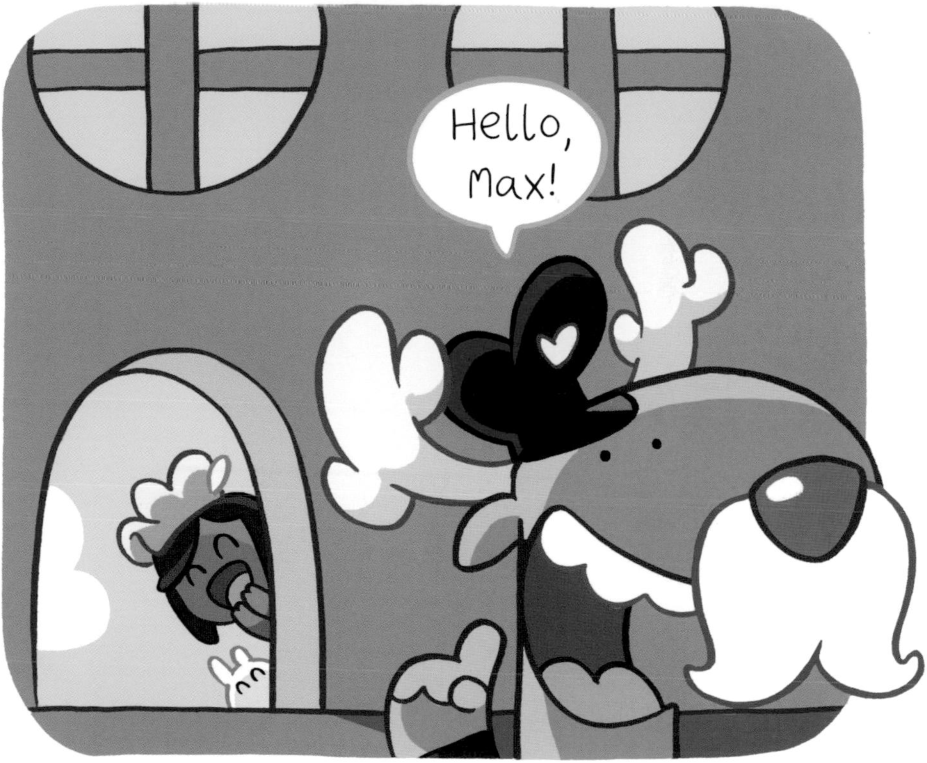
Hello, Max!

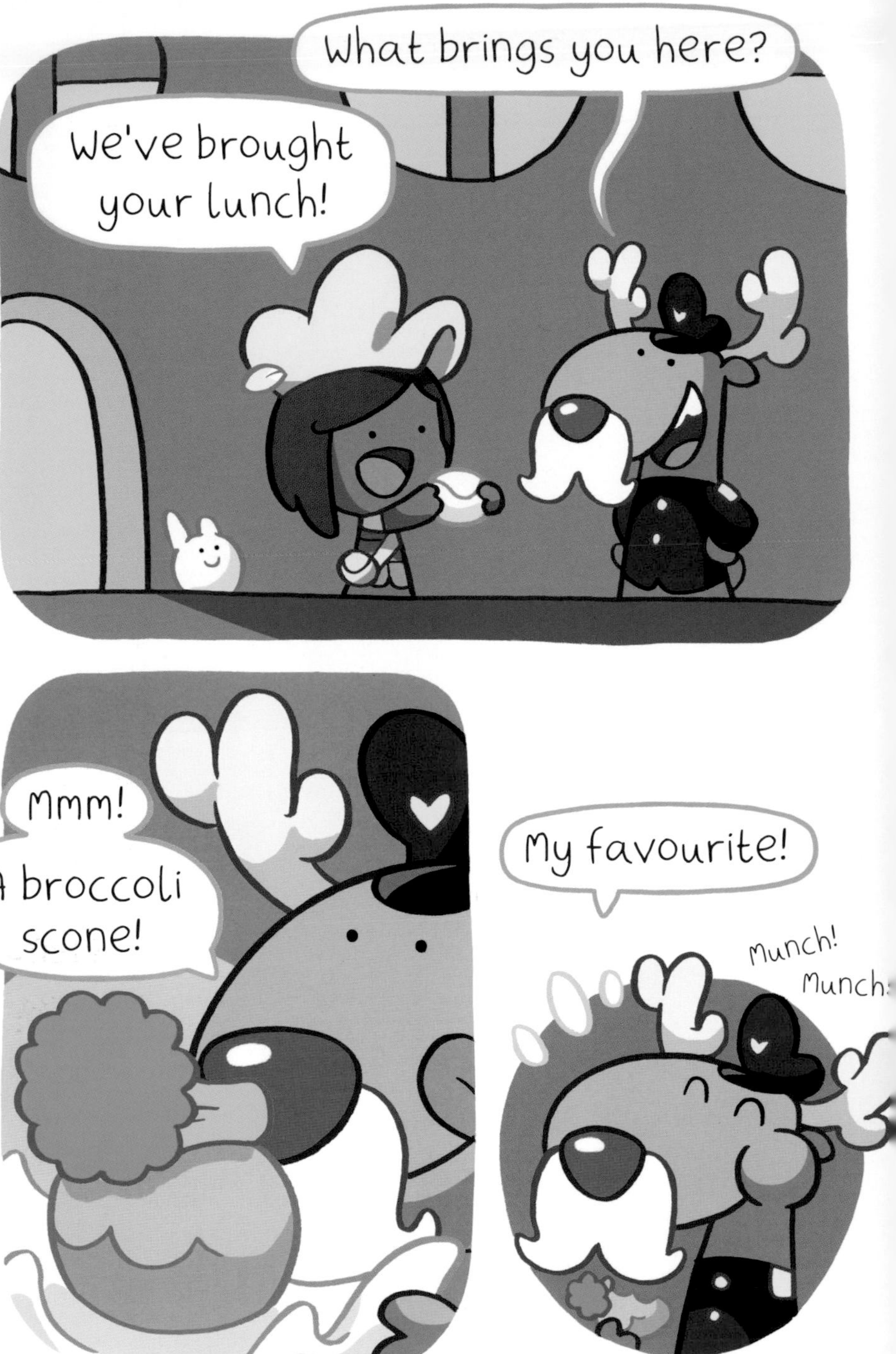
What brings you here?
We've brought your lunch!
Mmm!
A broccoli scone!
My favourite!
Munch!
Munch

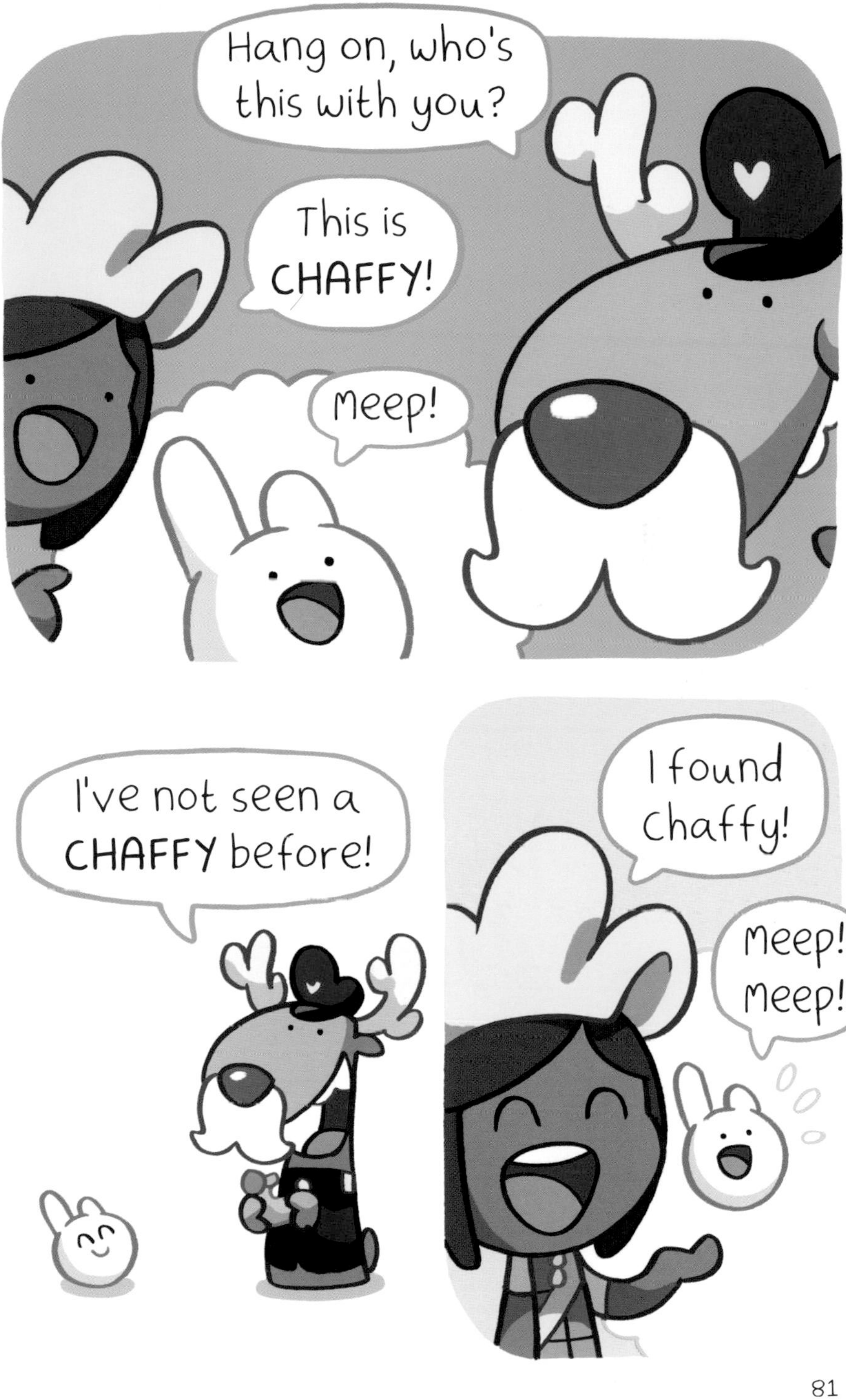

Hang on, who's this with you?
This is CHAFFY!
Meep!
I've not seen a CHAFFY before!
I found Chaffy!
Meep! Meep!

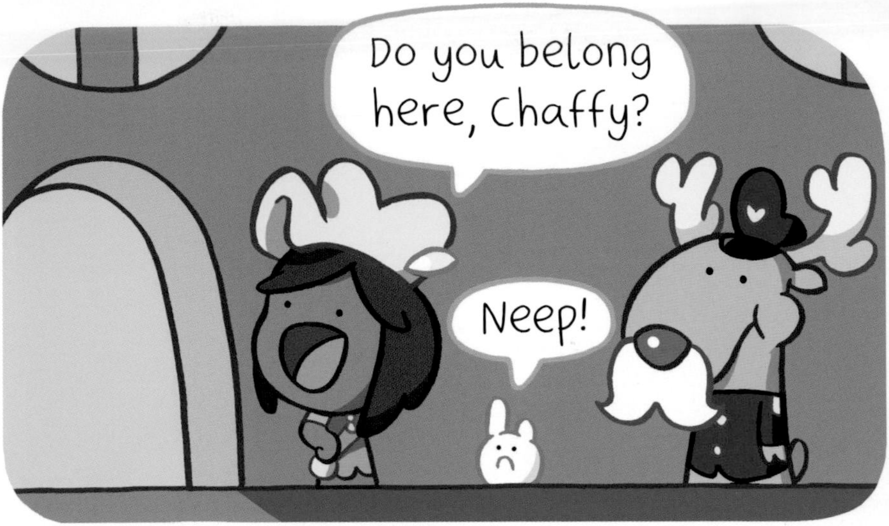
Do you belong here, Chaffy?
Neep!

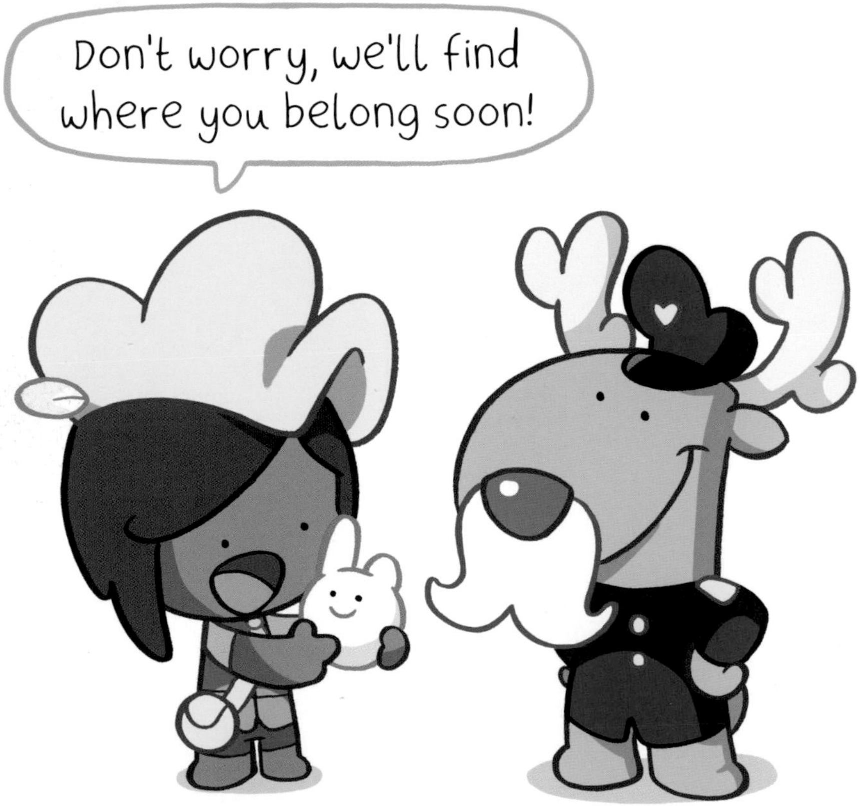
Don't worry, we'll find where you belong soon!

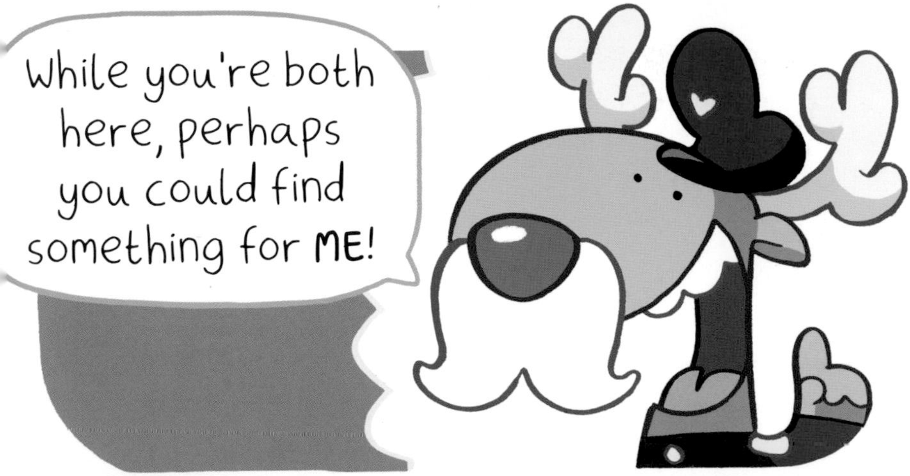
While you're both here, perhaps you could find something for ME!

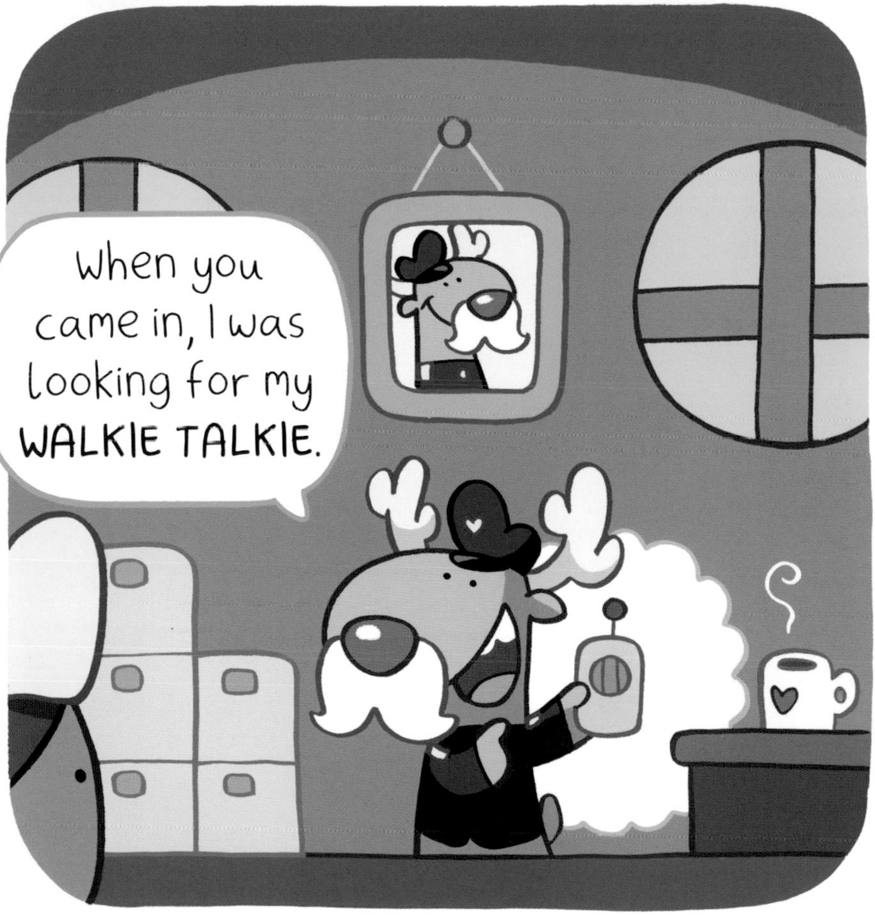
When you came in, I was looking for my WALKIE TALKIE.

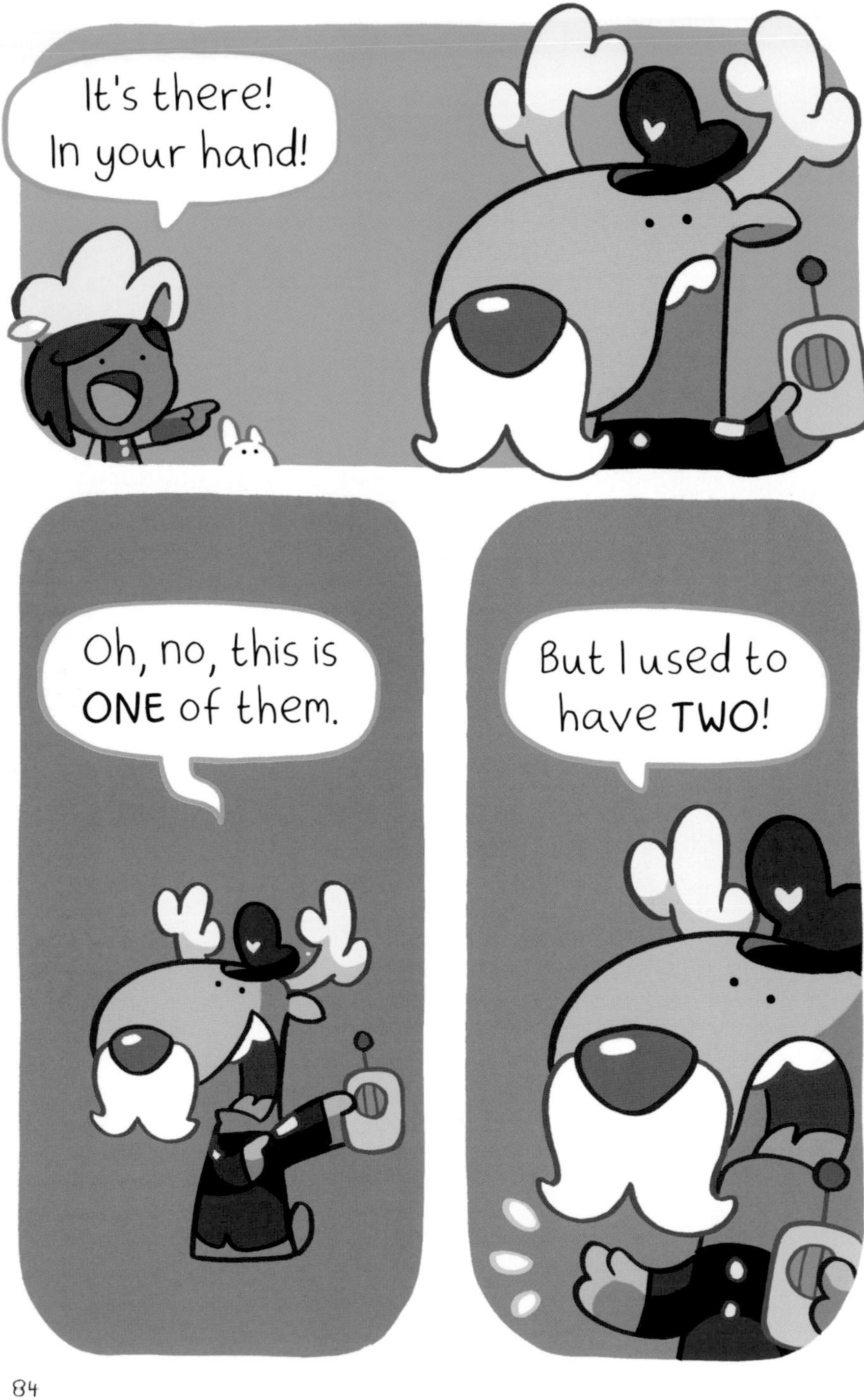
It's there! In your hand!
Oh, no, this is ONE of them.
But I used to have TWO!

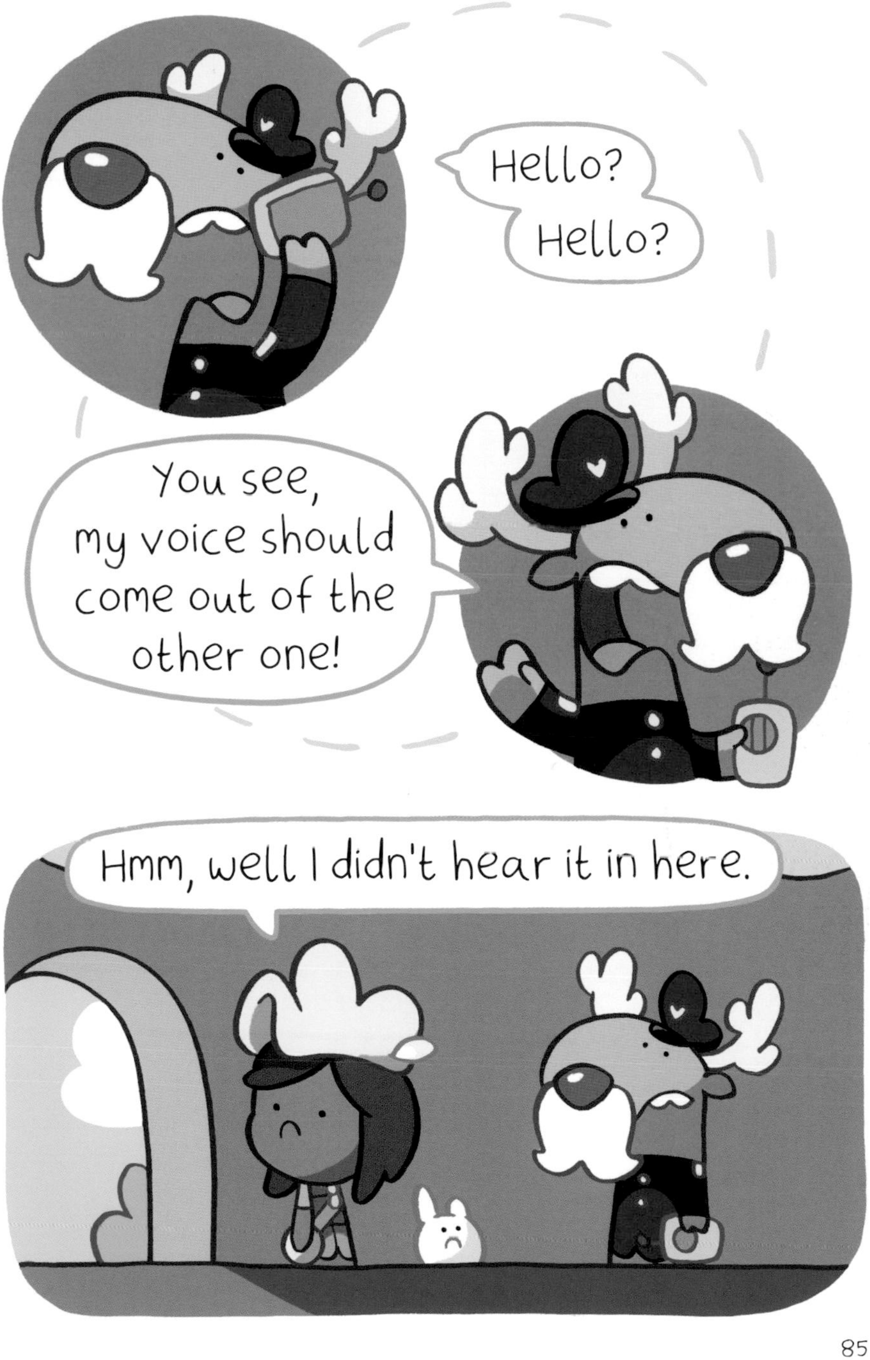
Hello? Hello?
You see, my voice should come out of the other one!
Hmm, well I didn't hear it in here.

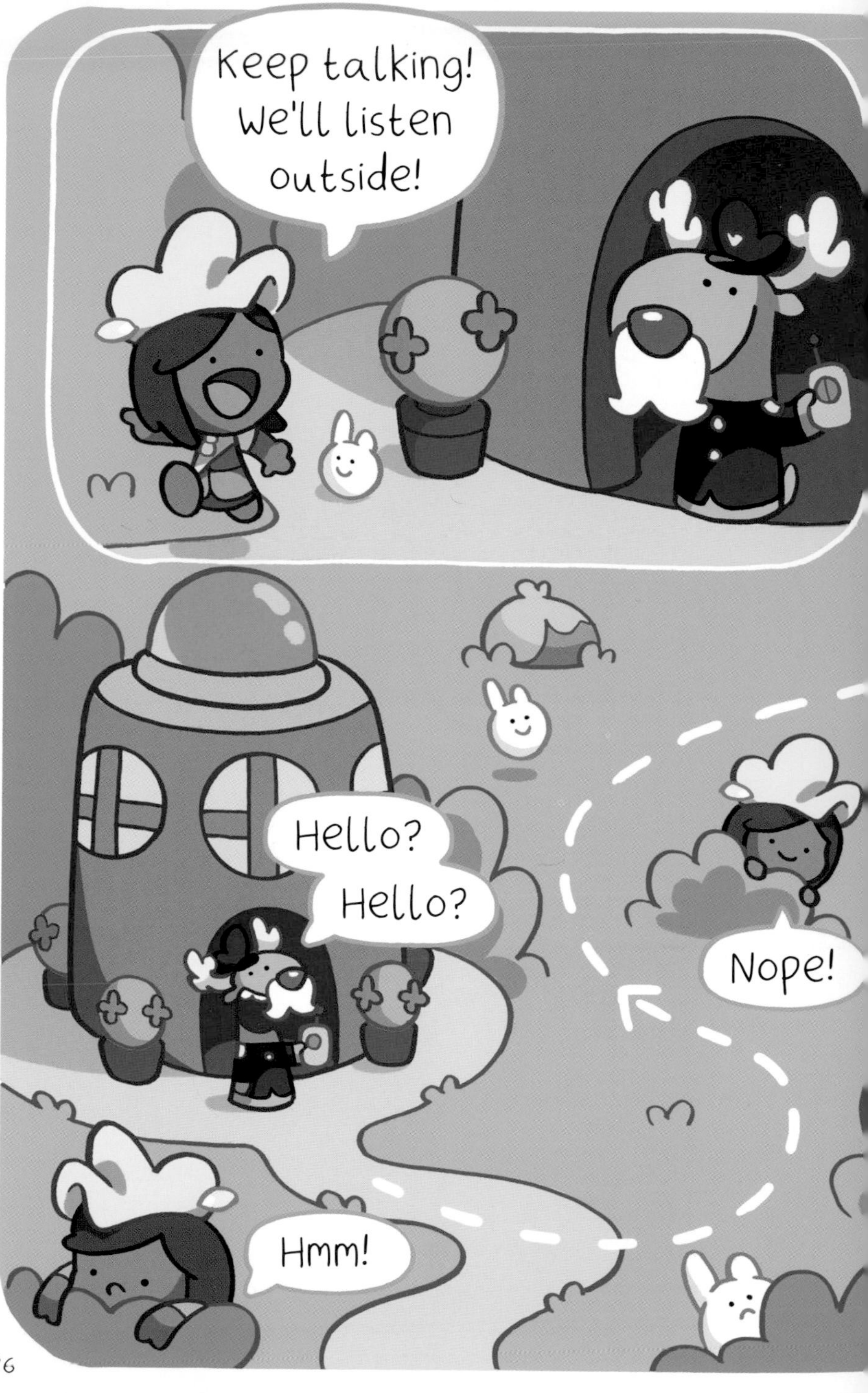
Keep talking! We'll listen outside!
Hello?
Hello?
Nope!
Hmm!

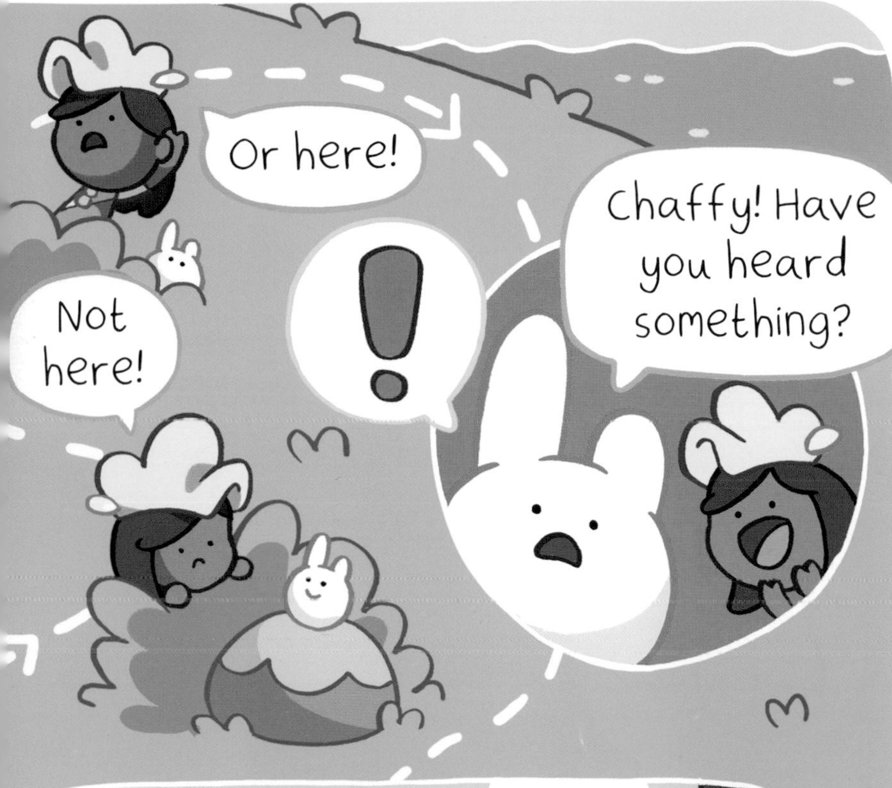
Or here!
Not here!
!
Chaffy! Have you heard something?

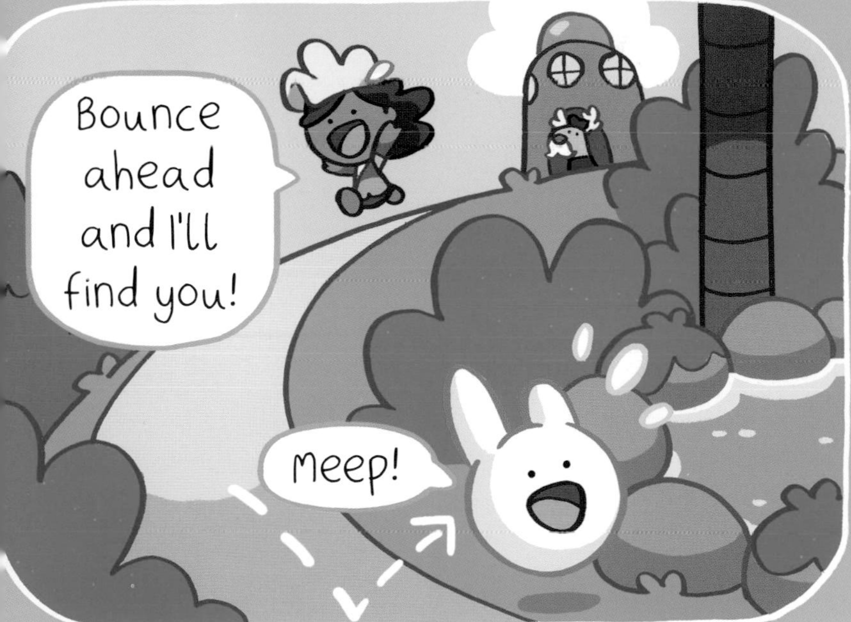
Bounce ahead and I'll find you!
Meep!

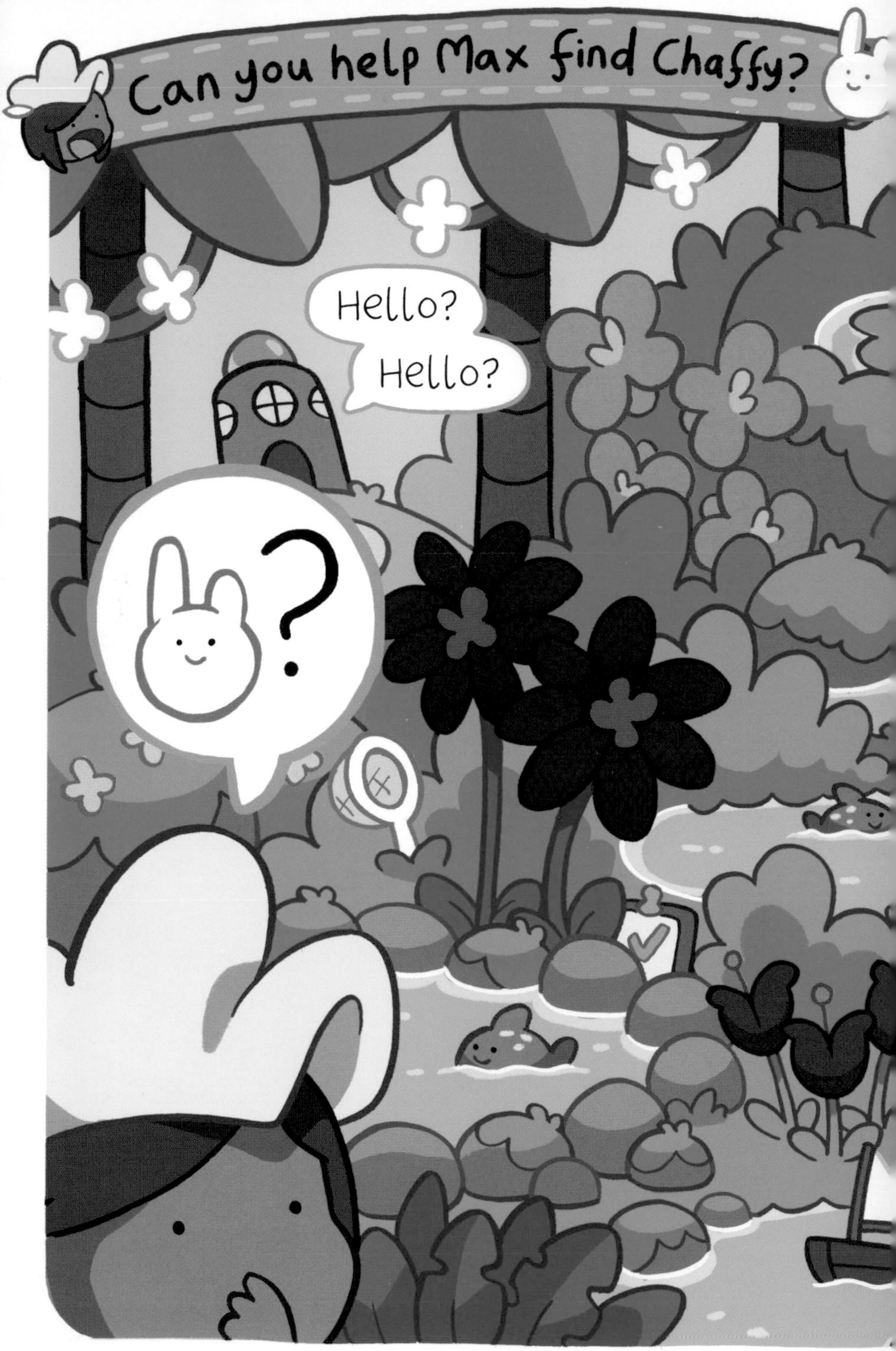
Can you help Max find Chaffy?
Hello?
Hello?
?

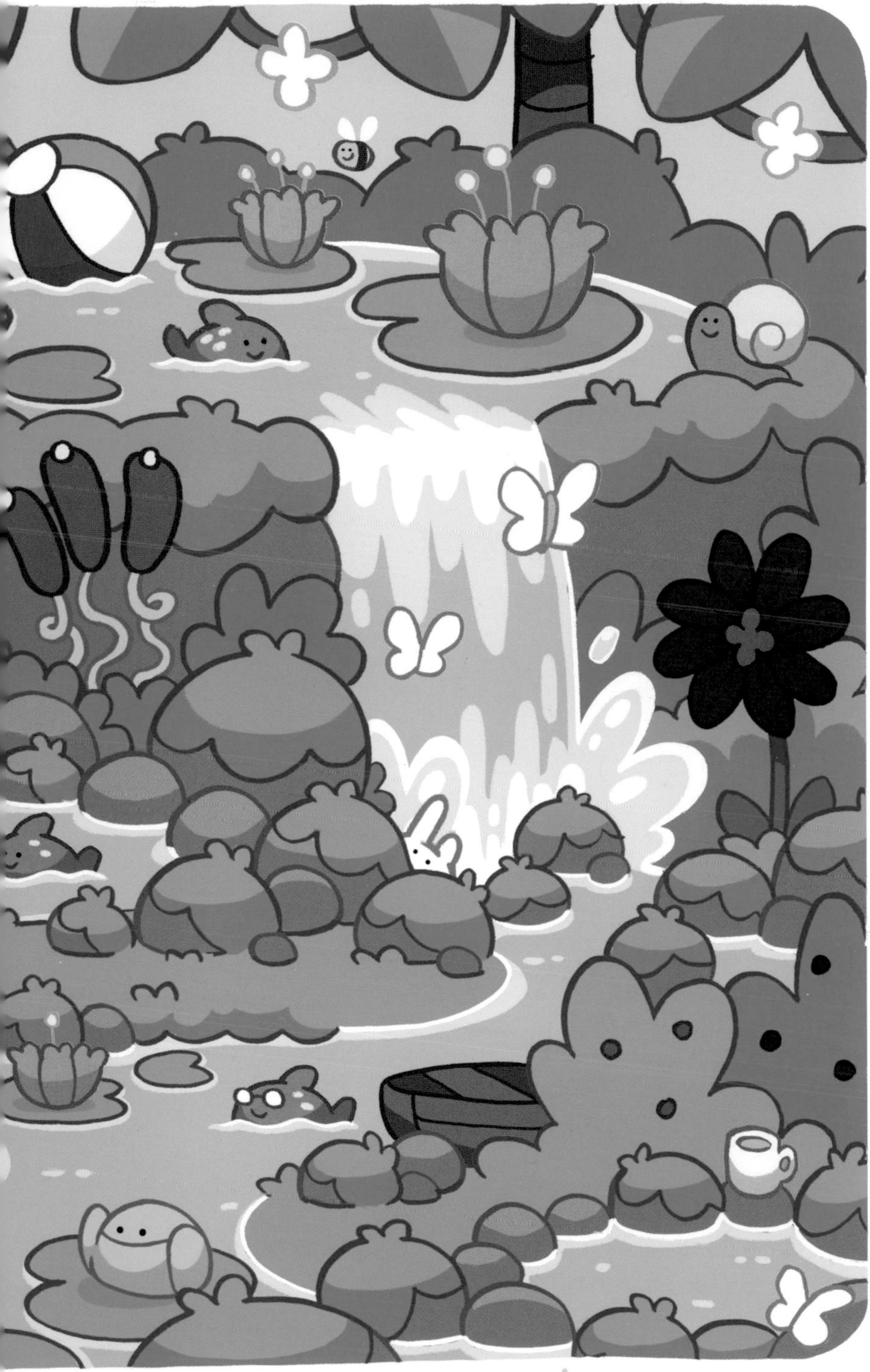

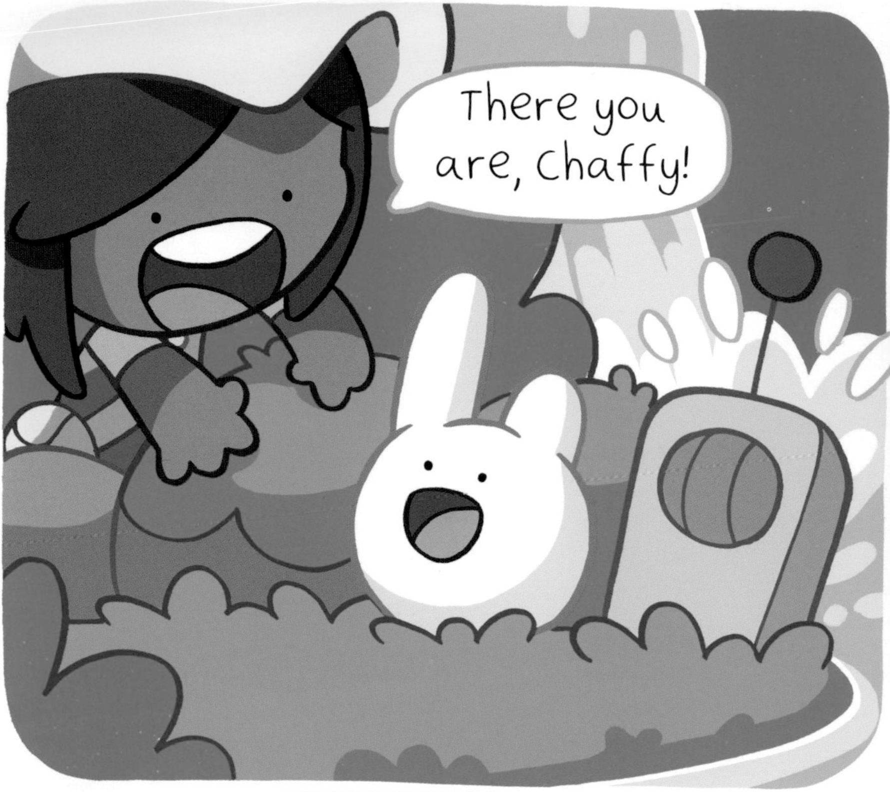
There you are, Chaffy!

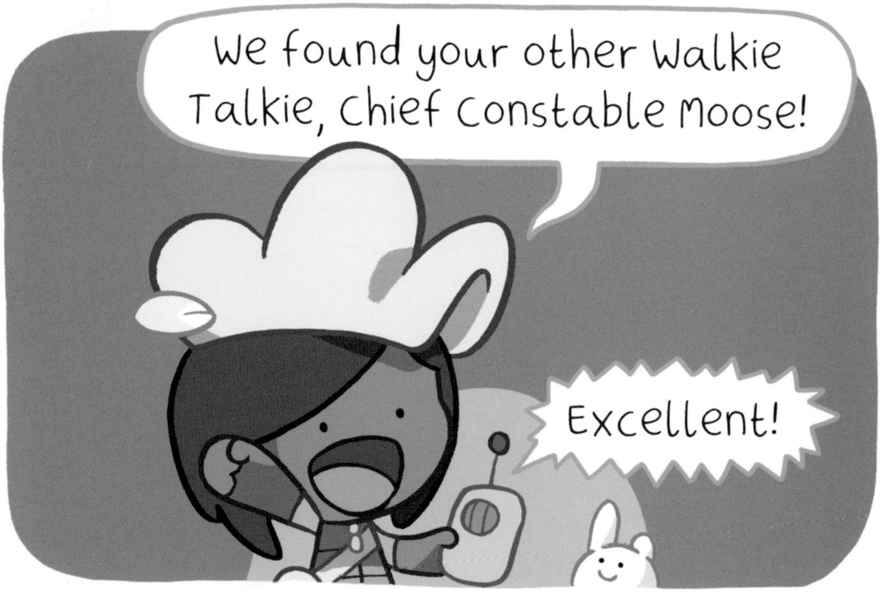
We found your other Walkie Talkie, Chief Constable Moose!
Excellent!

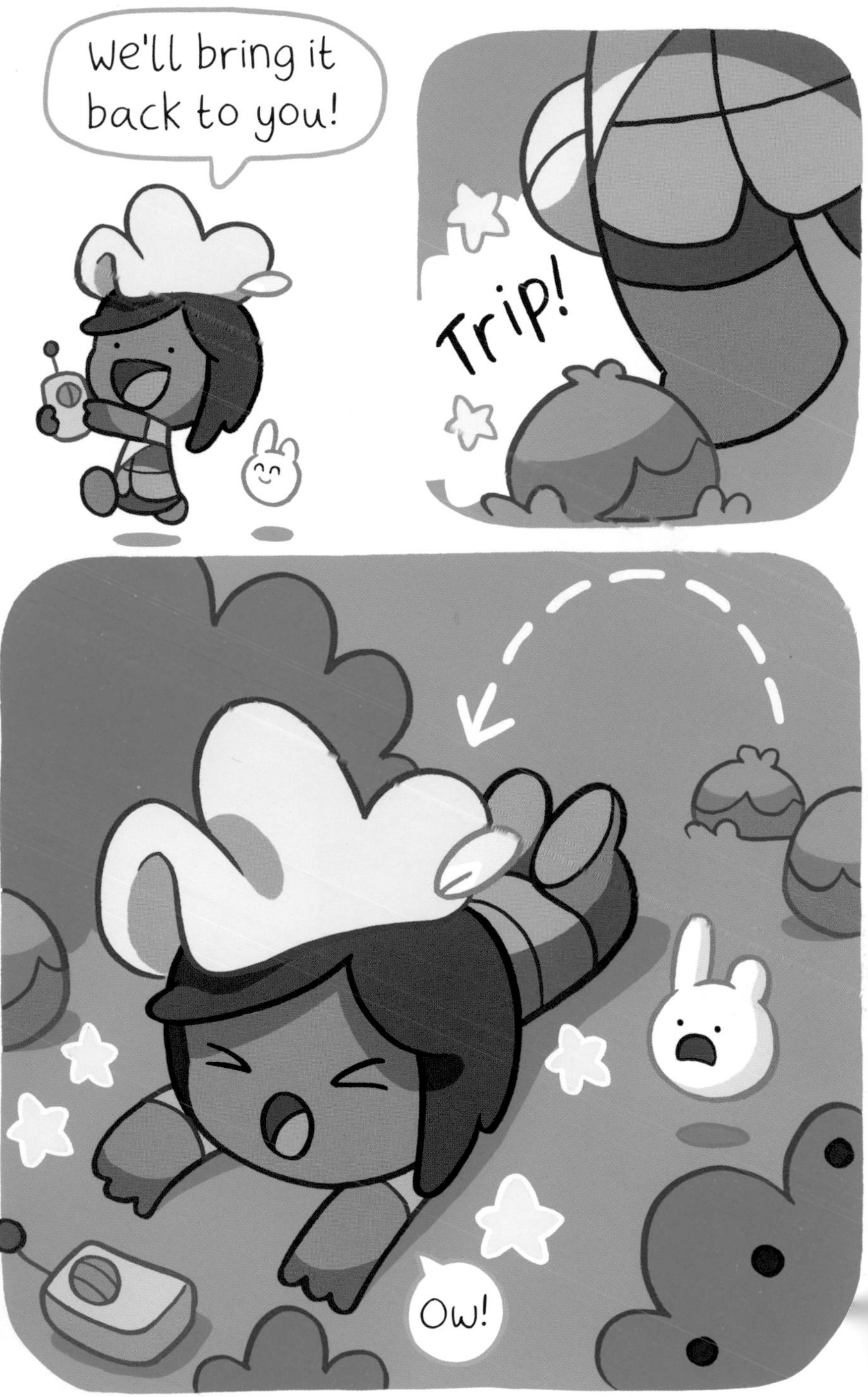
We'll bring it back to you!
Trip!
Ow!

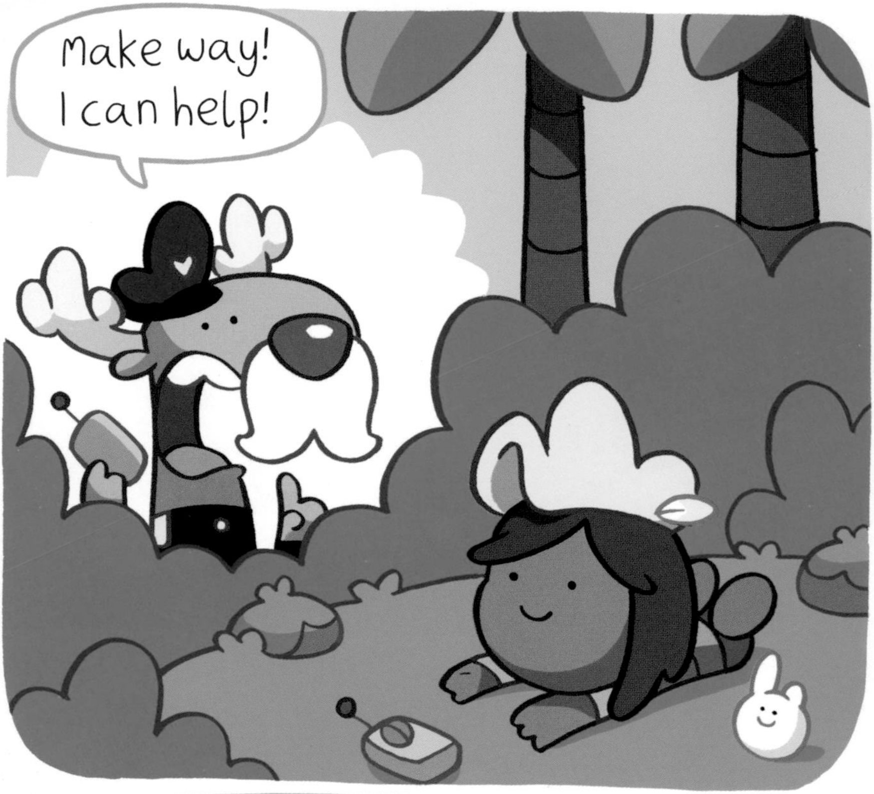
Make way! I can help!

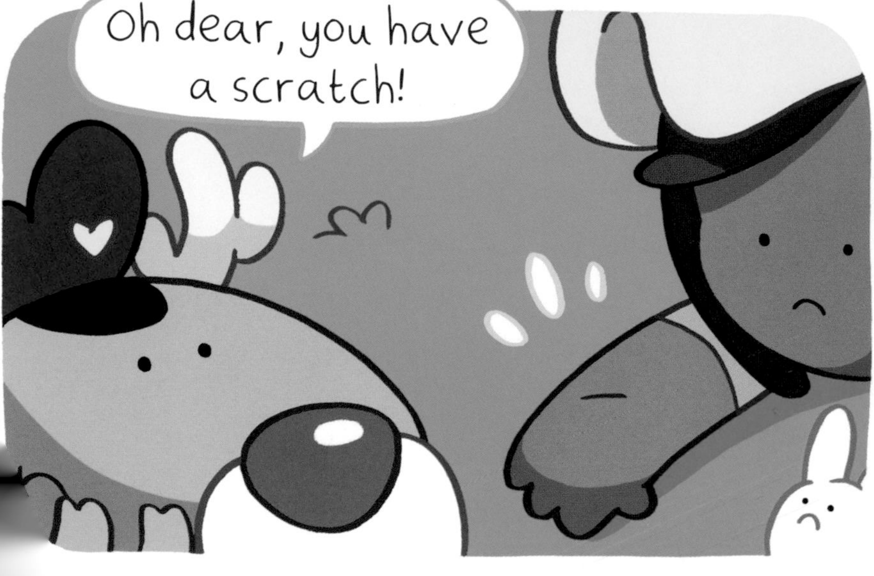
Oh dear, you have a scratch!

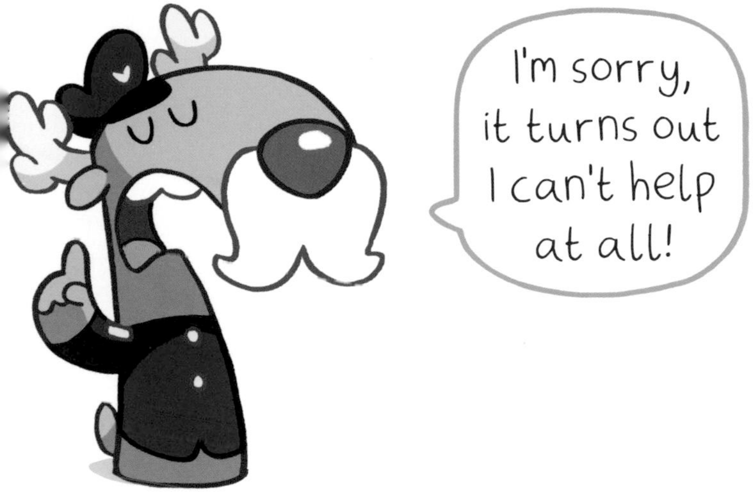
I'm sorry, it turns out I can't help at all!

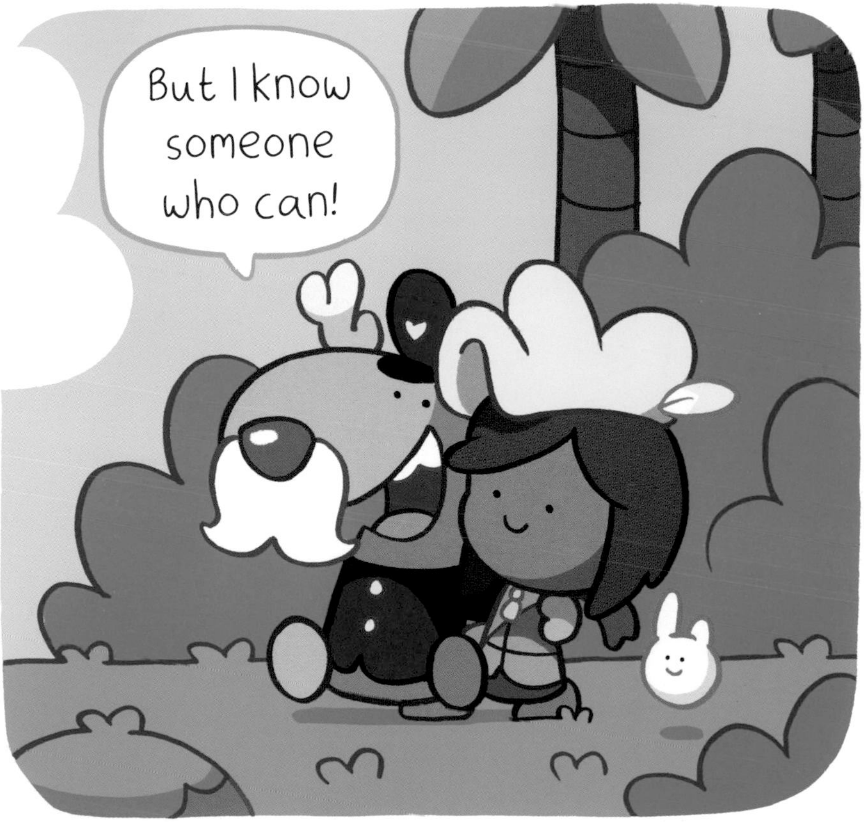
But I know someone who can!

Doctor Pedalo's Hospital!

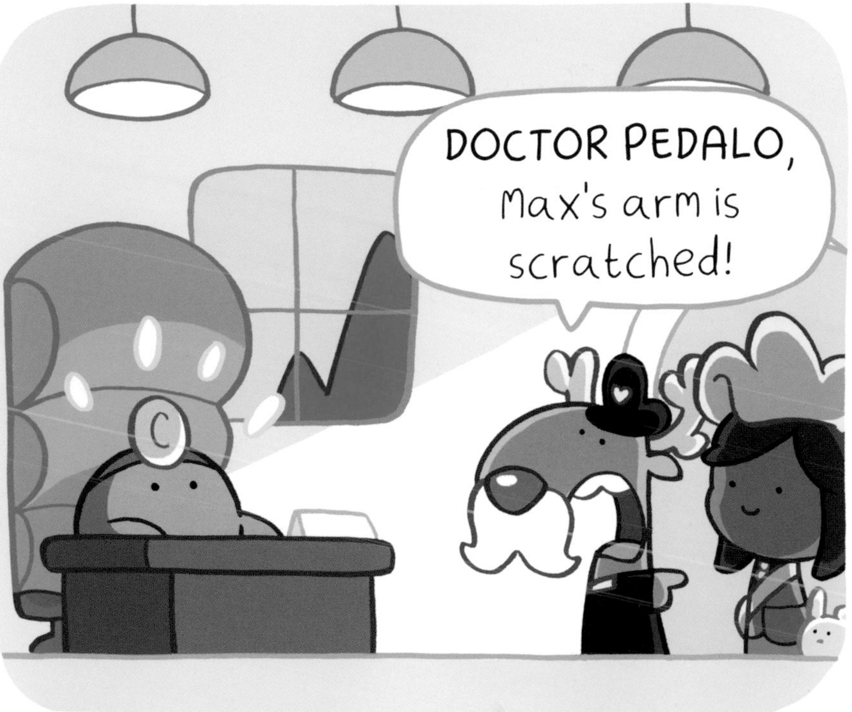
DOCTOR PEDALO,
Max's arm is
scratched!

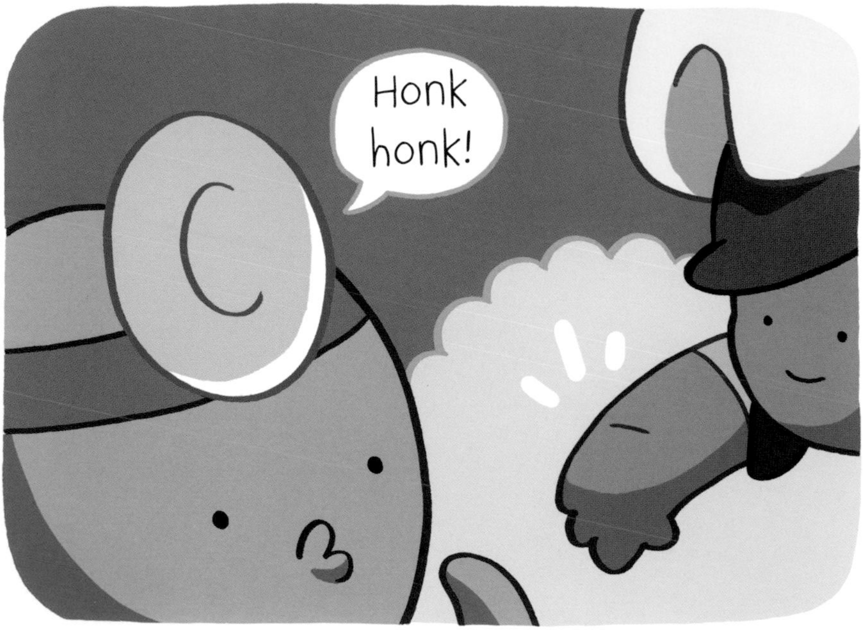
Honk
honk!

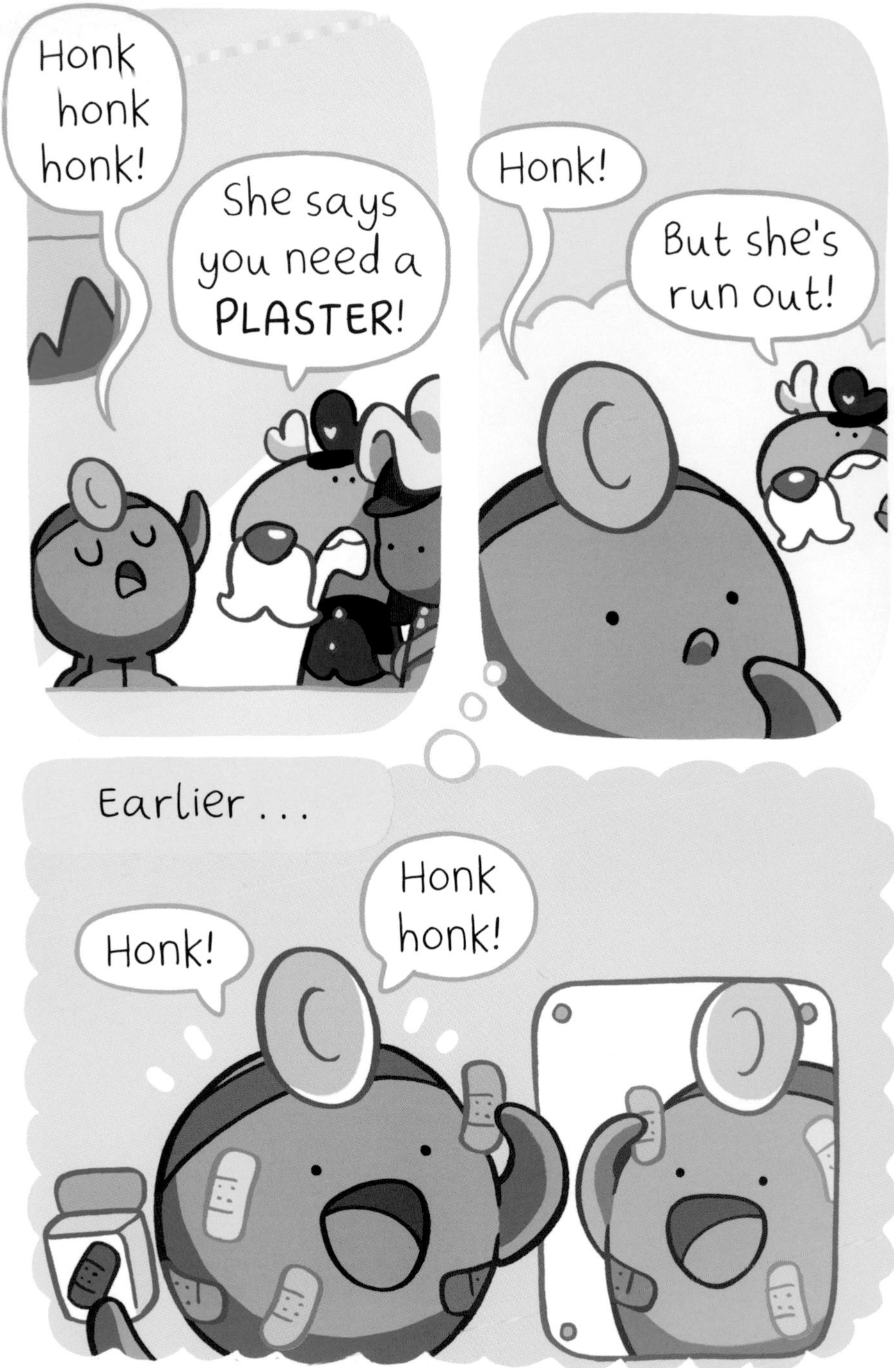
Honk honk honk!
She says you need a PLASTER!
Honk!
But she's run out!
Earlier ...
Honk!
Honk honk!

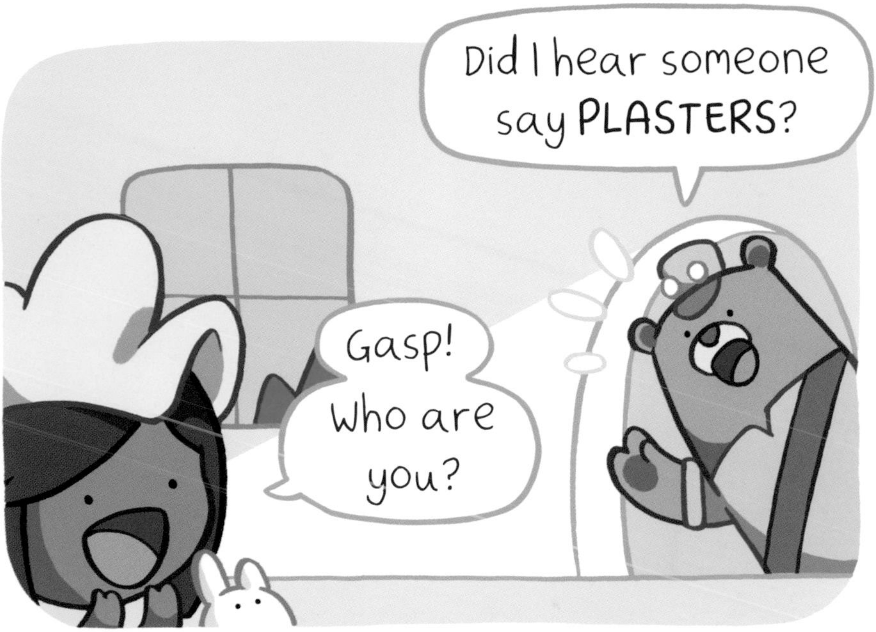
Did I hear someone say PLASTERS?
Gasp! Who are you?

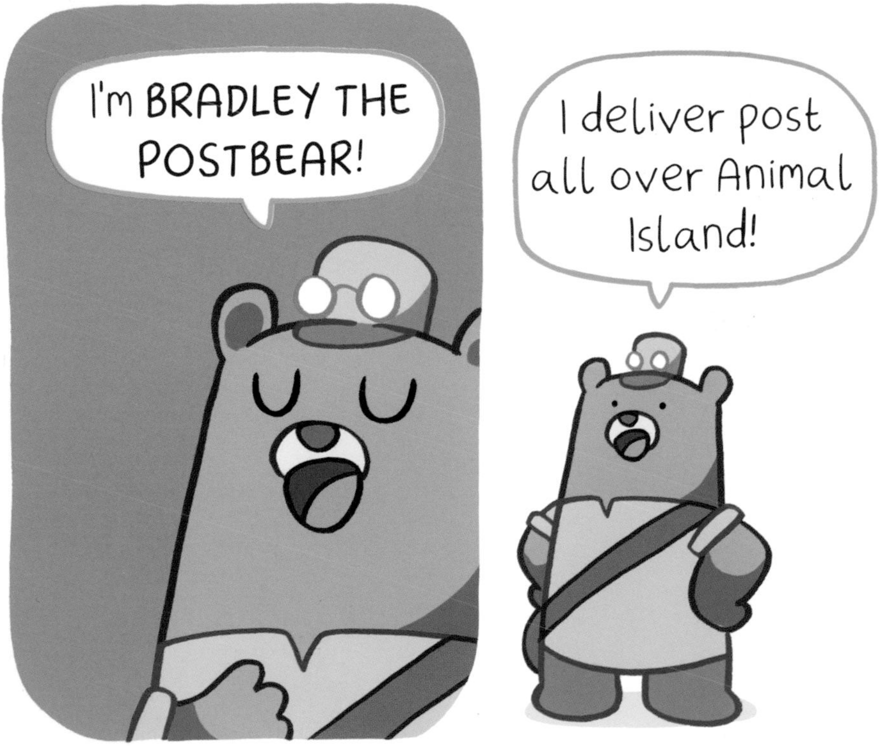
I'm BRADLEY THE POSTBEAR!
I deliver post all over Animal Island!

And I have a delivery of new plasters for you!

Hooray!

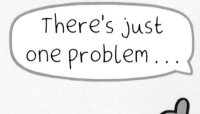

There's just one problem . . .

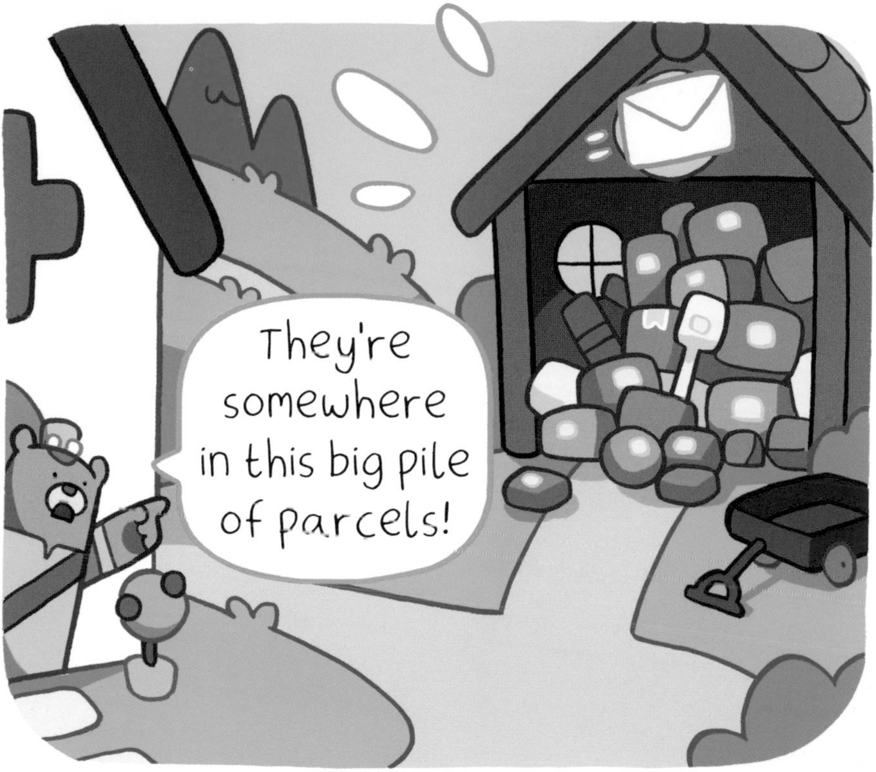
They're somewhere in this big pile of parcels!

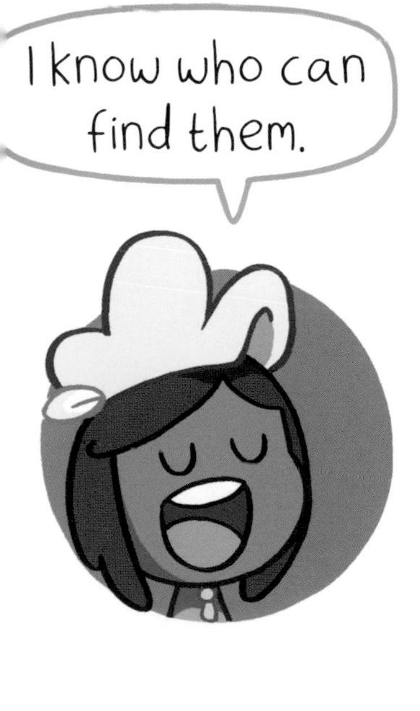
I know who can find them.

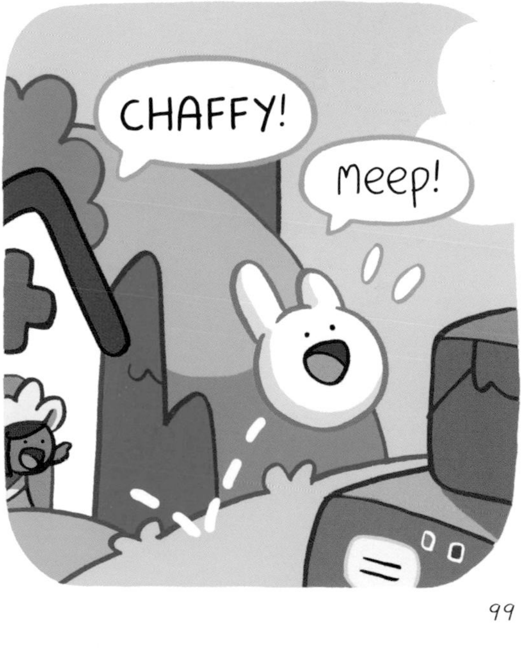
CHAFFY!
Meep!

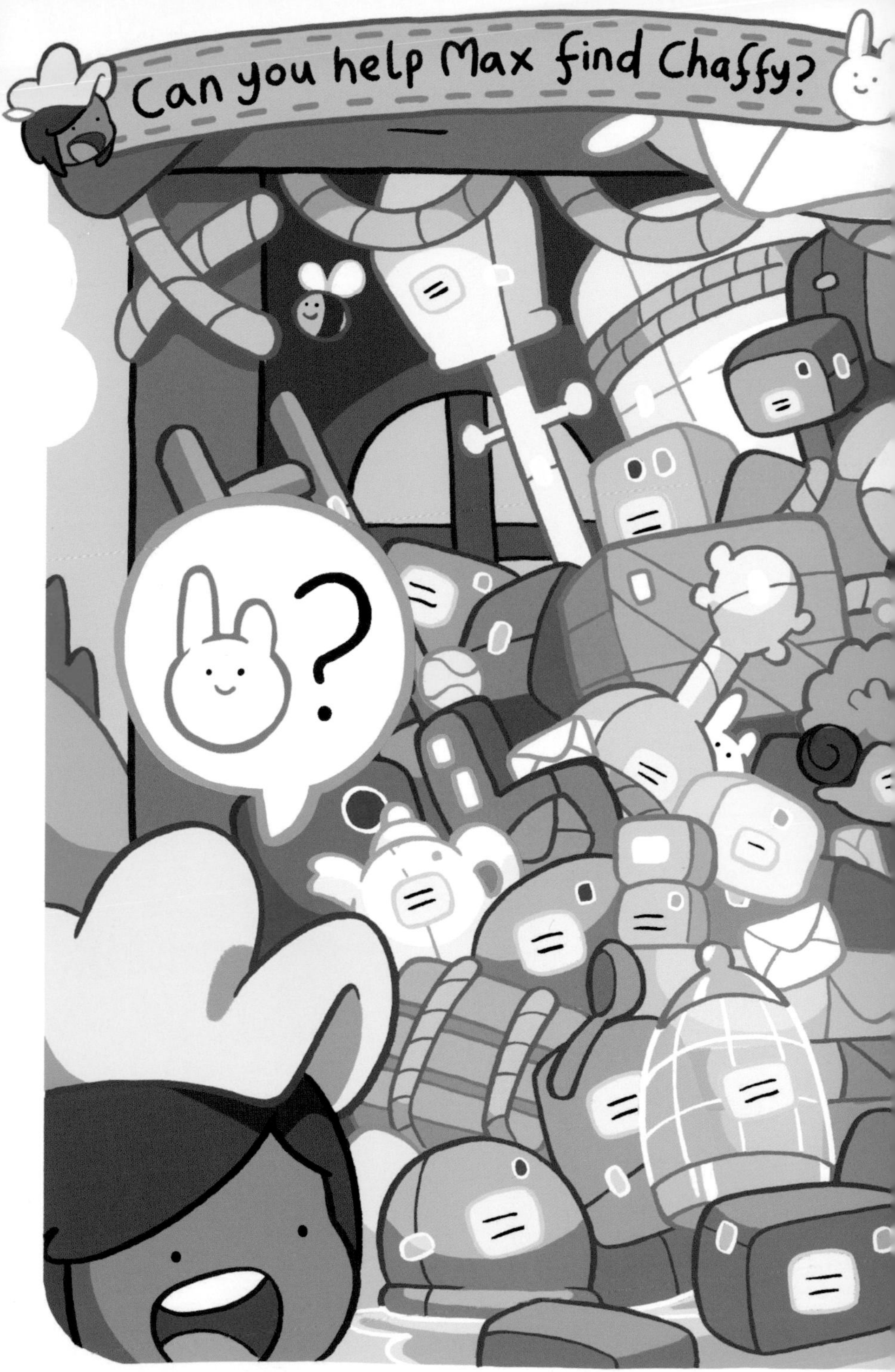
Can you help Max find Chaffy?

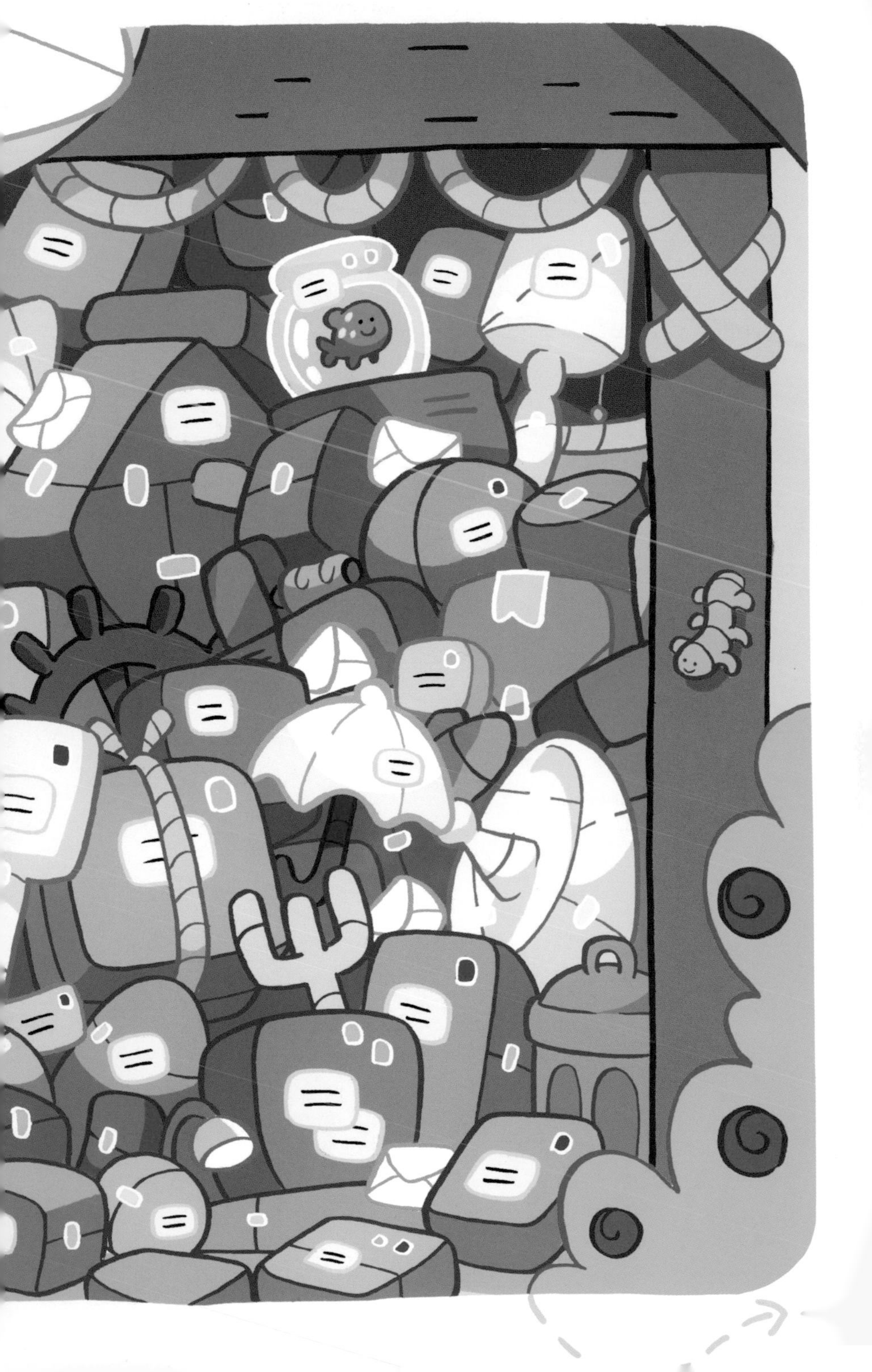

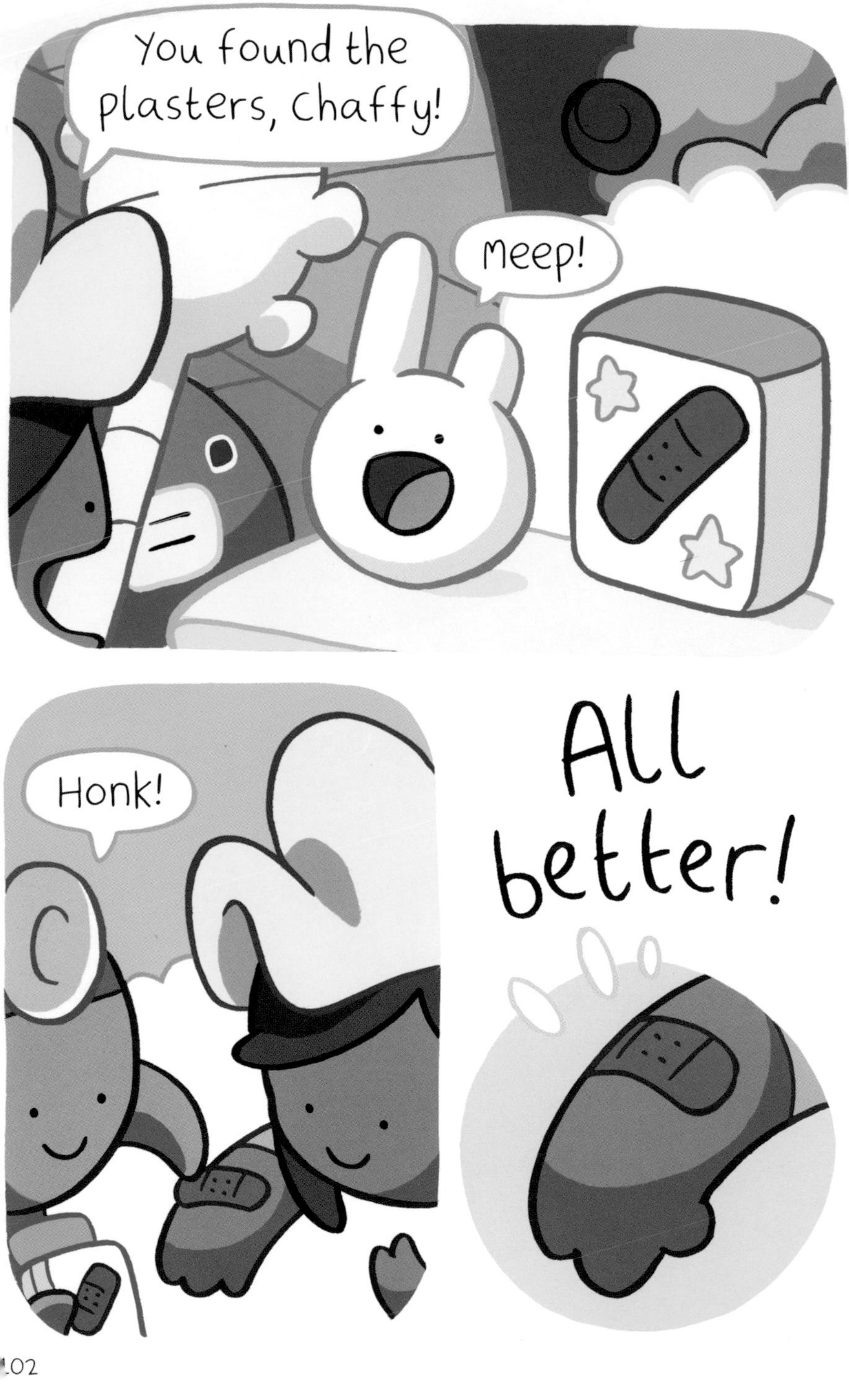
You found the plasters, Chaffy!
Meep!
Honk!
All better!

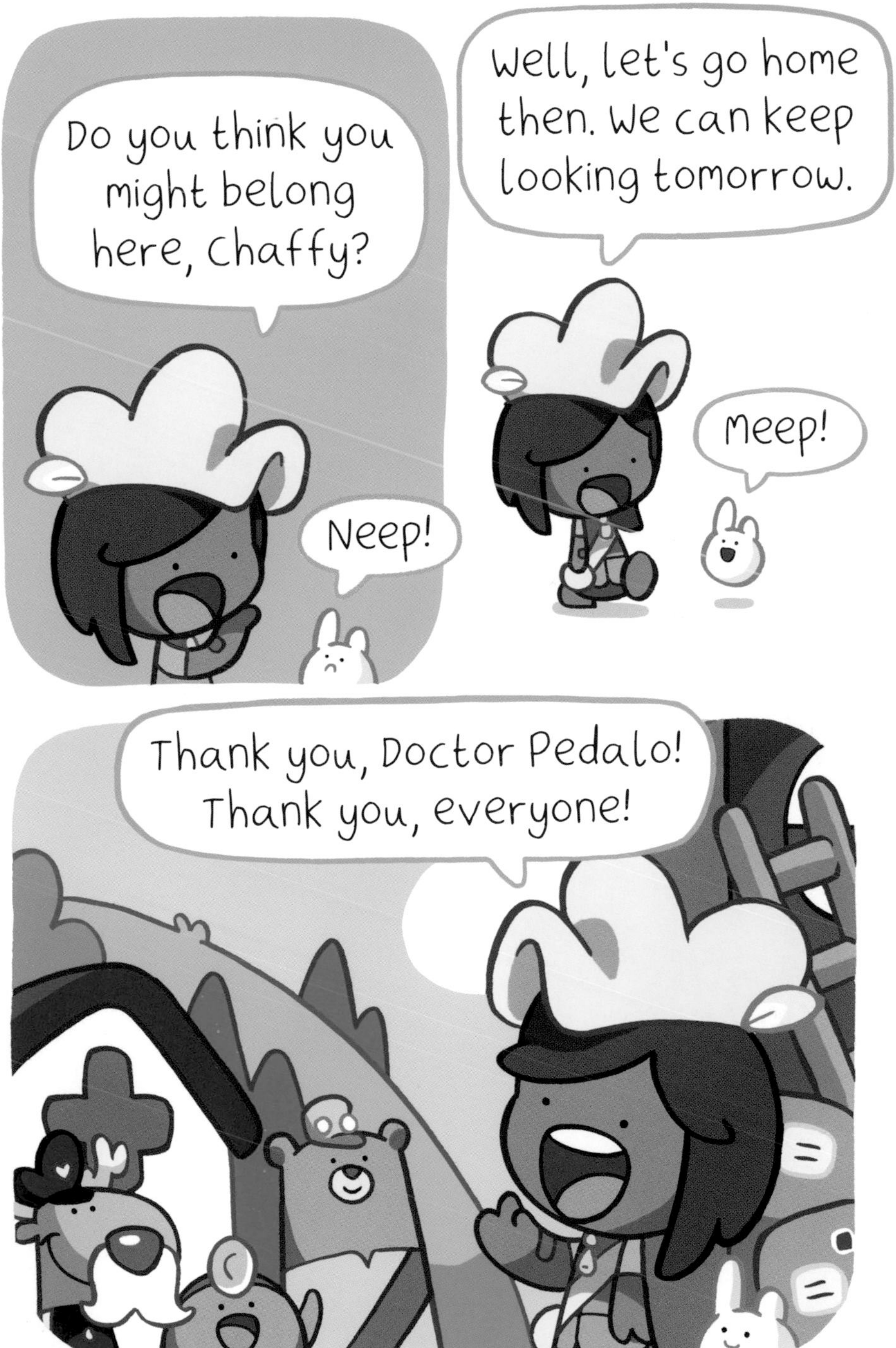
Do you think you might belong here, Chaffy?
Neep!
Well, let's go home then. We can keep looking tomorrow.
Meep!
Thank you, Doctor Pedalo! Thank you, everyone!

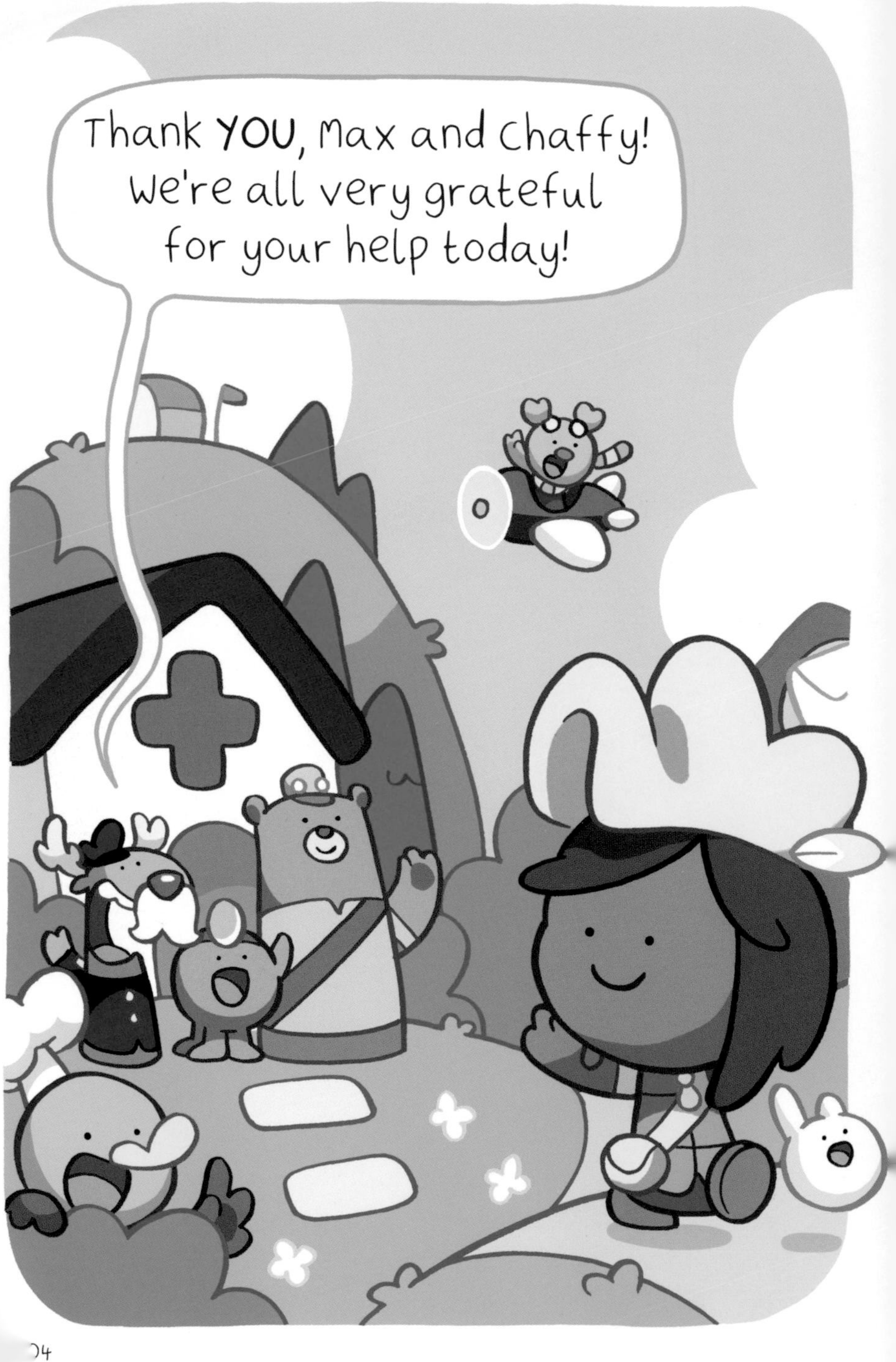
Thank **YOU**, Max and Chaffy! We're all very grateful for your help today!

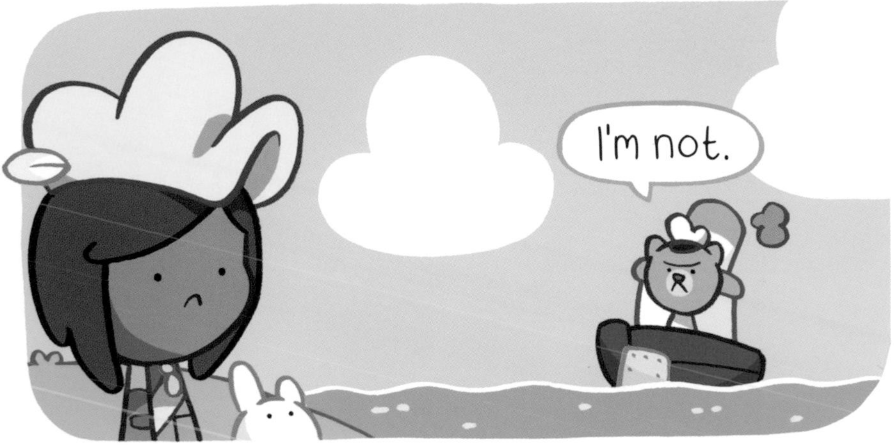
I'm not.

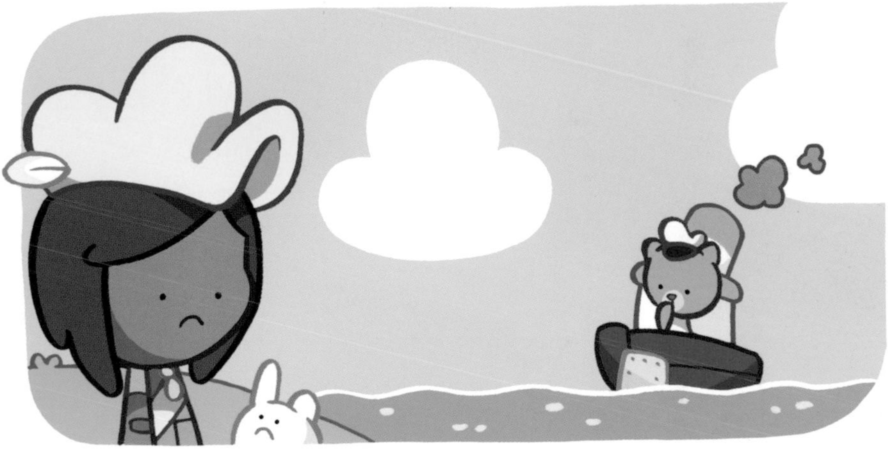

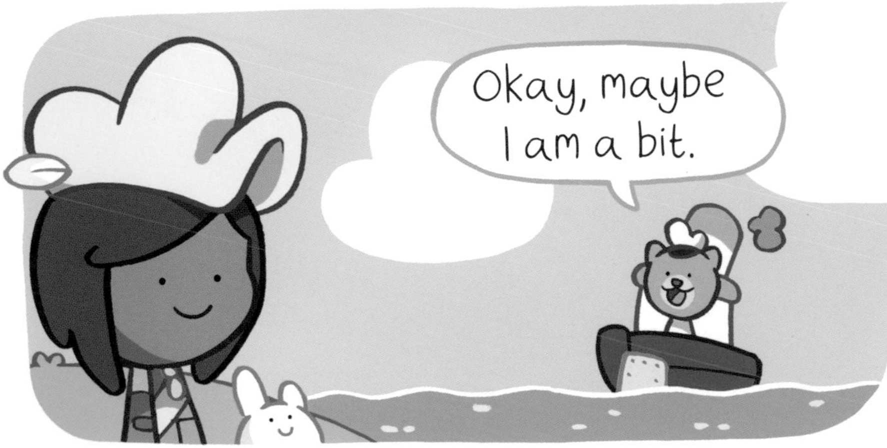
Okay, maybe
I am a bit.

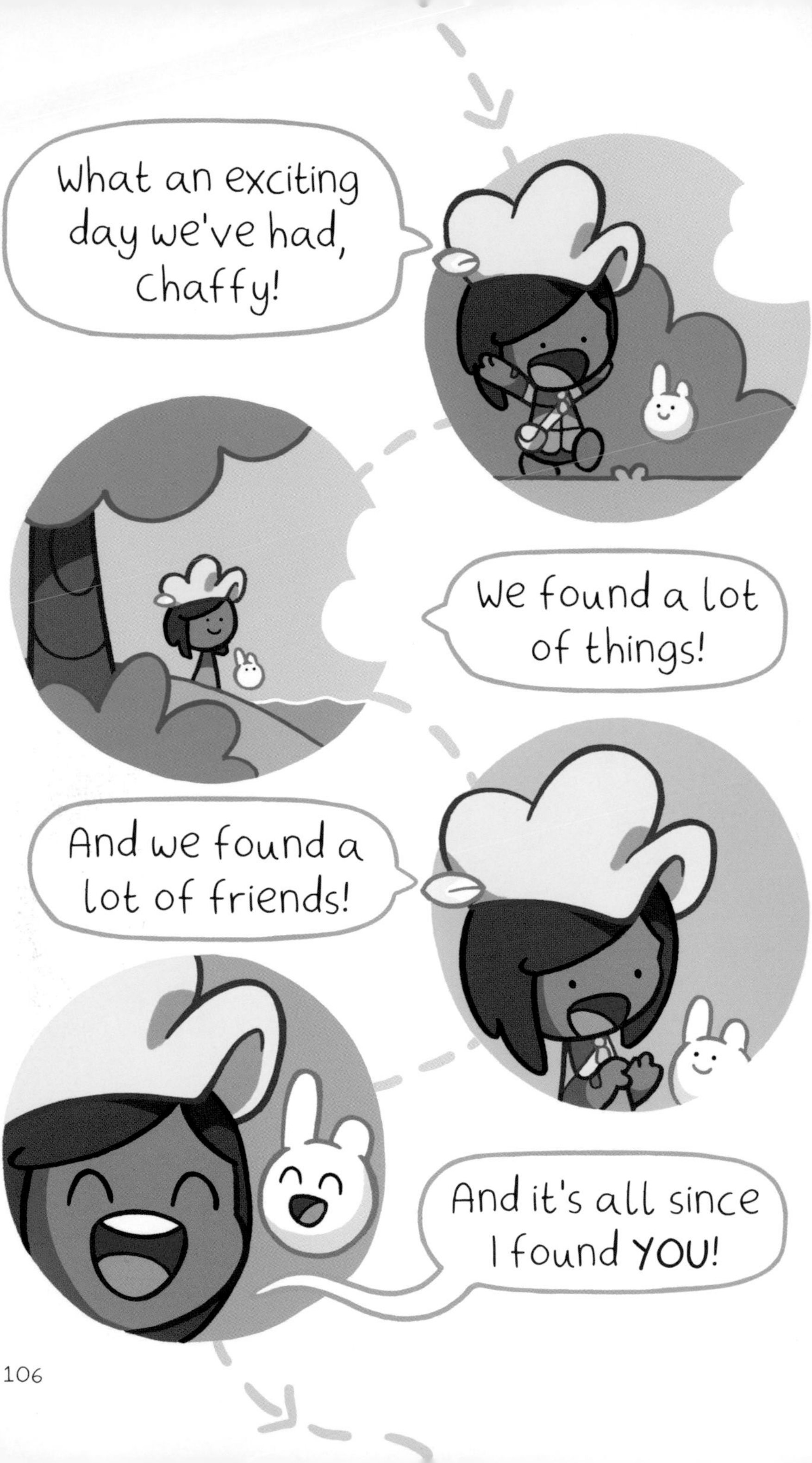
What an exciting day we've had, Chaffy!
We found a lot of things!
And we found a lot of friends!
And it's all since I found **YOU**!

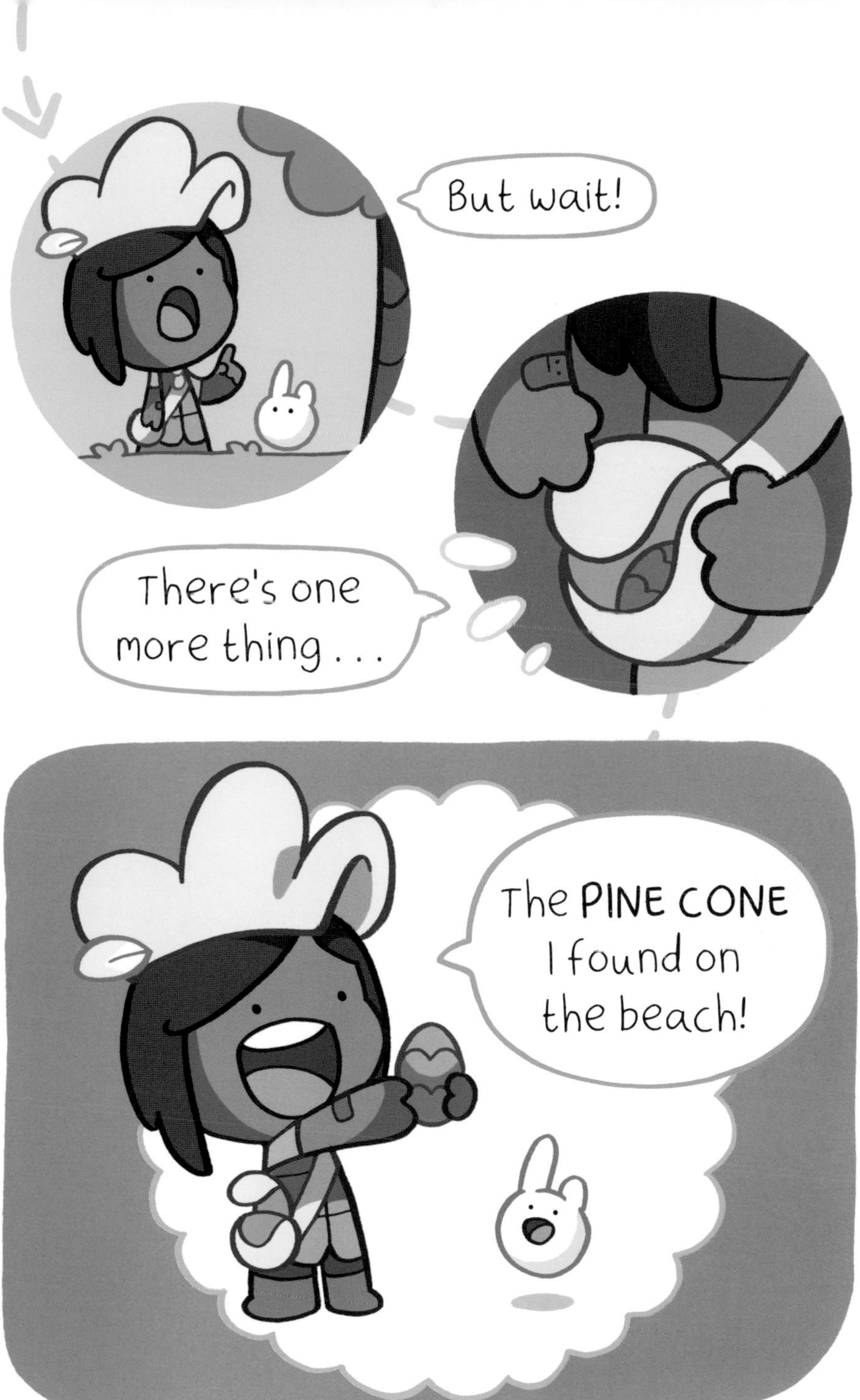
But wait!
There's one more thing . . .
The PINE CONE I found on the beach!

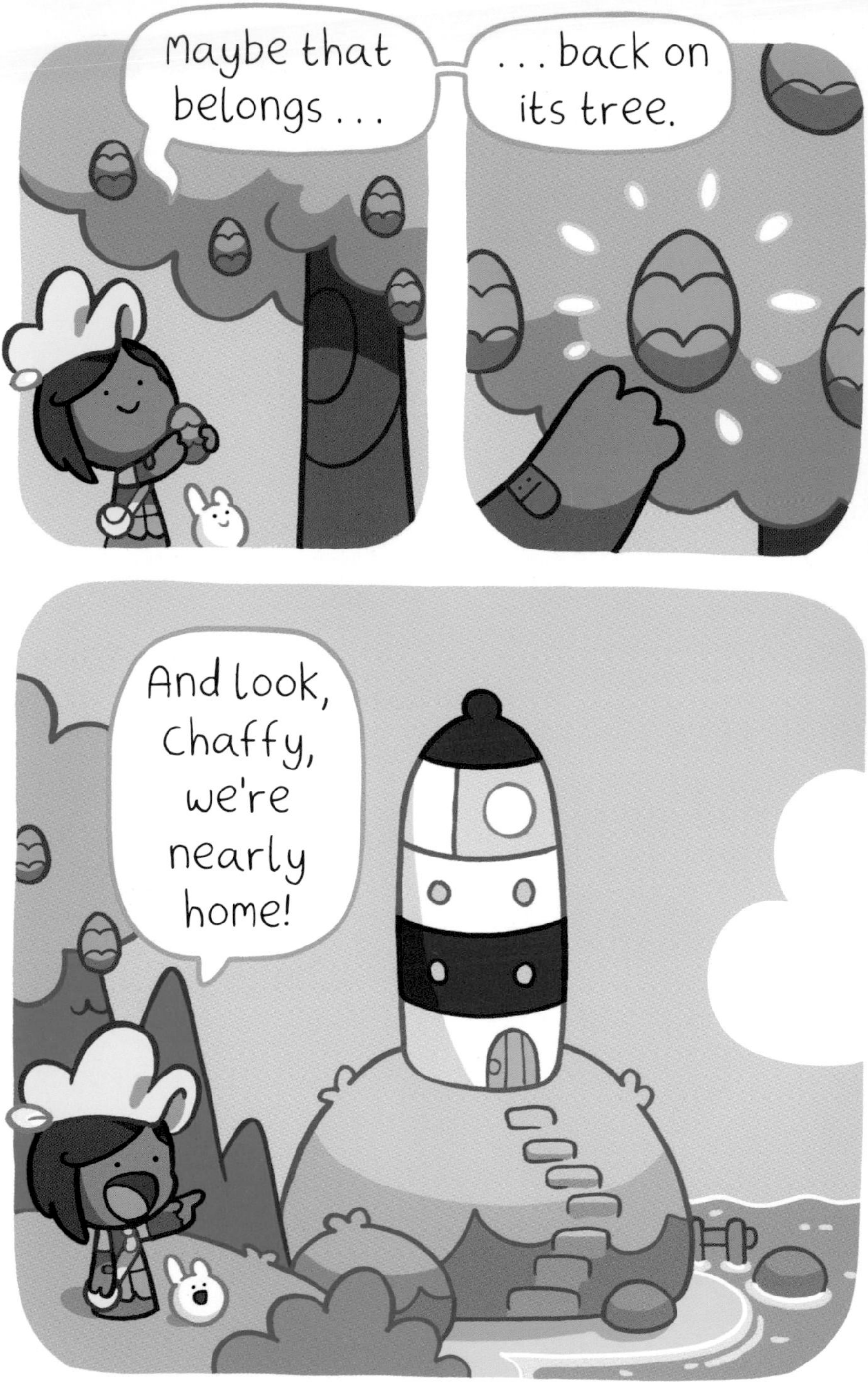
Maybe that belongs . . .
. . . back on its tree.
And look, Chaffy, we're nearly home!

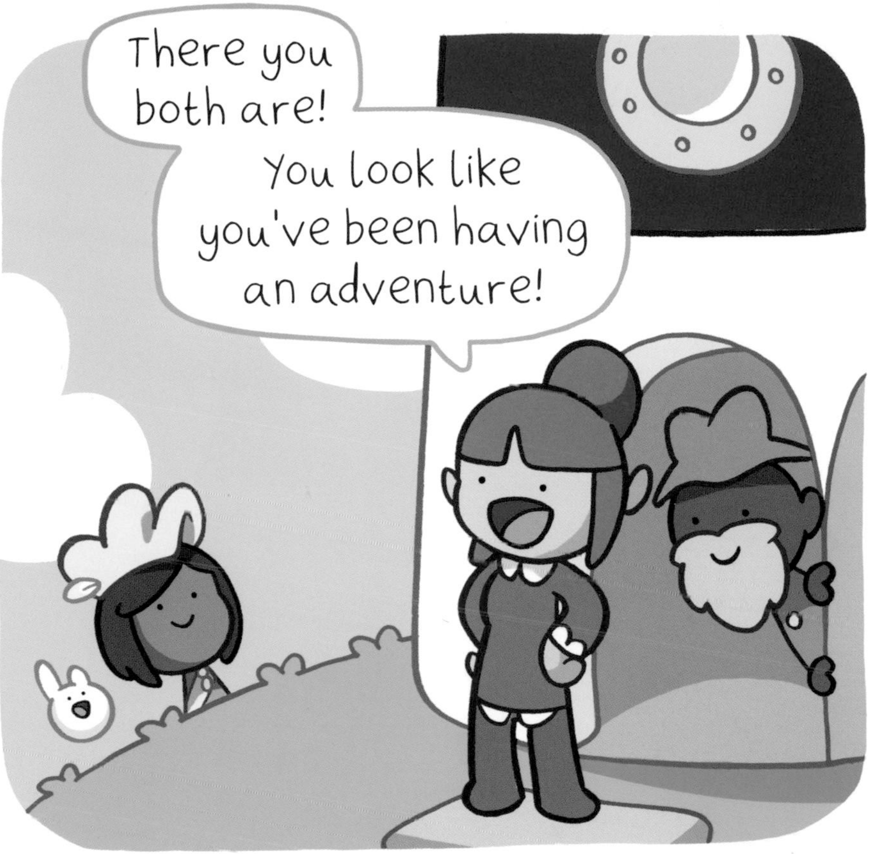
There you both are!
You look like you've been having an adventure!

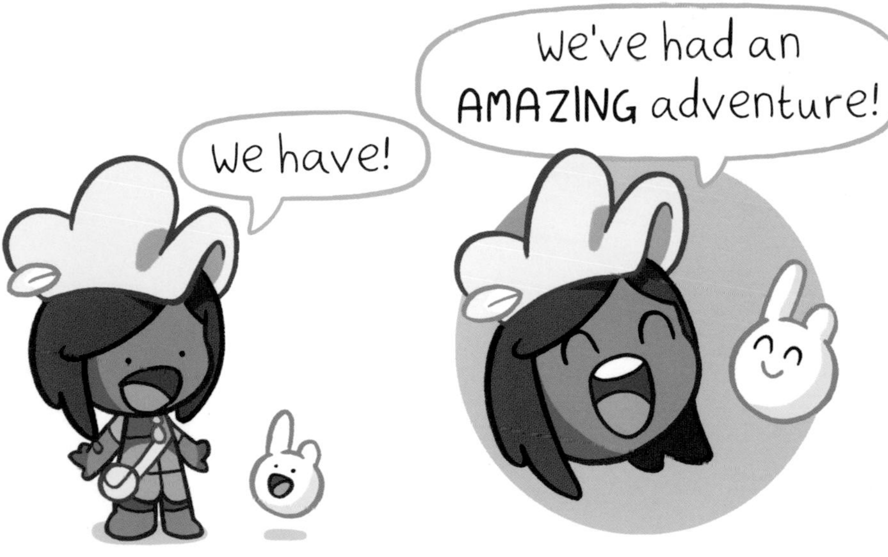
We have!
We've had an AMAZING adventure!

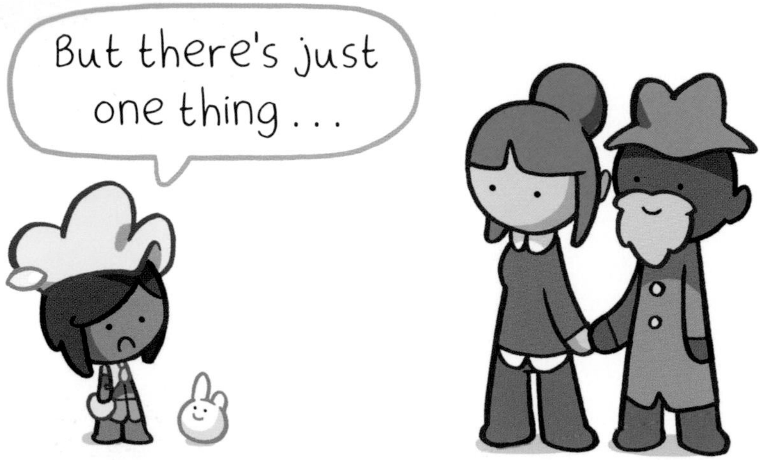
But there's just one thing . . .

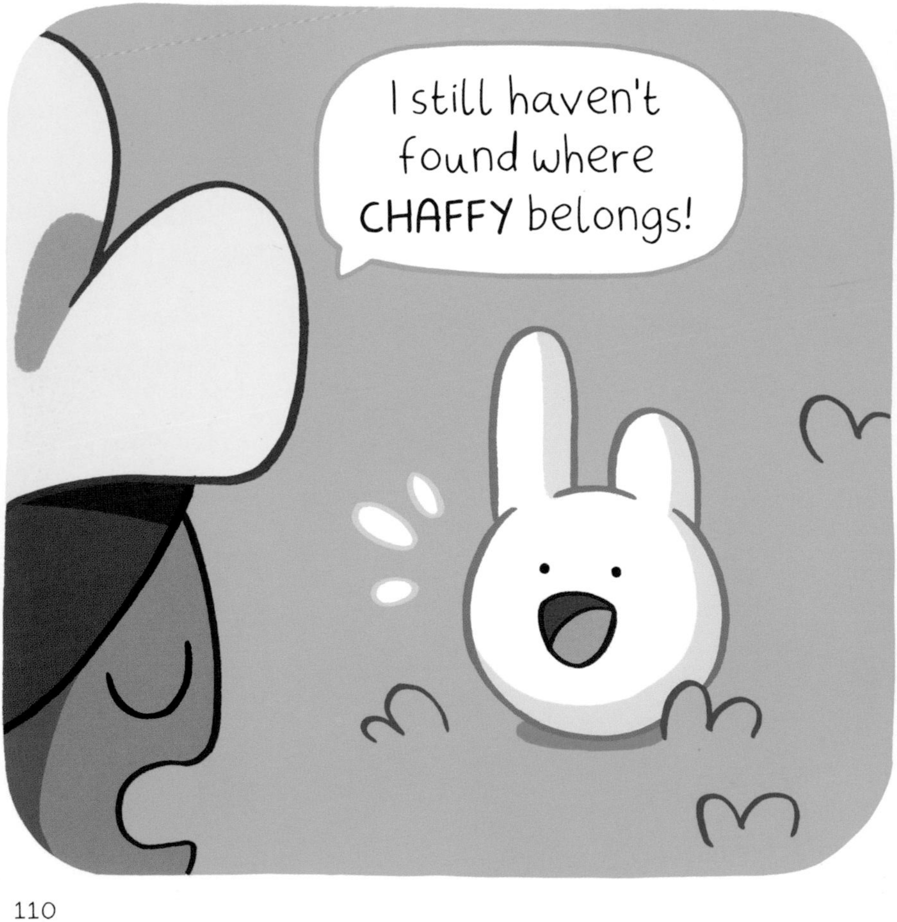
I still haven't found where CHAFFY belongs!

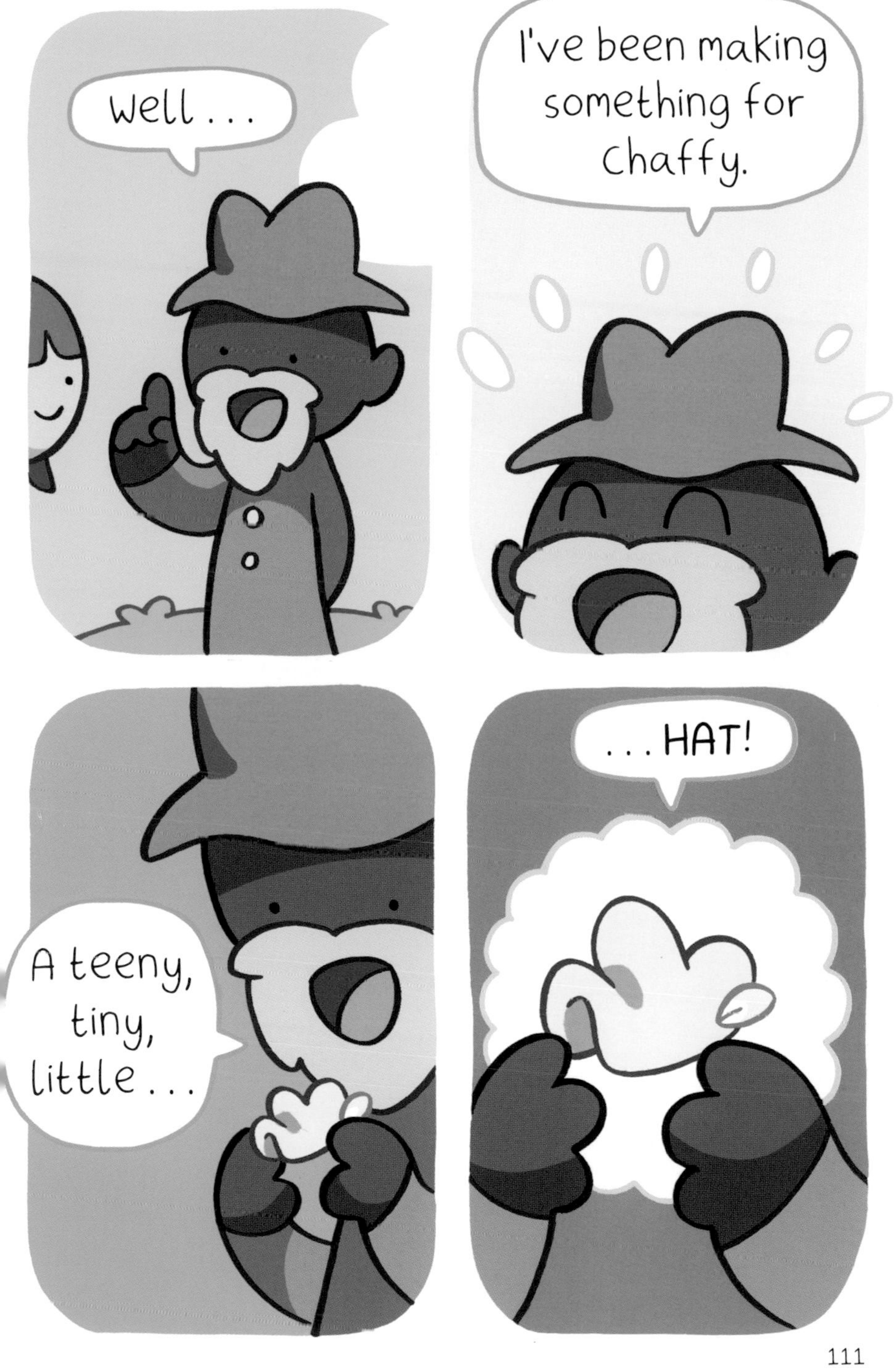
Well . . .
I've been making something for Chaffy.
A teeny, tiny, little . . .
. . . HAT!

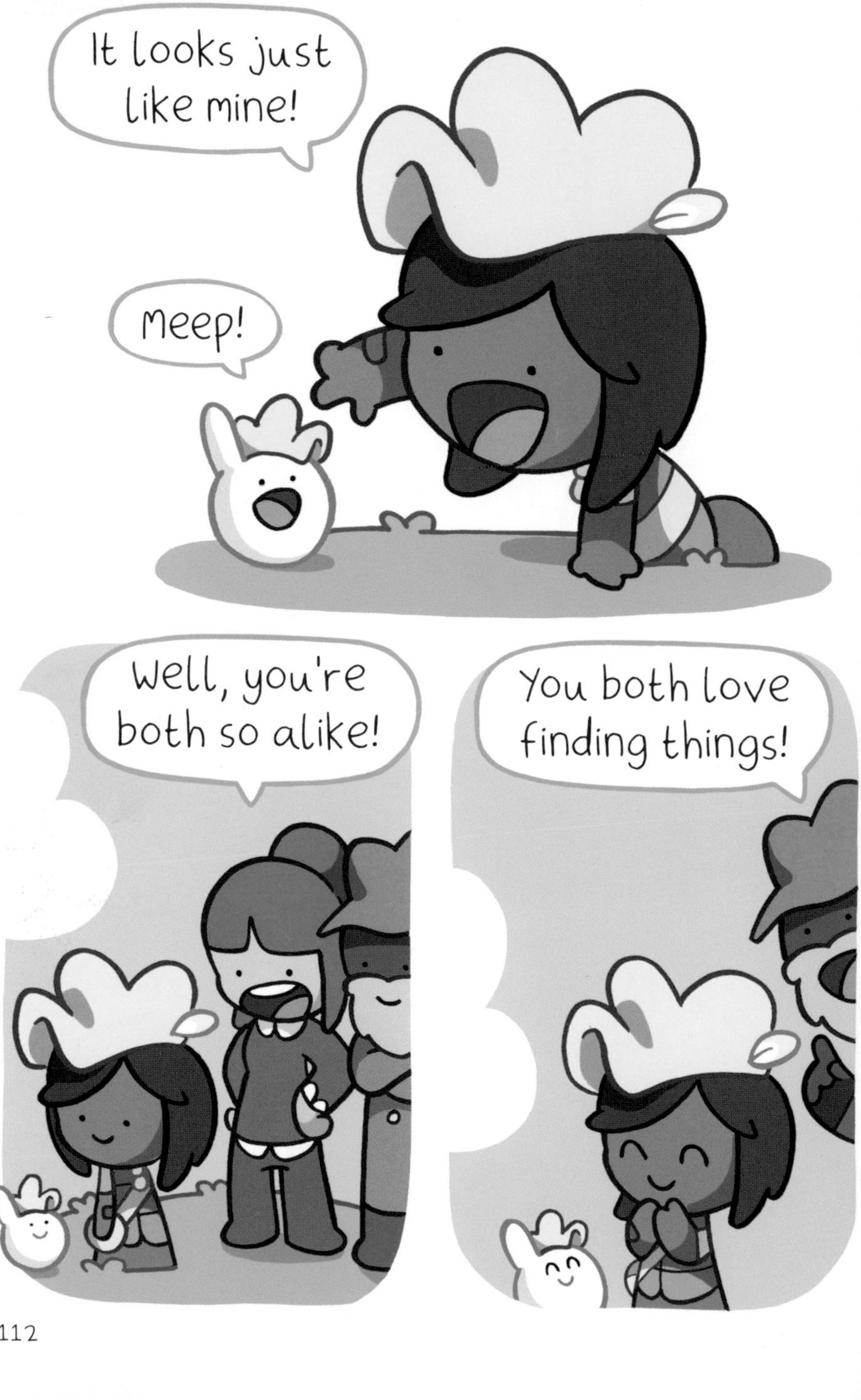
It looks just like mine!
Meep!
Well, you're both so alike!
You both love finding things!

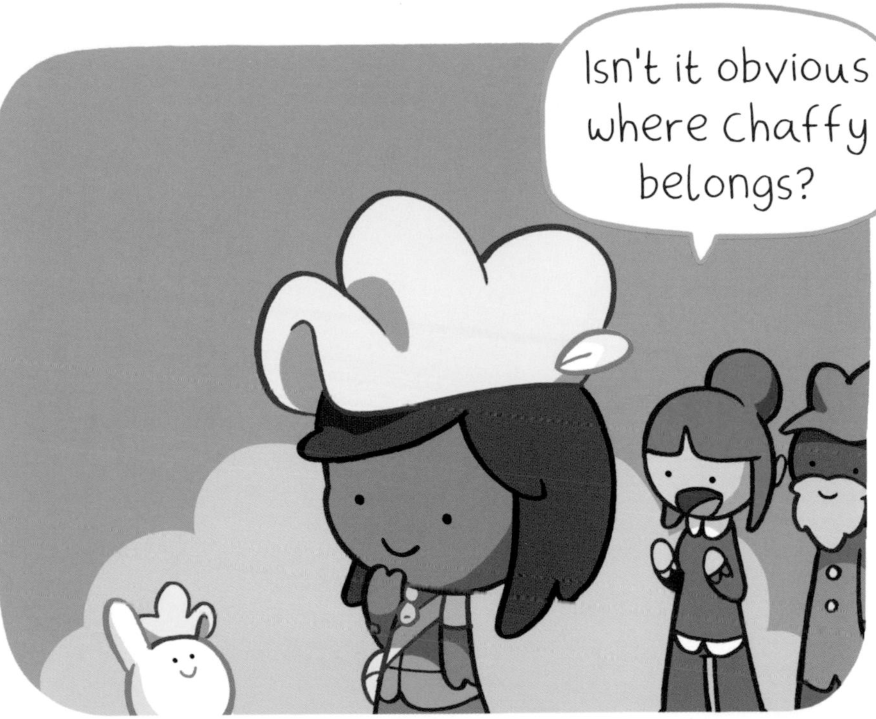
Isn't it obvious where Chaffy belongs?

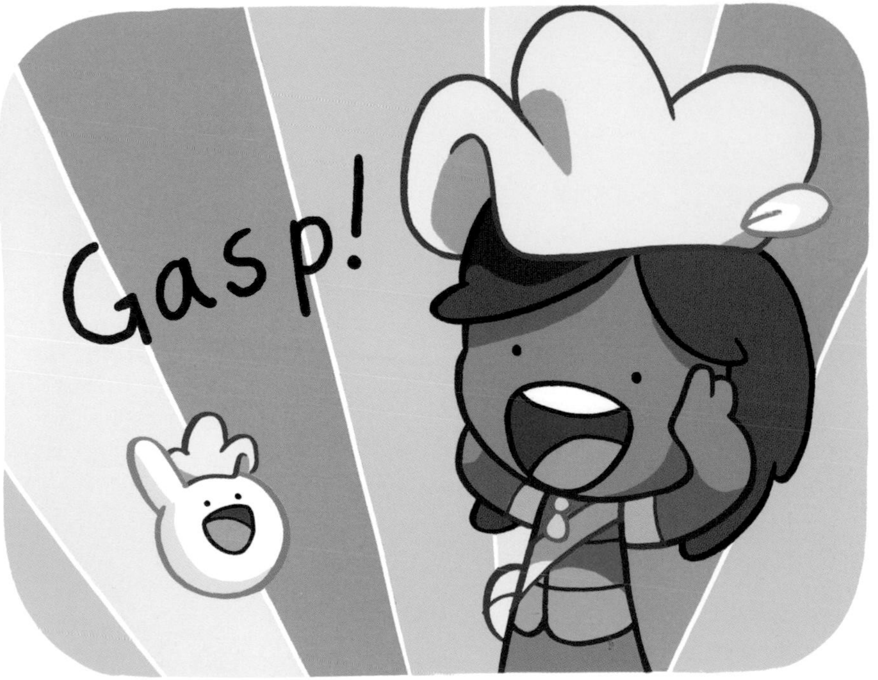
Gasp!

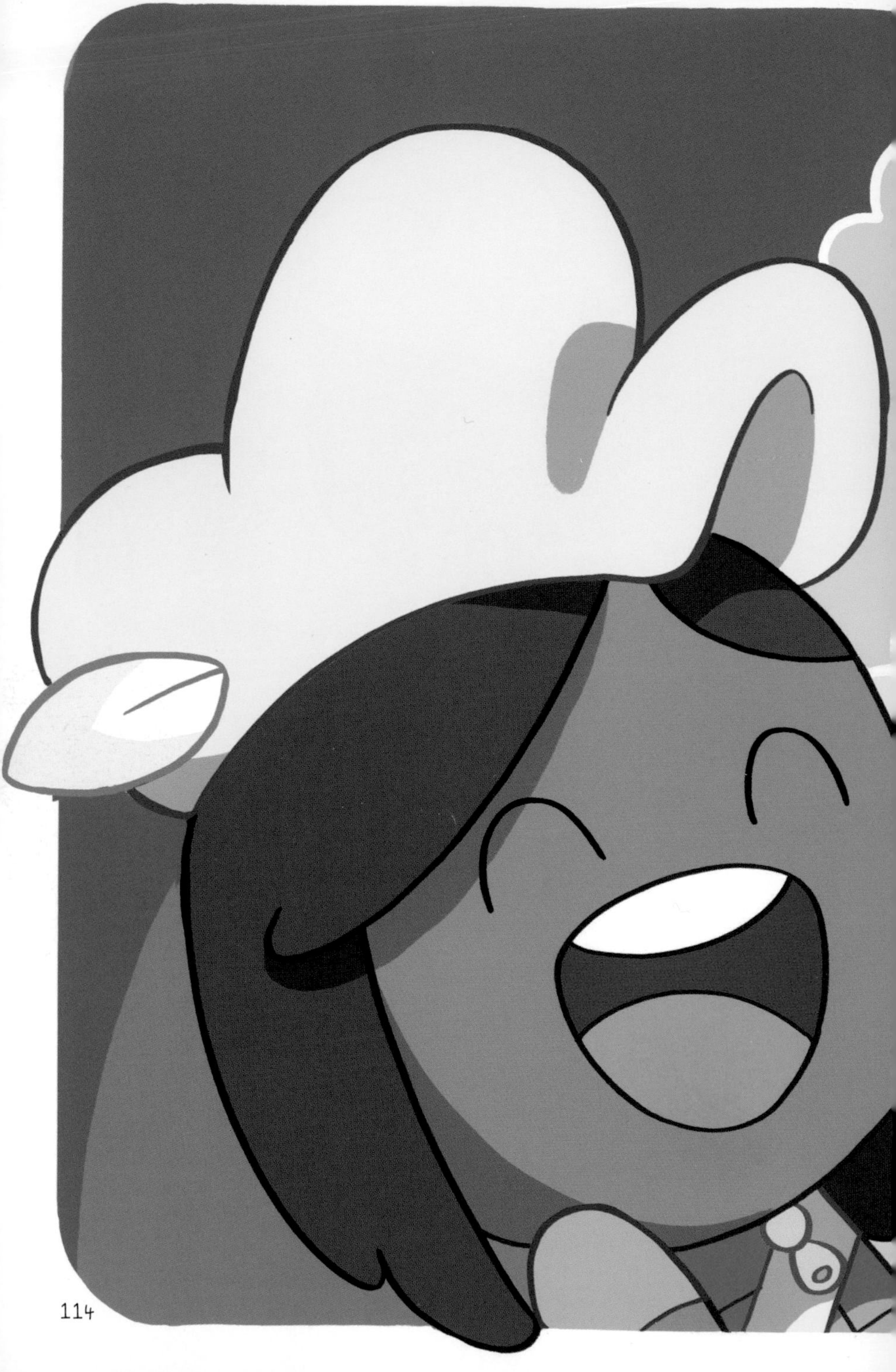

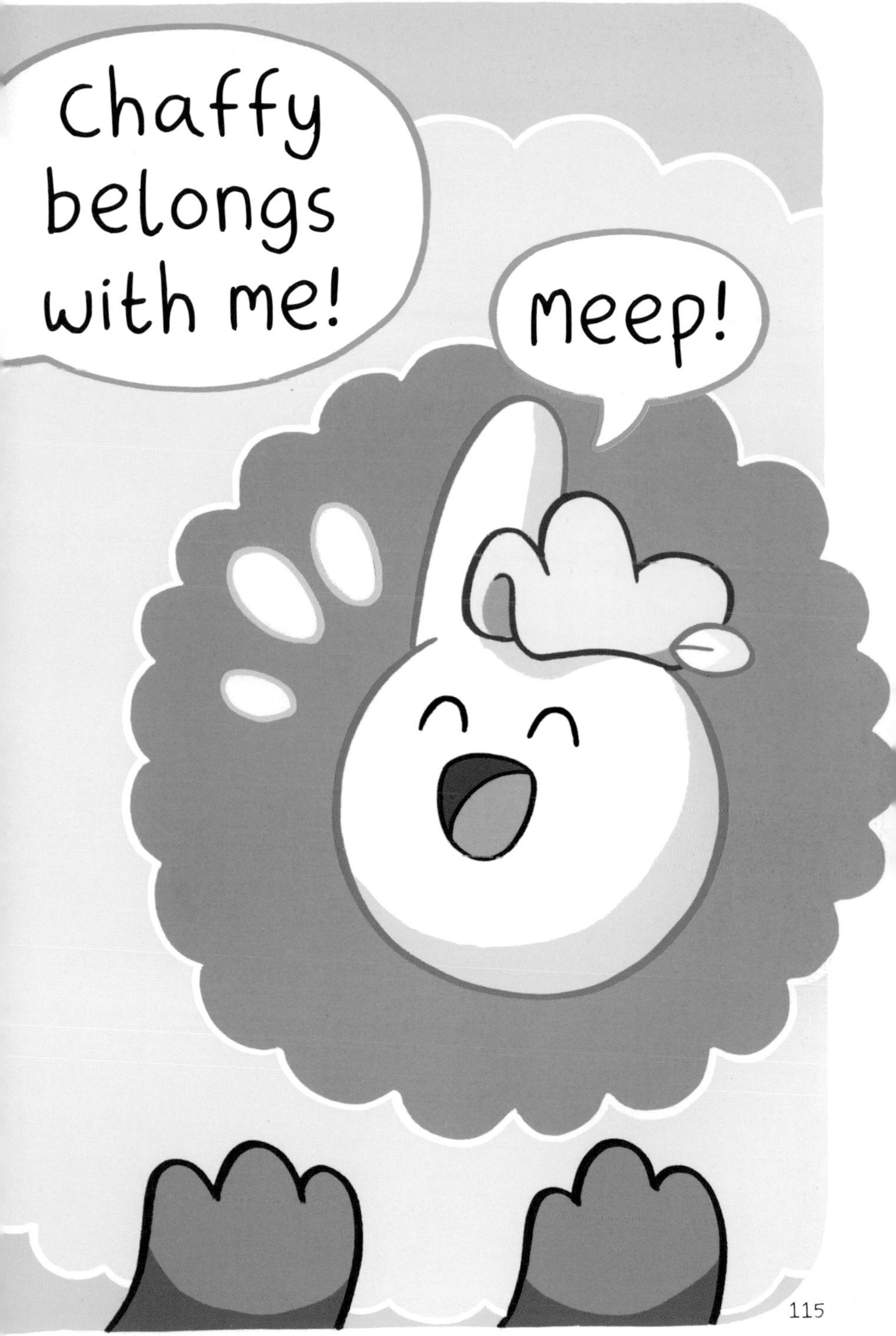
Chaffy belongs with me!
Meep!

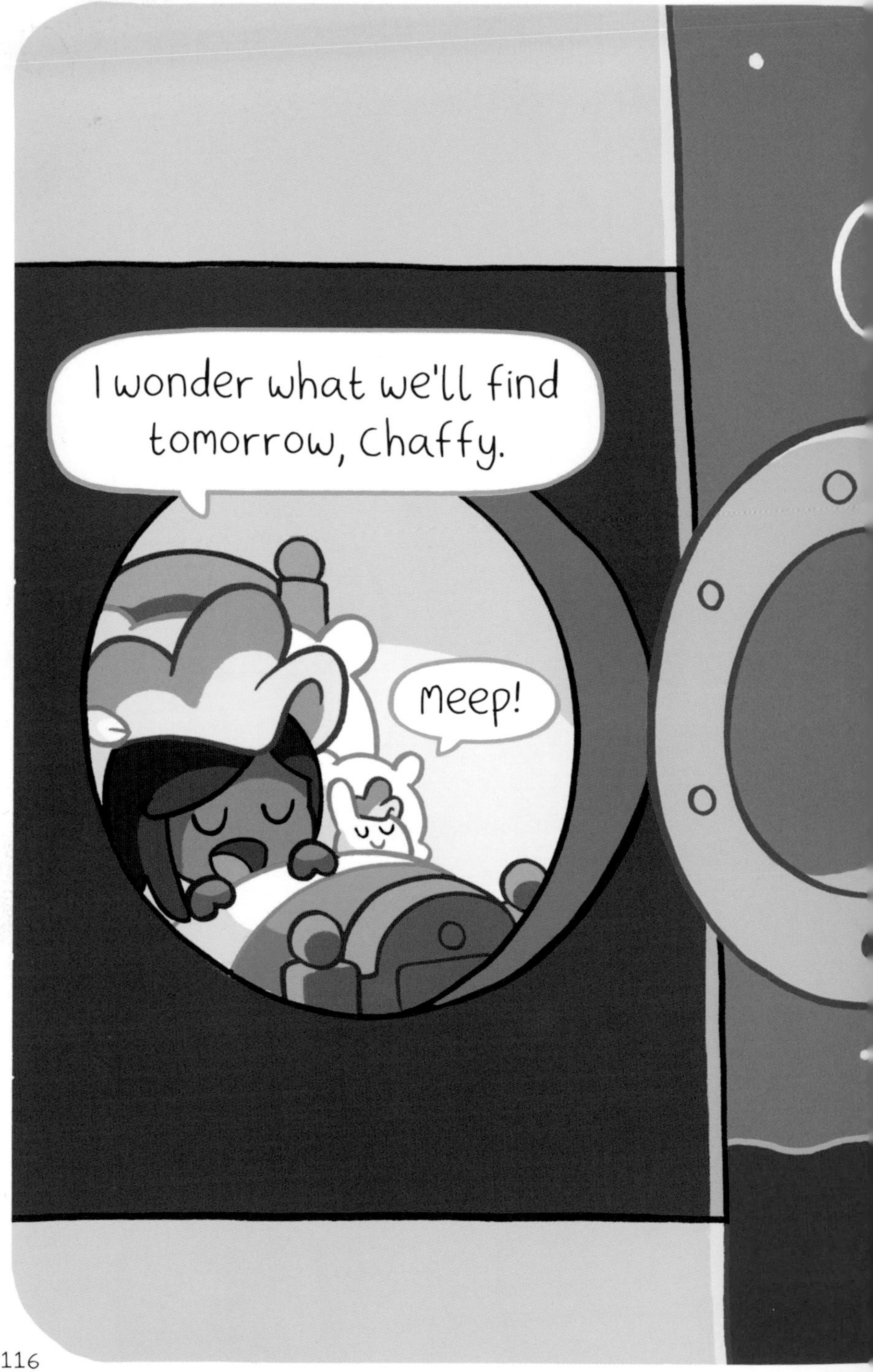
I wonder what we'll find tomorrow, Chaffy.
Meep!

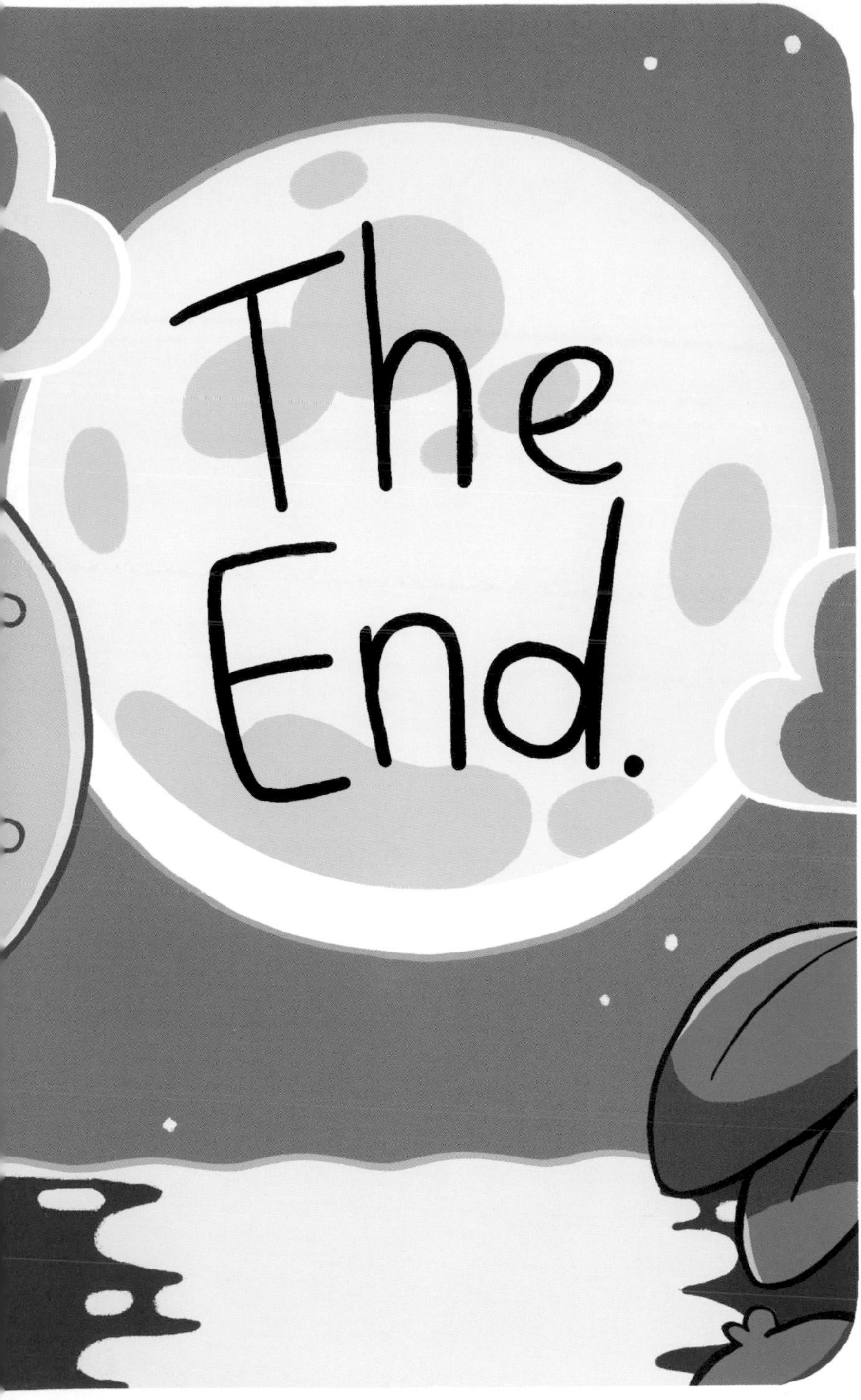
The End.

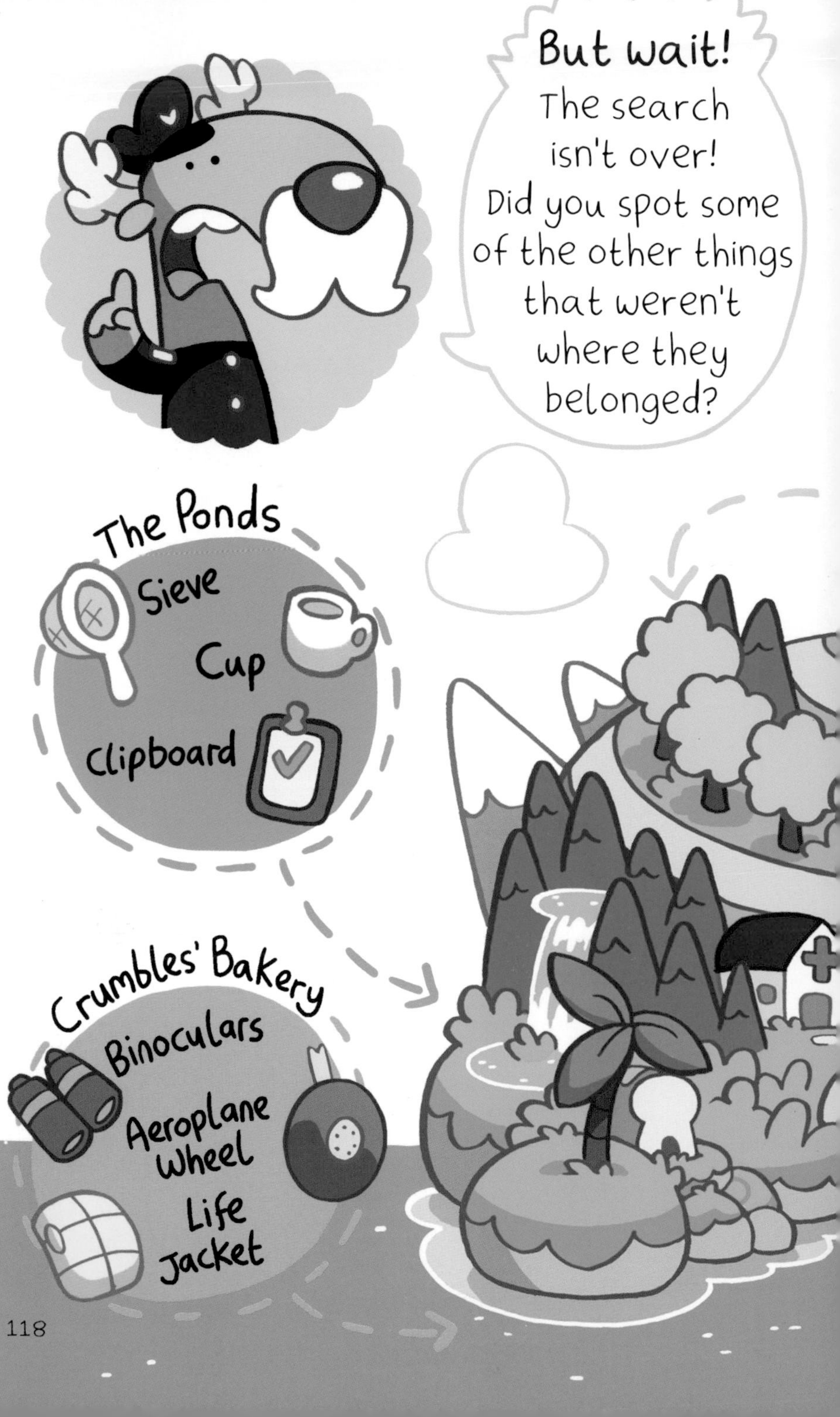

But wait! The search isn't over! Did you spot some of the other things that weren't where they belonged?
The Ponds
Sieve
Cup
Clipboard
Crumbles' Bakery
Binoculars
Aeroplane Wheel
Life Jacket

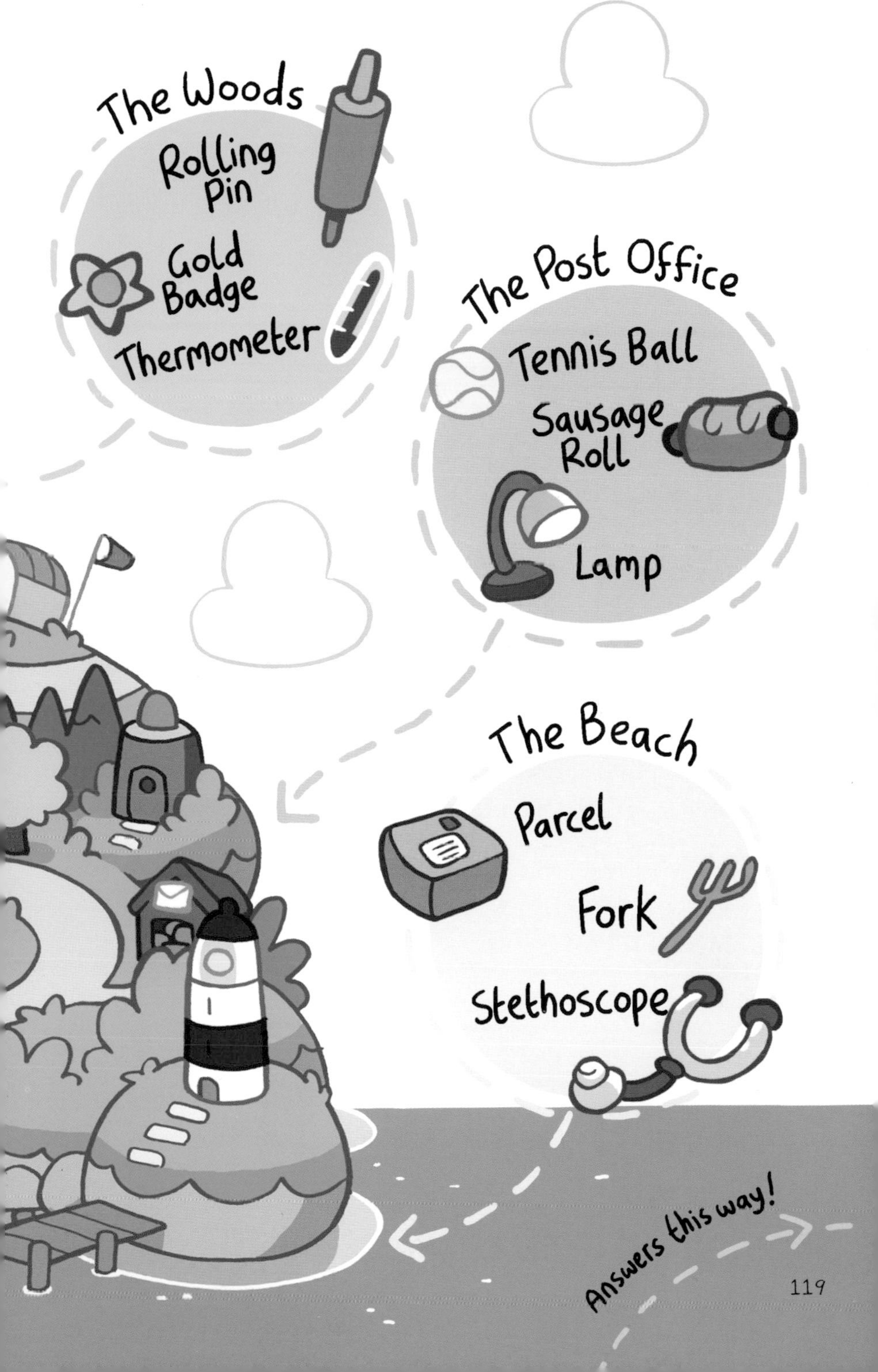
The Woods
Rolling Pin
Gold Badge
Thermometer
The Post Office
Tennis Ball
Sausage Roll
Lamp
The Beach
Parcel
Fork
Stethoscope
Answers this way!

Answers

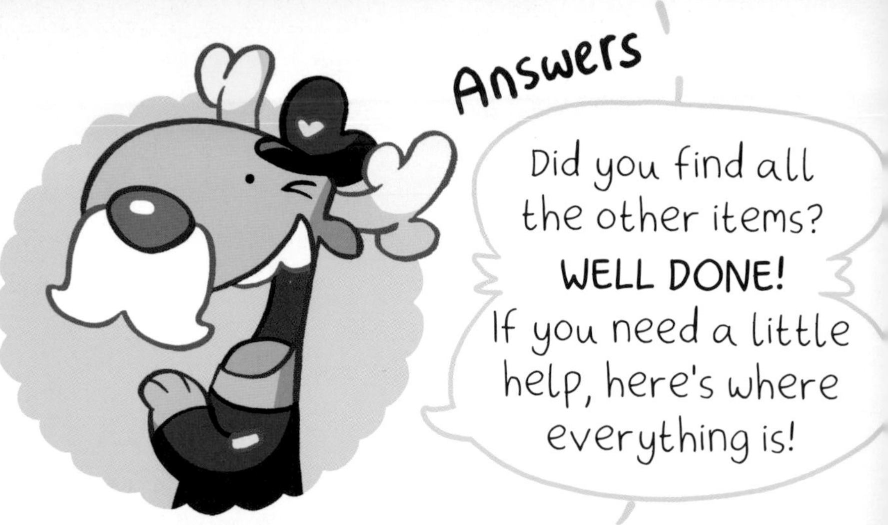
Did you find all the other items?
WELL DONE!
If you need a little help, here's where everything is!

The Woods

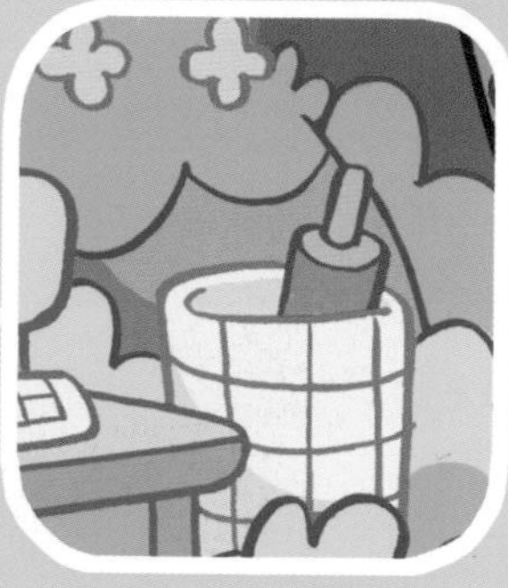

Rolling Pin

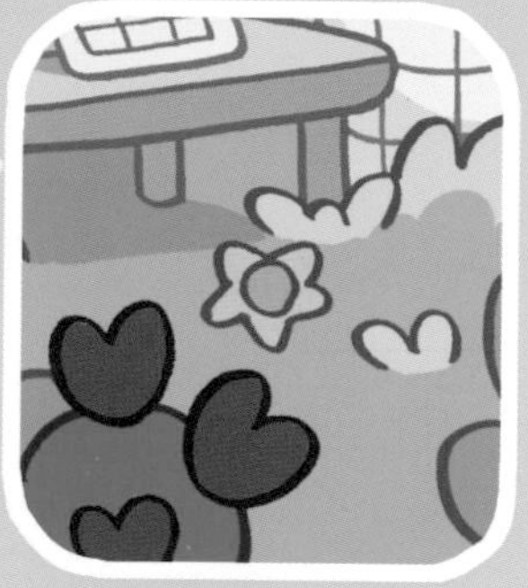

Gold Badge

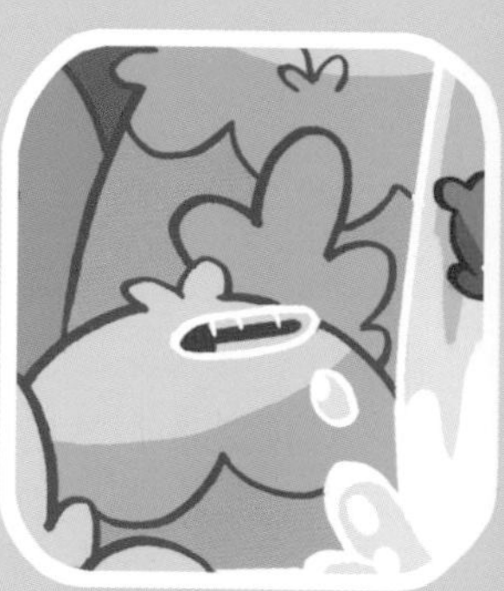

Thermometer

The Beach

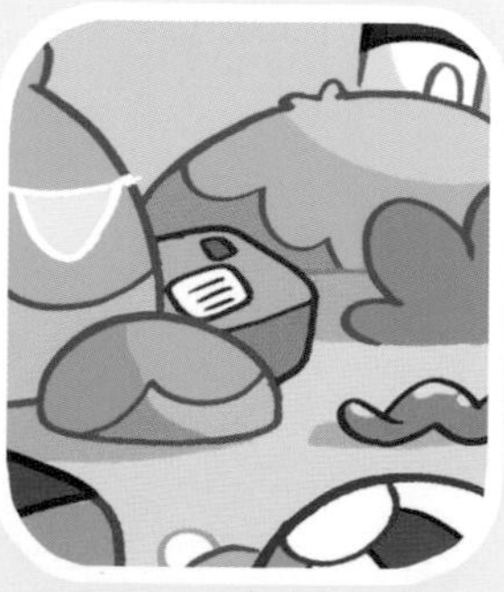

Parcel

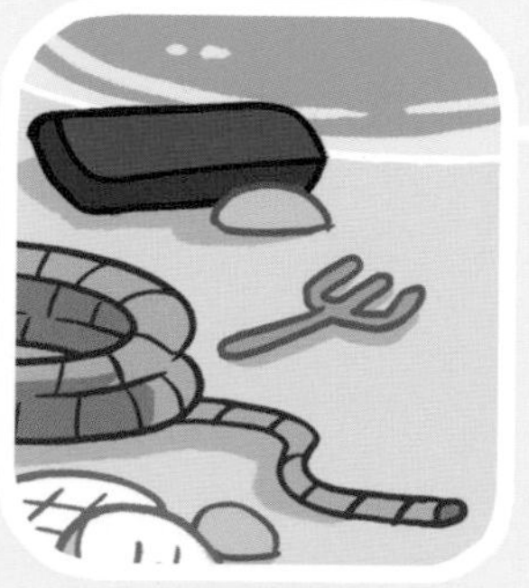

Fork

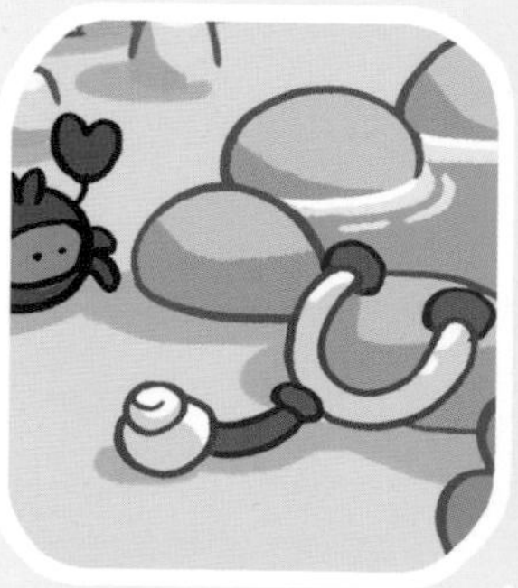

Stethoscope

Crumbles' Bakery

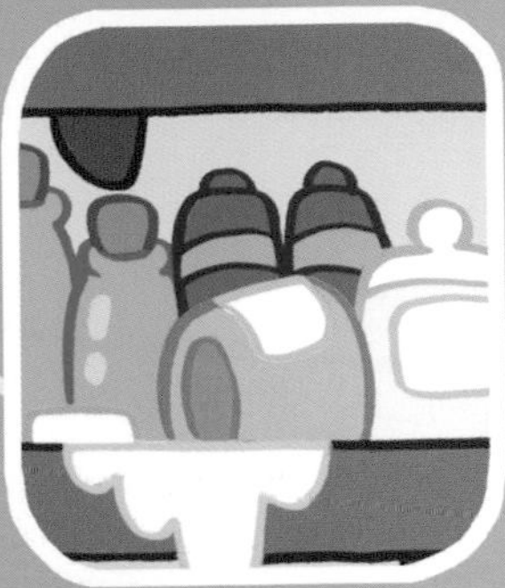

Binoculars

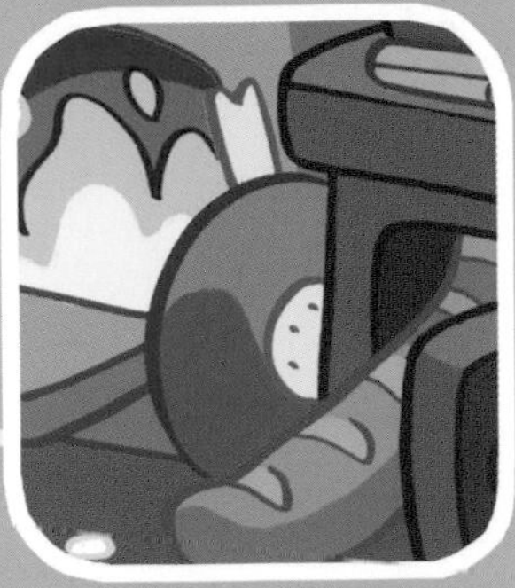

Aeroplane Wheel

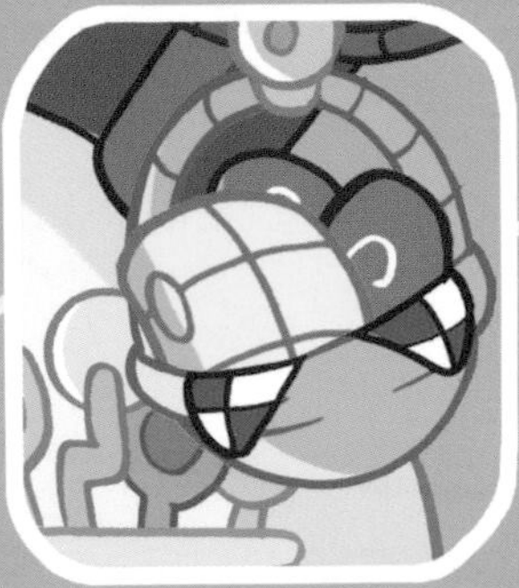

Life Jacket

The Ponds

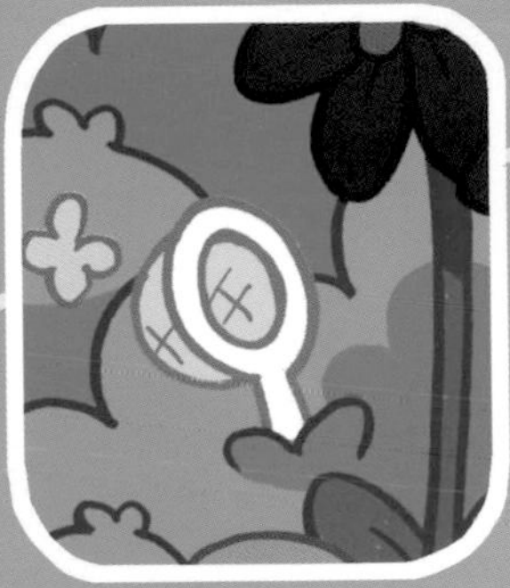

Sieve

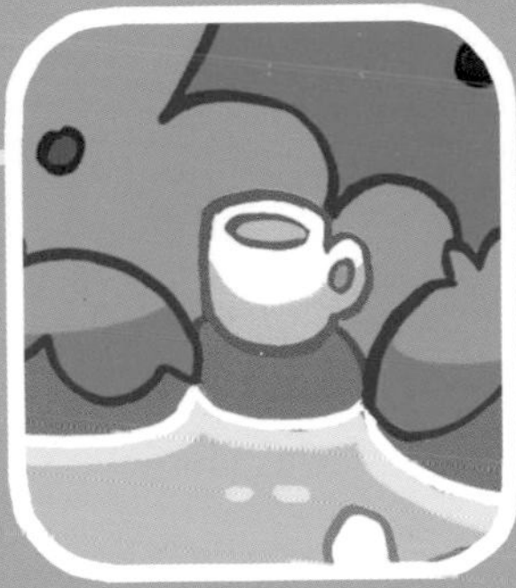

Cup

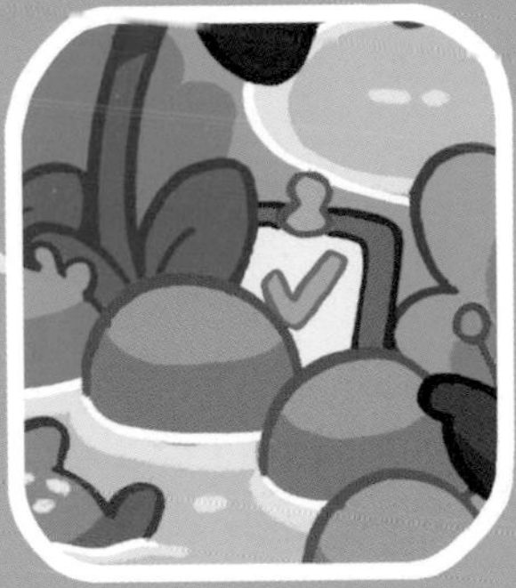

Clipboard

The Post Office

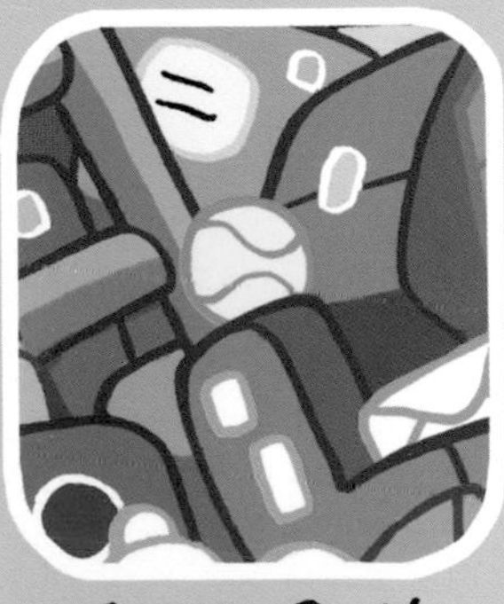

Tennis Ball

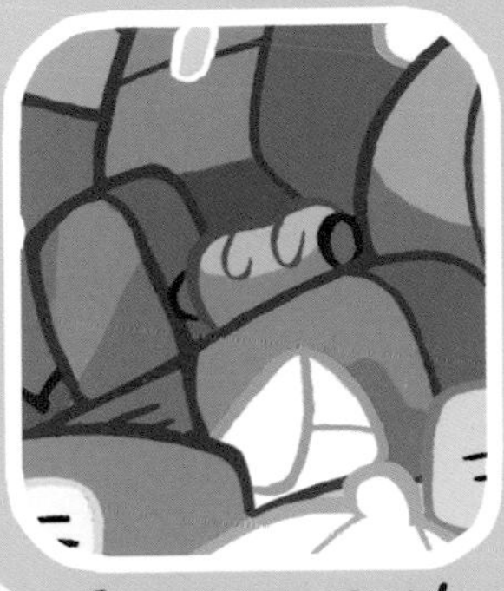

Sausage Roll

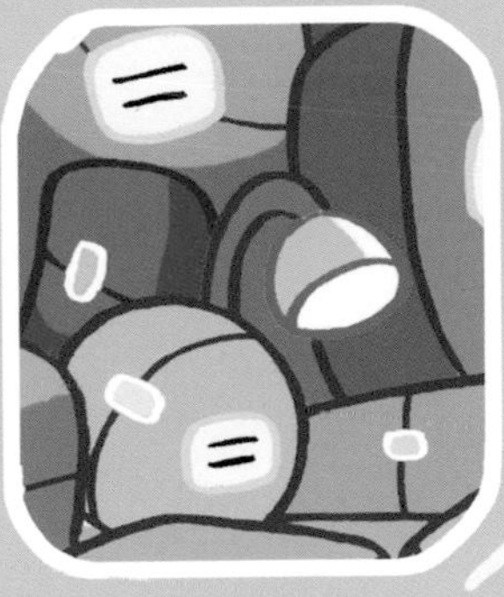

Lamp

More adventures with

MAX & CHAFFY

COMING SOON!

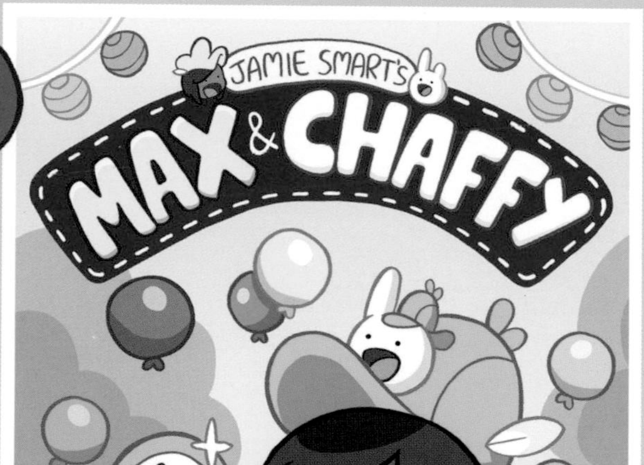
JAMIE SMART'S
MAX & CHAFFY
THE GREAT
CUPCAKE MYSTERY!

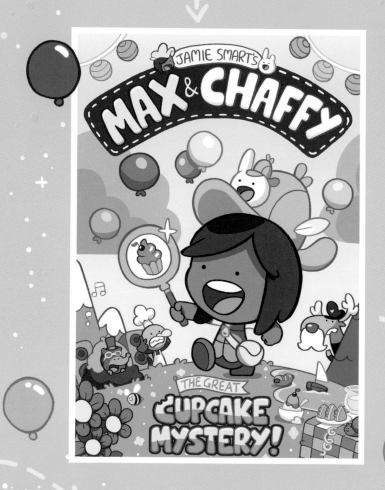

More adventures with

MAX & CHAFFY

COMING SOON!

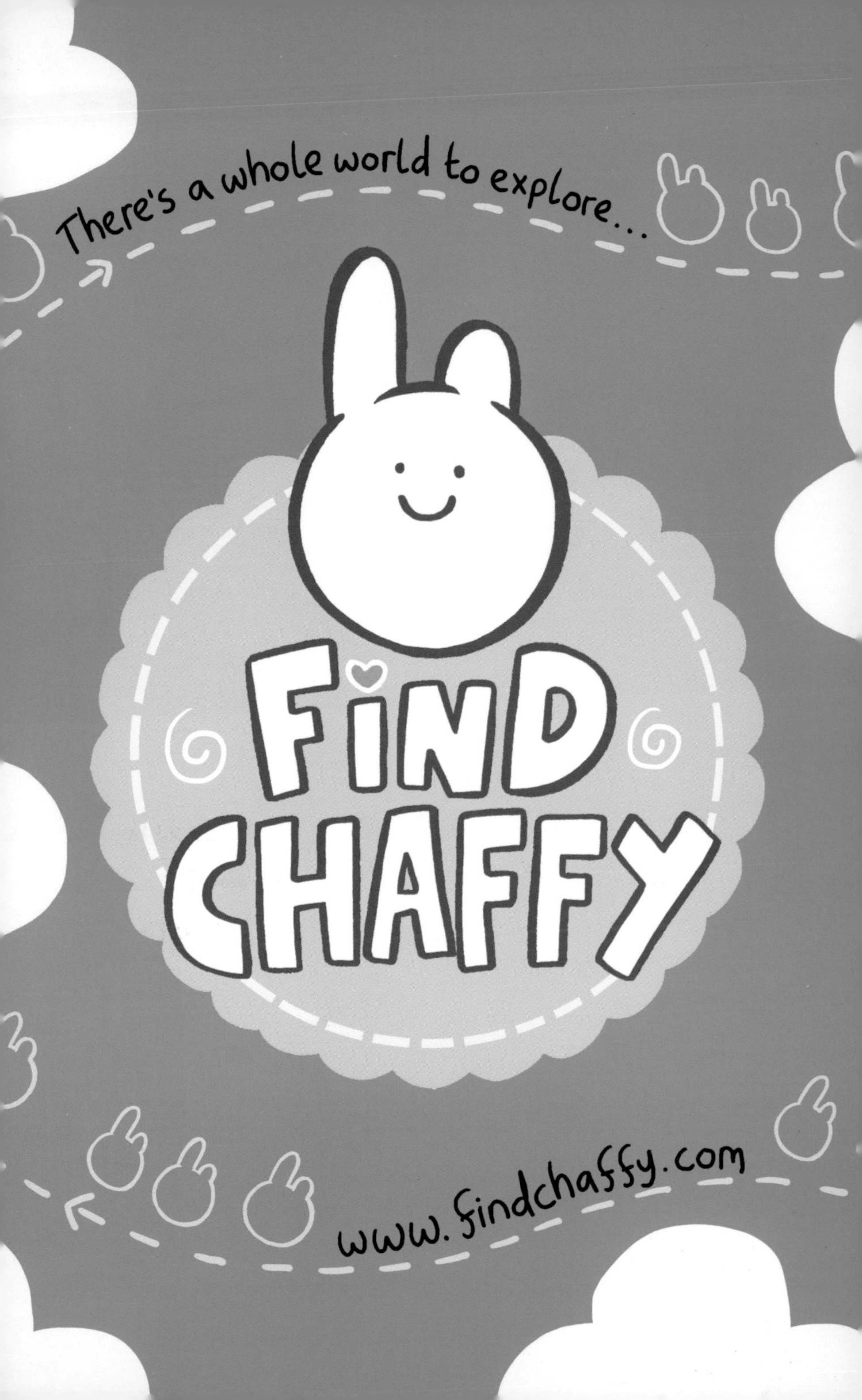

There's a whole world to explore...
FIND CHAFFY
www.findchaffy.com